DARK BEFORE DAWN

THE PROTECTOR GUILD BOOK 7

GRAY HOLBORN

Copyright © 2023 by Gray Holborn

All rights reserved.

No part of this book may be reproduced in any form or by any electronic or mechanical means, including information storage and retrieval systems, without written permission from the author, except for the use of brief quotations in a book review.

ISBN: 978-1-963893-06-9

Edits by: CopybyKath

Cover by: DamoroDesigns

❀ Created with Vellum

For everyone who's ridden the waves of grief - and continues to fight their way back to the surface.

AUTHOR NOTE

This book deals with material that may be difficult for some readers to engage with. Please visit my website at wwww.gray holborn.com/books for a more thorough and updating list of content warnings.

1

ELI

Two days.
Two days since I found Max in a puddle of limbs, crumpled on the ground, sobbing over Cyrus's body. Two days since she'd spoken a word. To anyone.

The sound of her screams had struck through me with more force than even Lucifer's creepy, glowing blade.

But something about the silence was even worse.

It felt more permanent, more irreparably broken. A familiar sort of fracture that I'd tried and failed to glue back together before. That kind of pain didn't come with any magical cures or easy fixes.

Grief was a bitch. A gnawing, ever-present ache that pulsed through the body like a poison.

It'd quiet down—eventually—but it would always be there, flowing through her veins, reminding her that it was there, whenever she got comfortable enough to forget.

Seeing her go through that—it felt like I was going through it myself. Her pain, an extension of my own.

"I can't even reach her in my sleep." Wade's voice cracked as he leaned against the wall. He slid down it, like his body just couldn't hold his weight anymore, until his ass landed with a dull thud on the worn carpet next to Darius.

Whatever animosity remained between the two of them had dissolved the moment they found Max. It was like a mutual understanding had bloomed where only anger had been before. Both of them were suddenly bonded over a common goal—making the shadow hovering over Max's head disappear.

Only problem? None of us knew how to accomplish that.

We were all huddled outside of her door. It had become the unofficial hangout spot—we could be close without crowding her, all of us desperately waiting for... something.

We'd found an old house a few miles from town. It wasn't the warmest place in the world—the electricity was off and I could see a visible trace of my breath with each exhale.

And every time I inhaled, I could feel a new layer of dust coating my lungs. But it was what we needed until we could figure out a plan—abandoned and safe. We needed to regroup. To figure out what the fuck we were supposed to do now. I sure as hell didn't have any ideas.

"This close to her," Wade shook his head and ran his hand roughly through his hair, "it should be easy as hell to dream walk to her. If I can reach her there, maybe I can get her to open up. Dream-walks have a way of doing that sometimes."

I didn't share his surprise, though I did empathize with his disappointment. She hadn't spoken to any of us. Not since we pulled her fingers, one by one, from where they clutched onto Cyrus's arms like a metal vise.

She'd nearly killed herself, trying to bring him back, trying to latch on to whatever magic her healing powers pulled from. Her body vibrated with it, the power thick and parasitic as it drained her.

I could feel her life force, her soul? Hell, I didn't know what it was that kept us around, but I could feel it fading from her.

Would she ever forgive us for making her stop, for calling time of death before she was ready to do the same?

Who was I kidding? She never would have been ready. Not if she had a choice.

No one was ever really ready to let go of someone they loved. No matter how much time they had with them. It was never enough. That was the cruel, double-edged sword of love.

Darius had carried her here, while she screamed, her arms flailing wildly as she fought desperately to get back to Cyrus—to the body. Eventually those screams turned into muffled sobs—until that too faded into whatever hollow place she'd sunken into.

"Maybe she doesn't want to see you." The vampire raised his brow, an echo of his usual playfulness—but his eyes looked haunted, a mirror of the misery cloaking us all. It made it almost impossible to breathe. The ache in my chest had been unrelenting since I'd found her. "And just so we're clear," he turned to Wade, "when we run into the man who spawned you, I *am* allowed to tear him piece-by-piece this time. And I'm only letting him sink into death when *she* says it's enough, yeah?" He asked the question in that odd, almost amused tone he often used, but there was a flash of something darker just underneath. That darkness used to terrify me, but now I was grateful that it could be mobilized on our side.

Wade stiffened at the comment, his body still like he wasn't even breathing, but he didn't lash out at him.

"I mean, it seems only fair, right?" Darius continued, oblivious to the shift in the atmosphere, "since he killed the man who spawned Max? And no one who makes her make that horrible sound should be allowed to keep living. To keep breathing. The echoes of that scream have been bouncing around in my skull on repeat since I heard it." He turned to me, eyes wide, imploring. "We can all agree on that, right? I'm not just being the," he made finger quotes, "bloodthirsty fanghole of the group." A pause. "Right?" He turned to Declan, eyebrows scrunched together. "Right? I'm reformed."

"Cyrus didn't spawn her," Declan tilted her head back against the wall and pinched the bridge of her nose. She was exhausted. We all were. We'd slept in shifts, but I wasn't sure any of us were able to fall asleep for more than an hour or two —we were all too afraid that Max might slip away, like the grief would permanently pull her if we left her too long, if we weren't careful enough. Like she'd follow some invisible thread to Cyrus and never come back to us. "He adopted her."

"Believe it or not," Darius crossed his arms over his chest and huffed—a hollow, noiseless chuckle, "even I can admit that some things are more important—more powerful—than blood."

"What do we do?" Wade's voice was scratchy, worn, like he had been the one screaming for Cyrus to wake up and not Max. "We can't just stay here forever like this, we can't just sit here while she's in pain." He ran his hand roughly over his face. "And we can't go back."

A sharp ache bit at my chest when I took a breath.

It was a strange thing—to know irrefutably, that we'd never be welcomed home again. Sometimes, when I was younger, I hated Headquarters so much that I'd spend hours dreaming of excuses to never return. I'd fantasize about running away—me and the rest of Six—imagine the kind of lives we might lead if we weren't beholden to our code. But those were the musings of a young, heartbroken kid under more pressure than he could withstand. Now that I really couldn't return, I couldn't deny the hole that realization left.

I had no home.

Other than my team.

Other than Max.

"And we need to figure out how to get Atlas—" the name

cracked on Wade's tongue, like giving voice to it brought the reality of the situation back into focus, "I'm not leaving my brother to the mercy of Tarren. Sarah either."

Bile burned the back of my tongue as I thought about them. They were both locked up in The Guild's labs. Labs that none of us had any access to anymore. We hadn't spoken about that particular clusterfuck much since we got here. Probably because the others felt as fucking useless and uninspired as I did.

All I had were questions, fears. No answers in sight.

How the hell did we go up against The Guild? Where the fuck did we even start?

Would my father truly leave Atlas to The Guild's whims and laws? Would he still stand by Tarren and the rest of them after what happened to his own brother?

If not, would they let him leave? Or would he be thrown behind those impenetrable glass walls just like Atlas?

The thought made it even more difficult to suck in a semblance of a breath.

"You're right. We do need to get them out, but we have to be smart about it. We're only going to get one chance, and we don't know what things are like back home—" Declan paused, and I knew that she was coming to the same realization that I just had—that the boundaries of Headquarters would never wear the title of 'home' again. She cleared her throat, expression flattening into her mission-ready-mask. "Right now, we need to get intel on what the fuck is going on there before we do anything reckless."

"You're right, we have to move slowly here—tread carefully," I said, ignoring the brief flash of surprise on her face. I wasn't exactly someone known for patience or restraint.

Maybe Darius wasn't the only one in the group who'd been reformed.

"As for Max," she continued, "I don't think she's going to let any of us in right now." She pulled her bottom lip through her teeth as she shook her head, her shoulders slumping. "We haven't earned that kind of trust—" she shot a lethal look at the vampire when he started to interrupt, "no, fanghole, not even you. Offering to chop off the head of whoever so much as looks at her wrong isn't the kind of support that will help her right now. This is big. Catastrophic. She's never felt this kind of pain before. Until a few months ago, she had exactly two people who'd been by her side—*on* her side. Now half of her family is gone, just like that." She paused for a long moment, as the truth of her words settled over us all. With a sigh she added, "she needs Ro."

I felt the rightness of that deep in my bones, and tried to ignore the small stab of jealousy that I might never be someone Max would turn to for that kind of support. We might all be her bond mates—a possibility that was becoming impossible to ignore or deny—but Ro had spent ten years in her corner, never once putting her through the sort of turmoil and pain we had. Their connection went beyond the strange threads of magic slowly tying us all together.

And hell, I'd done everything I could to push her away, to weaken and threaten the bonds drawing me to her. It was ridiculous of me to hope that she'd let me in when she was most vulnerable.

Still, it hurt to know that after months of push and pull, I'd succeeded in my endeavor.

I'd fucked any chance I had at finding that sort of happiness with her.

The best I could hope for was doing everything I could to make sure she found happiness at all, even if that meant shoving aside my own ego and desire.

If Ro could help, if he could get her to speak, to function—if he could bring back even a small shadow of that usual spark in her eyes, we needed to find him.

"You're right," I said, surprising her again, judging by the small lines carving through her forehead, "but how?"

We ditched our phones the second we could, none of us wanting to chance Tarren or anyone else from The Guild tracking us down.

"It's not like we can go storming up to his cabin door and ask if he can come out to chat for a few minutes. All that will earn us is a cozy spot in between Sarah and Atlas." Wade dug his fists into the mystery-stained carpet, every muscle coiled and ready for action, with no clear path to dispel it.

I felt his helplessness as if it was my own. It was a sort of stunted need for action that I'd felt more times than I could count since Max had stormed into our lives—the worst of which was definitely when she'd disappeared in hell.

Both times.

Once when she and Darius ditched us, and once when she, Darius, and Dec got stuck in hell for a month with no way to reach us. I thought I'd known fear before then—fuck was I wrong.

I was so fucking sick of disappointing her.

I sat up straight, the first tendrils of hope that I'd felt in days slowly unfurling in my chest. "The rendezvous point."

"Come again?" Dec asked, but all three of them were leaning forward, expressions attentive, like they could feel my excitement too.

"When you disappeared for a month—" I started.

"We didn't exactly have a choice," Darius interrupted.

Declan shoved him in the shoulder, shushing him.

"Right, well—Atlas, Ro, and I were all obviously pretty tense and anxious about it. We spent days waiting up for you all, or cycling through sleep on the off-chance Max might reach for one of us. When things started to get particularly desperate, we decided we needed to develop contingency plans. We knew that once you got back, things would inevitably ramp up—become more unpredictable. We decided that if shit hit the fan, if Max got discovered or we got separated and couldn't reach each other on campus, that we needed to find a rendezvous point. Somewhere close by that we could find in a pinch, but where no one would likely go looking."

"And?" Wade asked, his anxious energy now coiling into something more actionable. "Where'd you land?"

"Ralph's spot," I said.

"Ralph? As in the hellhound?" Wade tilted his head to the side, looking almost like a dog himself, his brows furrowing a bit. "Max's hellhound? He has a spot?"

I kept forgetting that he'd been gone for so long, that he was so out of the loop. It felt like my life had been split into two very different timelines: before Max and after Max. And the latter had somehow come to completely eclipse the former, like it was brighter—in sharper focus.

Wade had been absent for most of my After Max life. It was an odd discrepancy to unravel.

"Yes, he has a spot," I answered, figuring it was best to keep it simple.

Dec's face lifted into a grin, her eyes shining as she nodded. "Brilliant. Close to the action, familiar to all of us, but no reason for anyone other than us to go trespassing in that part of the woods."

"Still need to be careful though." I toyed with the hem of my jeans, trying to keep my focus on my team. I kept finding myself staring at the door, like I'd somehow be able to see Max through it if I just strained my eyes in the right way. The others had checked on her a lot, sat vigil next to the dusty bed she lay on, but I hadn't been able to bring myself to enter the room. I was afraid my presence would make things worse somehow. Our relationship was so complicated—filled with so much tension and unprocessed shit—I was afraid she wouldn't want me there. "After the attack, they're going to be a lot more vigilant—they'll be guarding every square inch of Headquarters."

Them.

I wasn't sure exactly when it happened, but I realized then that I'd stopped considering myself one of them—a protector aligned with The Guild. They were the enemy now, as much a threat to us all as the demons in hell were.

"We still don't know how bad things got," Wade said, a metallic edge to his voice. I knew he was thinking about his father, about Atlas. "How many casualties, who—none of it. We don't have any access anymore, no in."

"I'll go to the rendezvous point," Declan leaned forward, like she was ready to leave as soon as possible. "Sooner we find Ro and get a feeling for the others—for who we can trust—we'll be in a better position. Then we can start," her eyes hardened as they met Wade's, "then we can figure out how we're getting your brother and my cousin out of that hellhole."

I felt my lips tug briefly at her word choice. Dec had always been so ferociously by-the-book, so dedicated to The Guild—her hunger for hunting demons deep and unrelenting. To hear her align everything she'd believed in with our least favorite place—hell—it just went to show how much things had changed in the After Max era. For all of us.

"I'm coming with you," the vampire said, his forearms resting loosely on his knees as he studied her. They'd developed an odd bond over the last few weeks, another unexpected twist in her worldview.

He was growing on me too. Which, while annoying as fuck, was also a good thing. Lessoned the risk of me forgetting about our blood bond and attacking him—and therefore myself—at the slightest provocation.

"No way," she said, shoulders tight. "Chances are too high

that you'll land yourself in a cell right next to Atlas if anyone sees you."

He smirked, but there wasn't any humor there, only pity. "You forget that you're just as much at risk of that fate as I am now."

The statement hung heavy in the air.

He was right. We would be seen as no better than demons if we found our way back to the place we'd all called home for most of our lives. As far as they were concerned, we became traitors the moment we ran.

I felt the second this realization hit Declan too, just as it'd hit me, her skin even paler than usual, maybe even a tinge green. Not only did we have no home there—but everyone who occupied our old home considered us enemies.

Wade nodded, no doubt because he'd had enough time sitting by himself in the dungeons of hell to fully metabolize his new, strange reality.

"And I'm faster and better at killing protectors than you are," Darius continued, pushing past the strange stuckness we all felt, "it's a smart move for me to come along, not that I'm taking no for an answer. I'm your best chance at coming back alive."

"I don't need your protection," Declan snapped, though I knew her well enough to know that it was grounded in rage at our situation, not at the fanghole.

"I get it, you're strong and independent. I'm not arguing with that—I've seen you take out guys twice your size. But this is no time for pride." He paused, and a dark shadow seemed to cast across his face as he glanced at Max's door—somehow, I knew that the memory of her scream was reverberating in his head, loud and unrelenting again, just as it was in mine. "I'm not letting the little protector lose anyone else if I can help it."

Declan took a deep breath, nodded once. "Fine. You're

coming with me. But you aren't killing anyone—" she paused, jaw tight, considering, "not—not unless you have to."

I felt the possibility that we very well might have to do just that spark down my spine, like a splintering crack through ice.

Darius stretched his arms high, stretched his head from side to side until a sharp crack echoed around us. "Good. It's settled then. And someone should go out for supplies. If we're staying here for a few days, we'll need more food. Especially if we're adding another mouth to the party. And, at the risk of sounding needy, I could do with some blood."

"I'll go," Wade said, before I had a chance. "I'm not quite as strong or fast as the vamp, but I've got my own arsenal if I need it." He nodded to me. "You should be the one to stay with her."

Because I was the weakest link?

Ouch.

He wasn't wrong, but it stung all the same.

"Maybe go sit with her for a while," he continued, "It might —it might do you both some good."

My stomach sank. He'd noticed.

Something in his expression softened, and I wondered if I was really so goddamn transparent.

Declan squeezed my shoulder as she stood up, her other hand reaching to help the vampire up. "He's right." She nodded to Wade and handed him the cash she pulled from her back pocket. "Be careful. You see anyone you recognize, get the fuck out immediately. And make sure you're not followed back here."

He rolled his eyes and, for a moment, a flash of the old Wade shone through his expression—annoyed with being the youngest, eager to prove his worth—but then his features dissolved into solid determination, and settled into the distinct darkness that had wrapped itself around him like a shroud since his return from Lucifer's shitty dungeon. He nodded.

I felt everyone's anxiety coating the hall as they prepared

their things and left. This was all new territory, and none of us had even the illusion of a safety net anymore.

And then they were gone.

And it was just me—

Alone in the silence as I stared at the door, praying like hell for the courage to open it.

2

DECLAN

"He'll be okay." Darius bent down and picked up a small twig, watching as Wade walked in the opposite direction to us. Then he tilted his head sideways. "Probably, anyway." He exhaled, loud and slow. "Actually, if we're realistic, probably not."

My head snapped to his.

He shrugged. "He's been through a lot. And I know that look in his eyes."

"What look?" I pressed my palm into my chest, trying to rub out the ache that had lingered there, deep and heavy, since we left The Guild.

His eyes trailed to my hand, one gold and one black, flickering briefly before turning towards Headquarters. "Things have been... chaotic."

I snorted.

"But you have to remember that the Wade you knew months ago, is not the same as the one with us now. And I don't just mean because he can pull power from sexy dream time and beat his old record for running the mile." He tossed the twig in the air, only to snatch it back again.

Sure, Darius was capable of disemboweling a man in a few seconds flat, but sometimes he seemed more golden retriever than vampire.

"What do you mean?" I asked, craning my neck back towards the direction we'd come from, back towards Max. I tried to ignore the way my stomach had tightened into an impossible, unrelenting knot the moment we'd left.

"I mean, that his life has been turned upside down just as much as all of yours has." I felt the fanghole's eyes on me as he spoke, his words slow and questioning, like he was puzzling through Wade's experiences in real time. "But he's been alone through most of it. Being locked in a dungeon—for months—alone and malnourished—it's not a small thing, Declan. It's not something someone just snaps back from, sliding into their old habits and life like riding a scooter or whatever. Besides, even if he wanted to, his old life is gone."

"Bicycle." I stopped, my neck cracking as I turned back to him. Darius never used my name.

I saw it as soon as my eyes met his—the heaviness in his expression as he stared through me. The thin veil between the vampire I'd grown to almost tolerate and the strange darkness that occasionally eclipsed him.

My stomach lurched with guilt. I'd been so caught up in the impending doom of everything that I hadn't thought about the fact that Wade would be marked from his captivity—just as Darius had been. Both men had been starved of companionship, of kindness, of everything good for months on end. That kind of trauma left more than a mark—it left deep, permanent gouges on the psyche.

I'd never really thought about the fact that Darius had been put through experiments, torture, and god only knew what.

For years.

Because of us. Because of protectors.

For a moment, I found myself wanting to reach forward and

pull him to me, as if a hug could dissolve some of the lingering pain.

A shiver ran through me at the impulse. Hell certainly was freezing over.

"Whatever. Bicycle, scooter—human idioms are all absurd and strange anyway. Not to mention," he cleared his throat and started walking again, like he could see the empathy raging out of me and was as uncomfortable with it as I was, "that Wade also had to deal with the fact that he'd become the very thing he was trained to hate—to destroy—all at the same time." He shrugged, the twig dropping from his hand noiselessly as it landed on a soft pile of snow. "I'm not the kid's biggest fan, don't get me wrong—he's got some maturing to do, some confidence to find—but even I'm impressed that he survived all of that," he cleared his throat awkwardly, "and that he's come out on the other side with the ability to feign normalcy—with the determination and focus to help you all fight whatever battle it is we are going to fight, with the determination to be there for, well, her—consequences be damned." He shrugged. "I might find him annoying, but I can't deny that I admire that particular quality. Reminds me of Max in some ways. They have a similar quiet sort of strength."

I swallowed, my throat tight and thick with emotion that I didn't want to unleash right now.

"All I'm saying is, it's going to take time for him to be alright. It's no easy task—digging yourself out of that sort of darkness."

"I shouldn't have let him go out on his own," I said, my voice raspy and strange to my ears. Reading the group, monitoring the boys' scattered emotions had always been my job—how had I missed this?

"Yes," Darius craned his neck to look at me, "you should have. He asked to go for a reason. The kid was itching to stretch his legs, to leave the house—when you've spent that kind of time in a cell, it's hard not to see every set of walls as another version of the same, once you've slowed down and had the space to examine them for a day or two. He needs a few minutes to feel free from it for a bit, to dig himself back to the surface again." He turned back around and walked in silence for a few seconds that stretched and lingered like full minutes. "Like I said, his strength is impressive. And he'll be okay. Probably. But probably is going to have to be good enough right now."

"And Max?" I asked, "Will she be okay?" The question passed over my tongue and through my lips before I could reign it in.

His shoulders tensed, but his pace didn't change. After a long, drawn-out moment, I thought he was just going to ignore my question. But then his voice trailed softly behind him. "I don't know. She's also been through a lot."

That was an understatement. It was like the gas pedal had been pushed to the ground in her life since the moment she stepped foot on Guild territory—a lifetime of pain and surreal, haunting experiences crammed into a few short months. And now she'd lost one of the only things anchoring her to her old life—to her family. To herself.

"But I can give you exactly one guarantee." I heard the grin in his tone—feral and terrifying. "If she isn't okay, I'm going to rip every person responsible for her pain to shreds, one limb at a time."

I wouldn't blame him. If Tarren was in front of me right now, I wasn't sure I could resist carving his heart out of his chest myself—Atlas and Wade's father or not.

Was that love? The sudden urge to murder?

Max's sobs had been rattling through me for days, like they were my own.

I stopped, my stomach dropping.

"The body." How had we not thought of it until now? We'd just left Cyrus there, dragging Max away before anyone could find us. "We should go get him, so she can lay him to rest. Properly."

It would be a long journey towards healing, but maybe a small burial would help. Even just a little. There was a reason that the entire funeral industry existed, and I had a feeling that there was more to it than just capitalism. Probably.

Having somewhere to visit my parents had been a small comfort over the years. Not right away, but later as the grief transformed into something softer, something slightly more manageable. Even though I seldom made the journey back there, to the site—sometimes just knowing I could offered its own form of peace.

"I've never really understood that impulse," he said, pausing briefly, "the way your kind and humans almost play with the dead—building them small boxes that you shove into the ground, as if that's a comfortable way to rest or an honor that matters in the slightest." He tilted his head, eyes narrowing, then nodded. "But if it has even a small chance of helping her, you're right. We should go find the corpse."

We made our way towards the pond in silence for a few miles.

The memory of Max sobbing over Cy's body was vivid and painful and carved into the back of my eyelids. It was a pain I knew well, and I hated more than anything that she had to feel it now. Part of me wanted to stop, to turn back, to go anywhere but to the location of that scene, like visiting it again would drown me in the waves of her overwhelming grief.

Why did I feel it almost as deeply as I felt my own?

I pressed my knuckles briefly into the spot on my chest again, the skin probably bruised by now from all of my fussing.

He turned back, considering me for a moment, before continuing forward again. "You can feel it too, can't you?"

I didn't know what to say, so I didn't say anything, just

studied his back as he carved his own winding path towards Headquarters.

He stopped; the movement so sudden that I ran into him. He turned around, like he hadn't even noticed the collision, pressing the heel of his palm into his chest. "She's fractured. It's like—" his eyes narrowed, "like an echo of her pain?"

"It's such a hollow feeling, but it lingers," I murmured, not taking a step back. The shock that he felt it too kept me rooted, transfixed as I studied him. "What, how—"

"I don't know." He shook his head. "Mate bonds—true ones—have been absent from my kind for as long as they have been from yours. The knowledge we have is little more than lore, speculation. Those old enough to remember them don't speak on it. Vampires aren't known for discussing their feelings about even trivial things. But mate bonds? They're sacred. Protected. So I know very little about what to expect. And Max, especially, is—unusual. But I feel like," he stopped pressing into his chest, and I realized that I'd mirrored the pressure on my own, "this has to be related, doesn't it? You, Eli, Wade—I've watched you all the last two days, I think we all feel it, the ache. I don't know why, what's causing it, why we can feel it now. Maybe it's her grief—like it's found some way to take tangible shape inside of us all."

"Or Atlas's mate bond," I said, my thoughts suddenly churning faster than I could chase them. "He and Reza might have completed their ceremony before the attack." I looked up at him, "Do you think that could have caused it? Broken something?"

He shrugged. "I told you. This is as new and strange to me as it is to you."

I nodded, took a deep breath, and started walking again. It was strange—to be confiding in a vampire, to be seeking guidance and reassurance from him. Hell, I was alone with him and not the least bit concerned that he could kill me before I pushed out my next syllable if he wanted to. And somehow, the fact that he could feel the phantom pain too comforted me. So did his presence, if I was being honest. I never would have imagined myself thinking it before, but I felt safer walking on enemy territory with him at my side.

Another thing I'd never thought I'd consider: that Headquarters—home—would take shape as enemy territory in my brain.

Still, as we walked in silence, both of us masticating the heavy conversation, I couldn't help but feel that having Darius as backup gave me the same confidence that fighting alongside Atlas or one of the other boys always had.

Like he'd become my teammate, without me really noticing it happened. Like he'd crossed some invisible barrier into new territory—a barrier that I'd always guarded with a sort of rigid steadfastness that impressed even me.

Family.

I shivered, shoving the simmering emotion down, down, *down*.

It'd been a strange year, that much was for damn sure.

We'd crossed into Headquarters, and though we hadn't come across anyone, it wouldn't be prudent to lose focus now. All it would take was one moment of collapsed judgment, of losing myself in a trailing thought, to surrender the upper hand in an ambush.

We were getting close to the pond where we'd left Cyrus, only a few minutes or so more and we'd be there. The snow crunched beneath my feet. Darius moved soundlessly, like a cat, even as he kept to my significantly slower pace.

The cabin that we'd kept Ralph hidden in for a few weeks was only a short walk from there too. Two birds, one stone.

Though I was growing less confident that Ro would be there. It was too cold and the cabin was hardly even a cabin, let alone something that would provide shelter against the elements this time of year. It was scroungy and unimpressive housing, even for a dog. But where else would we start? How else could we get in touch with him?

There was so much we needed to accomplish, but no good place to start actually doing it. We just needed a frayed seam, a place to grip so that we could unravel even a small segment of the tapestry.

Darius stilled next to me, his hand pressing into my stomach to keep me from moving forward another inch.

I felt him stiffen against me. It was the odd, absolute sort of stillness that had a way of reminding me that he was a vampire.

I narrowed my eyes, trying to catch whatever sound or scent had stopped him in his tracks.

Not for the first time, I found myself sorry that I didn't have the acute supernatural gifts my teammates had garnered for themselves. Wade—an incubus, Atlas—a werewolf, Darius—a vampire, Eli—not exactly a vampire, but bolstered by his blood tie to Darius, and Max—well, she was a whole hell of a lot of things these days.

And then me.

Practically just a fucking human, throwing useless sticks at unmovable forces.

Weak.

Darius rushed us forward, dragging me with him like a ragdoll as he skittered through the woods like a ghost.

"What?" I asked, my voice a soundless whisper, but enough for him to catch with sharp clarity.

"We're surrounded," his voice was calm, but I wasn't pacified by it, "They're moving in. They know we're here. They've been waiting. Probably hoping she'd come back to the body."

Fuck.

My stomach tightened as I did all I could—wait for the shoe to drop and be dragged about by the vampire.

Was it other demons? Or was it The Guild? I honestly wasn't sure which enemy I was hoping for anymore.

Protectors would certainly be easier to kill, if necessary.

The thought was fleeting, but it made bile rise up my throat.

I grabbed my blade from the holster, all the same, the second Darius slowed to a thicker patch of trees that opened up to the small, usually tranquil, pond.

My eyes darted to the spot where Cy's body had been left. It was gone—a fresh layer of snow masking any blood or imprints left from us.

Of course they'd found him.

Of course they'd taken him.

They would have combed through every square inch of campus, a hundred times over by now.

My chest squeezed at the fact that we couldn't even give Max this, this one thing that might offer even a nanosecond of respite—the chance to say goodbye.

Two figures emerged a few feet from us—Guild. One of them I recognized, though he was a few years older than me and stationed at one of the other branches. Chris, maybe.

Maybe-Chris's lips curved in a dark, menacing smile as his eyes met mine. "So it's true, you are working with the demon dirtbags now. Are you a wolf girl too?" the corner of his mouth pinched. "Fucking scum."

"Wasted resources," the other one growled, his knuckles clenching around his blade as I felt the rest of their team close us in from behind. "All these years, all you've been given, all we've done for you—and you turn it against us. Your entire team disgusts me."

I rubbed my lips together, struggling to make my tongue form words.

"Am I allowed to kill these dickholes now?" Darius asked from the corner of his mouth, though he did little to muffle the volume of his voice, "or are we still operating on the do-no-harm-to-The-Guild's-charming-progeny platform?"

Before I could answer, they dove towards us, blades prone and eager to carve into any flesh they could meet—mine, Darius's, it didn't matter—they were aiming to kill.

I felt the familiar whir of darts blow past my ear as I dove to the side, punching Maybe-Chris in the gut, grinning as he grunted in surprise against me.

His blade swiped, finding purchase in my left bicep, but my adrenaline washed away any pain. "I'm going to watch them tear your wolf to shreds, you know? He's been the golden boy for so long, I have to admit," he punched me in the jaw, the crack rattling my skull like coins in a tin, "I'm almost looking forward to it. We're all taking bets on how long he'll last."

Something in me snapped into focus as I dodged his next blow.

"That's it," Darius yelled from a few feet away. He had one of the protectors pinned against a tree, as he fought off another from behind. "Executive decision time. I get to kill these fuckers."

But a few inches to his left, another man—his face vaguely familiar, part of the same team as Maybe-Chris—approached him, unnoticed.

As if the sight of him suddenly conjured it, Aunt Jay's story unraveled through my mind in a flash of angry bolts—The Guild's corruption, her suspicion that they'd murdered my parents, my uncle, the vampire mother and her child, slaughtered needlessly and blamed for crimes they didn't commit.

Not Darius.

They couldn't have him. He was not going back to those labs.

I threw my dagger with as much force as I could muster, waiting only long enough to watch it bury itself to the hilt in the man's eye, just before he reached Darius.

Maybe-Chris tackled me to the ground, his black eyes glistening and furious as we both fought for control of his blade, the metal already coated with my blood.

"You killed one of us," he spat, his forearm shoved against my throat, cutting off my air supply. "You fucking killed one of us. Have you fucking lost all semblance of loyalty?"

I kneed him in the dick, using the brief moment of shock to grip the hand clasping his blade and direct it towards his stomach. "No, I've just learned to carefully consider who's deserving of my loyalty." I pressed the tip into his abdomen, my strength somehow winning out over his, even though he was easily twice my weight, "and it's not you."

His eyes widened with shock, fear momentarily clouding the rage as he realized that he'd lost.

Blood seeped from the seam of his mouth and I shoved him off of me, twisting the blade deeper before removing it and slashing his neck.

For a moment, I was transfixed by the sight. It was strangely beautiful as a thin, almost invisible line suddenly appeared, red and angry, growing steadily thicker until dark blood eclipsed the pale skin of his neck.

Dead. Another one. I'd killed two.

I turned back towards the battle, ready to help Darius take out the others, but the small, wooded clearing was deceptively calm and quiet as he watched me, shoulder leaning casually against the tree he'd had the protector pinned to a moment before, his hand lazily gripping a severed head by a clump of blond, matted curls.

Three other corpses littered the ground in various piles of limbs—I couldn't tell which arms belonged to whom, and a thick, muscled heart sat half-buried in the snow, steam almost visible from the contrast in temperatures. The clean wintery scene was awash with thick coils of red, like a macabre Christmas card. It hit me then, harder, as I realized, slowly, that I was responsible for some of it—that I'd kill two protectors.

And that I felt very little remorse about it. Adrenaline pounded through my body, the steady thump of my pulse ringing in my ears.

Darius considered me for a long moment, like he was giving me a chance to scream or cry or attack him if I needed to—his expression devoid of anything readable.

"You're okay?" I asked, my voice piercing the unusually quiet scene. "Nothing important injured?"

His head dipped, slowly, his eyes roving over his crotch. "Nope, necessities are intact." I swallowed a chuckle as his eyes met mine again. "And you? Are you okay?"

There was something soft in the way he asked it, like he legitimately cared about the answer.

I shrugged my shoulders, the ache from where Maybe-Chris's blade punctured muscle, flaring deep and loud now that the heat of the moment was subsiding. "I'll heal."

"I didn't mean the blood wound," he said, his body stiffening as he dropped the head with an irreverent thud and surveyed the scene. "I meant you in a more cerebral sense. You'll be okay?"

Because I'd killed two people who were decidedly not demons. He was worried that I'd start freaking out because I chose him—a vampire—over the people who'd helped raise me my entire life. Over the people I was supposed to serve and be loyal to above all else.

"As okay as any of us are." I walked towards him and bent down to the corpse a few feet away, the man that had nearly attacked Darius from behind. With a loud squelch, I pulled my blade from the dead protector's eye, pausing only to wipe the blood and goo on his black jacket before resheathing it at my thigh. "We should get going. This slaughter won't stay quiet for long. Someone will come looking for them."

An entire team, dead, in only a few short minutes.

And I was part of the reason.

I paused for a moment, mentally probing for a flash of guilt, for the urge to vomit or serve myself up to Tarren and the council on a platter. But there was none. If anything, the thick knot in my stomach loosened slightly as I stood up, like something permanent shifted into place, my perspective clearer.

"In retrospect," Darius surveyed the scene, "might've been good to keep one of them alive. You know, intel and what not." He shrugged. "Ah well, next time, we'll remember to reign in the bloodlust. But yeah," he arched a brow, nodded, "we probably should get going."

He turned towards the trees, his hand sweeping over his hair and his face, messing both up with the carnage covering his fingers. He looked so tired. And it made sense. Vampire or not, he'd been through just as much as we had these last few weeks—maybe more. It wasn't like the guy got a vacation after spending half a decade in the labs either. He really did need blood. And soon.

I jerked my head towards the bodies. "You should feed."

His expression stretched in surprise. "Yeah?"

I shrugged. "No sense in wasting relatively fresh blood. It'll hopefully be the last we encounter for a while."

He nodded and I walked a few steps away, not really wanting to watch the feast as he indulged in it.

After a few drawn minutes, I felt him approach my back. "I don't actually know where exactly we are going from here—where this cabin thing is. You'll need to lead the way."

I nodded, carving a path towards Ralph's hideout without sparing the dead protectors another glance. We walked in silence, each of us lost in thought, but comfortable in the quiet presence of the other.

When we reached the tattered hut, my stomach sank. It was even more weathered by the recent snow storm. There was no way anyone would come here, rendezvous or not. Not this time of year. Not when there were so many protectors on guard out here.

There weren't any fresh prints lining the snowy path. I wrapped my good arm around the bad, like thinking about the chill sent a fresh wave of it through me, rattling my bones.

"This was a terrible idea," I said, turning towards Darius. "Maybe we should just get a few burner phones and hope Ro picks up without Guild intercepting the call."

"Even I know there's no chance of that happening." Darius shook his head, took a few steps towards the makeshift shack. His back stiffened, every muscle suddenly still. "Someone's in there. I think." He paused for a beat, both of us completely still. "I think I hear rustling. Breathing."

"Probably a rabbit or squirrel." But I took a few steps closer, hopeful all the same.

The door shifted slightly, a quarter of an inch, maybe, before whatever was inside determined we weren't a threat and opened it fully. I noticed a small, decorative banner hanging inside and bit back a grin. Max had tried sprucing the place up a bit, tried making it a home filled with warmth for her beloved hellhound.

That seemed like a lifetime ago.

Pale, blue eyes emerged from the shadows, set in a face far paler than I'd ever seen it, with dark circles that made him look more vampiric than Darius.

"Ro." I moved towards him, scanning him for injuries as his focus locked, briefly, on Darius.

"Where is she?" he asked, his eyes darting around like we were hiding his sister in some invisible pocket of the forest. "She's okay? She's alive?"

"She's alive," Darius answered, the usual teasing tone of his voice mellowed into something softer, like he was speaking to a feral cat. "Hiding out in an abandoned house, just outside of town. And, well," his head tilted as he studied Rowan, "about as okay as you are, I suppose."

Ro looked like shit. Like he hadn't slept or eaten in days.

When I reached out for his fingers, my own burned with the bitter cold of him. "Have you been out here for two days? You're half frozen; this weather is dangerous."

He looked at me, expressionless. "No more dangerous than The Guild would be for me right now. I couldn't go back. And I —" his voice trailed as he continued scanning the trees, his eyes darting with a hollowness that chilled me more than his hand had.

"You had no other way to reach Max," I finished for him, my chest aching that he'd been out here alone, in the cold with no company but his grief.

A twig snapped a few feet away from us and before I even knew what was happening, Darius had someone pinned to a tree, a few feet away.

I stepped towards them, my hand on the hilt of my blade.

I exhaled when a familiar pair of wide, gray eyes came into view. "Izzy?"

Her panicked, round eyes found mine as she mouthed 'yep' in response, her airway constricted by Darius's hand.

"Darius." I tried to keep my voice calm. He merely grunted in response, his body coiled and stiff as he stared daggers at poor Izzy. "Darius, not her. Let her go."

He turned to me, brows bent in question, eyes clearly screaming 'Did you already forget that protectors just tried to murder us both?'

"It's Max's best friend." I raised my hands up, like now Darius was the feral cat who needed to be handled with kid gloves.

The tension in his shoulders dissipated, and he let Izzy go. "Oh! That Izzy. I've heard a lot about you." He placed his hands on her arms, steadying her, before brushing up and down, like he was trying to warm her up.

... And make her forget that he'd almost killed her one second ago.

The corner of her mouth lifted as she gave him a bemused grin.

"Sorry about," he waved his hand from her to the tree, "You know," he mimed choking with his hands around his own neck, "that. Can't be too cautious these days, right? We were just attacked by a handful of protectors."

She shook her head, lips opening and closing like a fish trying to find food. I felt a wave of compassion for the girl. I was familiar with that feeling—trying to make sense of all that was Darius the Vampire. He needed his own cartoon series and an instruction manual to boot.

Giving up, she sidestepped Darius and walked over to Ro, her brows cinching as she studied him. "You're okay? Arnell got the alert that someone was near here. He was in a meeting, but I ran as fast as I could." She reached into her pocket and pulled out a small parcel that she handed him. "A few more hand warmers and some food. Arnell's going to bring more later."

Ro's expression was blank as he accepted the gift. "She's alive."

Izzy glanced between me and Ro, face blank as she put things together. "Max? Of course she's alive. There was never any doubt there." She turned to me. "We've been keeping an eye out for Ro, as best we can without getting caught. Things are," she exhaled sharply, the puff of air making the flyaway hairs at her temple float around her face like a cloud, "extremely tense. And developing rapidly on campus, as you can imagine."

I didn't doubt it. Headquarters had never been breached like that before... and well, the ambush had been nothing short of cataclysmic.

"You're okay though?" Darius asked, taking an exaggerated step, dramatically reinserting himself into the conversation. He stared at her, eyes narrowed, sizing her up. "Maybe you should come back with us too. Might cheer her up."

A small, almost sad smile crossed Izzy's features. "I wish that I could, but I'm the best inside sleeper agent that you all have right now for—" she took a labored breath, and I noticed for the first time that she looked a little unwell, weaker than usual, "well, for whatever it is you're planning to do now. I haven't seen Atlas, so I don't have much access to the high security stuff, and I only just got released from the medical ward this morning—" Ro grunted, and Izzy rolled her eyes, "Okay, I'm not *technically* discharged yet, but everyone's too busy running around with their heads up their asses to notice."

She took another deep, steadying breath, and Darius reached a tentative hand forward to steady her. She shrugged him off. "The important thing is that Ten and I are working on gathering any intel that we can. Council is in town," her eyes met mine and my stomach lurched with the heaviness I saw there. "Arnell's been eavesdropping on a camera he hacked. They're talking about implementing a lockdown on everyone, twelve hours a day. Everyone's being brought in for questioning. They're going to start blood testing soon, probably trying to make sure there aren't other werewolves in the mix after Sarah and Atlas. We'll figure out what we can. Plus," she straightened her posture, schooled her features—mission-mode activated, "Max can dream-walk to me. She's mentioned that she needs a connection with a person to reach them, that it helps sometimes. And she's done it before. I don't know if there's anyone else who'd stand a better chance at acting as a spy than me right now." She started pacing slightly, slipping slightly like she didn't have total control over her limbs, talking as much to herself as us, "I've just got to play up the shock and horror—" she flung up air quotes, "about what she is, you know? Pretend

I was clueless the whole time, and make it seem like I'm reinvesting my efforts into all things Guild-centric. And in the meantime, I can try and suss out who else can be persuaded of the truth."

Darius's nostrils flared slightly, his eyes hardening as he nodded. He clasped a hand on her shoulder, keeping her still. "That's brave and admirable. I can see why the little protector values you so much." His grip tightened, but Izzy didn't falter. "But betray her and I'll make your death slow and laborious—keep that in mind."

I held my breath, waiting for her to cower in fear, desperately searching for a way to apologize and explain away the complicated clusterfuck that was our vampire, but then Izzy's face split into a giant, dazzling smile.

"Don't worry, bloodsucker," she patted him on his bicep, "same goes for you. Anything happens to Max under your watch—I'll have an old-fashioned stake carved with your name on it. And I'll make sure it leaves some nasty splinters on the way to your heart. We clear?"

Darius beamed.

Fucking beamed.

And then he took her hand and dramatically shook it. "I like you, Izzy. My collection of protectors I find to be tolerable has expanded more than I ever thought possible."

A cloud of air obscured my vision as a grunt escaped my lips. Max had a way of bringing together the oddest assortment of people.

Ro was silent as he watched the exchange, impassive and distant—like he was here but also not.

"We should get going. We uh," I scrunched my nose, "sort of left a few bodies by the pond." I nodded to Izzy. "You should get out of here too, don't want them finding a reason to detain you in the labs either."

Izzy nodded, eyes hard and determined again. "Tell Max—"

she glanced at Ro, clearly at a loss as to what to say to him to ease the pain as well, "just tell her to visit me when she can. And that I'm with her one-hundred-percent—so is Arnell and the rest of Ten." She clenched her jaw and raised her head slightly. "The Guild can go fuck itself."

3

MAX

A strange, penetrating chill had taken up residence in my body. One that punctured my lungs and ricocheted against my bones. It was searching—hunting—as it pierced through me, creating craters like bullets.

The door opened and closed, the sound soft and delicate, but it rang through my ears with a sharpness that made my stomach lurch.

They kept checking up on me—Darius, Declan, Wade—trading off like sentinels in the night.

They'd bring food, tea, ask me questions, soothe me with a hand on my shoulder—a pressure I couldn't quite feel—cover me with blankets that did nothing to combat the persistent cold that made it almost impossible to move, my fingers and toes long numb and stationary.

I had vague recollections of Declan's thin fingers pressing softly into my arms, lifting me gently like a puppet on strings, guiding me to the bathroom a few feet away so that I could relieve myself—but I felt awkward and detached, like no matter how much guidance I had, I couldn't feel my limbs move or make them work the way I usually could.

Their concern lapped against my skin each time they opened the door. Part of me, deep down in a pocket I couldn't quite reach into, wanted to soothe them, to smile and chat, to make them laugh, to move my lips and tongue and say *something*, to erase the fear and concern I could feel pouring into me.

But even though it was like a thick tsunami wave, that buried part of me was imprisoned behind an even thicker glass barrier. The buried wave was visible, powerful, but not something I could reach from the other side of the glass.

Something about their presence made the chill sharpen, made my chest contract and my breaths come in short, painful gasps until my vision clouded over with black dots. I didn't know how to tell them that it was better when they left me alone, that when I was alone, the numbness hollowed out the cold—that when they were gone, I could sink into a strangely soothing nothingness. A nothingness where time slipped away and I could watch myself from above, a removed bystander from all of it—detached, floating. Nothing.

When they were close, images of *him* flooded my mind. Our last conversation playing on loop like a broken, warped record, the sounds and images creating caricatures that felt unfamiliar and strange. Images of his body collapsing against mine. Of his blood soaking my hands in a red so thick and dark that it almost didn't look real. The feeling of my chest cracking in half over and over and over again as I tried desperately to call on my powers to heal him.

But they didn't.

My powers were broken, useless—gone, maybe. I wasn't sure. I honestly didn't even care. It didn't matter. None of it mattered.

My body felt like it wasn't mine anymore, like I was occupying it, temporarily, waiting for the permanent owner to come back and claim it. And maybe when they did, I could be left in peace.

The hellfire that I'd slowly mastered felt distant and far from reach, an echo in a hallway I couldn't quite access.

I couldn't sleep, couldn't bring my lips to form words, couldn't think of what I'd say even if they could, couldn't focus on anything other than those final moments with him—and the relentless cold that only abated when numbness tempered it.

This felt more like hell than hell ever had.

The low, growly rumble of someone clearing their throat lifted me back to the surface, but I couldn't quite take a breath large enough to fill my lungs. Even that satisfaction was unsalvageable.

"The others left." His voice was quiet, strained, but somehow more familiar to me than my own.

Eli.

I felt the mattress dip as he sat next to me, his hip pressing softly against mine. The feel of him against me sent a sharp trill down my spine, lingering heavy in my chest.

I felt his eyes on me, watching, wanting me to say or do something, but no matter how hard I tried, I couldn't get my thoughts to latch onto anything concrete, couldn't bring myself to do much more than breathe in and out—and even that was difficult in the harder moments.

His hand gripped my shoulder and squeezed as he sighed. The back of his other hand pressed against my forehead, like he was checking for a temperature—the gesture gentle and filled with an empathy that made my heart thud thickly, like it was waking up, recalling, however poorly, how to function.

Time slipped, and I wasn't sure how long we remained that way—him leaning into me, like his body was searching for a connection mine couldn't match, me curled on my side, immobile. Minutes? Hours?

"I'm sorry you have to feel this pain." He pushed the words gently into the silence, his voice gravelly and strained with an emotion I couldn't mirror. "I'd give everything I had if I could take it away from you, if I could prevent you from going throu —" the word cracked and he took a deep breath, steadying himself. "Our world seems to keep hurling the impossible at you. It isn't fair. You haven't deserved an ounce of the hurt you've experienced. I'd hoped that at least—that at least this one thing, you'd be shielded from." A long breath of silence. "I'm sorry." I felt my fingers tingle slightly, begin to twitch and muscle their way out of the locked claw they'd formed into hours ago. "I didn't know Cyrus well, Max—" his weight settled against me, heavier now, and my stomach clenched tight around Cy's name, the cold dissipating into something else, something worse, "but he was good. And I'm sorry that he's gone. I'm sorry that I couldn't save him—that I couldn't give you that one thing."

His guilt settled heavy in the air and I tried like hell to understand why he felt it. None of this had been his fault. He wasn't the one who—

I swallowed, felt the dryness of my tongue as it rolled against the roof of my mouth, testing. That wasn't his guilt to carry. I wouldn't let him shoulder it. It was mine.

"I forgive you."

He froze against me as the sentence floated between us, my voice hoarse, little more than a scratchy whisper.

"But not for that. Nothing about what happened to him— nothing that happened the other day was on you." I licked my dry lips, tried to fill my lungs with a full breath of air, failed, but forced my mouth to keep moving anyway, to press through the sludge that had been burying me. "It's on me. But I can forgive you for before. For lying to me—for using me—and I'm sorry that I didn't say so sooner."

He took a shaky breath, like he was choking on air. "You shouldn't."

"I do. I think I forgave you a long time ago, Eli."

"Why are you telling me this now?" He sounded so lost, like a small child almost.

For a moment, I felt less lonely, as if the wandering, terrified child deep inside of me had found a momentary reprieve, a companion to walk alongside in the darkness. I wanted to cling to it, to him, to connect and feel—something. Just for a while. Something other than the clawing chill.

"Because forgiveness should be an easy thing to give once it's felt."

The words were coming easier to me now, but I only felt partially in control of shaping them. It felt like we were floating in a dream, me hovering peculiarly over our shapes on the bed, watching and participating, but not quite there.

"I wish I hadn't held onto it for so long. It seems so small now. Everything I've worried about, everything that's made me so angry and afraid these last few months. All of it so wildly, cosmically—" a chuckle escaped from my lips, harsh and unbidden and hollow sounding. "All of it so goddamned unimportant." I closed my eyes, my throat thick as I swallowed, the anger I'd felt in my last conversation with Cy flashing through me, the most vivid thing I'd felt in days. "He asked if I'd ever be able to forgive him. That day—when Ro came back with Jer's body. He'd said that he hoped one day I would be able to. And I didn't, not then, I couldn't bring myself to tell him that I someday might. Couldn't make myself feel it enough to want to voice it, to give him that hope. I was just so fucking angry. So tired of being lied to, so tired of feeling betrayed. And now, he's gone, and I couldn't give him that one crumb of peace. He devoted his entire life to keeping me safe. And I didn't even thank him. He died trying to protect me and he died thinking that I hated him—" I sucked in a sob, unable to continue, but no tears fell, like my lungs were feeling the raw ache that the rest of me couldn't wrap my mind around, couldn't quite reach.

I felt Eli cocoon me in his arms, the pressure strangely comforting, grounding, as he pressed his chest into my back and squeezed my ribs in a vise. His lips brushed against the side of my head in a soft kiss. "Max, he knew," I felt him shake his head, hug me closer, "of course he knew that you loved him. No one who's seen you two together for more than a fraction of a second could ever doubt how much you loved him. How much he loved you. He died the way he would have wanted to go—too soon, yes—but he died protecting you, keeping you safe. If he was given the chance to do it again, there's no doubt he'd make the same choice a million times over."

"I didn't want him to make that decision for me. I didn't want him to die. It—it should have been me. I wish—" I swallowed, suppressing a shiver. "I wish it had been me."

The chill sharpened, like my awareness of it made it flare. I felt Eli stiffen against me, his biceps tensing as they squeezed me, like he felt it too.

"Don't say that." His voice was low, strangled. "Don't ever say that." He took a deep breath, inhaling into my hair—not in a sensual way, but like simply being next to me grounded him too, like he could sense the disconnect and he was trying to weave us back together. "Please, don't ever even think that."

There was fear in his tone, pain. I could hear it, even if I couldn't quite feel it.

We fell back into silence, I could feel his heart beat heavy against my back, slowly drumming at the exact moments mine did.

My thoughts tunneled, swirling together at lightning pace until I thought I might throw up: the visual of Cy collapsing in my arms, the strangled stretch and tug of my magic as I tried to undo what had been done, the sound of my scream when I realized that I couldn't bring him back, that he was really gone, the feel of his warm blood coating my arms as it cooled and started to flake off like ash.

Too much. It was too much.

As if sensing the panic gripping my chest, he turned me around until I faced him, his face an inch away from mine, visible only in abstract features in the dark room.

I latched onto his eyes—dark and shadowed right now, but I could picture the warm amber that I was so familiar with all the same. Something about that familiarity squeezed painfully at my chest and I dropped my gaze, unable to hold his.

"I want it to stop," I said, my voice quiet and vibrating with something I couldn't voice. "Please."

"I know." His jaw tensed, his fingers tightening around me. "I know. I wish I could make it stop."

And he did know.

Eli was no stranger to pain, to loss. I saw it reflected there in his expression now—a frozen sort of torment that he carried with him, always. Occasionally, he found ways for it to thaw, but it never left him completely.

Slowly, like my limbs didn't quite remember how to follow my brain's instructions, I lifted my right hand to his face.

He didn't so much as breathe as I feathered the pads of my fingers against his brow, tracing down to his cheek. When my thumb swept across the corner of his lips, they parted as he let out a trembling exhale.

I felt his eyes on me, but I couldn't remove mine from the spot where my finger traced his flesh, while I watched his body respond to my every touch—like suddenly I was the puppet master instead of the puppet.

A familiar heat flared briefly, simmering low but unmistakably, battling against the piercing cold that had a grip on my chest—a grip that loosened, just slightly, with Eli's arms around me.

This.

This was what I wanted right now.

What I needed.

To feel something.

To break out of his horrible, apathetic purgatory I'd been simply existing in—floating in like a corpse—since they'd set me down on this bed.

Where were we even? Whose bed was this? Why hadn't I thought to ask before?

I pushed the thoughts away, chasing that need. I leaned forward, brushed my lips against his—not so much a kiss as a touch, and felt that simmering heat flare again, glow.

And then it was gone, a smudge wiped clean.

Eli gripped my waist as I leaned into him again, like he was caught between stopping me and pulling me back to him.

"You can," I whispered, my body feeling more my own than it had in hours, days maybe, my heartbeat galloping towards something just out of reach—like the organ itself recognized that this might stop the chill, even if for only a few moments. When my lips met his again, I kissed him properly this time, so there was no mistaking whether or not it was my intention. My lips felt cold against his, awkward, familiar and not all at once. "You can make it stop. Just for a few minutes."

He stiffened, took a deep breath, and pulled back until there were a few more inches between us. It was slow and laborious, like our bodies were magnets fighting to close the distance again. "Max, I can't—not like that, not like this. That would be taking adva—"

"You wanted to know what would make it better," I said, cutting him off, "this is it. I'm telling you that this is what I want right now. I know sex isn't a permanent fix. I just want to feel—something—even if it's just for a few minutes. I just need to feel connected to something—to someone. Alive." I exhaled, slow and steady as I met his eyes. "This is what you do, right? Drown your demons in a few moments of pleasure?" His grip tightened against me again, and he leaned back like I'd slapped him, something unreadable in his face. When I felt him start to refuse, I pushed further. "It's what you all do. Why can't I do the same? Show me how you do it. Please, you owe me that. If you don't want me, that's one thing, but I'm giving you my consent here—casual, meaningless sex. That's what I want right now." The sharp line of his jaw clenched, the muscles working overtime. "I just want the thoughts—the visuals—to stop. Just a few minutes of peace. Please."

I sounded needy and maybe a little whiny, but I didn't care. This was the first thing that I'd wanted, that I'd craved, that had stopped my thoughts from circling the drain of Cy's death since it happened. The first thing that had beaten back some of the numbness stretching down to my toes. That had at least drawn a tether between my thoughts and my body, if not fully making them one again.

I was a succubus. Maybe connecting with that part of myself would pull me back to the surface, help me breathe again.

I'd settle for one, deep breath right now. Just one.

I saw the indecision war on his face, saw the moment of hesitation, and the moment that he shoved it aside.

His lips pressed to mine, hot and hungry—and like a song I'd heard before, mine responded to each beat.

His fingers dug into my hair, gripping it as he deepened the kiss.

I trailed mine down the hard plane of his chest and under the hem of his shirt, my fingers tingling with the sparks of sensation as my skin met his. His warmth sank into me, a ferocious wave that shoved the piercing chill somewhere far—back, back, *back*.

I straddled him, needing more, needing it quickly.

His teeth snagged lightly on my bottom lip, pulling a low, intoxicating moan from my throat. Every atom of my body was suddenly burning. As I felt his thick, hard dick press against my core, something primal unleashed deep in my chest.

"More," I said, the word caught between a growl and a whisper. "Now."

Deftly, his hands peeled my shirt off, his movements slow and deliberate as the cotton ghosted across my body, pebbling every inch of skin it touched. With less intensity, he peeled off his own, the skin of his chest meeting mine in a tender heat as he flipped us over, my head landing softly on the pillow.

He kissed my jaw, nipping and licking his way down, one hand teasing one of my nipples as he sucked and bit at the other.

My body felt electric, on fire, something buried and needy emerging with a force that almost took my breath away. Everything but Eli evaporated from my thoughts—suddenly the only thing in the entire world that existed was him, was this moment. I wanted to live inside of it forever.

His fingers dipped into the hem of my pants as his lips found their way back to mine, two of them sliding low, low, low, until they slipped easily through the building wetness and entered me.

"Jesus fucking christ," he mumbled into my mouth, voice straining with a need that met my own and amplified it. "I don't think I'm ever going to stop wanting you." His thumb circled my clit in slow, consistent, delicious movements as the pressure built. "Tell me what you want." His lips brushed mine with every word he spoke, his teeth snagging again on my bottom lip as he pinched my clit. "Tell me what feels good. I want to make you feel good, Max." He moaned as I started riding his fingers. "It's the only thing that I want in the entire goddamn world."

I could feel his dick straining in his pants against my thigh.

Heat flooded my body in thick, intoxicating waves. I unbuttoned his pants and shoved them down. He throbbed when my hand met the skin of his shaft, the tip wet with pre-cum as he gasped into my mouth, his hand cupping my face. Clumsily, I shoved my pants down, any seductive, languid movements the succubus usually had when she was in control noticeably stunted. "You. You inside me," I moaned. He sheathed himself in one fluid motion, our low groans meeting as one. "Just you."

Our bodies fit together like puzzle pieces. It probably sounded like a cliche, but it sure as fuck didn't feel like one. Our heavy breaths mingled between us in the moments when our lips came apart.

Hand caressing my cheek, his eyes met mine. There was so much swirling behind them as he fucked me—slow, tender—and suddenly this didn't feel like meaningless sex.

"You have me." He whispered the words into my mouth and my chest tightened, breath catching. There was such an intense sincerity in the way he studied me, sliding in and out at a pace that kept me perched on the edge of mindless bliss.

It took a moment for my brain to catch up and realize he was responding to what I'd said before, about wanting him inside of me. But this felt like something else, something more.

His grip tightened as his hands moved into my hair, his pace slowly building until a pure, syrupy, liquid heat filled me to the brim. "You have me, Max. You had me long before my stubborn ass realized it, and you'll have me until my last breath."

On his next thrust I came undone and I felt him fill me as he followed me over, swallowing my moan and thrusting so deeply it was like he was trying to merge our bodies into one.

We didn't speak. The dark, cold room was filled only with the sound of our labored breaths as our bodies processed and came down from—whatever that was.

He lifted himself off of me slightly, but not enough to

remove his warmth, both of us still connected, still one. His eyes searched for something in mine—soft, open, so unlike any look I was used to seeing from him.

The piercing chill was gone, buried under a warmth that melted me like putty. The numbness, likewise, was nowhere in sight.

My floating form, that had been watching me from above for days, had fallen—crashing back into me with a force that stole my breath, grounding me so deeply in my body, I might as well have been buried.

And then, like a match snuffed out from a gust of wind, something inside of me shifted.

And then cracked.

I tried to hold my expression still, to swallow back the wave I felt rushing over me.

At first, just one ragged breath escaped from my lips.

Then, another.

And another. Only this one broke into a loud, deep, echoing sob.

My eyes clouded over with liquid just as I saw the tenderness in Eli's fade into concern.

Suddenly I was sobbing so intensely that I dislodged him out of me, my chest shaking in heavy, deep heaves as I tried to suck down a breath of air. The harder I fought it, the heavier it weighed me down.

I was suffocating.

Drowning in my tears.

I felt Eli's arms tighten around me, his hands frantically wiping the dampness from my cheeks—could hear him whispering hurried words and apologies, though I couldn't pick apart the words.

Crying.

There was only crying—the sobs loud and angry and filled with a pain I'd been trying to find for days.

Only I wish that I hadn't.

Now that I'd found it, I couldn't escape from its hold.

The blanket of fear, of grief, was so heavy that I found myself suddenly missing the featherlight bliss of numbness and that sharp, penetrating chill—almost as much as I missed Cyrus.

4

WADE

My skin was tight.

The crisp air helped me suck down a breath—not enough to fill my lungs, not enough to break through the lingering pressure around my chest. But it was better than the stale, compressing air of that hallway.

Even the forest felt fucking confining as I tore my way through the trees, carving my way towards town—the path familiar enough that I only had to focus half of my attention on tracing it.

I needed out of that house, away from those dark walls. I wasn't sure I could've survived another moment there without punching through them. I was suffocating.

After months of living alone, it was difficult being surrounded by people again at all times—even if it was my team, the people I cared about most of all.

Things were different now. I didn't fit the way that I did before, even though I'd never really fit with the team.

I'd always been the outcast: Atlas's little brother, a trophy from Tarren's weakest moment—his living reminder that condoms were important.

There'd been moments over the years when that feeling dissolved, flashes of how I might one day fit with my team. Especially when I officially joined Six. Moments where those strange fractures started to disappear; Declan would look at me as an equal, instead of as the little kid she always tried to coddle, or Eli would ask for my advice about a girl and actually seem to value it—even if he never actually followed it.

But they'd gone on living—fighting—while I'd been stuck in some weird fucking limbo, out of touch with all of them.

Except for Max.

Through it all, she'd grounded me—a steadfast anchor. The only thing that kept my mind whole during my imprisonment.

Mostly whole, anyway.

I felt the most like myself, the most steady, when I was with her.

Only now she was out of reach too—buried under a grief so suffocating that I felt it in my bones, as if it were my own.

Part of me wanted nothing more than to sink into a dreamscape. To pull her with me and erase the rest of the world for a few hours. For a few years, if we could manage it. Those moments with her, alone and consumed with each other, felt more real than anything I experienced in waking life.

It was like my dream self was taking over the physical. I didn't know how to exist in this world anymore.

I didn't know where I fit.

The dark look I saw in Tarren's eyes when they met mine fractured any lingering, naive hope I'd had buried deep that things might be normal again one day. Functional.

I wanted to kill him. Wanted to destroy his faith in the world, like he'd destroyed mine.

But I'd free my brother first. And we'd do it together.

Atlas.

A sharp stabbing pain gutted me whenever I let my thoughts linger on him for more than a second.

I shook my head, tried to shove the image of him away. If I let my ruminations go too far, I would break down. I couldn't handle the very possibility that he might be dead.

Would Tarren kill him? The prodigal son, now the embodiment of his darkest fears?

I dug my palm into the center of my chest, pausing for a moment as I tried to breathe through the invisible vise squeezing me.

I slammed my eyes shut, forced away the images of that small cell that painted my lids every time I closed them.

My pulse accelerated and I sat down, sinking my head between my legs, to keep the trees from spinning around me.

I was in a forest.

I wasn't there.

I wasn't in hell.

Neither a prisoner of Lucifer, nor The Guild.

My fingers dug into the ground, the snow cold against my skin before it melted to slush and left me gripping soggy leaves and clumps of mud. I sank into the sensation as I dug up a new snowball, trying to center myself.

I needed sleep. I hadn't gotten more than a few minutes here and there over the last few days—just enough to try and reach Max, to see if she was as desperate for that sanctuary as I was. But it felt empty without her there with me.

Slowly, I opened my eyes again, forced myself to see the trees and scattered vegetation around me. I wasn't there anymore. I'd escaped. And, so far, we'd all survived.

And I'd do everything I could to make sure that we kept surviving. No matter what. It was the only thing that mattered anymore, the only moral compass I could read.

Right now, that meant tracking down enough food and supplies to get us through this transitional period while Max came back to herself and we navigated the next steps.

Hopefully the others had ideas about what the fuck we

were going to do next, because I was fresh out. There were so many giant fires burning around us that it was impossible to plan a way to stomp each of them out. The moment we focused on one, we'd be consumed by another.

Intrusive thoughts whirred voraciously, hopping from one clusterfuck to the next, until suddenly the forest broke into a familiar clearing. It seemed like one minute I was sitting on the cold ground, the next I was standing on the outskirts of town, my feet robotically moving me towards the entrance of the small grocery store.

I shook my head, tried to dispel the low ringing pulsing in my skull.

Quick. I needed to be quick. Meandering around was reckless. I needed to get in, get out, and get back to them. I had no clue what time it was, but hopefully Headquarters would still be all hands on deck and the town would be empty of everyone but the humans who populated it.

I avoided eye contact and tried to walk through the aisles as covertly as possible, aimlessly throwing random boxes and bags into the cart, careful not to grab anything that required electricity to preserve or prepare. The labels and lighting were familiar but strange all at once, as I traced the same path through the store I'd frequently carved on late nights after drinking too much with Eli, desperate for a snack to hold me over until we got back to campus and real food.

I felt like an intruder now, like that life belonged to an entirely different person.

A set of footsteps broke their cadence, shoes squeaking slightly on the wet floor as they stopped suddenly.

I froze. My heart pounded heavy and thick in my chest as I held my breath.

I didn't turn, just made my way quickly to the cash register after tossing in some packaged, raw meat to tide the vampire over—I hadn't missed the way his eyes would occasionally dart to our necks, like the soft pulsing under our flesh was a beacon—and loaded my items onto the conveyor belt.

"Bags?"

I glanced up briefly to meet a pair of dark hazel eyes set into a face mapped with deep wrinkles.

"Bags," the man said again, shaking his head in frustration when I continued to stare at him. "Do you need bags? Or did you bring your own?"

"Bags." I cleared my throat, dropping eye contact as I fished for the cash Declan had handed me before I left. "Yes, bags. I didn't bring any. Thank you. Please."

The words coming out of my mouth barely made sense to me, but he seemed to get the gist.

Without waiting for him to help, I shoved the items haphazardly into the bags at the end of the conveyor belt, ignoring the old man's muttering as he moved through the items at a snail's pace.

"Hm." He paused, picked up a small bag of pears and moved a pair of glasses that hung on a lanyard up to his face, squinting through the lenses, "you remember how much these were? They aren't ringing up."

My stomach tightened as I shook my head. "No, just forget them. I don't need them."

He set them down, stretched the clear plastic bag, as he studied the small sticker on one of the pears. "Nonsense, nonsense. We'll get to the bottom of it." He grabbed a phone at the side of his screen and pressed it between his face and shoulder. "Price check." He cleared his throat, the sound amplified over the store. "I need a price check on—"

"Really, forget them," I said, interrupting him as I tried to shove the last few items closer to his scanner, to rush him along. "I'm in a hurry."

"Now now," caterpillar brows pinched, he covered the mouthpiece of the phone as he studied me, but it was half-assed and the words carried over the mic and rang throughout the store anyway, "it'll only take a minute. You kids these days need to learn the value of patience. It won't take more than a minute or two of your time."

My heartbeat pounded so ferociously that I could feel it from deep in my gut, all the way to my temples. I felt everyone in the store looking at us, the hairs on the back of my neck were prickling with awareness.

I needed to leave. Now.

"Wade?" a disembodied voice called from somewhere far behind me.

Fuck.

With a grunt, I left a few twenties from the stack on the counter, grabbed the items the man had already rung up, abandoning the pears and last few bags of chips on the counter.

"Hey," he reached for me, but I was too fast, "son, get back here."

Whatever else he yelled melted into the other, suddenly obnoxiously loud sounds of the store as I ran for the door, my head rushing with the pace of my pulse.

This had been reckless.

I shouldn't have been the one to make this trip. It should have been Eli. Word might not have gotten out to everyone that he was technically not on Team Guild anymore—but I knew that everyone would have been acquainted with either my death or my resurrection. Neither were ideal in this scenario.

I'd been selfish, desperate to get out in the open and dispel the pressure building up in my chest, but I'd only made it worse.

"Wade," a soft grunt, "Wade, wait."

That same voice, closer now, but my pace picked up into a steady run the second my lungs filtered in the fresh air, my feet thudding on the pavement for a while, and then the dirt and snow as I found my way back through the treeline.

I focused on the steady swish of the bags at my sides as they bounced together with each step. They were loud and clunky, and not exactly ideal for making a stealth escape.

After a few moments, the buzzing in my ears became unbearable, lights danced before my eyes, and my hands felt stiff and tingly. I leaned against a thick tree, trying to catch my breath for a few minutes.

I closed my eyes, fell back into the dank, dark cell of hell.

I couldn't breathe.

Fuck.

Fuck.

"You're not there, Wade," I whispered to myself as the bags slipped from my fingers and fell to the ground. "You're not there. You're here. Just wake the fuck up. Snap the fuck out of it."

I turned around and swung, burying my knuckles into the bark of the tree, the branches cascading me in powdery snow as they shook from the impact. I didn't feel it though—not the cold, not the pain of the bark biting into my skin, bruising my bones.

But I tried to focus on it anyway—the deep crimson of the blood as it ran through the cracks of my fingers.

"Wade."

That voice again, quieter now, but close. Too close.

I ran towards it, opened my eyes, and felt my fingers wrap around the slim, smooth column of a neck as I shoved it back against a tree, with more force than I'd intended.

Wide, blue eyes stared back at me.

They were set in a familiar face, framed by purple hair.

I blinked. Tried processing the wave of recognition that washed over me.

Thin fingers gripped at my hands, trying to peel them away.

"Dani?" I asked, my voice echoing strangely in my head, like it came from me but also not.

Her eyes bugged out even more, until she looked more fish than foe, as her lips mouthed my name and she slapped my hands.

I shook my head, coming to, and released her. "Fuck, sorry."

She doubled over, coughing and shook her head. "It's okay." Her voice was soft, scratchy, and while some part of me felt guilty for it, my heartbeat was pounding at too punishing of a pace for me to focus on it. "I shouldn't have snuck up on you."

"Dani?" I whispered again, taking a step away from her. I needed to get out of here. I walked back to where I'd dropped the groceries. They were spilled on the ground, caked in snow.

I bent, scooping them back into the bags, as quickly as I could, along with a few handfuls of fresh powder. Wet groceries were better than no groceries.

I needed to go.

Now.

Five minutes ago.

"Wade, wait." Her hand closed gently on my shoulder, but she pulled it away instantly when I jumped and spun towards her. She showed me both of her palms, and took a step away, staring at me like I was a startled animal. "I'm not going to hurt you. You know me. I would never hurt you."

I did know Dani.

She'd always been a friend to me, to my team. I wasn't as close to her as Declan and the others were, but I'd always respected her.

But a lot of people I trusted before would likely run a blade through my heart now. Before meant nothing anymore.

"I won't hurt you," she repeated. "Just talk to me for a moment."

Did she know what I was, what I'd become? Or had word not spread as quickly as I'd thought it would? Maybe in all of the chaos of the ambush, Tarren was trying to keep a lid on things, to quell some of the panic likely pouring through the campus.

Tarren. The expression on his face when he saw that I'd come back from the dead. Dani would hate me just as much as he did, as soon as she realized the truth—as soon as the shock of seeing a ghost dissipated into the harsh reality.

"Are you okay?" She stood taller now, dropped her hands, apparently satisfied that I wouldn't try and kill her again. "Are the others okay too? Declan? Eli? Max?"

She knew Max?

I clenched my jaw, stayed silent, and studied her. Waiting. Though I wasn't sure what I was waiting for.

She sighed, ran a hand over her face, massaging her temples briefly, like she could feel the world's biggest migraine coming on. When her eyes met mine again, they looked as tired as I felt. "Look, I know you don't trust me right now. I know that things have—" she squinted, searching for a word, "changed for you recently. About you. That you've changed," she let out a frustrated sigh, "that you're more than just a protector." She waved her hands in a chaotic circle. "Obviously."

Every muscle in my body tensed and I glanced around trying to assess which direction I was going to run in. I'd gotten so turned around after—whatever the hell happened to me.

"It's okay," her hands went up again in surrender, "I'm not afraid of you. Whatever you are now—werewolf—something else entirely," she shook her head, "it doesn't matter. You're you. I can help you. I can help you all. If you need it. If you want it." She tilted her head, took a deep breath. "And I think you do. Or at least you will, anyway. Eventually. When you're ready to accept it."

My body remained rigid, but I didn't flinch as she reached into the small pouch at her side and fished out a piece of paper and a pen. She glanced at me briefly, considering, before turning her back to me and using the tree as a surface to write on.

I didn't so much as breathe as I watched her, but the fact that she was willing to turn her back to me eased something.

Slowly, I felt my heart rate slow down, the buzzing quiet, but I still didn't feel like myself. The ache in my chest, the tightness, was sharper now, impossible to ignore.

"I think you were having a panic attack," she said, folding the paper as she turned back to me, "that it started in the store and got worse when I scared you." Her nostrils flared slightly as she reached her hand towards me with the paper clutched loosely between two of her fingers. "Sorry about that. It was thoughtless of me; I should have approached with more caution. To be honest, things have been wild these last few days and I'm not thinking as clearly as usual." She let out a humorless chuckle. "But something tells me you get that. You seem like you've been through a lot since the last time we crossed paths." She scrunched her nose. "Chasing you was also probably a really bad idea. Sorry. I was just so relieved to run into one of you. I've been worried."

Silently, I reached for the paper, not taking my eyes off her as I gripped it firmly between my fingers and palm.

"It's a number," she said, biting her bottom lip and glancing around, like she was just as nervous about being caught out here as I had been. "There's a safe place, a few hours from here. There's food, shelter, community—people who," her gaze flashed to me briefly, hardening slightly, "people who don't fit The Guild's mold either. People with more nuanced views on the supernatural world than the ones we've been raised with. They can help you. And I can take you there—" she paused, took a deep breath, "all of you. Even the vampire. When you're ready."

The vampire?

That jostled something in my memory and I suddenly felt

like I was settling back into myself, that my body was becoming more mine again.

During the ambush, we'd run into Dani. Briefly. I'd forgotten all about it until now. But now that the memory was stirred loose, I recalled her panicked expression, the flash of recognition on her face when she saw Darius.

Did they know each other? How?

"Look," she took a deep, steadying breath and straightened her back. "My loyalties aren't with The Guild. Haven't been for years now. That piece of paper has the number to one of my burner phones. I don't know what kind of shit you and the others are wrapped up in, but I know you. And Declan is the closest thing I have to a sister. I've been trying to find a way to bring you guys in anyway, without eyes on us, but shit's been a bit intense. Anyway, the point is, you're family. I know you're good. If you guys run into trouble, if you need help or a place to stay for a little while—call that number. Okay?" Her eyes narrowed with concern, and I watched her body tighten and shift forward, like she wanted to reach over and hug me, but was trying to reign in the urge. "Just take care of yourself, Wade. I don't know what's going on, none of us do, I suspect—but I know it's big. I can feel it. We can all feel it. Something is shifting—something major."

And then, with one more lingering look, she shuffled awkwardly to the side and then back towards me, like she was trying to decide what to do next, like she wasn't ready to leave me here but she also couldn't stay. "And you should be as far away from Headquarters as you can get. Coming here today was careless. You'll need to be smarter than that. Anyone else finds you out here—" she shook her head, a shadow clouding her expression, "it won't go well."

When her eyes met mine one more time, her lips flattened into a small frown. She nodded once, and then walked away.

I didn't linger. But I didn't really remember the details of my trip back to the dilapidated house much either. I made my way back, grocery bags cutting grooves into my fingers, in a daze.

The moment I opened the door though, I snapped out of it.

A deep, heartbreaking sob echoed through the walls.

Max.

Dumping the bags unceremoniously at my feet, I ran towards her cries, bursting through the door of the small room we'd claimed for her.

She was curled into a ball, naked and shaking, her face damp with tears and contorted in a pain so all-consuming—so visceral—that it made my stomach bottom out.

"What happened?" I bent down next to her, pressed a palm to her shoulder and tried to process the scene I'd walked in on.

Eli was pacing along the far side of the room, his hair disheveled.

He was also naked.

Wait.

Why was he naked?

And why the fuck was *she* naked?

My brain was working more slowly than usual, like my thoughts were churning through molasses, but the sexual energy in the room knocked me out of it like an ice-cold shower.

In less than a second, I had Eli pinned against the wall, my forearm pressing into his neck. "What the fuck did you do?"

His eyes were wild and glassy as they met mine. Lost.

For a moment, I almost thought he wanted me to punch him.

"What happened? What the fuck happened, Eli?" I pressed, but then I pulled back a bit. He wouldn't answer me if I kept his air supply cut off.

"She won't stop crying." His voice cracked and he pressed the palms of his hands into his face. "She asked—and it was good," he punched the wall, cracking the plaster, "she was good, I thought. Better. Talking at least. But after—n-now, she won't stop crying. I don't—I don't know what I did."

I took a deep breath, bent over and grabbed Eli's pants. Carelessly, I threw them back to him. "Get fucking dressed, you absolute raging prick."

I picked Max up until she was sitting, and leaned her head against my chest. She was shivering. Instead of letting her go and hunting through the room for her clothes, I peeled my shirt off and put it on her until she was swimming in it, wiping her cheeks dry with my thumbs.

But her tears just coated them again until her face was wet and slippery, her eyes swollen and red.

"What the fuck were you thinking?" I whisper-yelled at Eli, not wanting to startle Max or make her feel like I was yelling at her. "I'm going to fucking castrate you. Your dick causes more harm than Lucifer's blade."

"Not his fault," she sniffed.

Or I thought that was what she said. It was hard to parse the words from the heaving sobs wracking through her small frame.

When I squeezed her to me, she pushed me away, crawling back into the same fetal position I'd found her in, only now she had the added armor of my shirt.

I swallowed, ignoring the way her rejection made my chest tighten. I wanted to help her, but I had no fucking idea how to reach her, how to pull her out of the pool of misery she seemed to be drowning in.

My stomach clenched, guilt boiling in my veins. She'd reached me when I needed her. When she'd found me, I'd been lost and trapped in the dark, a prisoner of my own mind even more than I was a prisoner of the devil—and she shaped herself into a light so bright I had no choice but to climb towards it. Why couldn't I do that—be that—for her?

"What do we do?" Eli whispered, but he wouldn't take a

step closer. He looked lost. Feral almost, as he pressed his back into the wall. "I'm sorry, Max. So fucking sorry."

And it was only when his eyes met mine that I realized that whatever I thought had happened between them, hadn't. He looked just as broken as she did. Just as cracked open. Just as lost.

I clenched my jaw and knotted my fingers together in my lap. It took everything I had not to reach for her again. I wanted to comfort her, to calm her, to soothe whatever wound Eli had clearly ripped wide-fucking-open. But it was obvious that she wanted space. She didn't want us here. We couldn't fix—this. Whatever this was.

And if we could, she wasn't ready to let us.

Slowly, I stood up and made my way towards Eli, but I couldn't stand still, watching her like that for long. I started pacing in the same listless way I'd found him doing when I walked in, standing guard until she reached for one of us—or let us know what it was that she needed.

After a few long, silent minutes, I opened my mouth, searching for something to say to him, to her. Her crying hadn't subsided at all. If anything, she only seemed to sink into herself, like she was trying to contain all of the pain she felt, to keep it from spreading out to us.

The door opened, a loud crash, and then Declan's soft swearing.

She must've tripped over the groceries.

I felt the moment they realized something was off. Three sets of steps thundered and then stopped as one when they reached the bedroom.

Darius looked like he was going to kill Eli.

Declan scanned the room, looking for an intruder, trying to make sense of what could have possibly turned Max from a silent ghost into the bundle of exposed nerves she was now.

Rowan didn't even so much as glance at us as he made his

way into the room, dropping a bag with a heavy thud on the floor. I heard one sob crack from his chest as he knelt down next to her. His hand swept her hair back from where it curled against her wet cheek and he pressed his forehead to hers. For a moment, they both simply lay like that, curled up together, cocooned in a shared grief.

He didn't try to stop her tears, didn't try to soothe her pain.

Instead, he lingered in it with her, because it was his too.

I held my breath, not wanting to interrupt the tenderness between them. I felt the rage dissipate from Darius, saw Declan's eyes well up out of the corner of mine.

After a few minutes, Rowan shifted, sat up, lifted Max into a seated position, and hugged her so tightly to his chest that I was afraid he might hurt her.

Slowly, her breath hitched in a swallowed sob before evening slightly, and then her hands gripped him back, with a force I knew would bruise even a protector.

"Ro?"

5

ATLAS

"Damn it, Atlas." Tarren slammed his palm into the wall of my cell. It didn't shatter. It didn't even waiver. The thick material between us might have looked like glass, but glass couldn't keep demons—creatures like me—inside of a prison. "Just tell me the truth." I felt him begin to pace, even though I refused to look at him. "What happened to you? To your brother? Where's the girl? What *is* she?"

Like they did the first—and second and third—time he berated me with these questions, my lips remained closed. I sat in the middle of the cell. It was barren of everything—even my clothes. After a few hours, the chill of my bare skin against the ground numbed.

I hadn't met his eyes once since I woke up in this room. The tranquilizers still hadn't fully left my system, and something told me that they'd find a way to keep me dosed once they did. I felt my wolf buried deep inside of me, like he was locked in some room I couldn't access—whatever they had running through my veins was enough to quiet him. For now.

Strangely, I missed his presence. I felt incomplete without him.

I had no idea when that shift had happened.

"If you tell us what you know, I might be able to convince them to let you out."

Lie.

We both knew he was lying. I would die here, like all the other captive demons would.

As far as I knew, Darius and Ralph were the only demons to successfully escape from these walls once they'd been thrown behind them.

"If you give us something to go on, you can survive this, son. I'll make sure of it."

Lie.

His voice deepened when he said the word 'son,' like it left a foul taste on his tongue.

"We're on the same side."

Lie.

My side was Max. And even if my father still retained a small iota of loyalty to me, I knew that he had none for her.

"The council—" he sighed, and I knew him well enough to recognize the small trace of fear in his voice.

Tarren was a powerful man. But if the council was involved now, even his power would be checked.

I didn't care, not anymore. Not about him. Not about what happened to me.

She was safe. She was alive. She was free from my father's grasp. From the council.

I bit back a grin. I'd been worried at first, but the fact that he was asking about her confirmed that he didn't have her. That she'd gotten away.

They all had.

The events of the battle had been replaying through my head constantly while I was locked in here. Once Dec had met my eyes and I saw anger, fear, and, finally, understanding flash across her face, I knew that she'd understood. She'd grabbed Eli and they'd taken off.

I'd distracted my father and the others long enough for them to escape. It wasn't difficult either. The prized son, leader of one of the most prestigious teams in The North American Guild, a werewolf?

I hadn't planned on getting knocked out, captured. I'd intended on taking my father out with me before one of them inevitably landed a blade in my chest.

The wolf wanted Tarren's blood. But after what he'd done to Max, I wanted it even more.

He'd killed Cyrus—an unforgivable thing—but he'd been aiming for her.

Hopefully Dec and Eli had found Max and Wade by now. Hopefully she was okay.

It took everything I had not to vomit whenever that scene ran on replay in my head—Max, heartbroken, clutching Cyrus to her. My father's raw rage when he saw Wade, when he saw me—the real me.

Tarren had nearly killed a nineteen-year-old girl—a girl so selfless, filled with a capacity for love that outstripped any creature I'd ever met in my life—yet he thought *we* were the monsters?

I had no doubt that Cy was dead, but I hoped for her sake that he wasn't. That there was a tether of life that he still clung to, that her healing magic pulled him back from the brink like it had done so many times for us. That she and the rest of my team would find a safe place to hole up for the rest of their lives, while the rest of the world crumpled. That she'd have a chance at happiness. Even for just a little while.

Clinging to that possibility, that hope, made facing my own fate tolerable.

"Atlas!" Tarren slapped the partition between us again,

enough venom in his voice that my gaze met his compulsively. "What do you know? Tell me now, before things get very, very bad for you. For all of us."

He looked more disheveled than I'd ever seen him. There were dark circles under his eyes, his hair was uncharacteristically out of place, the shadow of his beard scraggly and unkempt. The buttons on his top were misaligned so that the right side of his flannel dipped lower than the left. There were red lines along his neck from where I was sure he'd been stress-scratching.

The cool, calm, collected Tarren—the mask that he showed the world—was now just an echo. He was a goddamn mess.

I'd been so focused on Max, on my team, that the bigger picture had evaded me.

The details of the ambush were so muddled, and it didn't help that I was knocked out for the latter half of the battle.

How many were lost?

Which factions had attacked The Guild?

Was Lucifer behind it?

Were they here because they hated protectors, or were they here for Max?

The muscles along Tarren's jaw pulsed and tensed. I wouldn't be surprised if he cracked a tooth trying to keep the rage washing through him buckled down, contained.

I swallowed my grin as I studied him. Good. He deserved whatever inner turmoil he was pulsing with. I hoped it consumed him.

His eyes narrowed. "Fine. We'll see if one of your friends has more to offer. Maybe Eli? Adding a little pressure and persuasion has a way of yielding interesting results." He turned on his heels. "And down here, we have plenty of tools with which to apply pressure and persuasion."

I stood up and rushed towards him, but with nothing more than a malicious smirk, he walked away.

My stomach clenched and my chest ached as I pounded my fists into the not-glass where his face had been moments before.

Eli?

Was he here?

Had he not gotten out?

What about Wade?

Declan?

The vampire?

Max?

～

"You know who's responsible for my son's death?" Sal asked as he stuck me with a syringe that poured liquid fire through my veins.

When I tensed in pain, he grinned.

Sal was Jer's father.

And Jer had been killed by a pack of wolves when he and Rowan were separated from the rest of Ten. Rowan had nearly been taken down with him.

I'd felt strangely relieved when they'd returned—that it was Jer who'd died. The thought of Max losing her family cut me as deeply as losing my own.

But then she'd lost one half of her family anyway, a mere day or two later.

"I've always stood up for you," Sal muttered, his voice wavering as he hovered above me. "Whenever your father took his own frustrations out on you over the years—I," he shook his head. "Why my son? Jer was good. Kind."

"He was. I'm sorry he's dead." They were the first words I'd spoken since being brought into captivity. And, strangely, I found myself meaning them.

I'd never been particularly fond of Jer—he and Sarah had

some baggage from when we were kids, but his greatest recent offense as far as I was concerned was flirting with—and kissing—Max.

But he was also her friend, and his death had fractured something in her.

I couldn't blame him for wanting her though, as much as it had made my stomach turn to see them kiss once.

He didn't deserve death.

My attempt at conveying my sympathy did little to quell the rage emanating from him. If anything, it only seemed to deepen, to burrow and sharpen.

Sympathy wouldn't bring back his son. Right now, he wanted someone to blame, someone to hate.

"Not sorry enough to give us any answers." He shoved me into the ground, my head thudding on the hard, concrete floor. "So, tell me boy, what use to me is sorry?"

Every nerve in my body felt frayed and exposed, my eyesight blurry as I tried to maintain focus.

I had no idea what he'd injected me with, but I felt weak and soft—my body a gelatinous form that I had no control over.

They'd tried so many different forms of persuasion over the hours—days? I wasn't sure anymore. I pressed my cheek into the cool ground, letting whatever substance they'd given me do its work while sleep pulled me under.

～

"ATLAS. *ATLAS*. WAKE UP."

The voice was soft, familiar.

I blinked a few times, my vision hazing and clearing until a familiar face, framed by blond hair, came into focus.

Reza.

She looked terrible. Maybe even worse than my father.

Her usually confident expression was deflated in despair, her wide eyes rimmed with red and sparkling with a fresh wave of unshed tears.

"Thank the gods you're alive." She let out a sigh and took a step closer to the wall separating us, fidgeting with her hands as a loud scream down the hall made her jump. "Are you okay?"

The noises down here had all but disappeared from my notice. I wasn't sure how many demons they'd managed to capture from the ambush, but I knew from Eli's report that the labs had already been overcrowded before then. Tarren's primary mission since stepping foot on our campus had been to retain as many creatures as physically possible.

He'd succeeded in that endeavor, like he did in most.

The floor I was on had been filled with the echoing sounds of brawls and screams. He just had no idea that his son would be a part of his bounty.

I blinked a few times as I watched Reza, trying to process her presence as I fought through the strange fog weighing me down.

I felt nothing as her eyes met mine.

The last time I'd seen her was right before the ambush—mere minutes after our bonding ceremony had finished.

My stomach had been a tangled mess of knots during the ceremony, but it wasn't until our masks were removed after the fact that I'd realized, for the first time, that Reza seemed a little hesitant about our union too. Nervous, maybe even a little afraid.

She'd always marched in the shadow of her mother—as desperate to please her as I'd once been to please my father.

We'd led mirrored lives, in many ways—both of us bogged down by familiar familial pressure and the desire to earn our place here.

It made sense that we'd been forced together—the progeny

of two of the most decorated Guild protectors, united as one, strengths bolstered.

And if there'd been no Max, maybe I would've even grown to value her. It was possible that her edginess, sharpened by insecurity, could soften—that I could value her the way I valued the rest of my team.

But there was Max, and Reza had stood no chance with us from the moment that Max had come barreling into our lives. The force pulling us all together was unlike anything I'd ever felt before—powerful and terrifying and exhilarating all at once.

I think even Reza knew that.

She watched me for a long moment in silence, her face unreadable. I wasn't sure why she was here—probably something my father had cooked up to get me to talk.

It was strange to imagine her tied to me in some fabricated, shallow way.

I felt no pull toward her now.

No stomach flip or gut-wrenching possessiveness. No lure that made me want to break down the glass and reach for her. I wasn't strengthened by her presence or hyper-aware of every beat of her heart.

I was as indifferent towards her as I'd always been.

How could The Guild possibly think its staged version of bonding was even a shadow of the real thing?

"When were you bitten?" she asked, her gaze piercing mine with a leveled focus that made it clear she was trying to give me a semblance of modesty by not looking at my naked body. "How long have you been—" she swallowed, "like this?"

I blinked, my mind still hazy as I fought for control over my limbs, my mouth.

"Since Sarah?" her brow arched as her voice caught. I tilted my head slightly, which she must've taken for a nod, because she pressed on. "I've heard that she's back. That she's like you.

But no one will confirm anything. Not even—" she shook her head and blinked away the tears glazing her eyes as I filled in the silent gaps. Her mother, Alleva, was keeping things from her too. That, or Alleva was just as much in the dark as her daughter now. How many members of the council were here? Had my father lost the small measure of control and power he'd spent a lifetime scraping to gain? "That's a long time," she continued, popping her knuckles, finger by finger. "But you didn't seem—I don't know—bad. Or evil. Is it true what they say? Were you infiltrating The Guild? Spying? Did you kill anyone? Change anyone? Or—" her eyes darted down the hall again. "How could you live with us for months without any of us noticing?" Her voice grew so quiet that I had to read her lips. "I don't know what to think anymore. None of this makes sense. And I don't know what I'm supposed to do. Who to trust. Things are bad, Atlas. Really bad. I don't know what to—"

Her hands balled into fists as her focus darted up and to the left briefly, where I knew a camera would be.

"What are they doing to you in here?" She took a deep breath. "Do you feel different?" her hand gestured between us. "Since the ceremony? Bonded? Is this what it was like with you and Sarah?" she tilted her head to the side and her voice dipped into another whisper that I could barely make out. "Because I don't feel anything. At all. I thought it would be different, I thought—" she shook her head and pressed a hand to the glass. "Maybe it takes more time, I don't know. But I feel just as far from you as I always have. I think they finally only let me down here on the chance that wasn't the case—on the chance that I could draw some answers from you. Or they could see if werew—" her voice broke on the word, "if werewolves could bond to protectors. If I might be tarnished by you, somehow. They've been running tests on me nonstop." Her chin dimpled, like she was holding in a sob, her posture slouched. "I don't know what to do. My mother won't even look at me. What do I do?"

It was the most I'd ever heard Reza say. Or maybe this was just the first time I ever really bothered listening to her.

She seemed so small, standing there; so vulnerable. Even though I was the one naked and drugged in a cage, there was something so fragile about her now, so lost. Maybe she always had been, and I just never let myself see her as she was.

I'd accepted the mask she presented to the world at face value.

Just as I'd hoped the world would accept mine.

∼

Hours and days rolled into each other. With nothing but the harsh, artificial light bathing me in an unearthly glow, I couldn't get a register on how long I'd been locked here. Time felt frozen, stilted.

Visits from researchers—the pain of their injections, the carvings etched with their tools—were my only clear tell that time was passing at all.

How had the vampire kept his mind, locked inside of here for all of these years? For the first time, I felt myself feeling sorry for him, admiring him even. I could feel my fingers slipping from the tenuous grip that I still held.

How had I not seen this place for what it was before? Had it always been so twisted down here? Had I really funneled demons into these cells without questioning anything?

While I was certain they were likely going harder on me because of who I was—who my father was—and because of how intense things were getting, I still didn't understand why they were so focused on keeping us here. On keeping these cells filled with demons. To what end? An ambush that size on Guild Headquarters was unparalleled. They were desperate to find answers, and they thought the way to unleash them was by digging through my skin, my mind.

Joke was on them though. I had no answers. Not anymore. The only thing for me to hold on to was the fact that she was safe. We'd rescued Wade from hell, and the rest of my team was with them—I hoped so, anyway. They'd find a way to push through all of the shit and hopefully build a semblance of a life somehow.

The heavy clang of the door opening echoed through the cell.

Sal again. He appeared in the small gap, hands locked around a dart gun. As if I was capable of rushing him. It took all of my energy right now to simply keep my eyes open.

His face was covered with a surgical mask, one speckled with splashes of dried blood, but I could see the disgust on his face, in the divot between his beady eyes. The blood wasn't mine for once. Who else had he been trying to pull answers from?

"You ready to talk?" he asked, though something about the tone of his voice convinced me that he hoped I wasn't. He didn't want any more of my words. Not really. Not unless they led him to more wolves to tear down.

He'd enjoyed the recent torture sessions—there was a quiet revenge in the way he'd stab my arm with the injections they were giving me. When he'd drawn blood samples. When he'd used The Guild's many creatively excruciating tactics to try pulling information from my lips.

My lips remained closed though. Every time.

I could feel his lip curl, even if I couldn't see it. "Didn't think so." He widened his step, tightened his shoulders, like he was bolstering himself. "You talk and your pain will end, you know."

Once I gave them what they wanted—the whereabouts of Max and the rest of my team, information about my transformation—they'd have no more use for me. I'd become another discarded body in next week's trash pile.

He'd witnessed enough of my pain—hell, he'd caused most of it himself—to know that death would bring a kind of peace. That it was the most I could hope for now. But I'd suffer for an eternity before I betrayed her or the others ever again.

"Just fucking tell me. You owe me that one thing. Was it you? Are you the demon who killed my son? He always competed with you, you know—his entire life, he aimed to be as good as you and your friends. Tarren Andrews's star child," he mocked, though his voice sounded so hollow in the cell. "You got all of the accolades, all of the attention. Hell, you even got the girls he was interested in—first Sarah, and now Bentley's daughter has you wrapped around her demonic little finger. Was this your way of permanently striking him down, ensuring that he never challenged you again? Never surpassed you?"

He was in pain. Desperately seeking a way to relieve an ache that would never completely disappear.

I despised him, yes. But more than that, I pitied him.

I knew that rage he held onto. It'd guided me for months. First when I chased retribution for Sarah's—supposed—death, and later when I watched Wade's body fall at the hands of Lucifer and his minions.

Sal's anger was mine—his dark eyes a mirror of the same grief I'd felt.

This was how The Guild stoked the flames in our bellies. It led us to believe that all of our sorrow, all of our grief was created by hell. Gave us solace in the fact that we were doing everything we could to avenge our families, our friends. Then, it armed our hands with weapons and sent us to fight in a war that none of us truly understood.

I shook my head, the movement stiff and painful. I could give him that at least.

His brows furrowed, expression relaxing with surprise. This was the most response I'd given anyone in days. Maybe weeks.

"Your friends then?" His voice cracked on the last word. He blinked a few times, drying the gloss coating his eyes. "They do this? Sarah? Someone else?"

Sarah?

Gods, I hoped she was still fucking alive. But if Sal and The Guild knew what she was, that meant they had her.

So maybe her death would be a kinder thing for me to hope for.

I shook my head again, though my neck was so stiff that I wasn't sure it actually moved. "I would never hurt someone unprovoked." Not anymore, anyway. Not unless they were after me or my own. "We aren't all the monsters you believe us to be. Though I think, deep down, you know that."

My voice was strained and unfamiliar, my throat screaming at me with every word I pushed out.

Something unreadable flashed across the small sliver of his face I could see. But it was gone as quickly as it came. He inhaled deeply, shook his head with a grunt. "Yeah. Right."

For a moment, we locked eyes. Did he see the younger version of me? The one he'd watched train and grow for decades?

"Sarah—" I croaked, "Wh—"

He sniffed, then nodded to someone standing behind the door, a shadow I only just noticed.

A burly guard, cloaked in black. I couldn't make out their features, but I recognized the crest on their chest. A member of council or one of their favored personal guards. And different from the one I'd met at the bonding ceremony with Reza. This one had broader shoulders, and something about their stance, the power radiating from them, told me they'd be a formidable match in a spar. Even with my wolf at the surface.

But I only spared them a quick glance, because a familiar

figure stood, crouched and naked at his side, with shackles on her raw wrists and ankles.

Sal nodded the guard in and gripped Sarah's shoulders before throwing her to the ground. I crawled towards her, but I was too slow to soften the blow. "Seems your brother isn't the only one to fake his death and join the demons. The gods only know how many more of your team members—or the students you've been training and infiltrating—have succumbed to the same fate." He glanced down at her, shaking his head. "A woman too. And a fine fighter if my memory serves me—which it always does. A shame, she would have been an ideal candidate to carry a child soon—and at a time when we could desperately use strong numbers."

My lip curled in disgust as I gripped her arm softly in my hand, fighting Sal and the guard with the only thing I could—a glare and a promise that they'd pay for whatever harm had come to her.

The guard left without a word, before Sal shook his head once more, a sigh parting his lips, and followed them out.

"Sarah?" I said, my voice a whisper—partly because my throat was still raw and partly because I didn't want any surveillance picking up on our conversation. Protectors didn't hear as well as wolves—one of the only tools in my arsenal still of use at the moment. "Are you okay?"

Her skin was cold to the touch—which was saying something since I'd thought mine had long gone numb—but clammy, with a sheen of sweat. She shivered and her muscles spasmed under my touch, but her eyes remained strong, unwavering.

"They got you too," she said, a statement pushed through lips parted down the middle with cracked blood. "The others?"

"Safe." I wasn't certain, of course, but the promise of them out there and alive was the only thing pushing me forward. I had to believe it. "How'd they get you? We looked for you." I cleared my throat. "We thought you might have taken off—gone to fare on your own." I scanned her form now, battered and bruised and withered. "I wish you had."

"Me too," she said with a soft grin. Her lip split further and she winced. "I was careless. I just wanted to see my mother. I knew she was on campus. I wasn't even going to approach her or let her see me. I just wanted one look at my old life." She shook her head, her dark hair landing in a fresh wound and sticking to the blood. It was strange for a wolf to have so many bruises and open wounds visible and unhealed. What had they done to her? Suppressed her wolf too, with whatever poison they'd been funneling into me no doubt. She shrugged. "I got cocky, went closer, got lost in the moment—in the feel of the past, in the sight of her and a few familiar faces—" a harsh exhale, "fucking reckless. They got me," her lips twitched into a shadow of her usual smirk, "obviously."

Her piercing eyes met mine and warmth flooded through me at the fire still alive and well inside of them. Sarah was strong, and they hadn't broken her. "How'd they get you?"

"Ambush on campus. Hundreds of demons, some with powers I've never even seen before. It was right after my bonding cer—" I choked on the word, the last moments with Max flooding my mind before I abandoned her one last time. "Tarren tried to kill Max, even after she'd saved so many of us in front of his eyes—" I didn't hide the disgust from my voice. "He killed Cyrus instead. And then I distracted him long enough for the others to get away."

"Fuck." If possible, her face lost even more of its color. "Cyrus Bentley, gone from this world? That's a steep loss. And at the hand of one of his own."

It didn't escape me that she hadn't said 'our.' Sarah embraced her wolf, her lack of place in her old world with far more grace than I had.

The corner of her mouth twitched into another echo of a

grin, the movement so small I was surprised I saw it. Guess that's what a lifetime of friendship made possible. "Of course you sacrificed yourself though. And you went through the bonding ceremony with Reza?" She let out a humorless chuckle. "Just can't help yourself, can you? So goddamned determined not to let yourself have anything that you want in this life. Careful—I'm beginning to think you enjoy being the sacrificial lamb." Her eyes met mine, wild and teasing. "I can only contain my prey drive for so long."

I dropped my gaze, the truth in her stare too much for me to stomach right now. I scanned her instead, noting deep gouges all over her body, like the kind of marks left by claws. Deep hatred boiled low in my gut to see one of the strongest women I knew defiled like this. "What did they do to you?"

"Believe it or not, it wasn't them." She ran a hand through her hair, her fingers tangled in the mats of blood. "I think you're the only one in here with a cell to themselves. The rooms are jam packed—from what I've gathered, some having as many as six or seven demons in them."

Jesus. I remembered Eli mentioning something along those lines when he and Max made their ill-advised trip down here recently.

"I was lucky, all things considered. They only stuck me with Mavis."

My head shot up at that, my neck crimping in pain from the sudden jolt. "Mavis?"

The corners of her eyes dipped as she nodded. Even with as fragile as her body looked right now, the strength in her eyes was unwavering. The old Sarah didn't have that spark. This was the true testament of how much her transformation had changed her. She was more alive, more ferocious—just *more*. Even with all the pain she'd endured. "He's a wolf. When Ten brought him back a few days ago after that attack, he changed."

The memories of that mission were murky at best. I'd been

so focused on Rowan, because of Max, and once he'd returned, that concern shifted to Jer's death. I'd all but forgotten that Mavis had been attacked, that I hadn't heard any updates about him at all. That I hadn't even bothered to ask. Now, I understood why.

"His wolf is feral, reacting terribly to the prison they have him in, and even more so to the injections they keep giving him." She grunted, laid her head back against the wall and leaned her arms on her bent legs—no concerns for modesty, all pretenses of it stolen from her these last few days. "Whatever they've given me has suppressed mine."

Her eyes glazed over and I saw true sadness glistening there. She missed her wolf. It was an essential part of her now.

I cut my gaze to the floor, unable to hold her eyes. She was so much farther along in her journey than I was. There was so much power in her acceptance of herself, in the way she embraced her new reality—even the gritty, terrifying bits of it.

It was the same thing I'd seen in Wade' eyes the last few days—like he'd been reborn in his absence; a stranger now, but one I desperately wanted to know.

I was ashamed of how long it had taken me. The Guild's grip on me had been ironclad.

My nails bit into my palms and I relished the pain that poured through me. If—no—when. *When* I got my wolf back, I'd do things properly. He was my strongest weapon.

Fucking fanghole was right all along.

"I think they have new tools down here, new creatures," she whispered, oblivious to my mini existential crisis. Or perhaps just unconcerned with it. And she was right, if so. Now wasn't the time. "My mother visited me when they first grabbed me," she cut her eyes to me, "they haven't let her back of course, but after getting over her shock that I was still alive, she told me what she could."

Hope, or something suspiciously like it, sparked along my

spine. I sat straighter and felt my mind push through the fog, my body fight through the pain. Lowering my voice as much as I could, I leaned towards her, angling myself so that the back of my head blocked Sarah's face from the camera's sight. "What did she tell you?"

"Nothing too specific, but she suspects some of the researchers down here have found a way to extract our magic. Like its physical manifestation—they can harvest it. It's why Tarren and the council have been so adamant about capture over murder."

The truth of her words sank over me like a weighted blanket. Our number one goal on missions, on par with the grandiose mission statement of protecting humanity, had always been to bring the demons back. We were never told the specifics, and I'd always assumed that they were looking for a cure, a way to save more lives when protectors were bitten.

Of course, recent realities called any benevolence on behalf of The Guild into question.

Since my father's return, that desire for capturing demons seemed to only grow more insistent. And the cells were now overrun down here.

They wanted the most powerful, the most rare. But why?

"They need them." I paused a beat, then corrected course. "They need us. They want our power. And they're taking it."

"I gathered that much." Sarah narrowed her eyes, her face moving closer to mine. "But how? Why?"

We sat in silence for a few minutes, each lost in the labyrinth of our own thoughts. I was missing a crucial piece of the puzzle, or else unsuccessfully trying to shove a middle piece into the corner.

Threads started to weave and connect, but I still couldn't grasp them.

Was this a recent discovery or had The Guild always been able to separate a demon from their magic? What happened to a demon who was drained of it? What were they using it for? Had they already drained some of mine? How did Darius survive for so long?

The heavy groan and buzz of the door interrupted my musings.

Tarren stood in the gap, staring down at us with an expression I couldn't parse.

A man stood at his side—tall, lean, and shrouded in a mane of tangled dark hair.

Like Sarah, his wrists were bound with cuffs, and his body looked recently starved and pushed to the brink.

With a shove, the man fell to his knees a few inches from where we sat.

"You two have proven pretty physically resilient to our techniques," Tarren said, his voice metallic and cold—like he was speaking to a stranger and not his own son. "But we need answers." He nodded to the stranger, and I thought I saw a flash of fear, and then regret, cross his features. "So we're going to try a new approach."

That sent a wave of terror icing through my veins.

My father was never afraid. And if he was, he knew how to mask it.

I watched the man, but he hadn't moved an inch since landing on the ground, his face sheltered by the shadow of his hair.

Tarren's eyes met mine—steady, distant, and almost... sad.

I knew with a sudden, irrefutable clarity that he was in mourning—that whatever he had planned next, he didn't expect me to survive it.

"Let's see if your minds are just as strong."

6

MAX

Ro was here.

He was here.

We sat, clasped in each other's arms for what felt like ages. I noticed the others leave the room after a few minutes—Wade only briefly interrupting to apologetically place a bag of wet food on the floor near us.

And then we just were.

Both of us together, trading off crying and emptying ourselves into a strange, tearless, numb state. For a while, neither of us said anything. But I could feel some strange, integral part of myself stitching itself back together, healing.

I could survive this grief. I could survive it so long as Ro was here to carry it with me.

"They found you," I said, a few hours later, the single window in the room now long blacked-out with night. "I can't believe they found you."

He nodded, took a deep, choked breath in.

Ro's entry into the world of protectors had had such a physical effect on him. At first, I could see him getting stronger—filling out, growing into himself, finding a place in the new world we were a part of. But then he seemed to be in a rapid decline, deflating, his face lined constantly with concern, the circles under his eyes almost blue with fatigue. He was thinner. Dimmer.

I knew I was to blame for a lot of that deterioration. I'd done nothing but worry him since the moment I tangled myself with the members of Six. Every rash decision I made pulled us further apart, put more strain and concern on his shoulders.

"I'm sorry," I whispered. We were lying down, both of us facing each other, our cheeks pressed against the rough wood floor. I pressed the pad of my thumb to the swollen bag under his right eye. "I'm sorry you've been through so much. I'm sorry that I've put so much stress on you these last few months. If you had done that to me—I, I don't even know if I could've survived it."

He snorted, but his chin dimpled with the ripple of emotion he tried to swallow back. "You would have."

"Maybe. But you'd never put me in the position to need to. Not like I've done to you. Over and over again. And now, Cy—" my voice caught for a moment, "I'm sorry for that too. That you lost one of the few people you love."

He swatted my hand away from his face, threading his fingers through mine in a harsh grip as his eyes narrowed on me. "Don't."

"I—" I didn't know what I wanted to say, what I could say.

"Don't apologize for Cy, Max. That wasn't on you. His death, his blood—they're not on your hands. Tarren carries that tragedy, and he carries it alone. It's not on you."

"He put himself in front of me. That—" I didn't bother holding back the sob that slipped through, "that arrow was meant for me. If I wasn't there, Cy would still be here."

Using our twined hands, Ro pulled me to him until my face was buried into his chest. "No. Tarren made a choice. And Cy made a choice too. One I know he'd make a thousand times over if given the option. You can grieve, Max." He exhaled against my head. "And you can let yourself hurt—to feel the pain of losing him. But I won't let you blame yourself. It dishonors the choice he made, the sacrifice. And I won't let you destroy yourself that way, do you understand? It's the last thing he would want and it's the last thing that you deserve."

I pressed my eyelids tight together as I breathed him in against his chest.

"That ends here, okay? Promise me."

My stomach flipped as I gripped my fingers into the cloth of his shirt.

"Promise me."

I nodded, sniffling. When he squeezed me, tight enough to nearly crack a rib, something inside of me loosened. Breathing felt easier, like my body had suddenly become lighter.

"We'll get through this together, Max. Whatever is coming for you, you won't be alone. It's us against the world. Until the end." He snorted, the air from it lifting a few pieces of my hair through the wind. "And I guess we'll just have to carve out some extra space for the strange collection of creatures you've been saddled with. If you want them, that is."

If I wanted them. Declan, Wade, Darius, Eli, and Atlas.

Did I want them?

Maybe more than I wanted anything.

My body seemed to crave them, like they were extensions of myself.

But I understood now—why they'd all spent so much time pushing me away.

Letting people in, at that level, it was opening yourself up to new ways to be hurt.

And opening myself up to five people I cared about as much as I was starting to—that wasn't just opening myself up to pain. To grief. That was opening myself up to full on devastation.

"How did they find you?" I asked, changing the subject.

"After the fight," his eyes went distant for a moment, like he was retreating into himself, "I went looking for you. I searched —" he cleared his throat, his voice thick with emotion. I squeezed his hand softly. "I searched for hours. Couldn't find a trace of you—of any of you. I knew if I could at least find Eli or —someone—that they'd lead me to you. But you all were just —" his pale eyes met mine, looking lost and scared. "Gone. And it was just me. I couldn't go back there. Didn't know what they'd do to me if I did."

My chest felt tight and my stomach bottomed out at the realization that all this time, I'd been so wrapped up in my own angst, at war with my brain, fighting to breathe—and Ro had been alone. Scared. With nowhere to go.

"Arnell found me later that night," he continued, "he wanted me to go to a safe house he knew about." Ro shook his head. "But I couldn't leave—not without having some way to reach you, to find you if you—in case you came back for me."

His features blurred as a fresh wave of tears glazed over more of my vision. I did everything I could to keep them back.

"Last time you disappeared—we'd all decided that Ralph's hut would be the meeting place. So I stayed there. Refused to leave. Just on the off chance I'd get a hint as to where you were."

"It's so cold," I murmured, a chill running through my bones at the mere thought of him out there all this time, alone and freezing.

"Arnell visited every other day, when he could," his lips lifted at the corner. "Izzy too. They brought me food, any information they were able to smuggle out. Things are—" he shook his head, "not good back there. We can't go back, Max. Not ever."

Hearing those words sent a jolt down my side. He was right. We could never go back.

Did I want to?

It was the last place I'd felt at home—however briefly. It was the last place I'd shared space with Cy.

That first night, eating dinner in the dining hall with Cy, Ro, and Seamus—it felt like a lifetime ago. Had it really only been a few months? Everything had felt so fresh—so new and hopeful, like the world was suddenly awash in vivid colors, the contrast on high. We were so naive back then. I'd been so naive.

"Seamus," I whispered, the memory of him stirring fear in me. "Is he okay?"

I knew that Seamus and Cy had been working together—that Seamus knew some of what was going on with us, with our world, if not all of it. And he was the last and only connection we had to Cy. Part of me just wanted to see him again—to see his face, his familiar dark eyes. Like if I could just see him, I'd see a distorted version of Cy looking back.

Ro shook his head. "No one has seen him. Not since the end of the battle. They—" he bit his lip, considering, "they collected the bodies after. And he wasn't there."

The bodies.

The breath caught in my lungs. "Cy—"

Ro sat up, crawling to the small bag he'd dropped earlier. "Arnell hacked into one of the interfaces down at the morgue. Less security since people rarely go searching through the dead. There are too many other atrocities for the living to deal with right now. He switched some things around—people rarely argue with or question what technology tells them. He made sure they cremated him, that they thought it was someone else—some nameless departed. And then he brought him to me." Ro pulled out a small, plain black box, latched closed with a metal clasp. "It was frivolous—put him in unnecessary harm. If he'd been caught," Ro swallowed, his focus dipping to the container in his palms, "I don't know what I would've done. Stormed the place, probably. But he knew that I couldn't stand the thought of them having him. Of Cy resting forever in that place. Not after what happened. Not after what they did. He doesn't belong there. They shouldn't have him."

My gaze rested on the small box. Cy was in there.

Well, not Cy. But the only thing we had left of him.

My heart warmed at the thought of Arnell doing that for Ro.

But the thought of him remaining at The Guild sent a fresh wave of fear crawling down my skin. "We can't leave Arnell there. Or Izzy. Or anyone who's been close to me," I said, the words falling from my lips in a chaotic rush. "They'll be targets. Tarren will—I don't know what Tarren will do, but we need to get them out."

Ro's expression hardened, something unreadable in his eyes. Strange. I wasn't used to not being able to read his every thought as if it were my own. "I tried to convince them to come with me, as soon as it was decided that I'd wait at the hut for you. But they're staying."

For a moment, I felt ill. Now that they knew the extent of my abilities—of what I could do—now that there was no ambiguity about whether or not The Guild would take my side—did that mean—

"Not because they are on their side," Ro said, apparently having no problem with reading me still, "but because they are going to infiltrate it. Spy. Be our eyes and ears as we do—" his eyes lifted to mine, "whatever it is that we're going to do. Save the world, I guess. Knowing you. You don't really do things halfway, so I'm assuming that's the path we're on now. Right?"

I bit my lip. I had no fucking idea what path we were on. I'd been too busy sinking into my mental purgatory to even spare a thought to Lucifer or the collapsing hell realm since losing Cy. But the ambush certainly aligned with Lucifer's warnings. There were far more demons in the human realm than there'd ever been before—or at least more than The Guild had been made aware of.

"Izzy did request that you dream walk to her at some point. Or, and I quote" his face split into a grin, "she will develop dream-walking powers herself, just to visit and throttle you for scaring her half to death."

I felt a smile tug slightly at my face, but it felt strange and not entirely my own—like my face wasn't quite sure how to achieve the goal, but the muscle memory lay buried deep down all the same.

"They're on your side, Max. Arnell, Izzy—and they won't be the only ones to question Tarren and the council in these coming months." Ro scooched back towards me, one of his large hands encapsulating my shoulder as he squeezed. "Time, Max. It'll take time. But we'll survive this."

I didn't think it was the end of the world he was talking about.

I lifted the small container from his hands, the feel of it cold against my skin. It was grief.

It was Cy.

But he was right, we'd survive it. Cy would kill us himself if we didn't.

For a long while, we simply sat together, occasionally snacking on a few chips or cookies, though my mouth was dry and I might as well have been trying to swallow gravel.

Eventually, with my head pressed to Ro's shoulder, I let myself set down the fear and pain that were weighing me down. Instead, I felt myself slip into a quiet, dreamless sleep—breathing deeply and completely for the first time in days.

∽

"SHOULD WE GO IN?" A rough, muffled voice, filtered through the emptiness.

"No, fuckface—she needs sleep." Also muffled, but filled with more gravel than the first.

"I don't know if she's actually even asleep. I still can't reach her. I tried a few minutes ago," a third voice.

"If you tools keep arguing outside the door, she certainly won't be." This voice was softer than the others, but it seemed to shut them all up.

"They're an odd bunch, aren't they?" Ro shifted, his own words groggy with sleep. "Jesus, I needed that nap."

I could feel the others standing on the other side of the door, could almost sense the strange anxiety vibrating through to me. A small grin tugged at my lips at the thought of them all out there. I wondered how many times Wade and Darius had come close to murdering each other in the time that we'd been here.

I scanned the dark room, sitting up. Not that I was exactly clear where here was.

"Where are we, anyway?" Ro asked, as if he'd plucked the question from my thoughts. "Kind of creepy, no?"

I scrunched my face, taking in the scene. Everything was coated in a layer of thick dust that was even somehow visible without a single ray of light. When I stood and flicked the light switch up, nothing happened.

Ro shivered, running his hands up and down his arms. "Cold too."

"No heat," I said, as I moved towards the door. "Looks abandoned, so no one's paid the electricity bill in a long time, if I had to guess."

When I pulled open the door, Wade tipped onto the floor, hitting his head with a soft thud. He'd been sitting, leaning against it.

"Sorry," I muttered, extending my hand for him to pull himself up.

He didn't take it. Instead, his eyes grew wide as he stared at me. "You are awake." He flashed a dark look to the others—all of them just as wide-eyed. "Told you."

"I was asleep," I said, clearing my throat as I studied the strange, motley crew assembled outside in the hall.

Declan was leaning against the far wall, her shoulders angled towards Darius like they'd been whispering something —judging by the slightly annoyed tilt of her lips and the mirth in his eyes, he'd been teasing her. It was probably his favorite pastime these days.

Eli was a few feet away, his cheeks splotching a bit as he avoided meeting my eyes.

My stomach clenched as the memory of our last encounter came flooding back to me. I tugged on the shirt I was wearing —Wade's from the smell of it—though it covered almost down to my knees.

"And you're speaking," Declan said as she took a step towards me, her posture hesitant like she was approaching a scared animal. "How are you feeling?" She paused, shook her head, then started again. "Awful question, thoughtless. Would you like some more food? Something to drink?" Her soft Irish lilt was thicker than usual, as she stumbled through the words.

I stepped through the door frame and looked down both ends of the hall. I felt my brows pinch, and a fleeting bolt of unease charged through my chest as I turned back to her. "Where's Atlas?"

The others all looked at each other, the tentatively hopeful aura of the decrepit hall suddenly drifting into something decidedly more severe.

Declan's eyes dropped to her hands, where her fingers were a tangled ball.

Eli, if possible, looked even more lost, his gaze completely unreadable.

I turned to Darius, studying his mismatched eyes as I closed the distance between us. "What happened?"

He took a deep, slow breath, then brought his hand up to my cheek, his calloused thumb brushing the sensitive skin under my eye. But any hesitation melted into a dogged determination as he pulled me into a hug.

The air rushed out of me, thick and fast, but I melted into him, my skin buzzing as it came alive at his nearness.

"We'll get him back, little protector," he whispered into my hair, "you have my word."

My heart stuttered briefly, before it ramped up pace. With an ounce of regret, I untangled myself from his arms and took a few steps back. "Back? Back from where? Where is he?"

Wade exhaled, cursing under his breath, his elbows balancing on his knees as he hid his face between his legs.

I bent down to him and pressed a hand to his shoulder. "What's happened?"

He didn't emerge from his self-imposed cocoon, but he didn't shrug me off either.

"After you teleported," Declan said, pulling my focus to her. Her expression was cool, collected—back to the protector mode she often donned whenever shit truly hit the fan. Like the only way to hold the team together was to smudge away her own anxiety—blotted and polished, but not truly invisible. Not to me, anyway. "Atlas stayed behind, to give us time to run. But —" she cleared her throat, struggling to maintain her composure as her eyes met mine, piercing and slowly glazing over with unshed tears.

"But they got him," Eli finished for her, sheepishly meeting my eyes for the first time. I didn't see regret or anger there. Only concern—shyness—and maybe a little bit of fear. "The Guild. He's in the labs. We're assuming anyway."

Ice filled my veins as my fingers dug into Wade, using his solid form to keep myself from falling over. "He's where?"

"Maybe we shouldn't have told her yet," Eli whispered, turning to Declan. "She needs more rest. More time to," he ran a hand over his face, through his tousled hair, "to process. We can't just throw everything at her."

I felt strong hands grip my shoulders and steady me.

"The one thing Max needs," Ro said, hugging me to his side, "is the truth. Whenever we can give it to her."

"You're right," Eli said, shoulders dipping as his dark gaze drifted and then settled on me. "From now on, only the truth. And the truth is, Atlas was definitely taken. We don't know where, but we assume he'll be down in the labs, unless he's—" Declan cleared her throat, cutting him off, as Wade sucked in a deep breath. Eli squared his shoulders and took a step closer to me. "Unless he's dead, but we don't think that he is."

Dead.

The word struck me, landing in my chest and ricocheting through my ribs. Could Atlas be dead?

The mere possibility filled my lungs with icy terror—a chill that seemed to permeate through the group around me.

"He's alive," I said, and though I had no reason to know for sure, I felt the rightness of that statement deep in my gut. "He's definitely alive."

Eli's features softened, and I could almost feel the same shift in the others, though my eyes didn't leave his.

"That's one of many problems," Darius said, one brow arched. There was a sort of distance about him, his focus split between our conversation and something else. It was the way he got sometimes when he sank into himself—when he went to that other place I was never able to access. "We're still no closer to discovering the source of shadow magic that Lucifer sent you after, and now our ability to infiltrate The Guild and hunt it down has been severely compromised. Plus, in addition to an angry camp of protectors after us all, it appears that the breach between realms is far more complicated than we realized. I saw creatures that day that I've only heard lore of. I haven't the slightest idea where they've come from or how they've found their way to this realm. And, more worrisome still, we have no idea of the extent of their powers or whether or not those powers will be fighting on Lucifer's side—or another side altogether. If I had to guess, I'd say there's another big baddy in the picture that hasn't revealed themselves yet."

"The shadow magic," I said, my voice piercing the ominous, dark halls. The jolt of excitement shifted into a tangle of knots as the memory of it came flooding back. "That day—" I paused, shaking my head. The day Atlas bonded to someone else. The day Guild Headquarters were ambushed. The day we lost the only place we had to call home. The day Cyrus died. Clearing my throat, I shook my head and began to pace, the energy and emotions fighting for control, desperate for a way to dispel themselves. "That day, I accidentally shifted to the ceremony."

"The ceremony?" Wade stood up, studying me with an intense focus as he leaned against the doorway. "What ceremony?"

"Atlas's bonding ceremony." It felt more dream than memory as I tried to conjure that room back into focus. The council member standing between them, Reza standing there shivering with covered eyes, the pool of shimmery liquid, the mysterious stone. And Atlas. Atlas choosing to forsake whatever connection he had to me and pledge it to another person instead. I swallowed, willing the bile rising through my body back down. "I was in a vent, watching while Atlas bonded to Reza."

"Fuck," Eli muttered, his hands closed into a fist that looked almost painful. "The fucker actually went through with it, didn't he?" His eyes met mine and I saw the ghost of my own pain reflected there. He could see the cut Atlas had carved through my chest, as if it were made boldly and cleanly by a blade. "I'll fucking kill him."

"After we save him, you mean," Darius offered, his tone almost feral with the promise of violence. "First, we do the good guy thing, then we take out the trash. The universe likes balance."

I raised my palms to stop the riot before it began. "No, it—" I shook my head, trying to believe my words as I uttered them, "that doesn't matter. I saw it. I saw the shadow magic. They used a pool of it—and this blade." I could feel five pairs of eyes focused on me—the hall filled only with my voice, no one so much as breathing. "The blade they use to bond protectors—it's made out of the same material as Lucifer's dagger, I think. Something uncannily similar to it at least. And it's surrounded by a pool of shimmery, liquid, shadow magic—like a moat." I closed my eyes, trying to picture the iridescent liquid. It had called to me, willing me to reach out and touch it—something so familiar, so peaceful, like I'd seen it before.

"Shit," Declan whispered, her back landing against the wall with a soft thud. "What the fuck is The Guild doing with shadow magic?"

"Stealing it," Darius said, his tone clipped, "does that shock you, after everything?"

"But for forging mate bonds?" she continued, not responding to the antagonism in his question. "How? Why?"

"True mate bonds—actual life bonds—haven't existed in years," Wade said, pacing just as I had been a few moments ago, his gaze flitting to mine briefly before he continued. He touched his shoulder—naked now, but where the temporary runes carved by Serae had been. "In some cases, with users powerful enough to wield it, it can be shaped. What if using shadow magic is the only way that The Guild can create an echo of a true bond? We knew they forced them; we just never knew how—the ritual is so private. Even when you're part of it. I remember with Sarah—I was sliced by a blade—" his eyes narrowed, like he was lost in thought, chasing a memory just out of reach, "and I did touch something—something smooth and cold, air-like almost. And it seemed to radiate power. But the specifics, my memory of it, it's so disjointed. Hazy."

"Hmm," Darius tilted his head, his eyes following Wade's

every step, like they were the key to deciphering his words, "and I suppose it's no coincidence that Max would be drawn to that." His focus darted to me, "or that she'd be the first creature in perhaps centuries to forge not only a single, true mate bond, but five of them."

My stomach dipped, his words ringing through my ears, hollow and loud.

True bonds. It was a reality I think I'd known for a while. But it had lingered unacknowledged among us for so long, alluded to only in whispered moments, it seemed startling to hear it on Darius's lips now.

It made sense though. Why else would I be so drawn to Six? To a vampire I was supposed to despise? But I'd been so resistant to the idea. Partially because something about it seemed too inevitable—like we didn't have a choice in the matter. And I didn't want them forced into anything.

But now I understood: bonds might be initiated by fate—but they could be rejected if they weren't wanted.

Atlas had done just that, hadn't he? He'd chosen The Guild's version of a bond to Reza over whatever strange magic had been twining us together.

Eli's mom had broken a bond with Seamus—it was why he was so repulsed by the idea of being bonded himself.

And me—well, I wasn't lying when I told Eli that the only thing I wanted right now was meaningless sex. I didn't want to strengthen my ties to them. Didn't want to open myself up to the vulnerability of loving them. To the raw torment I'd feel if I lost one of them. It was too much. The look in Eli's eyes when we'd been together—the shadow of emotion I'd seen there, the utter rawness of it. It was too intense. It had cracked me in half. If I was going to get through what we needed to do, I couldn't tie myself to them, not like that.

"Um," Ro cleared his throat and I felt him take a step closer to me, "what?"

Darius rolled his eyes, a vicious smirk plastered on his face. "We're not seriously going to keep pretending like that's not what's happening, are we? It's been exhausting getting everyone on board. Protectors are all so... blocked up. And while you are all the most stubborn creatures I've ever encountered—which, by the way," he waved his hand in front of his face, "is saying a lot because I grew up with Claude—I think we're all a bit past that. So let's just get on with it. Reject the bond, don't, that's all up to you and Max. But I know where I stand."

My cheeks warmed as his eyes met mine, the challenge and declaration clear.

"I only raise this now because Rowan should know what he's walking into here," Darius continued, unblinking, "the connections you share with us all, little protector, can be as dangerous as they are powerful. And if anyone—even your brother—gets in the way of protecting you, I will end them. It's as simple as that."

I opened my mouth to argue, but Ro's quiet laugh cut me off.

"I'm fine with that," he said, his shoulder nudging mine as he came closer. When I turned to him to argue, he just shrugged. "What? You're basically the chosen one now. Which is cool and all in the movies, but this is real life. And that means you're in a world of danger. Knowing that a vampire and other supernaturals will do everything in their power to keep you safe? That's only a win, as far as I'm concerned. Plus, if true mate bonds are anything like the bonds The Guild forges, strengthening them will only serve to strengthen you too. And you're going to need all the strength you can get." His gaze darkened as he lifted his focus to Darius. "Whether or not any of you actually deserve her—well, that remains to be decided." He narrowed his eyes, fists clenching at his sides. "But you should know that it goes both ways. She's my sister. And if any of you get in the way of her safety, bonded or not—

I won't hesitate to pierce my dagger through your heart either."

Darius's face split into a wide grin—one that read as both dangerous and impressed. "Deal."

I cleared my throat, annoyed now. "No one is killing anyone on my account. Period." The thought of losing anyone standing in this room made me feel like vomiting. And thinking about the warped, complex connection between me, Darius, and Six—it felt how I imagined Lucifer's blade might feel if it were sinking into my chest. "We're here and we're going to work together to do—" I waved my arm around the dark hall aimlessly, "whatever it is we're going to do after we get Atlas."

"You have an idea—" Wade stood up, took a step towards me, his expression darkening at whatever he saw in my eyes. "What is it?"

"I can teleport." I stood taller, took a deep breath. "And I can teleport with another person now," I pushed away the memory of Cy's body clutched in my arms, pulling through space. I didn't have the luxury of working through the grief of losing him. Not now, anyway. Maybe one day I could. "Apparently. I can just pop in right now—pull him back to us."

"No." Eli's jaw was clenched so tightly, the word barely made it past his lips.

"Absolutely not," Declan echoed, shaking her head as if the word 'no' alone wasn't enough.

"Fuck that." Darius's eyes narrowed.

I raised my hands, stopping Ro and Wade before they could add their thoughts on the matter. "I can do it. And we can't leave him there. He's already been there for—" I closed my eyes, trying to remember how long it had been while I wallowed in my own pain—completely neglecting everyone else. If something happened because of me—if Atlas was—I shook the thought away. "How long have I been—"

I didn't know how to finish the question. How long had I

been a blubbering mess? Shutting the world out? Selfishly sinking into grief?

"It's been a couple days." Ro's fingers twined through mine. "And stop whatever twisted mental path you're taking right now, Max. You're allowed to process your trauma however you need to."

He was right. And it was decided—for now, I was going to process that trauma by ignoring it. By shoving it into the ever-growing pile of clusterfuck-boxes in my head. I'd deal with it later.

When my friends weren't in danger.

When the world wasn't collapsing.

When it was convenient.

No more falling apart, until then.

I nodded, dropped Ro's hand from mine, took a few steps back, and closed my eyes. I focused on Atlas. On the color of his eyes as they swirled from brown to yellow when the wolf was at the surface, on the rigid posture of his spine whenever he was stressed or tense—so, always—on the way a few strands of hair would occasionally fall into his eyes when he was too focused to notice, on the way his muscles rippled and moved during sparring sessions, on the deep, gravelly sound of his voice, the ferocity with which he'd kissed me when we finally gave in to the heat simmering between us—

But something was wrong. Vacant.

The quiet, invisible tether I often felt between us—the one I'd cling onto when healing—was gone.

Panic welled in my chest at the loss of it.

No—a wash of something soft flitted through me. Not gone. Not completely. It was fractured. Almost imperceptible. But I latched onto it, clung to him with every ounce of my focus.

I breathed in deep, felt my breath ripple through it. Focused on reaching him, on collapsing into millions of particles that reformed wherever he was.

When I opened my eyes, I didn't see Atlas.

I saw the same five familiar faces huddled around the same abandoned hallway I'd been standing in a moment before.

"What happened?" Darius.

"What's wrong?" Ro.

I shook my head as I felt hands land on my arms and took several steps back. They protested at first, but didn't press.

Maybe teleporting was too much right now. I hadn't eaten properly—maybe I needed more sleep.

Or maybe Atlas's bonding with Reza had damaged my link to him, severed it.

I rolled my head from side to side, shook my hands. I just needed to warm up.

I'd start with the easier stuff first. Build up to it. Teleporting had always been the most difficult for me to master.

I thought of the flame, the way the warmth spread through my veins, the tingling sensation along my skin.

Then I looked at my hands, twisting my wrists in front of my eyes, searching. But there was nothing. Just the soft flesh of my palms, dented with half-moons from clenched fists.

"Max?" Declan's oval face was above me, concern mapped clearly in the bend of her brow. "What is it? What's wrong?"

"My powers," I whispered, feeling suddenly more vulnerable than I'd ever felt before. "They're gone."

7

DARIUS

Her arms fell limply to her side, and her dark eyes widened with fear as they met mine.

It was a fear I felt too, though I tried to keep from broadcasting it back to her. I felt like I'd failed her. Like she was looking to me to fix things—and fixing things for her was the only thing I wanted to do—but I couldn't.

"Gone?" Eli asked his posture stiffening. "Like completely?"

She closed her eyes and focused, the skin around her eyes nearly bruised purple from crying and no sleep.

With her deep inhale, we all held still, perfectly quiet, waiting for something to happen.

I scanned the hall, clocking every possible exit point that I could.

Most of my worry these days had nothing to do with Lucifer's impending apocalypse. I honestly couldn't give a fuck if the hell realm collapsed or all protectors were wiped from the planet.

My worry stemmed from the possibility of something happening to the little protector.

And that was a worry that I felt deep in my bones, even

when she could light up like a firecracker, scorch a pile of werewolves with one breath, and pop her body through time and space

Without her power?

What chance did I have of protecting her during this war? This tearing of worlds?

"Nothing," she said, her eyelids slowly peeling open as her eyes dropped to her hands, a flash of anger in their depths, like her very hands had betrayed her. That anger softened back into the grief that had been shrouding her for days. "I don't—" she licked her bottom lip, and I could hear the tremor in her voice, "I don't know what I did."

Declan reached for her shoulder and squeezed. "You're probably just tired. Hell, exhausted. It's been an intense few days—you might just need more rest."

"I don't even feel it—" Max's eyes narrowed as she studied her arms like her body had betrayed her, "not a single breath of it. I never," she nibbled softly at her bottom lip—looking so lost and adorable that I wanted to just pick her up and tuck her into my arms, carry her away from here, protect her from being constantly impaled by pain, "I never really noticed that I could feel it, like a gentle hum, a heat. Now that it's gone, the absence of it feels so—hollow." Her arms wrapped around herself, folding around her waist, like she wanted to sink back into herself—to collapse back in that room and float in the abyss she'd been drifting in for days.

"I don't think it's gone." My voice sounded harsh in the hall. We'd spent so long trying to be quiet, to give her space to grieve and breathe. Filling the abandoned house with so much talking, so much activity, felt like sending a parade through a church. "Not permanently anyway," I added, lowering my volume.

Everyone's attention swept to me. It felt odd, being in their spotlight—all of them looking to me for answers, trusting me to give them. Especially since, only a few months ago, these very people had wanted me dead. I knew that my place was next to Max, and I'd grown closer with Declan over the last few weeks, but I still wasn't sure how I fit with the rest of them.

"What do you mean?" Wade asked, his brow arched. It wasn't quite a challenge, but his expression was shrewd enough to make his distrust clear.

"The kind of power that runs through you," I said, speaking directly to her, "that runs through many supernaturals—it's tied to you physically, but also emotionally. Deep emotion can influence how your power mobilizes."

"Like bonding?" Wade asked, his coldness evaporating into curiosity. "The way that bonding and connection strengthens both parties—are you saying the reverse can happen too?"

I nodded. "Grief is a deep pain—perhaps the deepest anyone can really feel. And while it's rare, every once in a while, someone can lose their connection to their power—like a switch has simply been flicked, their access revoked."

"How do I get them back?" she asked. "Can I get them back or are they just gone forever?"

"For some people, once powers are lost, they don't come back," I said, wishing for once that I could just lie to her—shelter her from at least some pain, if only for a little while. "But others can get them back, or at least partially get them back." I cleared my throat and met her eyes. "Mine came back." I shrugged, "mostly."

A thick silence cloaked the hall, making the small space between walls feel even smaller.

I didn't want to remember how empty I had felt when I noticed my powers dampened—after I'd left Claude, after our sister—

Max's fingers curled around mine, the pressure soft and comforting.

Instantly, I exhaled, air no longer feeling obtrusive and

threatening. I no longer wanted to escape from this hall, from these people and their unspoken questions. I just wanted to stand here, next to her.

How did she do that?

"How long?" Wade asked, his head tilted slightly as he studied the space where Max's hand clutched mine. There was a depth of understanding there, not pity but maybe empathy, as his eyes lifted to mine. "Before you got them back?"

I shrugged, hating that I didn't have a concrete answer. I wasn't really sure—I'd spent months drowning myself in blood, booze, and sex, trying to fill the crater that had smashed through me, to keep the darkness—and my demons—from eclipsing me completely. "Vampires aren't the same as," I squeezed her hand in mine, "well, all the things Max is. I didn't lose my vampiric nature. And the circumstances for me were very different."

What I didn't say is that I still didn't have complete control of my powers, that the shadow magic had distorted and twisted something inside of me—irreparably. That it wasn't just grief that stripped my strength, it was selfishness—cowardice.

I gained more control over time, but then I became a lab rat for The Guild.

The day Max showed up outside of my cell, something inside of me woke up. Max—giving in to the connection I felt with her, with the others—it was the closest I'd felt to my old strength coming back to me. Like she was lending me her own.

Wade and Eli both looked like they wanted to push the issue, and Max's brother looked like he was debating whether or not he should pull Max away from me—like he could see the stretch of darkness I kept buried deep, deep down.

But Max ran her thumb against the back of my hand, sending a wave of chills through my body and shrugged. "We shouldn't stay here. We can figure all of this out later, but for now we should find somewhere safe, somewhere warm, and start plotting a plan to get Atlas back."

"Where do we go?" Declan asked, sounding quieter, smaller than I was used to—like she was suddenly feeling as lost as I was. "Nowhere is safe."

No one moved or answered her question. None of us had an answer, a solution to the absolute mountain of shit we were buried under. Hell, I didn't even know how to find a shovel to start digging us out.

But after a long, heavy moment, Max's features softened—the fear and intensity simply melting off of her as she turned to her brother. She moved towards the room, but I wasn't ready to let her hand part from mine, so I followed her like a dog on a leash. She bent down, picked up a small box on the floor of blankets and rags, before returning to the others.

She handed the box to Ro, with a gentleness that felt almost reverent. "We take him home, where he belongs."

∼

THE JOURNEY back to Max's old home was a long one. One that required a *borrowed* minivan that we abandoned during the last twenty miles of the trip, and a very long walk. Thank the gods we had her brother with us, because there was no way in hell she would've been able to navigate the trip on her own.

Max squinted through a thick patch of trees and took a confident step forward. "This way, I'm pretty sure."

"Actually," her brother scrunched up his nose, like he was debating letting her save face, even if it meant leading us on a long, winding detour, before his lips curved in a small grin. There was a fondness when he looked at her that made me feel full somehow—pleased to know that I wasn't the only one in this world to know how precious she was. Granted, the rest of the dunderheads we were with also looked at her like that, but with her brother it was different. I wasn't competing for her affections with him in the same way I was with them. "It's this way."

Max stopped, her posture slinking slightly as she changed course. "Right, that's what I meant."

The girl was hopeless at navigating. Strange that she held the fate of the world in her hands, but couldn't track her way back through the forest she'd grown up in.

Strange, but adorable.

I had to hand it to Cyrus though. I'd never properly met the man, but this place truly was well hidden. I couldn't imagine anyone accidentally stumbling across their doorstep—even with clear directions and Ro's unfailing memory, we took a couple of slightly loopy turns before the clearing finally opened onto a small, well-camouflaged cabin.

When Max set eyes on it, all the muscles in her body seemed to relax at once. She discreetly wiped the corner of her eye when her brother stood next to her, squeezing her shoulder softly. She'd spent the entire walk clutching that small box in her hands, and when she set it down by a large tree that shaded the cabin, she let out a heavy breath.

With a soft smile—one that didn't quite reach her eyes like I was used to—she turned back to us. "Come on, we'll give you the tour."

The tour lasted all of thirty seconds.

The cabin was small. The three bedrooms were cramped like closets, and Cyrus's bedroom seemed to double as weapons storage. There was one equally tiny bathroom, a kitchen with two square feet of counter space, and a living room with a patched up, oversized couch. And with all six of us crowded around, it felt like we were giants standing in a dollhouse.

Still, there was a warmth to the place that charmed me all the same. Maybe it was the way Max's face got some of its glow back as her fingers traced the door frame, the bookshelf by her bed, her father's mostly-empty wall of weapons; or maybe it was that everywhere I looked, I could almost feel her energy envelop me. Whatever it was, the cramped conditions didn't bother me. I'd happily spend months in this place, trying to imagine what she'd been like all of her life—what conditions had manifested this person in front of me who took up nearly all of my brain space.

"I suppose it's not much," she whispered, her expression suddenly shy, "and we'll be a bit cramped."

"It's perfect." Eli fell down on the couch, his eyes focused on her in a way that made it clear he was feeling the same electric charge of the place that I was—that this place was Max, boiled down and without all of the heartache.

Being allowed to see it, to see her here, was a welcome gift amongst all of the horror and angst in our lives. Maybe she'd even be afforded the chance to heal a bit here—to work through her grief.

Oddly, I found myself wanting to help her do just that. I'd spent years running from my own pain, fighting to stay three steps ahead of the grief that haunted me. I didn't want that for her. It was the last thing I wanted for her.

It was strange how clear my mistakes became when I was terrified of someone I loved making the same ones.

"And the good news is, Cyrus is—" Rowan paused for a moment, clearing his throat, "was one of those off-the-grid sorts, super paranoid." His brows furrowed as he gestured towards Max, "well, I guess now we know that he had his reasons for the paranoia and secrecy, but back then, when I moved in, I remember thinking he was a bit of a conspiracy theorist."

"What Ro's trying to say," Max said, her face glowing again as she looked at her brother, "is that we have enough electricity to bunk here for a while if we need to. There are solar panels, a generator if we need it, tons of canned food, hunting supplies, and enough movies and books to keep even Darius happy," her smile dipped slightly, "though I do think I took all of my favorite paranormal romances to The Guild when we left."

I'd developed a bit of a—tolerance—for vampire novels. Mostly because the best revenge for Declan's attempt at teasing me was to not let her win. But now, I was a full-on fan. That shit was good.

And vampires were always the mysterious and hot love interest. My kind of storyline.

"I'll find ways to amuse myself, I'm sure," I answered, unable to swallow back my smile at the red coloring her cheeks.

Declan surveyed the living room, like she was clocking every exit and possible hiding place this cabin had. There weren't many, but I admired her commitment all the same. "This will be perfect."

"There, er," Max shrugged, "are only three beds and a couch, so things might be a little tight, but we have camping gear and stuff in the shed out back with extra blankets and stuff."

"Not to mention the bunker," Rowan added as he rifled through the kitchen drawers, brows furrowed in concentration. "It's got most of the canned stuff and I think a cot or two down there. I'm not really sure though, haven't been down there in years."

"A bunker?" I asked. I didn't have any judgment in my tone, I just was trying to create a mental image of this Cyrus. He was the person who raised Max and I'd never get a chance to properly know him. A bunker and this set up? The guy was clearly running away from something and even more clearly terrified of what would happen if that something ever caught up to him.

"Yeah," Rowan scratched the back of his head. He looked just as exhausted and lost as Max. "Makes sense now, of course.

Why all the secrecy and preparation. Back then, we just assumed he watched too many zombie movies."

"Haven't gotten into that genre yet, so I'll be sure to add it to the list," I said with a forced smile, my voice a little too loud. Declan shot me a confused glare and I shrugged. I was as thrown off by my awkwardness as she was. Generally, I was the suave, mysterious one of the group, not the baboon. That position was reserved squarely for Eli. Maybe the blood bond was fucking with us? Tying our personalities as well as our bodies?

No. I shook my head, waving the idea away, which only seemed to make the divot between Declan's brows burrow deeper. Right. Channel the normal.

Shit, were my fangs showing with this ridiculous Cheshire smile? I tugged my lips back over my teeth and gave Rowan a more normal-looking grin instead. "Cyrus sounds like a cool guy. Would've been fun growing up here—away from the noise." I paused a beat, trying to ignore the silence and all the wide eyes lingering on me like a trainwreck. "And people. Like one of those wilderness shows. Very cool. Bet he would've done great on one of those survival shows."

I cleared my throat and looked down, twirling my finger around a few loose strands of Max's hair. The repetitive motion and her nearness calmed the strange gallop of my heartbeat.

I found myself wanting desperately for this Rowan character to like me. Like my entire future depended on whether or not he approved of me.

Max seemed to like me—usually—and I knew for certain that she was attracted to me. How could she not be? But something inside me was terrified that if her brother wanted me gone, she'd send me packing. And the thought of leaving her side again, after everything I'd seen and felt these last few months, made my stomach curl.

Would I go if she asked me to—at the end of this, if she didn't want me around anymore?

"Er, yeah, I guess," Ro said, saving me from answering the dark thought. "Anyway, I should probably head into town, get us some more supplies, make sure there isn't anything out of the ordinary."

"Would be good to do a perimeter check," Eli said, pulling himself up from the couch with a groan, "I'll go with you."

"Me too," Declan added. She stretched her head from side to side. "I'll sleep better knowing we're safe. And if I don't get a good night's sleep soon, I'll be useless."

"Guess that leaves me with the little protector," I said, slapping an arm around her shoulders.

"And the little incubus," Wade said, his eyes flashing to me, voice laced equally with teasing and threat until I couldn't tell which was which. Fucking incubi. Their animosity was always so tightly wound with their power. It was cute at first, but grew exhausting almost instantly.

"Goody." I let the creepy smile spread across my face again. This time, with fang most definitely out.

"Should we all just go?" Max asked, positioning herself between me and Wade. "All of us staying together is probably best, no?"

She was afraid I was going to eat her little incubus. I hoped he was afraid of that too.

Rowan shook his head. "Stay here, get set up, and rest. Too conspicuous with all of us walking around and I'll feel better knowing you're safe here with two demons, now that your powers aren't accessible." His nose wrinkled with amusement. "What a weird statement that I never thought I'd be uttering."

Ha. He does trust me with her.

I'd assumed the thought was a silent one, but judging by the flash of confusion spreading through the group, my tongue got away from me.

"Too much time alone." I shrugged. "Sometimes my filter isn't always working. Carry on."

"Same here," Max whispered, her hand gripping mine again. "Did I ever tell you about the time I woke up in the hospital and loudly told every member of Six they were hot?"

Though my stomach tightened briefly with jealousy, it dissipated just as quickly. She was comforting me. Trying to make me feel like I fit here—if not with them, at least with her.

I winked. "Feel free to tell me how sexy I am whenever you want."

The warmth in her eyes, coloring her cheeks, washed away any lingering anxiety I felt. All that was left was a blistering heat. Thank the gods I'd fed recently. She was damn delectable.

"This is so weird," Rowan muttered, his face pressed to his hands like he was rubbing out a headache. "I'm out of here before this turns into an orgy."

Max tensed, but I couldn't hold back the peel of laughter. One that Wade echoed—and then immediately quieted when our eyes met.

"I'm going to like having you around, Rowan Bentley." This time, my grin felt natural, easy even, as I patted him on the shoulder. "You and Declan—I'm declaring it now—you are my two favorite people." I paused for a beat. "After Max, obviously."

He arched his brow, expression blank, body frozen and rigid under my palm.

"Jackass." Declan rolled her eyes and walked to the door, but I didn't miss the way her lips pulled up at the corners. "You'll get used to him, Ro." She paused, hand on the handle, then turned back to us. "Well, I can't promise that. He's never really normal. But I can promise you'll, at the very least, often be entertained. And a laugh is good when the world goes all wonky."

She left.

Eli followed. His eyes lingered briefly on Max, softening with the sudden lightness in the atmosphere. It was the most relaxed any of us had been in days. "Stay inside. Get some rest."

Rowan cleared his throat.

My hand was still crushing his shoulder.

"Off you go, Rowan," I started peeling my fingers away from him but stopped. "No. Ro. I'm going to go with Ro from now on. More Jovial. Off you go, Ro." I chuckled. "Rhymes, see?"

He ducked away from my grip, bemused, before running a hand roughly over Max's head—the two of them locked in a silent conversation with nothing but an unbreakable stare and furrowed brows.

"Right," he glanced from me to Wade. "Anything happens to her while we're out, I'll kill you both. That's a promise. Even if I have to enlist the help of some other demons to get it done."

With that, he left.

As in left me with his sister.

Yeah, we had a surly incubus supervising us, but he trusted me with her. Which meant he liked me. Or at least had very specific conditions about murdering me. Judging by Declan's trajectory, that was adjacent to downright approval. Friendship, even. I was basically officially part of the family now. Declan fucking loved me. I was confident Ro soon would too.

I pulled Max against me, squeezing her bicep.

When I caught her eyes, I expected them to be bursting with excitement, like I was sure mine were, but she only looked confused and mildly amused.

Still, it was the lightest and most like herself she'd looked in days. Maybe even weeks.

Slowly, she made her way from room to room. She picked up the remote, ran her fingers over Cyrus's pillow, grinned at a discarded paperback that was left open on Ro's nightstand. When she got to her room, she went to the window, staring out at it for a long while, like she'd missed the view.

Wade and I watched, following quietly, reverently, as she

took in the small cabin—watched as her body relaxed into the setting with every passing moment, like a huge weight was being lifted from her.

The circumstances were terrible, but I was glad to be seeing her in her home, in the place she'd felt most like herself.

I found myself wanting to watch her life, as if it were a TV show. What were her holidays like? Her favorite things to read? Her favorite ways to pass rainy afternoons, or sunny summer days? Did she always get along with her brother or did they occasionally fight in that way only siblings could?

"Does it get better?" she asked, her eyes still focused, unseeing, on some invisible point through the window.

"The magic?" I asked, taking a step further into her room. It smelled like her—even though she'd been gone for months—like time couldn't erase her essence, no matter how improbable.

She shook her head and turned toward me, her eyes filmed with unshed tears. "The pain."

I felt Wade tense next to me. I wasn't sure what it was, but something told me he'd felt deep pain too—beyond what he'd been through in that cell. That he'd felt the kind of grief that made breathing seem impossible.

"Grief doesn't go away," I said, wishing I could give her a better answer. "It's heavy and it lingers with you. But, slowly, you grow stronger. You heal and you reshape yourself around it. And then one day, without even realizing it, the grief doesn't feel as heavy."

"Because it's become easier to carry it with you," Wade added, the words almost a whisper, "more like a companion than an enemy. A part of you that you learn to value because it's tied to the parts of you that care."

His eyes met mine briefly.

Maybe the dickhead wasn't as awful and childish as I gave him credit for. That was almost elegant.

Max considered for a long while, then sat on her bed.

The comforter was simple, like the rest of her decor. Nothing that really screamed nineteen-year-old-girl. It felt almost like an adult's taste—all neutral colors and minimalist-looking. Bare, even, but warm and cozy all the same.

"Your—" she took a deep breath, hands fisting into the comforter, and then she met my eyes, "your sister. That's who you meant before? Claude mentioned that she died. Is she the reason you lost some of your magic before?"

A rock lodged in my stomach. I stared at the shag rug at my feet, trying to find the words.

It wasn't often that I let my thoughts linger on her.

"I'm sorry," she said, the words a rush, "I shouldn't have asked. It's not my place."

For a moment, I considered her words, the edge of compassionate panic in her voice. I met her eyes and took a seat next to her on the bed. I could feel Wade watching us both, but didn't bother looking in his direction.

"You can ask difficult things of me, Max. If answers are what you want, what will help you right now, then I want to give them to you. I'm just afraid of how you'll think of me when you hear them. Nessa isn't an easy thing for me to discuss." I exhaled loudly, "I haven't even let myself utter that name in years, if I'm being honest."

She grabbed my hand in hers, twining our fingers together, and studied me in silence, urging me to continue. It wasn't a promise. She couldn't—and shouldn't—forgive all things, but it was a commitment to listen.

It was more than I deserved.

"We made a deal, years ago, when we left the hell realm," I said, needing to start somewhere, but knowing there was no good start to this story, "Nessa was in trouble and we wanted to get her out. Back then, it wasn't easy leaving—especially with all of us together—and the portals were incredibly difficult to find and navigate. As were the guardians who controlled them. When you did, a sacrifice would need to be made, a ritual or trial completed, the balance maintained in some fundamental way. I suspect one of the reasons that the barrier between realms is so messy right now, is because with the new tears, there is no way to maintain that balance. But at the time, Claude and I, as twins, became guardians on this side of the realm. That was the sacrifice we made to protect Nessa."

"How did you become guardians?" Wade leaned against the wall and studied me, but there was no animosity in his tone.

Still, I flinched.

"We took over the previous pair's post. Most guardians do not last long in their positions—Claude is, well, Claude is a special case." I left out the part that in doing so, that pair chose death, to be consumed completely by the shadow magic that corrupted them. It was the future Claude and I would one day succumb to. "Nash and Nika took over the duties from the other side."

"Nash as in the guy we met in hell?" Max's voice was soft, and she rubbed her thumb over the back of my palm. I wasn't sure she was aware she was even doing it, but it was comforting all the same.

"The one and only." I grinned down at her, but it felt stiff, stilted. Nash and Nika's story was not one I wanted to dwell on at the moment. "In exchange, Nessa was permitted to come with us, with no risks or sacrifices made beyond that. Things were fine for a while. The shadow magic was intoxicating. It was like a constant high, feeling that kind of power flow through my veins. But shadow magic has its own motivations and can't be controlled, even through conduits. I started to spend a lot of time lingering in the portal, being consumed by the magic. Too much time." I looked down and saw that I was now squeezing Max's hand, so I eased the tension in my hand, took a deep breath. "I started to hear voices and, eventually, just one voice. A girl—something about it sounded almost like Nessa."

"What did she say?" Wade asked, and I noticed that he'd moved several inches closer to where we sat.

"She was stuck." I closed my eyes, trying to recall anything else about her, but it was like trying to catch a dream in the morning, the memory running away at a pace I couldn't match. "I don't know much more, but I remember seeing these horrible visions. Nessa, Claude—both of them being ripped apart by the portals. At first, I tried to brush them away, but it became all-encompassing, any time I came near the shadow magic, the visions would get darker, more visceral, more detailed. The voice suggested that I leave, that in doing so I could save them both."

"That's why you left?" Max whispered, her eyes wide and watery and filled with a kindness that I couldn't accept.

"It was reckless, but yes. That's why I left. The voice had convinced me that if I wanted to save them, I needed to go. I thought I was making a valiant sacrifice—giving up the allure of the shadow magic, the power, to save my family. I know now how naive I was. That voice was no prophecy, it was the cruel game of a drude."

"A drude?" Wade asked. "What's that?"

Max furrowed her brows. "I heard you say that word during the ambush. There was a drude there, wasn't there?"

I nodded, my stomach tightening with disgust that one had been released on this realm. I wasn't certain Max's hellfire could truly kill one of them, but I hope that one burned to a crisp anyway. "Nightmare demons."

"Like an incubus?" Wade sat on the floor, no more than a pace from our feet, like a child in school.

"Darker," I said, trying to keep my voice even, "more vicious, more powerful. I'd only ever heard whispers of them. They weren't in hell. Or if they were, they weren't in my pocket of hell. We'd always been taught that they became extinct when hell's prison was created. They feed on a person's worst fears, can trap you inside of them until you don't know what reality even is anymore. When they've controlled you enough, they use that gap in reality to create their own—they possess their victims and control them. Their existence otherwise is ephemeral, like shade." I took a deep breath, tried desperately to suppress the building darkness from leaking out of my pores. "The fact that one made it here—" I shook my head, "I don't know who was leading that ambush, but they managed to mobilize wendigos all while accessing a drude. It's not good. If even one drude is unleashed, I can't imagine what else will unravel."

"And so you left," Max said, the sound of her voice pulling me back from the edge, "and Claude said Nessa tried to take over, right? For your post? That's when she died?"

I nodded, swallowing the lump in my throat. It took me a few moments before I could find my voice again. "She was related to us, so she and Claude must have tried to fill the gap I left, after they couldn't find me. But while she was our sister, she wasn't a twin. Eventually, the balance broke, the magic turned on her, and she died."

"You never returned, did you?" Wade asked, his stare stripping me until I was bare bones and flesh. "That's why your brother hates you so much. Your sister was killed—her life sacrificed to maintain the disturbed balance—and you never returned."

I leaned over, elbows on my thighs, and ducked my head down, to hide my face. I nodded, unable to respond with even a single word.

"Does he know?" Wade asked, "Claude, I mean? Does he know that you were just trying to protect her? That you were trying to protect them both? Losing her—I can't imagine that, but it wasn't like *you* killed her. You were trying to save her life, not end it. How could you've known what would happen? That the creature was using you? Hell, maybe it wasn't. Maybe it was true. Maybe if you'd stayed you would have lost them both. There's no way to know."

I stiffened. I was expecting the frustration and ire in his voice, but I wasn't expecting it to be mobilized on my behalf. "There was no point in telling him," my voice cracked, "she was gone. Nothing I did or said could have brought her back. The best gift I could've given my brother was to disappear from his life, to stay away. I was clearly too easy to manipulate, too weak to be trusted with such an important position, with such power."

"So the first time you saw him since that happened was when you brought us to the bar?" Max's face was expressionless, her focus on the wall across the room as she processed the truth—of what I was, of who I was.

Did she finally see it? That she deserved so much better than me? So much more than my cowardice? My selfishness?

"Shit." Wade let out a single, humorless chuckle. "No wonder he was so pissed."

Max turned to me then, her palms raising to cup either side of my face. It took every ounce of courage I had to meet her dark stare but, when I did, all I saw was an empathy so strong it ripped the air from my lungs. "What happened to her—you couldn't have known. A decision you made may have led to her death, but it was not a path you chose knowing all the options." Something flashed in her eyes, her body tensing, and I wondered if she was applying the same nuance to her own story. To Cyrus's death. She closed her eyes briefly and tightened her hold on my face, before meeting my gaze again with unflinching demand. "You went through something horrible, Darius. But it doesn't define who you are. I know you, and I know you're good. That's all that matters to me."

When she dropped her hands, letting the weight of her words sink in, Wade kicked my foot with his.

"Your brother deserves to know the truth, when you're ready to tell it. You shouldn't have to lose him too. Not now. Not when," he ran a tired hand over his face, "not when we need every motivation—every connection—we can find to fight this battle. To win. Not before it's too late."

As his eyes met mine, I felt something shift in the room—like any residual animosity and distrust between us was slowly evaporating away. Maybe it wasn't all gone yet, but for the first time since we'd met, it felt like it one day would be. One day soon, even.

And I found myself suddenly overwhelmed with warmth and gratitude. For my bond with Max, more than anything. But also because, for the first time in a long time, it felt like I had a family again.

8

MAX

I woke up to a dark room and a heavy, warm weight pressed into either side of me. A quick, cursory glance showed Wade on my left, the side closest to the wall, Darius on my right, his arm curved around my body, pulling me into him.

Heat pooled low in my belly at the thought of both of them in my bed. With me. Tangled together like we've been sleeping like this for our whole lives.

I wasn't sure when we'd fallen asleep, but I sensed the others were long back. And by sensed, I meant that there were now three water bottles left on my nightstand. They were placed carefully on a pile of old paperbacks, alongside an unopened box of crackers and some over-the-counter pain medicine.

Whoever grabbed that had read my mind before I could. My head was pounding, a dull, ever-present ache.

I wasn't sure what the cause was, mostly because there were a million to choose from:

Crying for hours? Check.

Emotional conversations? Check.

Losing my powers? Check.

Very little sleep? Check.

Long journey to my childhood home? Check.

Honestly, at this point, with the way things were going, I was happy that I woke up with any head at all.

For a moment, I considered reaching over and grabbing the pills—I could do with some water too—but the thought of disturbing either of them in the process kept me still.

I wasn't ready to disentangle myself from the two men who'd come to occupy way too much of my brain space. It was a rare, coveted moment of peace.

And I never really got to see either of them like this.

Darius's brows were relaxed, his lips curved slightly, like his perpetual smirk followed him even in slumber—any remnants of his earlier distress erased by sleep. His skin was smooth, pale in the soft moonlight glow shining in from the window.

If I didn't know any better, I'd think him just a man. Not a vampire, not a demon or former portal guardian carrying his weight's worth of guilt. Just a man. And a goddamn beautiful one at that.

He'd removed his shirt at some point, the heat of three bodies in one bed likely too much for him, and I traced the gentle swells and sharp planes of his shoulders, his arms, his chest with my hungry eyes.

His arm tensed around me. "If you keep looking at me like that, little protector, you'll make it impossible for me to get any sleep." His voice was a soft caress, barely a whisper, his eyes still closed—as if he could feel the way I was drinking him in with my stare. "Your scent changes when you're aroused. It's subtle, but I find myself often hunting for it like a parched man in the desert chases the illusion of just one drink of water."

I froze—the shock and guilt of being caught enough to send a bolt of electricity through my body. But then as I processed the rest of his muffled sentence, my stomach clenched with a different feeling altogether. "Looking at you like what?"

"Like you want to eat me alive." He grinned and I wondered if that subtle scent was growing stronger.

My desire certainly was.

"Sorry," I murmured, trying to keep my voice as quiet as his, so that I didn't wake Wade up too.

Darius's lips curved into a sharper grin, his thumb drawing lazy, featherlight circles against my shoulder where it lay. Intoxicating tingles spread out in a web from his touch, like my entire body was an instrument only he knew how to play.

"I don't mind. I'm yours to look at. Yours to devour." He opened his eyes, the contrast between black and yellow as startling as ever, even in the grayish hues of the dark room. "I'm yours to do whatever you want with. Whenever you want."

Something about the cover of dark, the silence of the cabin, made me feel suddenly bold—like I could turn off the problems the day would bring, if only just for a few moments.

Lifting my left hand carefully, so as not to disturb where Wade's arm pressed against my back, I brought it to Darius's cheek.

His skin was both firm and soft, and I traced the outline of his jaw, down his velvety neck, his shoulder, his arm—watching greedily as his eyes bore into mine, his body as still as a lion's—just before he devoured his prey.

He opened his mouth to say something, the heat in his eyes stoking the fire already burning low in my belly, but I pressed my finger to his lips, quieting him before the moment broke.

I just wanted one. Just one minute to devour him with my eyes, my hands, to abandon the whirlwind of emotions and worries that had set up permanent camp in my brain. In my body. I was wound so tight that I was sure I'd snap any second now.

His lips were soft, and he parted them, drawing the tip of

my finger into his mouth. A quick, cool dart of his tongue against it had me squeezing my thighs together. I could feel the familiar wetness already soaking through my underwear.

How did they all have this instant effect on me?

Darius exhaled sharply, the breath of frustration hot and tingly down my finger as he nipped at my flesh, teasing.

But I didn't want teasing.

I shifted my finger until the pad of it pressed into his canine.

Darius held his breath as his eyes found mine, a warning flashed there.

With a small, greedy smile, I ignored it.

A small prick of pain, and then I felt my skin pierce. He groaned, softly—quiet enough that I didn't feel Wade shift next to me, but loud enough that I felt a mirrored moan lodge in my chest, just as needy.

He bit down on my soft flesh until his lips lined red with my blood, eyes closed now as if savoring the taste.

I couldn't imagine what I tasted like to him, but the rush of power that filled me was like a drug. It was no small thing rendering a man like Darius feral with need.

I pulled my finger from his tooth, dragging it over his full, lower lip, watching with a morbid fascination as my blood smeared down his chin, as his tongue dipped to wipe it clean.

The sight of his tongue lapping me up sent a wave of heat pounding through me, like I could feel him doing the same between my legs if I just thought about it hard enough.

He pressed into me, his dick hard and thick, throbbing with the same pulsing need I felt between my thighs.

For a long moment that seemed to drag for hours, we stared at each other, our chests heaving in tandem, both of us trying and failing to quiet the cloud of lust slowly drowning us both.

His eyes darted to where Wade lay behind me, before

meeting mine once more. There was a vicious glint, a promise of danger that drew me in like a moth to flame.

"Fuck it," he whispered, voice still soft as a breath. He slid his hand between my legs, thumb pressing down my clit as I whimpered.

It took everything I had not to thrust against him, not to claw him to me with the same wildness I had the last time we were in a bed together.

It was intoxicating—the way that my desire seemed to amplify his own. I might not have access to the succubus at the moment, but that also meant I could no longer blame her powers for the electrifying connection Darius and I had. Whatever this was, it was real—lodged deep and permanently in my very marrow.

I wanted him just as badly now as I ever did. Maybe even more, now that I knew how good it felt to give into that want.

He leaned forward, just slightly, but it was enough for him to press his lips against mine in the whisper of a kiss.

As he pulled my bottom lip between his, his hand dipped carefully beneath the waist of my pants until his fingers slid against me, the slickness of the friction alarmingly obvious in the silence of the room.

My heart beat wildly in its cage as I felt, more than heard, Darius's growl. It flowed into me, like I was swallowing his desire so that it could dance against mine.

I used every ounce of willpower I had to keep myself from thrusting my hips against him, to ride the movement as two of his fingers slid into me, his thumb drawing slow, delicious circles against my clit.

The slick sound of him moving inside of me felt like an echo down a hall—too loud.

He pressed a smile to my lips, like he could feel my struggling restraint as my body fought to grind against him, to set the pace.

"We shouldn't be doing this," I mouthed, even as my eyes closed at the waves of sensation rolling through me. Fucking hell did I want him. My entire body was heated with need—the warmth so intense I was almost shocked I hadn't burst into flames. If there was any cure for my missing powers, Darius's dexterity with his fingers had to be it.

"That's what makes it so delicious, little protector," he mouthed back, with a soft pinch of my clit.

I throbbed—ached—but I kept still. Wade was still pressed against my back, asleep. His deep, melodic breaths swept against the shell of my ear, pebbling my flesh. Every sensation was heightened.

For a moment, I closed my eyes, imagining what it would be like to have both of them touching me at once, our limbs wrapped together in a sweaty pile, both of them inside of me, consuming me.

Darius's languid circles picked up pace and I clenched around his fingers, unable to suppress the moany exhale from parting my lips.

The orgasm washed over me, fast and dramatic, my body shifting just slightly as I rode the waves.

Stars clouded my vision as my body recentered itself, satisfied but not nearly ready to be done. I wanted more. So much more.

A hand clenched around my hip, digging into the soft flesh there, as Darius pulled his fingers out of me.

It wasn't Darius's hand.

Now that I wasn't lost in sensation, I noticed that Wade's breathing was jagged and heavy, his heartbeat thudding against my back.

For a moment, dread pooled in my belly, concerned he'd be upset and that this would start another war between the two of them, the subtle peace they'd come to erased in a single, reckless moment.

But then I felt him hard against my ass, straining in his sweatpants.

Darius brought his fingers to his lips, sucking the taste of me off of them as he stared past me—meeting Wade's eyes, I was certain—taunting him.

Or maybe daring him? The moment was so tense, so fragile, I couldn't be sure.

All three of us were silent and still for a moment, waiting. All I could hear was the heady rush of blood through my body as my heartbeat worked overtime.

I felt Wade's power lap against my skin, pulling from me even as it stoked the flames building between my legs again.

Then, like a bubble, the tension popped and Wade flipped me on my back with a low growl, his lips furiously covering mine as his tongue slipped into my mouth—searching and hungry.

My succubus energy might've been taking a backseat right now, but Wade's incubus wasn't.

His fingers grazed under my top, lifting it over my head, while Darius pulled down my pants—every inch of my skin on fire as they both touched, licked, bit me.

Frantically, I shoved Wade's pants down to his knees, terrified this moment would collapse before I got what I needed. My fingers wrapped around his dick as I shoved him back on the bed and leaned over him, stroking him in long, fluid pumps.

All three of us groaned as Darius slid himself against my soaked core, the sound of his skin moving against mine echoing around us.

I muffled my moan with Wade's dick, taking the tip slowly into my mouth, feeling powerful as his body tensed and his breath hitched.

Darius massaged my lower back as he kneeled behind me and continued to slide against my slickness.

"Easy," Darius coaxed as Wade fisted the sheets, "relax your throat, you can take him. All of him."

I did as he suggested, drawing Wade in deeper, his skin salty against my tongue, until my lips closed around the base of his shaft. My eyes watered with the fill of him.

"Good girl," Darius whispered, as he thrust into me from behind, pelvis bone hitting my ass, so that I was filled completely with both of them at once.

I moaned around Wade, pumping my mouth around him in time with Darius's thrusts.

Wade's hand crept down my side, every inch of skin on fire with the feel of him. I felt his power in the air, encasing us, amplifying every sensation until it was almost too much to take while conscious. He traced along my thigh until he found my clit.

I whimpered, needy and pliable as the two of them worked me closer and closer to the edge.

I teased the tip of Wade's head, pumping him with my hand as my tongue traced the ridge of him, then the veins lining his shaft.

A wave of his power radiated around us, and my vision went blurry as Darius groaned, bending over me, his lips tracing along my shoulder, up to my neck.

I nodded subtly, groaning my permission as I took Wade fully into my mouth again, my vision dancing as I struggled for air.

Darius's teeth pierced my skin, and the euphoria of the connection flowed through me, the orgasm ripping through me as he released into me—warm and full.

Wade stiffened, his indigo eyes bright and alert as they glared at Darius.

"It's okay," I whispered, basking in the glow of sensations, my body already diving towards another one. "It doesn't hurt."

He opened his mouth to protest as Darius unsheathed

himself, my thighs growing wet with the remnants of our union. "But—"

Darius chuckled behind me, then lifted my hips, settling me over Wade's, until my entrance hovered just over the tip of him. "Don't be a hypocrite. My feeding off of her is no different than what you're doing, incubus. She's ours. She can take it. It will not weaken her—only make her stronger, our bond deeper."

As Wade's eyes cut to his, Darius pushed me down, sheathing me on Wade until I was full and warm again. We both moaned.

I tried to roll my hips, but Darius's hands kept me still, pinned.

A needy whimper pulled from my throat.

"I want him to," I said to Wade, my head leaning back into Darius's chest, begging, until he gave in and worked my hips. Darius controlled the rhythm as I started to ride Wade, slow at first—watching with reverence as his eyelids hooded and I hovered above him, teasing, before taking him deep inside of me again.

His fingers dug into my thighs, a silent plea to pick up the pace—for more, but Darius didn't give in. Not until he would.

This was a game between them—both of them used to being the dominant one when it came to sex. The heat of that clash only turned me on more.

"Don't you want our girl to have whatever she wants?" Darius asked, and I could feel his brow arch even if I couldn't see it. He scraped his teeth along the other side of my neck, pulling away as I arched into him. With a grin, he pressed a kiss against my collarbone, wrapping his hands from behind me until they each palmed one boob, teasing the hard peaks.

My need built so heavy that I thought I might explode with it if I didn't get what I wanted—from both of them—now.

"Please," I begged, my fingers digging into Wade's chest as I ground against him. I sounded needy and pathetic, but I didn't care. In this moment, I just wanted to bask in the feel of them—in the heated glow of everything they each had to offer. And I didn't want to apologize for wanting it from both of them.

Wade's eyes narrowed as he studied us above him, but then something shifted and he nodded once, the single motion all Darius needed.

Darius left me to my devices on top of Wade, to find my release as he nipped playfully at the inside of my elbow. Then he sank his teeth into the soft flesh there.

I moaned, loud, as I felt the warmth of my blood pool into his mouth. My pace quickened as I rode Wade, clawing him towards me with my free hand until he was seated, his lips a hair's breadth from mine.

Darius's hand closed tighter against my throat where it rested, a gentle, teasing warning to quiet myself. But the new pressure made my vision dance in a delicious way, ushering in another orgasm. It rolled through me, like a wave, as I collapsed against Wade's chest, my body jello.

"Fuck, you're perfect," Wade whispered, his voice a growl, as he swallowed my noises with his mouth.

Our tongues fought for depth, for control, as the third orgasm continued to pull through me, or else rolled into a fourth.

With a final groan, Wade met me there.

Darius licked the small bite he'd made, grinning smugly at Wade as his eyes cut to the mark he'd left.

The three of us collapsed back onto the too-small bed, a pile of sweaty limbs.

For a second, I thought I felt the gentle flicker of my powers, like I was pulling energy from the moment like I occasionally did—but when I tried to focus on them, to harness them, they were as absent as they'd been before.

Darius handed each of us a water bottle, and I reached for

the painkillers I'd been plotting to grab before. After I took them and drained half of my water, I curled my head onto Wade's chest as Darius wrapped me in his warmth from behind.

"I still hate you," Wade muttered to Darius as he pressed a gentle kiss into my hair.

"Good." Darius's forearm tugged against my stomach until my back was sealed against his chest, sandwiched between the two of them.

My head rose and fell with each breath Wade took and I did nothing to hide the giant smile stretching across my face.

My thoughts were filled only with the two men cocooning me, and I basked in that warmth until a deep, much-needed sleep took me under.

～

I WOKE up sated and content, the warmth of the sun heating my skin.

Darius and Wade were still wrapped around me, their soft skin against mine as I breathed them in.

The moment of peace lasted a full five seconds, before the bubble burst and I remembered with a sinking sensation where we were and *why* we were here. Before I remembered everything that led to this moment.

Before I remembered that Cy was gone. That Atlas was locked in a cage. That the foundation of the world—of everything—was falling around us.

Guilt cannibalized any lingering contentment I'd had the audacity to feel.

My room smelled musty from our absence, but everything looked the same. The scattered posters on my wall, the crack in my closet door from when Ro and I played a chaotic version of catch we'd made up one rainy afternoon. The view out the window, that I could only see a small fraction of from bed, though I knew if I stood, I'd find the same trees and paths framed perfectly, as they always were, just for me.

Except everything felt heavy with the absence of Cy.

The shadow of him lingered everywhere, in every memory I had of this place, and it just made the cold reality of it all sting more acutely. The ache turning sharp, acute.

I understood why Six had been so difficult to get close to now. They'd all lost people they cared about. This horrible feeling that had buried itself deep in my bones, carving craters of emptiness, had lived in them for years.

Love was the greatest vulnerability of all. And when the ones we loved were lost—I couldn't see a way out of that pain, a way back to normal. Everything else paled in comparison.

I wouldn't do it again. Wouldn't put myself in a position to face this kind of loss. The tattered pieces of myself wouldn't survive another fracture of this magnitude.

Wade shifted against me, burrowing his face into the crook of my neck, and I held in a sob.

For a moment, I wanted nothing more than to hold onto them. To bask in their comfort, to build a life together. But I couldn't. We didn't live in a world where we were afforded such luxury.

And right now—I cared too fucking much about all of them. The bonds between us were impossible to ignore. I wanted to be like Eli—able to fuck whoever I wanted, to take my feelings out of the equation and get on with my work.

But I wasn't. I didn't know how to remove the intimacy from sex. Every moment I spent touching them, the more attached I grew. I wasn't sure if it was the bonds or just how I was built, but I couldn't do this anymore.

As much as I tried to ignore it, I was falling in love with them. With all of them.

I refused to open myself up to more pain, to the possible

devastation that came with it. Not right now, anyway. There was too much on the line. I couldn't risk falling apart at the seams again—there were too many vulnerable points to attack.

This pain flowing through me had already caged my powers.

I finally understood the coldness that was badgered into Protectors from such a young age.

The callousness of Lucifer and Samael.

There was power in detachment. A power I needed to harness.

Loving them would make me weak.

Right now, I needed strength.

I needed to save Atlas, to infiltrate The Guild, to figure out where I fit in Lucifer's war.

To save as many people as I could.

My pain was so small in comparison to what the world would feel if the barrier between realms grew more unstable.

I understood what I had to do now.

Slowly, carefully, I climbed out of the tangle of limbs, my chest tight as I silently slid on some clothes.

Darius's eyes met mine, his expression unreadable as he watched me. His mesmerizing, mismatched eyes cataloged every muscle I moved until they lingered, finally, on my face, his jaw clenching at what he saw there. I wasn't sure how long he'd been awake, but he didn't disrupt the stillness in the room, the quiet, as I turned to the door and left.

It wasn't until I was in the bathroom, brushing my teeth, that I noticed my cheeks were wet with tears.

I climbed into the shower and let the water beat down on me, soaking in the familiar scents of my old body wash and shampoo.

As familiar as so many things were, I couldn't blink away the strangeness that coated the cabin now. This was such a different life.

The version of myself who grew up here was gone now. Or at least broken and reshaped until she was almost unrecognizable.

And without Cyrus here, this place would never feel like home again—not the way it once had anyway.

By the time I was done taking up way more than my fair share of the hot water, I found Declan and Ro in the kitchen, cobbling together a delicious breakfast for us all as if they'd been cooking together for years.

Eli was leaning against the counter, trying to swipe sizzling strips of bacon while Dec swatted his hand away with a spatula.

Darius was working on a crossword puzzle in the living room, shouting out clues he couldn't parse, Ro and Wade shouting back answers as they came to them.

It seemed so calm. So normal.

So familial.

But it also felt incomplete.

We were missing a few too many people. Some we could never get back, but others we could.

And we would.

I was going to do everything it took to keep them all safe and to rescue the ones who weren't.

"I'm going to get Atlas," I said, ignoring the tightness in my belly when all of the jovial commotion came to an abrupt stop.

Every pair of eyes landed on me, nailing me to the spot.

I stood taller, took a deep breath. "I'm going to get him out and I'm going to do it alone."

"Like hell you are."

"Over my dead body, little protector."

"Don't be ridiculous, Max."

"You actually expect us to just be okay with that?"

"Think again."

Their voices cobbled and climbed over each other until the stillness turned chaotic, the gentle peace uproarious.

I was expecting this though.

We'd had a version of this conversation yesterday, but I'd been hoping that they'd had time to see the truth. This was our only option.

"None of us have access to the labs anymore." I kept my voice even. "They'll have him under so much security that not even Izzy and Ten could get him out. We can't trust anyone other than them right now. And I'm the only one of us capable of bypassing those measures. I can use my connection to Atlas to find him and pull him out of there." Like clockwork, all five of them opened their mouths to protest. "I'm all ears if any of you has a better plan."

And, as expected, five mouths closed into flat, tight lines.

"Why by yourself though? Why not take us with you?" Eli asked.

"She's not strong enough." Declan cursed under her breath, completely oblivious to the piece of bacon burning to a crisp in the charred frying pan. "If she takes any of us with her, we'll be weakening her—making the mission more difficult, opening it up to further risks."

"Yeah, but Max—" Wade's eyes cut to mine, imploring, "you can't actually expect us to let you go into the lion's den alone? I mean, there's no way. Even if it worked, even if you got him out —Atlas would turn around and kill us all for taking that risk."

"And rightfully so," Eli added, his jawline rigid as he spoke through the tension. "This idea is batshit. It's going to get you killed. We're not going to let you do it."

"It's a moot point anyway." Darius wasn't looking at me anymore, the echoes of the moment we shared earlier carving a new space between us, a gap that wasn't there before. It was the space I'd silently begged him for, but I couldn't ignore how tight my chest felt at the chill. "Her powers aren't working, and it's going to take a hell of a lot to get them strong enough to pull Atlas with her. She was only able to take—" his eyes flashed briefly to mine before they found the floor, "to take Cyrus with her because of the adrenaline boost of the fight."

Would it forever more feel like a punch to the gut whenever I heard Cy's name?

I hoped not.

Darius was right, but I had a plan.

From this moment on, no more drama with the group. No more romance or sex or any of that. We didn't have time or energy for it.

I was going to spend every waking moment training. But I was also going to give myself the space to process Cy's death. To let myself heal that gaping wound. To stitch it up, even if I was bad with a needle.

"Yet," I said, my voice little more than a whisper. "I don't have enough power yet."

"There isn't an invisible switch, Max." Darius's expression softened as he took a step towards me, then stopped. "Your power won't just suddenly turn back on because you want—or need—it to. It will take time to develop again if you want to maintain any control over how you wield it. Likely a lot more time than Atlas has to spare."

I nodded, acknowledging Darius's point, not needing to press the matter further. We'd brainstorm options until we landed on something to try. But I was determined to restore my powers as soon as possible. I'd spent time training with Lucifer and Sam. I knew how to push myself. I just needed to push the process along much harder this time.

They weren't gone. Not completely. I could feel the ghost of my powers in the recesses of my mind, a shadow slowly taking shape.

And once I had them back, the others wouldn't be able to do anything to stop me from saving Atlas.

I was only telling them now because it was important to me

that I let them know my intentions before I acted on them—I owed them that.

"What's for breakfast?" I asked, grabbing a seat at the small wooden table, the flat top worn down with knife cuts, the front leg bolstered by a stack of magazines to keep it level.

Ro set a plate piled high with eggs, bacon, and toast down in front of me. "Dec's a decent cook."

"Only breakfast." Eli handed me a fresh cup of coffee. "Trust me."

"No bacon for you," Declan yelled as she lobbed a piece of dry toast at his head like a frisbee.

Without missing a beat, he caught it with his teeth, then frowned with wide eyes, a muffled "please-I'm-sorry," contorted around the bread.

Everyone filled their plates and sat around the table. Darius and Eli took the couch and Dec tossed the former a bottle of what I assumed was pig's blood they'd likely bribed the butcher for.

He curled his nose at it, but downed it in one gulp.

Surprisingly, no one batted an eye. Not even Ro.

I squeezed Ro's hand under the table, swallowing my last piece of bacon. "After this, I think it's time we lay him to rest."

His teeth sank into a bite of buttery toast and froze for a long moment.

I watched him chew, silently watching as the others tried to stir up conversation—giving us the illusion of a private moment.

Ro's fingers gripped around my hand, like I was a balloon that might float away, and he nodded.

We didn't even need to discuss where we'd scatter Cy's ashes. After washing the dishes and listening to everyone work out a shower schedule, Ro and I went outside and walked the fifty feet to a large, thick tree with thin, hanging branches near the back side of the cabin.

It was one of Cy's favorite spots and we'd frequently find him meditating underneath the swaying branches, or reading a book while Ro and I ran through our training exercises, screaming obscenities at him from afar.

Occasionally, on nights of heavy drinking, he'd lean against the trunk as if it were an old friend, his eyes dark and lost in thought as he scanned the treeline.

I'd always wondered about his past life, about what demons he'd tried burying behind the bottle.

Now, I looked back at Cy's paranoia, at the sadness that occasionally cloaked him with new eyes.

"He's really gone," I whispered, as I pressed my palm against the bark. "I can't believe he's really gone."

Ro laid his hand over mine. "I know. He was an odd man—impossible sometimes," Ro let out a watery chuckle, "but he was a good man too. I'll be forever grateful that he brought me into this family, into this life."

"It was an odd home that we created—the three of us here—" I paused, my lips quivering as I tried to push through. "But it was a good home, too."

Ro nodded, sniffling as he lifted the lid off the small box of ashes. "It was a good home."

Cy's presence was always larger than life. He radiated an energy that you could feel the moment that he stepped into the room. How was this all that was left of him? Nothing but a pile of ash and the memories we shared?

"The world feels like such a strange place without him in it. Unrecognizable, even. And I—" I felt a tear stream down my cheek, so I shut my eyes to prevent more from escaping. "I feel scared. Lost. I don't know how to stop feeling so lost. I don't know how we are supposed to just keep going without him here with us."

Ro tilted my chin until my watery eyes met his. "You're not lost, Max. You're exactly where you need to be. Cy devoted his life to giving us the tools to protect ourselves, the ability to choose between right and wrong, even when those boundaries blurred. We just take one step at a time. And we'll do it together."

I nodded, unable to form a single word in response without breaking down.

We each grabbed a handful of ash to scatter at the base of the tree, my tears watering the ground below me, both of us lost in thought as we said our private, silent goodbyes.

A loud, snapping twig sounded a few feet from us.

I felt Ro freeze next to me, body instantly poised and ready for a fight.

A tall, dark shadow emerged from the treeline.

A shadow that, through my blurred vision, shaped into someone so familiar that my heart squeezed in my chest.

"Cy?"

9

ELI

"Dad?"

A loud shattering of glass broke my focus.

It took me a second to realize that it came from me—my cup of water now in shards on the floor.

"Dad? Ugh, Daddy if you must, I suppose," Darius said, his lips tipping in a wicked grin, "Dad is far too paternal for my tastes." His head tilted to the side. "Daddy Darius? Never mind. I don't like it. Find a new superhero name to adorn me with. Or stick with fanghole—that one's actually growing on me. I might even be quite fond, if I'm being honest."

"You're insufferable." Declan stood and walked over to where I was at the window.

We'd given Max and Ro their privacy, but I'd been watching their ceremony from here—a witness to her pain, as if I could somehow hold some of it for her. A ridiculous idea, but I'd acted on it anyway.

"Eli?" Declan shook my shoulder softly, trying to pull my focus from the third figure that had just emerged, as if born from the branches, joining the siblings under the large tree.

"What's going—" Her words were swallowed up, stunned into silence when her gaze followed mine. "Is that—"

Without waiting for her to finish, I ran outside, not breaking my pace until I stood two feet in front of the man who'd raised me.

"It's you."

Seamus's shoulders visibly loosened as he closed the distance between us, enveloping me in a hug. "Eli. You're alive. Thank the gods you're alive."

For a moment, I simply stood there, enveloped in the warmth and coming to terms with the fact that he was okay—that he was here. I wrapped my arms around him and buried my face into his shoulder, swallowing the sob that threatened to escape. I hadn't realized how terrified I'd truly been about what had happened to him until now.

After watching Cyrus die—a man I thought would never fall—death seemed so much closer to us all now.

"How did you find us?" Darius's voice was laced with menace. I felt the animosity lap against my skin as he approached, only stopping when he stood just a few feet behind us.

My father's arms tightened around me, briefly, before he pulled away and stood next to me, studying the vampire. Recognition flashed in his eyes as he reached for the blade I knew would be hidden beneath his coat. "You."

I put myself in between them, raising my hands, desperate to diffuse the tension before shit got more out of control.

My father's eyes widened. Protectors never showed a predator their back, unprotected.

Even though I trusted Darius now, not least of all because his life was linked to mine, my instincts still prickled at the back of my neck.

"He's with us, Dad. He's good—" I turned around, cringing at the undeclared promise of death in the vampire's eyes, the teasing expression he'd worn just a few minutes ago now long gone, "ish. He's with us, and he won't hurt you." The latter I spoke more to Darius, than to my father, hoping he'd de-fang and dial it back.

Darius's eyes darted to Max though, and whatever look she gave him seemed to do far more than my plea. The vampire walked to her, standing as a silent sentinel by her side, like a good little minion, but he backed down all the same.

Who was I kidding though? We were all willingly and completely beholden to Max now.

"How did you find us?" Max's question was void of the aggression in Darius's, though her words were exactly the same. Her eyes were wide with genuine curiosity. "Cy—" the name stuck, briefly on her tongue, but she pushed forward, "Cy's always been so careful about keeping this place hidden."

"After the battle," Seamus cleared his throat, his gaze cutting briefly to Darius—trepidation—and back to the rest of us—genuine warmth, "Declan," he nodded, "Wade—good to see you again. Your resurrection is perhaps the only bright spot in my week."

Wade snorted in response as Declan grabbed my father's hand in a warm embrace—somewhere between a respectful shake and hug. He'd been like a second father to them both.

"After the battle?" Darius pressed, brow arched. He was clearly uninterested in the reunion.

Seamus grunted as he leaned against the old tree, letting his guard down more now that attack didn't seem imminent. "I saw them take Atlas and knew I wouldn't be able to get him out. I also knew they'd likely take me in for questioning, after everything came to light with Six, with Max. But after watching that fucking asshole," his eyes darted briefly to Wade, wincing in apology, "after Tarren killed Cyrus, I knew that any hope I had of changing things from within The Guild was gone. So I focused on the most important thing, tracking you lot down, to make sure you were safe—to do what I could to keep you that way."

"How'd you get out without them catching you?" Ro asked. It wasn't an accusation, but genuine interest.

Seamus shrugged. "Honestly, the place was left in chaos. After Max singed most of them, the remaining demons hightailed it out of there. Everyone ran around like chickens with their heads cut off. Not only was there a breach at Headquarters—a rare occurrence—but a huge one. And with creatures and powers no one has seen or heard myth of before. I used the chaos as an opportunity to go looking for information where they wouldn't—Cy's cabin."

"Why there?" Declan studied him, her posture vigilant, but I could tell that she felt the same relief that I had when I'd stepped through that door.

"Don't know if you noticed," Seamus's forehead cracked with familiar lines as he smiled, "but the man wasn't exactly an open book. I knew I'd find a few clues there, and I did. He had several safes buried beneath the floorboards, two that opened to a code I knew. I found this." Seamus produced a large, well-loved notebook and handed it to Max. "I don't know that you'll find many answers there—I hope you will—but the first page was addressed to you and Ro in the event of his untimely death, so it's yours to do with it what you will. Cy was always a bit doom and gloom, wasn't he?" He paused, a grief that he'd worn so often in my childhood now fresh and familiar, like a scab ripped clean, revealing the tender flesh below. "Still can't believe he's gone. Doesn't seem real."

Cyrus's loss hung around us all, a heavy shroud, as Max clutched the leather-bound tomb in her hands.

"Oh!" Seamus patted his pockets until he found the one filled with what he was looking for. "Also this, this was in an envelope of things he'd left for me, but I think he'd want you to have this particular token."

Max took the small, silver pendant with shaking hands. She ran her thumb over one side, her eyes welling up. "It says my name."

My father's face softened and he folded his hands over hers. "It was also our mother's name. She wore this necklace all her life—I hadn't realized Cy even had it until now."

"Grandma's name was Max?" I blurted, my cheeks burning with embarrassment that I'd never asked before. She'd died long before I was born, but it still seemed like a thing I should've known.

"Maxine," Seamus corrected, with an amused grunt. "If you paid closer attention to your history lessons, you would have remembered that."

I shrugged. Maybe I had known. That name had never meant anything to me until I met Max Bentley, though.

My Max Bentley, not my ancestor.

"He named me after her." The words came out a sad, reverent whisper and my gut twisted as Max's eyes brimmed with another wave of tears. "I've hated the name Maxine all of my life—I had no idea that he'd named me after his mother."

I pulled her into a hug, wishing desperately for a way to pull the pain from her—to drown in it myself so she wouldn't have to. With quick fingers, I unfastened the locket she wore around her neck and held it out to her.

Silently, her eyes met mine, wide and watery, and a soft smile smoothed the dimples in her chin from holding her grief in. She slid the pendant onto the chain and it hit her locket with a soft metallic clink. I fastened it around her neck again, pressing a soft kiss to her forehead.

I wasn't used to this kind of tenderness, to wanting to shield and comfort the girls I was sleeping with. But something about Max rewired something in my brain. I didn't just want to connect myself to her physically—I wanted all of her.

Her arms tightened around me with more force than I'd

anticipated, and she buried her face into my chest, breathing me in through her tears like I might lend her my strength, even if I couldn't quite remove her pain.

My chest cracked in half as I clung to her, and I didn't care that everyone stood around us, witnessing how completely gone I was over this girl.

Because I was.

I hurt because she hurt.

When I thought about the future—the only thing I saw was her.

Every decision I made, as ill-thought-out as most of them were, was made with her in mind.

This was more than friendship. More than romance. More, even than the tender pull of a bond.

I was so fucking in love with this girl that it was going to tear me to shreds.

And the strangest part was that I didn't even care, not anymore.

I wasn't sure how long we stood there like that, her crying softly into my chest, fingers digging into the fabric of my shirt as if she couldn't get close enough, but when she finally pulled away, I had to blink away the mist in my eyes as the strange memorial came back into focus.

"Yes, but how did you find us?" Darius pressed again—bloodlust gone from his expression, though distrust still lingered. "Literally, I mean. How did you get here? The little protector said no one could find this place. I doubt a man as secretive as Cyrus would tell you—brother or not. You work for The Guild and he didn't trust them."

"Worked," my father corrected.

Darius snorted. "Semantics."

"Cyrus trusted Seamus implicitly," Max's voice was strong, though tears still streaked her cheeks. Something about that—the confidence in her posture, her willingness to grieve and love so openly—made her seem untouchable. Like she could handle anything the world threw at her, even the apocalypse. "It's one of the last things he told me. And that means I trust him implicitly too."

Seamus ran a hand through his hair as he cleared his throat, swallowing back the fresh wave of sadness etched into his features. He handed me a letter and I studied it. It was written in some code I'd never seen before—part symbol, part alphabet.

"What is this?"

"Secret map of sorts." A wistful expression softened the harsh angles of his face as he tapped the center of it. "Your uncle and I made up a language when we were young. A way to communicate. It's how we spoke to each other for years, when he was in hiding, just in case someone intercepted any of our letters."

Rowan frowned, but there was a warmth in his eyes as he wrapped an arm around Max's shoulders and squeezed softly. "Sounds like Cy, alright."

Seamus nodded, eyes sparkling with a rare tenderness. "He left me a map to find the cabin he'd raised you both in, and I hoped like hell you'd find your way here. I had no other way of finding you, of knowing if you were all alive. The paranoid shit had me going all over the place for days until the last clue led me here." He shook his head, face splitting into a slow, amused smile. "Last clue poked fun at me for going through all of his scattered directions, instead of finding a way to trace the mail forwarding services we'd used for years—would've cut my time to get here in half with a well-placed bribe or two. Stubborn and smug, even from the grave."

Max chuckled—the sound soft and gone as soon as it started, but my chest clenched at the sound. Her laughter had been so rare lately that I hadn't realized how badly I was craving it.

Darius studied my father for a long, tense moment, his expression blank, but I could see the calculations running rampant behind his eyes. When he cut his gaze to Max, he relaxed slightly, nodding once before he took a step forward. "Okay, the little protector trusts you. And you don't smell like a threat. So you can join our team. But it's going to be on a trial basis."

My father's brow arched, confusion distorting his features as his eyes met mine.

"Team?" he mouthed.

Declan shook her head. "You'll get used to him."

Wade snorted. "Doubt it."

"So what do we do now?" Rowan asked.

Everyone was looking to my father, hoping he could be our guiding light out of this mess—center our chaos with strategy, a plan—to do the thing that Seamus did best. I felt the tendrils of hope tingle along my skin too, the familiarity of it.

Direction, someone to make decisions, to figure out what the fuck we were supposed to do.

But then I saw the flash of confusion, then regret in his eyes. My father had always had an answer, a path for us to charge down with precision and clear objectives.

He didn't anymore.

In fact, the rest of us probably had a better grasp on what was happening with the world than he did.

Still, he might be of some help with navigating The Guild.

The group seemed to deflate at once as they came to the same realization I had. My father's arrival wasn't going to solve the epic fucking mess we'd found ourselves in.

We weren't children, desperately seeking an adult to shelter us anymore, no matter how badly we wanted that security.

"I'd like to chat with Eli for a few minutes and then maybe we can find a bite to eat somewhere, talk strategy," he said. Darius narrowed his eyes, shoulders tensing slightly. "No secrets, just some sensitive family stuff," he added, hands raised.

"Of course," Max said. She froze for a moment, considering. Then, decided, she slowly closed the distance between them, threw her arms around him and buried her face into his chest. "I'm sorry, Seamus. I know he loved you very much, even if he had a strange way of showing it over the years. I'm glad you found us."

Her voice was muffled against the fabric of his jacket, but I could hear the emotion building in the back of her throat.

My father looked startled for a moment, but then, slowly, he sank into her, collapsing against her small frame until I thought he might capsize her. His vulnerability was palpable—as if he too suddenly felt his inner child searching for comfort, for stability, for someone to guide him to and through whatever shitshow came next in this strange life of ours.

Maybe we never really stopped looking for that—for guidance—no matter how old we got or how much authority we had.

It struck me then that he was feeling just as scared, just as lost as the rest of us. That this was probably the first moment he'd had to grieve the loss of his brother, to share that pain with someone who felt it as deeply.

Cy and my father weren't close in the traditional sense, not in the way Max and Rowan or Atlas and Wade were—especially since Cy spent most of their adult lives MIA.

But even apart, I knew that my father cared deeply for his brother. Time and distance didn't lessen that kind of connection.

The rest of us averted our eyes, witnesses to the tender, shared wound between them. It was a feeling we all knew well.

Seamus cleared his throat as he pulled away from Max, pinching his eyes with his fingers as he turned to me. "Right, then. Eli, lead the way."

We were quiet for a long time as we carved a winding path around the perimeter of the property. It was comforting, in an odd way, being in the place Max had spent most of her life. The woods felt alive with the energy of her in a way that I couldn't really put into words.

"Right, then," he repeated, staring straight ahead into the distance, as alert as always. "There's no easy way to say this, and I know that we generally don't talk about them, but I want to touch base with you about your mother and Levi."

My stomach twisted into knots at the mere mention of them. But the familiar anxiety and pain that usually accompanied any conversation we had about them turned quickly to dread—to fear. "The ambush," I said, struggling to find words, "I didn't see them. Are they—"

I couldn't put voice to the words. I'd spent most of my time since their arrival avoiding them completely. I'd only seen Levi a couple of times, but I'd managed to avoid my mother entirely. She'd been so busy with the work that brought her to Headquarters that it had been easy enough. She'd also long given up trying to win me over.

After she'd left, she did everything she could to try and repair her relationship with me, if not with my father. But I'd made it abundantly clear over the years that I wanted nothing to do with her. Not after what she'd done to him. Not after she'd torn my entire world apart with her selfishness.

Eventually, she let me be—understood that the only thing I wanted from her was to sever every connection we had.

My goal had always been to live out the rest of my life without carving a space for her or Levi in it—for us all to go off fighting evil on parallel paths, meeting as infrequently as we could. But the thought of them dying sent a cold rush of panic through my gut. Of regret.

"They're not dead." Seamus settled a hand on my shoulder,

squeezing softly. "I don't think they are, anyway, but I can't be sure."

I narrowed my eyes, unsure where this conversation was going in this case.

Seamus took a deep, steadying breath. "I haven't spoken to her—your mother—since she arrived. But I've been studying her patterns, her work. She's been poking around in things beyond her pay grade. And that boy—Levi—there's something odd about him, something sort of... off. So I looked into him, had Arnell fish around in the databases to see if he could dig anything up." His focus cut to my surprised expression. "Yes, I'm very much aware that Wade and Arnell know their way through our systems. I've done my best to cover your tracks when you've meddled with things that you shouldn't have been meddling with. Seemed only fair that Arnell return the favor." His expression softened with a smile. "He's a good boy. A good man. I hope that he and his team are doing everything they can to protect themselves. Who knows what kind of hell council will rain down on the teams now that they know about Atlas. About Max."

My father was a hardass most of the time. But he'd trained most of the young teams The Guild employed and watched my peers grow from children into battle-ready adults. He might not show it often, but I knew he felt responsible for them all—that every loss pierced him like a knife.

"What did he find?"

Seamus shrugged. "That's the thing. Not much. I don't know why I never really looked into him—maybe because he was so rarely around, maybe because thinking about him was too painful—but there's very little on Levi. He wasn't trained in one of our academies from what I can tell, and he seemed to spend the first decade of his life living somewhere else, outside of Guild purview altogether."

It made sense, though I'd never really thought about Levi

and his origin story. In fact, it took all of my focus when he was around to pretend that he didn't exist. Hell, I didn't even know that he did until long after he was born. Another secret my mother kept from us all. "Is that an issue?"

"Not on its own. But his position within the system is an odd one. He doesn't belong to a team, and there's no clear record of what he does for The Guild. He seems to come and go as he pleases—existing parallel to the system. Your mother has him behind so many security blocks, he might as well not even exist at all. At first, I thought it might be because of the nature of your mother's betrayal. That the broken mate bond would mar his reputation as it had hers, simply for being a product of it. But now I wonder if there's something else there. Your mother—she's been almost as difficult to track down, to trace. And has only really come into Guild prominence again after her return in the last handful of years. She's gotten quite high up, traveling constantly on missions I can't access. Even Arnell has had difficulty hacking into their files. He's also suspicious that a lot of the information we have on them both is fabricated—or altered in some way. He explained it to me in plain terms, but it's far out of my understanding if I'm being honest. She's always done things her own way, but I wonder now if it's a coincidence that the ambush—that so many security breaches on campus—happened to coincide with their arrival."

Without asking my permission, my body tensed, my legs stiff and no longer keeping pace alongside my father. Would they have betrayed us? Betrayed Max? Let in a horde of demons to take her away from us? To kill us?

I knew my mother was ruthless, but the realization that she could be responsible for such tangible harm made my blood boil.

"He was very interested in her." My voice didn't quite sound like mine. "In Max. In fact, the only times I saw him, he was extremely fucking focused on her, on getting to know her."

At the time, I thought he'd simply been trying to get a rise out of me, flirting with the girl that I was clearly bent out of shape over. And then, jealousy had clouded any other possibility from shining through.

His mouth flattened into a straight line, disappointment etching into the lines around his eyes. "I see."

"You don't really think they'd betray her like that do you? Betray all of us?" How many people had died during that ambush? Too many. The Guild as an establishment was an enemy to us now, but that didn't mean that all of the unsuspecting people there, the ones kept in the dark of the lab's nefarious activities, the warriors barely of age, deserved to be torn limb from limb like that—ripped apart in the one place they'd been made to feel safe.

It was the very catalyst that had led to Cyrus's death. To Atlas's capture.

Could my mother really be responsible for the grief tearing my team apart at the seams?

My father let the questions hang in the air.

She'd betrayed us before, without even once looking back. Who was to say she wouldn't do it again?

"I don't know," he answered eventually, his voice softer now. "I hope not. I'm telling you that it's a possibility. To warn you." He shook his head, eyes pinned to the ground, like it held the answers he sought. "I know there is more going on than I can see—that you and the others are wrapped up in the center of it. I don't expect you to trust me with whatever burdens you bear. But I want you to understand that you shouldn't trust anyone, not anymore. Not The Guild, not the council—not anyone. For so long, I thought I was doing good, that I could weed out the bad from within the belly of the beast—that by working with the small network of protectors I thought I could trust, we'd uncover the truth and restructure The Guild's values, align them with reality, with good. But I don't think that anymore. I don't know how to make sense of this world now. Good and evil are such unstable concepts—they're fabricated and reshaped—and I'm finally just now understanding that all of our history, the very foundation of The Guild, has been written through a very particular lens—one that doesn't serve us all. One that doesn't serve the reality of the world we live in. It's a strange feeling, to suddenly feel so out of the loop, so disconnected from everything I thought I knew. So—unnecessary." He cleared his throat, blinking a few times before he met my eyes. "I thought I was doing good, but I'm not so sure what that looks like anymore. So now, I just want to protect you. To help you—and the others—where and when I can. That's the only thing I know, the only thing I care about anymore."

For the first time in a long time, I let myself really look at him. His golden-brown skin was duller than it had been, the skin around his eyes loose and baggy, the lines cutting through his forehead, more dramatic. There was a weariness in the way he carried himself. The vigilance was still there, sure. It always would be, it was carved into his bones at this point. But he was tired. And whether it was his brother's death, or his suspicions and fears around my mother—hell, probably both—he was cloaked in a shroud of pain that was almost tangible.

I realized, suddenly, that he'd aged.

I wasn't sure if it really was a sudden thing, or if I'd simply taken a moment to stop seeing him as Seamus Bentley, and finally start seeing him as a whole person. My father, yes; the head of teams, yes; but also, someone who'd spent a lifetime floating in heartache. Now, the thing that had anchored him to this world for years was gone.

"I'm sorry, Dad."

His brows bent in confusion. "For what?"

"I'm sorry that the world is so fucked right now. That the people you thought you could trust, you can't. That you lost your brother, your position at Headquarters. That now Mo—"

my voice faltered on the word, "that she's back again, that because our world is the way that it is, you can't ever really escape her. Or the pain she put you through when she left us."

"Not one of those things are things you should be sorry for, my boy. It's a bit silly," he said, with a small, sad shake of his head, "all this time, I thought I'd lost the great love of my life. I'd spent years mourning your mother's absence, Eli. Never truly living because of one heartache. It was an acute heartache, sure. A supernatural one that burrowed into me, stole something. But it was just one relationship. One fracture. And then I watched my brother, my best friend, die in front of me. I haven't felt a pain that sharp in all of my life, watching him sacrifice himself for the daughter he loved more than anything in the world." His words caught in a rare show of emotion. "But when I couldn't find you, when I turned around and you and the others were gone, when I realized what you all had coming after you, even if you survived Tarren's tactical teams and misguided claims of justice—that's when I understood how wrong I was." He placed his hand on my shoulder, squeezing. "I loved her—deeply, yes—but your mother was not the love of my life, Eli. You are. Just you. And I'd happily go through the heartache of losing her over and over again, everyday if I had to—because your mother gave me you."

I cleared my throat, searching for a response, but I didn't have one.

We walked for a few more minutes in silence. I soaked in the chill of the winter air and the fresh smell of the woods, letting them sharpen and reshape my thoughts as I turned our conversation over and over in my mind.

My father didn't exactly bring any answers with him, but at least now I knew that he was safe. Well, as safe as anyone could be in a time like this. I no longer had to waste mental energy worrying that he had been tossed into a cell like Atlas, or that he was unintentionally working against us.

Right now, any win was good—and this one was huge.

"I spent too many years focusing on what I'd lost instead of on what I had. You, protecting Cy's sacrifice—Max, Rowan, your team—that's where my alliance is now. Nothing in this world matters to me if you lot aren't in it." He snorted before adding, "even if it means I have to apparently get the approval of a vampire."

I grinned, wondering what his response would be when he found out that not only was Max bonded to a vampire, but I was as well. "If it helps, that vampire saved my life once, at great expense to himself."

Seamus's eyes widened, his mouth stretching in surprise. "It helps." He nodded, expression softening. "Actually, it helps a lot. This world of ours is a strange one—I expect this won't be the first time in the coming days when I'll meet with the unexpected."

When I looked up, I realized that we'd found our way back to the others.

Max was looking far more chipper than I'd seen her in days. Her mouth contorted into a reluctant smile. "I'm also the daughter of Lucifer, so I'll bet you didn't have that on your bingo card, either."

"And I'm an incubus," Wade added with a grin, "though I suppose you expected something was up with me. What, with the whole me clearly not being dead thing and all."

Seamus's eyes cut to Declan, like he was expecting her to lay claim to another secret, equally shocking heritage.

She shrugged. "I'm still just me," she tilted her head, considering, "but the hell realm is at risk of collapsing and taking our world as we know it out with it. So, there's that if you haven't had enough surprises yet today."

He looked stunned and turned to me for confirmation.

"It's true," I said, feeling suddenly like our roles had reversed at some point on our walk, and now I was somehow the one offering guidance and assurance. "Unfortunately. But we'll take it one step at a time and fill you in on whatever we can."

"At least I'll never have to worry about life growing dull in my old age." He wrapped an arm around Max's shoulder and directed her back towards the house. "Spawn of Satan, eh? I knew your mother was a handful the moment I laid eyes on her. Should've guessed you'd be just as unpredictable. Especially with my brother's influence guiding you all these years. How about you show me to some food? Knowing Cy, you've probably got all kinds of bland non-perishables stocked here—enough to keep us full and happy for months." He snorted a gruff laugh. "I could use a decent meal and a shower before we start mapping out a plan to jailbreak that werewolf of ours."

10

MAX

The days bled together, all of us racking our brains, trying to find a way to get to Atlas.

Days. And we still weren't any closer to rescuing him. All of our ideas were just iterations of the same thing over and over again. We'd gotten nowhere, even with Seamus's knowledge of Guild infrastructure.

"Security will be tighter than ever before," Seamus said for the hundredth time since his arrival, "I'll have no access of course, and he will be kept under tight surveillance. Assuming he's still even—"

"He's alive," I said, cutting him off before he could voice the fear that cloaked us all. "I'm sure of it."

I wasn't sure of it of course. Not really. But something in my gut told me that I would know. That if Atlas had been killed, I would feel it in some deep, fundamental part of my being. It was silly—a childish thought, really, but I clung to it fiercely.

We had no other hope, and we desperately needed hope. Now more than ever.

"Max getting her power back is our best option. I know it's not ideal," Seamus's eyes cut to his son who was glaring daggers back, none of them exactly stoked by the idea of me going off on a solo mission into enemy territory, "but I've been over all the possibilities. Anyone I trust at Headquarters will be lying low. Council will be in charge of everything. Tarren himself is even likely under heavy surveillance, his loyalties questioned with the breach happening under his supervision. With his own son—" he paused, nodding towards Wade who was making us all a canned meat concoction that smelled pitiful, "sons proving to be demons and no one the wiser. If any of us set foot on campus, we won't stand a chance. Max is our best bet."

The others were sullen, and I'd often catch them whispering in huddles together when I walked into a room, splitting apart the moment I appeared, like they were desperately trying to find a different answer, a magic solution that would prevent me from getting my hands dirty. But I didn't need the kid gloves.

Having a mission, a clear goal, helped shield some of the pain. It gave me something to focus on.

I'd tried dream walking.

To Atlas and to Izzy.

I'd even tried to reach Wade, hoping his proximity would help ease the strain on my powers.

Even that I failed at.

It was beyond frustrating. All of my hard work honing and strengthening my power, simply gone.

Wade was able to reach out to me, at least, to carve a dreamscape for us at night, where we'd work for hours in my slumber to pull out even a spark of my abilities—no minute wasted, even in sleep, as I tried to call them back to me.

Still, nothing. Not even a stirring. And I could never start the dream walk, could never reach in and craft or shape the dream myself. I always had to be pulled in by him.

He was getting stronger, better at it at least. He'd crafted us onto a glacier, into a club in Tokyo, onto a beach in Greece. It was an entire new world that he could explore, the only limit his imagination.

Slowly, day by day, surrounded by them all, the tightness in my chest started to ease.

I still felt Cy's loss acutely. I'd probably always feel it—a deep, heavy ache, a gaping hole.

And I spent my early mornings, when darkness still shielded the sun, huddled on the floor of the shower, crying as the water rained down on me, hoping to protect the others from witnessing my pain, from seeing how fragile I still was.

I was sick of the pity rounding and softening their eyes whenever they looked at me or Ro.

Even Wade and Darius had stopped bickering when either of us entered the room, everyone working overtime to cushion us in our grief.

As much as I hated them all for it, for seeing me like this, for seeing me so weak and powerless, it helped.

And Seamus's quiet, stern presence acted as an unexpected balm.

He was very different from his brother. Softer, more open. But every now and then, I'd see the shadow of Cy in his occasional scowl, the same eerie wisdom in the depths of his dark eyes as he watched us train in the yard.

It made the pain of living with Cy's memory—haunting every inch of the cabin like a silent ghost—more tolerable. Like Seamus was a link to Cy, to home, that I hadn't known I'd needed.

We hadn't spent much time together before now, often only seeing each other in passing or when he was helping out with training, but I'd grown unexpectedly fond of his quiet, surprisingly gentle presence. He'd even spend the occasional evening relaying stories from their childhood.

It was days before I could bring myself to open the journal he'd given me.

When I was ready to take the plunge, I sat on a cleared path in my closet, sheltered by the familiar scents, now laced with the must of abandonment.

I ran my hand over the soft leather cover, imagining Cy's long fingers doing the same.

The paper was cream, yellowing at the edges from age. Cy's almost unreadable writing scratched in black over almost all of the pages.

I'd never seen him with this book, but it was obvious that he'd cherished it for years, finding solace with his isolated thoughts.

Many of the pages were filled with random, isolated phrases—fragments of ideas that were completely decontextualized from me, that I didn't know how to make sense of.

There were lists of names, a few hastily drawn maps to places I didn't recognize.

But it was the very first page that cracked me in half.

The first line of the journal made my eyes well until I almost couldn't read it:

She's small. Spends all hours of the night wailing. I don't know what the fuck Sayty was thinking, leaving her with me. What do babies even eat?

The next entry:

I can't do this. I'm working on finding a family I trust to take her in. Hopefully, by the end of the week, she'll be out of my hair.

A few days later:

A girl in town took pity on me. Loaded me up with formula and diapers, put in a special order for what was supposed to be some simple necessities. But now the child's things take up more of the cabin than mine.

One month later:

The girl has a strong grip. Holds on to my finger with a quiet fierceness while she eats.

Watching me. Always watching me. She's going to be smart—stubborn, too—I can see it in her eyes. Good. She's going to need her wits if she's to survive in this world.

I turned the page:

Maxine. It's a good name. I need to call her something. Mother would have liked her, I think.

One of my contacts got back to me finally, might know a spot for her to go to. Not sure I trust it, so going to keep looking. Still no word from Sayty. Assuming she's dead. Poor girl, no idea what she's gotten herself into.

Tears dropped, smudging the ink as I flipped through a few pages:

First word—fuck. I'll need to start watching my language around her.

She took her first step! Fell almost instantly, but not a single tear. Kid's got grit.

Went to the bathroom, came out and she had one of my blades swinging around. Terrifying. Need to secure them better from now on.

I flipped through a few more pages:

The girl never stops badgering me with questions. Gets annoying as hell, but she's smart. She looks more like her mother with every day that passes. I wish she was here, that she could meet this child. I think she'd be proud, albeit unsurprised by the number of gray hairs sprouting from my scalp.

Well, it's happened. She saw it in a movie, and begged me for one, so now I've had my first tea party. What has become of me? The girl smiled for hours afterwards.

She's officially read through every book I own. Ordered more, but I can't keep up with her. I think she's bored. Was naive of me to think this quiet life would be enough for her. Selfish.

Netty and Jay were murdered. They were on the run, I think. Guild, most likely. Their son can't go back there. He's Max's age. Going to take him in for a few days until I find somewhere safer for him.

I'm outnumbered. These kids are going to be the death of me. The girl hasn't stopped smiling since I brought Rowan home.

They took their first trip into town without me today. Followed them down anyway, just to be safe.

She's eighteen today. No sign of extraordinary powers, thankfully. Hoping whatever bind Sayty had put on her lasts for a few more years. I need to tell her the truth, but I don't know how. Hell, I don't even know the whole truth myself. All this shit I've kept from her.

She'll never forgive me.

Can't say I blame her either.

The letters became little more than blurs as my eyes welled with emotion, scanning each page like it could somehow bring me closer to him—like it could bring him back to me.

"You okay?" Darius stood above me, his white-blond hair curling over his golden eye as he studied me. The harsh angles of his face and the rigidity of his posture made it seem like every muscle in his body was working overtime to keep him from murdering someone.

I wiped the liquid from my cheeks and nodded, closing the journal with a silent promise to show it to Ro later tonight. I nodded. "I'm fine."

He grunted before climbing into the closet and sitting down next to me, his side glued to mine. "You don't really seem fine, little protector. I've been listening to you weep for an hour now."

I handed him the heavy journal, the cover slick with my tears, as if it could answer for me.

He studied it carefully, eyes narrowed as he turned it in his hands, before glancing back to me for permission to open it. When I nodded, he did, his long fingers soundlessly feathering across the weathered paper.

I watched his eyes scan the first page. It was strange, seeing Cyrus—my childhood—through his eyes. Even more strange to realize I was sharing this with him. I'd spent so much time denying how I felt about him, but now that fear of connection stemmed from something darker, a deeper pain. Now, I only feared losing him.

He soaked in the words greedily, his lips twitching every few seconds, like he was fighting back the urge to grin or frown, the movement too subtle to distinguish which.

I could tell he wanted to pore over every word, but he didn't read more than the first few pages before settling the book reverently on the floor in front of us.

"I'm sorry that I didn't know him." His voice was unusually contemplative and serious. "But I can tell that he loved you, deeply. And I'll forever be indebted to him for saving your life that day—and all the days before that. For shaping you into the person you are now. The person I—" he cleared his throat, his breath catching as he changed course, "I know it doesn't feel like the truth right now," he said, tipping my chin up until my eyes met his. The gesture was surprisingly gentle and it sent a shiver down my spine. I'd been avoiding him since the other night, but here, there was nowhere to hide, and suddenly my closet felt impossibly full of him, of all the unspoken things sparking between us, until all of my senses were vibrating with the closeness of him. "You won't always carry so much sadness, little protector. And while it might carve you up inside right now, that book will feel like an immense gift in years to come—a way to hold your past tight, to carry it with you."

I swallowed, unable to form words as I studied him.

His lips were soft and only a few inches from mine, his skin uncommonly smooth and pale in the shadow of the closet. It would be so easy to sink into him right now, to open myself to him and let him inside, to bury the pain for a few minutes in a wash of pleasure instead.

To let him take my pain, shape it and reclaim it until it sparked with something wilder.

Slowly, his hand traced my jawline, his expression growing more intense like he could read the tempting path my thoughts were traveling.

My skin was fire where he touched, until I was certain that Darius would be the very thing to reignite my powers. Every inch of me throbbed with desire, my body craving his touch after so many days locked in this house with all of them—lying next to them each night without a single caress.

I'd reached my breaking point. I could feel the invisible pull between us, my body a magnet to his that it took every ounce of my willpower to resist. The bond linking us was tightening and sharpening—hungry for the connections I'd been depriving it of since the other night.

I wanted desperately for him to sink his teeth into me, for him to press me up against the wall and torture me with pleasure and pain in equal parts, until every thought in my mind evaporated—until I was limp and a puddle before him, putty in his hands.

I whimpered, the sound whiny with need and shaping between us without my permission.

His eyes dilated, every muscle in his long, lean body tensed.

The desire to fuck him, to give in to the bond forging between us completely and entirely was almost as strong as the desire to protect the remaining fragments of my heart.

Almost.

I dropped my eyes, my stomach clenching with shame instead of need now.

How was this what I was focused on right now?

What the fuck was wrong with me? Cy was dead. Atlas was in danger. The literal world was ending.

And yet my thoughts kept drifting to the team that had eclipsed my entire world—to the desire to lose myself to the pleasure—to the warmth—only they seemed able to pull from me.

It was selfish. I was selfish.

"I can wait." He groaned, shifting slightly as he leaned in closer, his mouth so close to mine that his words felt like a caress against the soft, sensitive skin of my lips. My eyelids grew heavy, every inch of me sparking with the electricity between us. "I want you, little protector. But not just the parts you're ready to share right now. I can feel you shielding yourself, protecting yourself. And that's okay—the wounds on your heart are raw, fresh. I get it." He chuckled, the sound low and vibrating through me. "Believe me, I get it. One day, when you're ready, I'll fulfill every single fantasy you can dream up—but not a moment before you're ready to take that dive with me." His lips ghosted over mine, featherlight and not enough. "Take the time to figure out what you want, how you want to exist and live in this strange world of ours. And I do mean what *you* want—not because of the mate bonds. Not because of what we want or the power coursing between us. What you want. That's the only thing that matters—everything else is just noise. Even the apocalypse." He smiled a slow, lazy smile. "When you're ready for me, you'll have me." His breath tickled the shell of my ear as he leaned impossibly closer, tightening my belly. "All of me. And, though it may surprise most, when it comes to what I want, I'm a very patient man."

He pressed a surprisingly gentle kiss to my forehead and leaned back, creating what suddenly felt like a crater of distance between us. My chest strained with the desire to pull him close again.

I didn't. I couldn't move, couldn't even breathe as he studied me with an unreadable look in his eyes.

"And you are the thing I want more than anything else in this world. I'm confident you'll be more than worth the wait."

~

"Your form is good," Declan panted, lunging towards me again, "and it's good to know that your strength and speed aren't affected by the power loss." She wrinkled her nose. "Suppose I shouldn't be surprised though. Even before your powers kicked in, there was always something... more about the way you sparred."

I crouched to dodge her as she came at me again, then used her own momentum to knock her off balance. She fell to the ground but I cushioned her as much as I could on the way down.

When she turned, her chest was nearly pressed against mine, each inhale bringing us closer together, each exhale pulling us back apart.

"You don't need to do that, you know." Her brows bent inward, bright green eyes hard with frustration. "I don't need to be coddled."

"I— I know that. There's no use in you getting more injured than you need to though, not from just sparring."

And not when I didn't have the capacity to heal her, though I kept that part to myself. Not having access to my powers put more than just me in danger.

She grunted as she sat up, pushing more distance between us.

We hadn't spent much time together since reaching the cabin—since Cyrus, really. I'd been holed up in my room with Ro, dedicating all of my time to training when I wasn't sinking into the memories this place held.

I'd been present enough to feel her distance though, to know that something had been eating away at her. She'd been retreating since we got here, isolating herself from the group as she trained harder and longer than any of the rest of us—up before dawn for a run, gliding through her stances and meditations well into the late evening. She'd even stopped her verbal taunts with Darius for the most part.

"Dec?" I stood, reaching for her as she started to pace, but stopped in my tracks when the sun reflected on her glistening eyes.

Every muscle in her body tensed until, for a moment, I was

certain she would retreat even more, stop our session and go for a jog—holding the tension inside of herself until she could work it out her own way. Alone.

But then she squeezed her fists at her side, considering for a long moment, before releasing them and turning back to me.

"I hate this." Her jaw pulsed as she tried to combat the emotion threatening to spill over.

I furrowed my brows in question—there was so much to hate about our situation, I wasn't sure what she was centered on right now.

She took a deep breath, started pacing again. "I hate being the weakest link. The one who can't protect the group. Who can't protect you. And now that your powers are suppressed, it's all I can focus on. The entire supernatural world is after you and I'm just a measly protector." She paused in her stride, a harsh laugh spilling from her lips. "You know, when Atlas first turned, he was devastated. And I was devastated for him. Because we thought, we thought—" she shook her head, hands pinning her waist as she stared at the ground, "and then Wade. And now Eli's linked to a vampire. And Darius is a supercharged fanghole with a power boost from being a portal guardian. Is it ridiculous that now I'm almost jealous?" Her gaze cut to me briefly before she looked up at the sky, the frustration emanating from her softening now, as she took a deep, wobbly breath. "How horrible is that? I'm fucking horrible."

My chest squeezed as I closed the distance between us, pressing my hand to her cheek until her eyes reluctantly met mine. "You want to protect the people you care about—and you're frustrated because you feel paralyzed right now. That doesn't make you a horrible person. It means that you're scared—because you care about your family, you don't want to lose them. That makes you the very opposite of horrible, Dec."

My words hit me double, as I recognized my own fears mirrored in hers.

She opened her mouth to protest, but I pressed on before she could.

"And you're not weak. You're the strongest person I know. From the moment I've met you, you've given every ounce of yourself to protect your team, to protect me. When Atlas turned into a wolf, you went against everything you believed in to protect him, to keep him safe. You put your family before yourself, every single time. You watch out for us all. Hell, even Darius is drawn to the good, to the selflessness radiating from you. You're anything but weak. You're the backbone of this group—the very heart of it." The truth of the words settled between us, and I watched her chin dimple as they washed over her, as she soaked them in. "There are many kinds of strength, Dec. And this group—Atlas, me, all of us—we would be nowhere without you." I smiled at her, trying to imagine Six functioning without her. "Hell, are you kidding me? Atlas, Wade, and Eli probably wouldn't have even made it through their first mission without you there keeping them in check, keeping them alive."

She snorted. "Atlas did almost get killed on our first mission together," she said, with a watery smile and wistful distance in her eyes as she chased the memory. "He was trying so hard to prove himself—for Tarren's sake, thought if he earned his approval, proved he could lead, that he'd be able to carve out a spot for Wade—take charge of a team on his own —" she grunted, the tone in her voice turning sour at his father's name, "anyway, the night of the mission, he ditched the team we were working with at the time and went after the vampire we were tracking on his own in the middle of the night."

Honestly, not surprising. It sounded like Atlas. Stubborn, ruthless, ready to sacrifice himself for the cause he believed in —but far less careful and precise than the version I knew. Sarah's disappearance and his transition into a wolf had changed him—marking him and shaping him into something new.

"You stopped him?" I asked, though I knew with every fiber of my body that she had. Declan was always there, always had his back.

She nodded. "Followed him and dragged him back before the vamp caught sight of him. Turned out there were two others there our intel hadn't accounted for. He would've been dead within the first two seconds." A big grin stretched across her face at the memory, at the history between them. "Chewed him out for hours before he finally admitted to being reckless. Got a lot better about precision after that. Until—"

"Until Sarah, and the attack," I guessed.

She nodded. "Yeah, the bloodlust outweighed our training after that. For all of us. We'd lost one of our own, and on our watch. It's one of the most terrifying things to happen to a team —the stuff of nightmares. It happens to most of us eventually, but we were so young, we had no idea how to process all of that then. The guilt was overwhelming."

My chest tightened, the familiarity of the sentiment taking me by surprise. I understood them so much better now. Their overprotectiveness, their stubbornness, their distrust. But more than anything, I understood why they'd all kept me at such a distance for so long.

Why it was so difficult for them to let me in.

The only thing more painful than not letting yourself care was losing the one you cared about.

I wasn't sure it was something I could survive more than once. Cy's loss had carved a crater through me, until I was little more than the shattered pieces of myself, held together with string.

Declan studied me for a long moment, her expression hard and unreadable, the vulnerability paving way for something else. "We were wrong though. What happened to Sarah—to

Atlas. It wasn't our fault. And it doesn't excuse our carelessness. When I look back at that time now, I wish I had done many things differently. The Guild uses our grief—weaponizes it to make us better soldiers, to fuel our anger. I watched my friends harden themselves—" she shook her head, "hell, I practically wrote the manual on how to do it. It takes a lot of work letting that go, creating fractures in the steel walls I'd constructed. I won't—" she took a deep, steadying breath. I could feel her eyes on me again, but couldn't bring myself to meet them.

"Look, I won't tell you how to go about protecting your heart, Max. I know I have no business leading that lesson in the first place. You're in the midst of a terrible loss, one compounded by more pressure and stress than any single person could reasonably manage on their own. But I will tell you that if I had the chance to process my own grief again, I would do things differently. As a kid, after my parents—" the word wavered on her tongue, her accent growing thick through the emotion, "I did what I thought I needed to do, what I thought would keep me safe in the long term. I shut down. I shut everyone but my team out—and I only even kept them close in the first place because I saw my own trauma reflected in theirs, like peas in a pod. It was only recently that I realized the fault in the logic that all of us seemed hellbent on following. That sometimes there are worse things than opening yourself up to being hurt."

I was saved the tragedy of cobbling together a response when the treeline a few feet away from us started rustling.

The hairs on the back of my neck stood up as I glanced at Dec. My fear echoed on her face. We communicated soundlessly, both of us frozen.

Ro, Wade, and Darius had gone to get more supplies and a couple of burner phones. We wouldn't be expecting them for another hour or so—unless something went deeply wrong.

But even then, they would never sneak up on us. They knew

we were on high alert; they'd announce their presence immediately.

The air around us felt static and wrong and I knew with a fluid certainty that we were being watched.

As one, Dec and I slowly reached for the blades we'd tossed to the side during our sparring session before pressing our backs to each other to keep our eyelines clear.

My sweaty skin stuck to hers and I felt her heartbeat pummel through her spine into mine. We both held our breath, waiting.

Slowly, a tall figure emerged in the clearing—a lean, white man with deep brown hair and shadowy black eyes.

"You've been a difficult girl to track down, Miss Bentley. We've spent days scenting you through the better part of the state." He arched a brow, a thin smile smirking across his face. "You're lucky I enjoy the hunt so much—most would've given up the search days ago."

And then, he started to strip.

"Um," I turned my neck slightly to catch Dec's eye from the corner of mine. "What the fuck?"

I watched him, stunned, as he unbuttoned his jeans, climbing out of them one leg at a time as if he was in the comfort of his bedroom and not in front of strangers, in the middle of winter. It was the sort of awkward introduction I expected during a bachelorette party, not in the middle of the woods.

He pulled down his boxer briefs, and I immediately averted my gaze as he piled them on top of his shoes. "No use wasting clothes, finding new ones will only slow us down."

Then, his body started to pop, crack, and warp—skin bleeding into fur the same color as his hair.

"Fuck," Dec muttered, both of us catching back up to the reality of the situation at the same time. "Eli! Seamus!"

Four more figures emerged from the clearing—two large

wolves slinking around their friend as he shifted and two women, still in their human skin.

The door behind us slammed open and I felt the heat of Eli and Seamus as they pressed close to me and Dec, weapons raised before any of the new guests moved an inch closer.

"We'll let the rest of you go," one of the girls said, her voice silky and smooth, her face almost doll-like in its ethereal beauty, "if you give us the girl. I don't like being wasteful, there's no need to kill you all."

I felt Declan stiffen against me, Eli shifting closer until his shoulder positioned slightly in front of mine.

"What do you want with me?" I shoved him to the side slightly so that we were on even footing. I couldn't fight properly if he was defending me, and he wouldn't either—we needed to keep our heads level, work as a team. I didn't have my powers but I was still a damn good fighter—Cyrus had made sure of that.

The girl arched a single brow, a thin smile spreading across her face until the white tips of her fangs pierced the seam. A vampire then. I wondered if the other girl was too. "Rumor is your blood holds great power." Her eyes narrowed, erasing the deceptively dollish expression, reshaping it into something feral, dangerous. "And we're going to need power for what is coming."

Eli growled under his breath, his body coiled and ready to attack.

"What exactly do you think is coming?" Seamus asked, his voice steady, though I could see him discreetly scanning and assessing the five demons in front of us, calculating and crafting scenarios in his head. It was a posture and presence that made me feel like Cy was standing with us.

"Demons will walk this realm. More than ever before. They will fall or they will control it. We will not fall. The girl is the key. The key everyone wants. And with her, we will find the lock." The other girl spoke now, her voice monotone and strange, like she was in a trance. There was no malice in her eyes, no bloodthirst or aggression, but something about her sent a bolt of terror straight through to my gut.

"Enough of this," the vampire said as the wolves flanked her side. "Let it be known that you had your chance to save yourselves. It's the only one you will get."

And then, as one, the three wolves lunged towards us.

Instinctively, I called for my fire, knowing from experience that it wouldn't harm my team, but no fire came.

I grunted, that momentary lapse enough to cost me, as one of the wolves bowled into my chest, knocking me to the ground and my dagger from my hand.

I felt and heard, more than saw, the others clashing with the demons, and hoped like hell they were okay.

The wolf's teeth grazed my shoulder, but I knew that the venom would do little to harm me.

It used its considerable stature to try and pin me to the ground, and I felt it shift on top of me, searching for one of the others to help keep me from fighting out from under its weight.

I could tell the creature was aiming to capture, not kill, which gave me an upper hand—I didn't have that same limitation. And after everything we'd been through, I no longer felt the same moral weight of my kills—if me or mine were attacked, there was only one option to consider.

I took a deep, centering breath, but my chest was too compressed to suck in enough air. For the first time in a long time, I felt weak.

My teeth clenched as I considered my options. The others needed me. There were too many for us to take on all at once. I might not have my demon powers, but I had eighteen years of Cy's training to pull from. And that was no small thing.

Using my forearm to keep the snapping wolf back from my face, I fished for my blade with my free hand. Relief and adrenaline spread through my chest as my fingers brushed against the cool, metallic tip.

I bent my knees, shimmying and shifting until my feet were level with the wolf's chest, and then I shoved the heavy canine off of me with as much force as I could muster.

It wasn't enough to cast it across the field, but it created enough space between us for me to grab my dagger and crouch, ready and primed, before the creature reached me again.

This time, when the wolf lunged towards me, I lunged back, both of us meeting in a clash of muscle and bone.

My wrist snapped from the force, but the high of the fight kept me from feeling the immediacy of the pain—at least long enough for me to wedge my blade through the ribs of the wolf, using all of my strength to shove the dagger forward until it grazed the fleshy muscle of its heart.

Just one more inch, one more thrust, and it'd be dead.

The wolf landed, heavy and panting on top of me, its weight difficult to maneuver off with only one functioning arm.

The animal snapped and spit, teeth inching towards my neck as its impending death shifted its goal—it no longer aimed to capture me, it wanted revenge before sucking in its final breath.

With a grunt, I gave the dagger one final shove, my muscles relaxing into the ground as I watched the light dim from behind the large, yellow eyes.

I shoved the wolf off of me, my wrist screaming with a sharp, deep ache, now that the immediate threat was gone. Seamus and Declan were taking on the two other wolves as Eli squared off with the vampire, a deep, angry slash bleeding through the back of his T-shirt.

I sent up a silent prayer to whoever the hell was listening that the cut was deep enough to trigger his bond with Darius, but not enough to do any permanent damage.

We hadn't tested my healing powers, but I knew in my gut

that they would be locked and unreachable, just as the fire and teleportation were. I was nothing but a protector right now. And we needed back up. Desperately.

It had been reckless to let Wade and Darius go off together —our two strongest fighters. We figured they'd be better use out in the world, protecting Ro. This place, this was supposed to be safe—a quiet oasis for us to catch our breath while we deliberated over our next steps.

We should have known we weren't the type of people who would ever be granted that kind of peace for long.

My scan took less than a second, but my gaze latched on the other girl, the one who'd seemed so robotic before. She was watching the battle from the sidelines—her expression as dull and removed as it had been before.

The sight of her there, simply spectating, made fear bleed into my stomach, angry and acidic, but I didn't have time to give in to that fear. She was the dangerous one, I could feel it in my bones, but if she wasn't going to act on this fight yet, then I'd use the time to help the others and worry about her when the time came.

So, instead of going after her like every atom in my body seemed to want me to do, I tugged my dagger from the carcass at my feet and moved towards Eli as fast as I could, ripping the vampire's head away from his neck with as much dexterity as I could manage with one hand already holding a blade.

It wasn't much, and not enough to keep her away from him for long, but I clung to her hair as she screamed, scraping her neck with the edge of my blade.

"Max," Eli panted, wrestling her back from me, his attention catching on the arm I kept awkwardly tucked in to my chest, "get the fuck out of here. You're not at full strength. You need to run—"

I shot him a look until the words dried on his tongue, both of us working together to slow the vampire down.

Eli was strong, stronger than most protectors thanks to his blood bond with Darius, but the two of us still weren't enough to outmatch the strength of this girl. So much for cute and doll-like. This little shit was more Bride of Chucky than docile Barbie.

I heard Seamus grunt in pain, and felt Eli stiffen, his attention momentarily dragged to his father as mine was momentarily dragged to him.

It was enough for the girl to shove him to the ground while shaking me off.

With a wicked grin in my direction, she stepped with all of her force onto his leg, snapping his femur in half—the loud crack echoing around us all, blocked out only by Eli's scream.

"Enough of this." The girl from the sidelines spoke quietly as if she was watching a boring show instead of a deadly attack. "No more playing, you've had your fun. We've already lost two and my patience is wearing thin. Kill them and take the girl."

Two? That meant Dec and Seamus must've taken out one of the wolves. Thank the gods.

We just needed to hold them off long enough for the others to get back and help—Darius would be here. He'd feel Eli's pain. I knew he would. I just hoped he wouldn't be slowed down too badly by the break, assuming that had mirrored in him as well.

The vampire turned to me with a wicked grin, then glanced at Eli. "Goody, you'll get to watch me eat your boyfriend. Don't worry though, I'll be sure to save room for you."

Gripping my bloodied blade, I used all the momentum I could muster to tackle her to the ground, both of us rolling in a mess of limbs and rage. Her teeth grazed me, just as my blade bent into her. I felt my back land against Eli, heard his groan of pain as it reverberated through all three of us.

The vampire clutched her thin fingers around my neck, the

pressure making lights dance across my vision as I tried to pry them off.

Giving up, I wrapped my arms around her in a hug, wedging the tip of my blade through the bones in her back.

And then, everything seemed to freeze and speed up all at once.

The cold ground shifted and molded, until it felt like we were falling through the earth, the tanginess of the blood-soaked air dimming into something warm and familiar instead. The taste of magic coated my tongue, until I was suddenly aware of every atom in my body—atoms pulled apart and squeezed and reshaped until they came back together.

When the world re-righted itself, the girl was still on top of me, but her body had stopped moving, stopped fighting.

I heard Eli wretch behind me, his body shaking against mine.

"Well, this was two more bodies than I'd planned for," a gravelly, familiar voice echoed around me.

"Lucifer?" I asked, my body sore and strangled from the trip. We were in hell? How were we in hell?

"The very same." He pulled the girl from me, a look of disgust curling his lip as he tossed her aside.

Her eyes were open and wide—a shadow of wrongness in her expression, her body stiff.

"She's dead." Eli's voice was little more than a whisper and I pulled myself from him as slowly and carefully as I could. His skin was clammy, pale. "How the fuck are we here?"

Lucifer's brow furrowed as he glanced briefly at Eli, before cutting his gaze to the vampire who was indeed very dead. "I called Max here, through our oath." He bent down, grabbed the girl's chin, shifting her face from side to side, studying her. Then he turned her, pulling my blade from her back. "Interesting. Her body could not survive the shift here. It tore her apart, internally." He shot me a chastising look, clicking his tongue. "Your blade only pierced her lungs, not her heart. Bad form."

I turned to Eli, ran my hand over his chest, his arms, bridging them to his face so that I could see into his eyes, needing to know that he was okay, even though he was breathing, he was speaking.

He grabbed my good wrist. "I'm fine, Max. It's just my leg and a little jet lag from the trip. I'm okay."

"The boy is bound to you, however weak and tenuous that bond may be. He is fine. So long as I pulled you together, it would not kill him—I do not think." Lucifer narrowed his eyes, his jaw muscles clenched as he studied me. "You're welcome by the way. I gather there's a very good chance you'd both be dead if I hadn't pulled you when I did. Samael said Ralph had been especially antsy. Now I understand why."

"The others—" my body tensed as I stood, still clutching my wrist to my chest, though I could feel the bones knitting themselves slowly back together. The process was absurdly painful. "We need to go back. The others are still there."

Lucifer shrugged, reaching for my wrist and examining it in his hands, his fingers unexpectedly gentle. The flare of pain quieted and then disappeared entirely. He let my arm drop to my side, the break now unbroken. "The others are of no concern." When I opened my mouth to argue, his nostrils flared with annoyance, "and if they were dead, you would know it. The death of a bond is an unbearable—impossible to ignore or miss—pain." An unreadable emotion flickered briefly in his eyes before his face froze back into its typical marble mask— notable only because the mask always seemed immovable. "Why did a single, measly vampire leave you so close to death? You should be practicing your powers. You could've easily incinerated her, or—as a last resort—at least teleported yourself away from danger. This was a careless brush with danger.

Do you not yet understand the stakes of your existence? The role you must play in this war?"

"Can you heal Eli too, please?" I rolled my wrist around, the bones cracking and popping as they settled.

"He's yours, do it yourself."

Mine. I hated that a shiver ran down my spine at the thought of that—at the thought of us being permanently and irreparably connected. There was an ache in my chest that preened at the idea and clamored against my protest.

"I can't," I whispered, my jaw and teeth locked.

"I'm fine," Eli leaned forward and stood up on his good leg, his face looking green as he gripped the arm of a large leather couch. We were standing in what I guessed was generally used as Lucifer's study. It was one of the only rooms in his creepy castle I'd actually gotten to see. "What are we doing here?"

Lucifer ignored him and took a step closer to me. "You're regressing?"

"That's one word for it," I bit out, though I couldn't tell if I was angrier at Lucifer or myself. After a moment, I took a deep breath. I didn't want to owe this man anything more than I already did, but maybe he could help, maybe he'd have a way to wake up my powers, bypass the waiting period Darius seemed certain I'd require. "After Cy—" I cleared my throat, trying again, "the man who raised me was killed recently. And since then, my powers seem to be locked—there but not accessible, like they're trapped inside of a safe I can't open. Or even find."

Lucifer's hand touched my chin, just barely, and turned my face towards him. I got the idea that he didn't like touching me. He dropped his hand as soon as he had my full attention.

His dark eyes weren't legible to me—I could tell there were hidden depths there, that if I had the tools or language to tug at the seams of the man in front of me, I'd find more than cruelty. But I didn't.

"Grief?" He shook his head once, lips twisting into a dangerous, angry smirk. "I don't have time for grief."

I wasn't exactly a fan of it myself, but I swallowed the retort shaping on my tongue. Not now. Messing with this man when he had that dangerous gleam in his eyes would never bring us any good, I'd learned that lesson by now.

He fidgeted at his side briefly before pulling out the strange dagger he carried with him. My attention locked on to the iridescent, blue glow that emanated around the blade as he held it before me. I knew now that this was a shadow blade—a blade crafted from the very magic that wove the realms together—or perhaps partitioned them apart, I wasn't very clear on which.

Shadow magic.

Atlas, Reza, the bonding ceremony. I'd located the shadow magic stores, or at least one of them.

But when I parted my lips to tell him as much—that, though everything else had gone to shit in our lives, we'd made progress on the mission he'd sent us on—he shoved the blade into my abdomen.

"Oh," is the only word my lips could form as he buried the strange dagger until the hilt met my flesh. And then he twisted it in further, carving up.

"I'm sorry, my girl, but there is no time," he whispered, but it was almost entirely edged out by the tenor of Eli's angry, agonized yell.

The world went black around me, cushioning me in its dark embrace. And then, there was nothing.

11

ATLAS

There was only pain.

Pain and a radiating fear that burrowed far deeper than anything physical ever could.

I closed my eyes, trying to erase everything from my vision, and when I opened them again, all I saw was hope.

Warm brown eyes, wide with worry, an oval-face framed by dark wavy hair, full pink lips that were moving and shaping words, though I couldn't process them.

My breathing slowed, the pain easing slightly—not gone necessarily, but like it was compartmentalized for a moment.

"Max?" My voice was cracked and ragged, my throat raw.

Her hands pressed into the sides of my face forcing my gaze to lock onto hers. I shivered under her touch. "Atlas? Are you okay? Where are we?"

Okay? I wasn't sure that was a word I could use to describe myself right now, so I chose to ignore that question.

Where were we?

I forced myself to drag my eyes away from her, to focus on our surroundings instead of on her. The room was dark, cold. A bed in the corner, a simple desk next to it. Nothing was out of place.

I licked my lips, preparing for my throat to protest against every word. "My room."

She paused, lost in thought, then shook her head. "Atlas I've seen your room, this isn't it."

My focus latched onto her lips as she bit the bottom one, studying our surroundings, and me with equal focus.

"My childhood room."

How had we gotten here? Where was Sarah? The monster?

The questions drifted away as soon as I thought of them—concerns for later.

She was here.

She leaned back, scanning the room with a renewed interest, lingering on the empty walls, the perfectly-made bed. I wondered if she saw what I did—a sterile, cold place.

I'd only spent a few years in this room, before dorming at the academy, but I didn't have particularly fond memories of it. It was a place for study and sleep—nothing more.

When I wanted company, fun—I went to Wade's room, or hung out at Eli's. There was no warmth here.

"Atlas." Max's hand was back on my face, tilting it towards her. I leaned into the soft pressure, my breath hitching at her familiar scent. "Atlas, I think this is a dream." Her thumb ran a circle along my cheek, her face scrunched in concern. "I need to know what's going on—if you're okay. Where they're keeping you. What can you tell me, to help us find you?"

I straightened. Find me? Were they coming for me? Hope and fear battled in my chest.

Where were they keeping me? Who were they? What was going on?

"Max?" I repeated, panic constricting my chest as I tried to reach for the answers, the memories floating away like balloons in the wind.

She grabbed my hand and stood. I followed her bonelessly as she moved to my bed and sat down. I sat next to her, but my body didn't feel fully in my control, didn't feel like mine.

With a single nod, she met my eyes again. "You're alive. We'll start with that. It's not the worst place to start at least."

"Where are you?"

She opened her mouth and closed it, her brows furrowing. "You know, I'm not entirely sure? Things feel a bit fuzzy. A bit disoriented." She ran the hand not holding mine over her stomach, checking for something though I wasn't sure if she found it or not. "Why did you choose this room?"

The question seemed entirely disconnected from the previous one, but I tried to follow the pathway of her mind, to anchor myself to her, since my own was less steady.

"I've been hiding here. I think."

"Hiding? From what?"

A chill unfurled down my spine. "I don't know. I don't remember."

She sighed, nodding again. "This conversation isn't getting us anywhere, is it?"

With a small grin, she bit her bottom lip, shaking her head.

She might have said something else, but my focus was locked on the small imprint of her tooth on her lip.

Suddenly I had an impossibly strong desire to trace that mark with my tongue.

So I did.

"Oh. Atlas I—" Her words were unintelligible around my mouth, but they created soft vibrations that hummed along my skin, lighting me on fire.

I pressed my lips against hers, sliding my tongue into the seam of her mouth, my mind going fuzzy and clear at the familiar taste of her.

"Atlas," she said, her voice breathy now. I swallowed whatever else was going to follow that with my tongue sliding against hers, until the only sound she was making was a soft moan.

I pressed her closer, a feverish need suddenly taking over as I pulled her onto my lap. My fingers combed through her thick hair, tugging at the base of her skull, tilting her head so that I could go deeper.

More.

I needed so much more than this.

I needed her all around me, consuming me.

I was hard as a rock, my head growing dizzy as she tilted her hips forward, her body sliding against me, teasing.

Why was it like this with her? Why was just being in her vicinity enough to make me feel like I was going to combust?

Slowly, I slid my hand down the front of her pants, desperate to feel her, to be consumed by her. My fingers were soaked as I slid against her, circling her clit. She was more than ready for me, but I teased and pinched for a minute, savoring the delicious gasps she made as her body spun out of control.

Every inch of my skin tingled, my body somehow just as sensitive as hers, like I could feel the pleasure raking through her core too.

She tensed, her hand pressing into my chest as she looked up. The dazed look in her eyes cleared as she came into focus.

"No, this—" she shook her head, closed her eyes tight as she climbed off of me. "This isn't what we should be doing. This isn't right."

Panic stabbed through my chest. "What's wrong? Did I hurt—"

She shook her head, cutting me off. "No, no it's not that. It's just, Atlas." Her eyes met mine, only now instead of glazing them over, it was the glassy sheen of tears. "Atlas we can't do this. You bonded to Reza. You made that choice. You didn't want whatever," her hands waved between us, the movement jagged and filled with her frustration, "whatever bond is—was

—developing between us. This is just the haze of a succubus dream."

Reza. I'd all but forgotten that she existed. What was she even talking about?

A cold, sharp stab pierced my chest at the expression on her face.

I stood, adjusting my pants as I tried to focus. "Max, I don't want Reza. I've never wanted Reza. From the moment my wolf tracked you down in that town, I've wanted no one but you. I've thought of no one but you—" I exhaled sharply, trying to contain the emotion clogging my throat, "I tried everything I could to resist it—I tried to stay away from you, to protect you —but I can't. You're all I fucking see."

For a moment, something in her face softened, but she reconstructed the hard mask she'd learned to wear almost instantly. It was a new skill she'd developed, her thoughts and emotions no longer displayed on her sleeve for all to witness and dissect. It was a hardness The Guild manufactured quickly. It would serve her well, protect her—but I hated that she needed it in the first place, that she needed to shield herself like that. The thought that she'd been forced to abandon the gentle openness she had when we met made me sick. "Atlas, no. You bonded to her." She let out a frustrated laugh. "I was there. I watched it happen."

"You—" I paused, trying to understand what she was saying. The ceremony came flooding back into my mind with the force of a train. My memories of the last few weeks were hazy at best, but I was certain that Max wasn't there. I wouldn't have been able to go through with it if she was. It was hard enough already. "I— Max, I was trying to protect you."

The lines of her jaw sharpened, her posture stiffening as she studied me. "Hurting me wasn't protecting me." She let out a frustrated sight. "You ended things between us, Atlas—*you* chose to stop whatever connection was solidifying between us.

You made that choice. Not me. And I— I'm not interested in being your plaything whenever you deign to allow it. I deserve more than that." Her hands curled into fists at her sides. "And, honestly, Reza deserves more than that too."

"I feel—" My jaw was tight, but I forced the words out anyway, tight and angry, "I feel nothing for Reza. The bonding ceremony did nothing—whatever paltry magic The Guild uses to forge bonds between protectors is nothing compared to the connection between us. Nothing." It was laughable to even think of those bonds in the same breath. I ran a frustrated hand through my hair, took a step towards her but paused when she met that step with one of her own—away from me. I swallowed the hurt, pressed past the way the fury on her face burned through me, flaying me alive. "I was trying to protect you, Max. My father—I didn't want him to find out about you. I was fucking terrified that he'd kill you, that I wouldn't be able to protect you from him. I made a sacrifice—"

"No one *asked* you to protect me. I'm pretty damn good at protecting myself. And no one asked you to make that sacrifice, Atlas. That's the point." Her teeth rolled over her lip, her onyx eyes animated by her rage. Why did she look so fucking beautiful when she was angry. And why the fuck was I focusing on how beautiful she was when she was pissed off at me? "You made that choice on your own. You make every decision on your own—you carry the weight of the world on your shoulders and then get pissed and lash out because it's so fucking heavy. You could have talked to me. We could have discussed your fears about your father. We could have made a plan—together. All of us. And now—" her jaw clenched as her eyes cut away from mine, locking my access to emotions she wasn't willing to show me. "Now you've damaged something between us." She shook her head. "And I'm not sure it's damage that can ever be repaired."

I couldn't pull air in through my lungs, my vision clouded

as I studied her. I did all of this. *I* caused the pain lancing through her now—me, not Tarren. And it was all for nothing. I tried to protect her and it blew up in all of our faces. The ceremony with Reza was irrelevant now. My father knew the truth about her—about me. Didn't he? It felt like the truth, though I couldn't isolate the history of it. My forehead furrowed as I tried to remember, as I tried to grasp onto the last thing I could remember. Bits and pieces were clear, but so much was missing.

She ran a frustrated hand over her face, massaging her temple. "You know what's strange?" Her voice was quiet, strained. "I actually feel bad for Reza. Because she's become the innocent collateral damage in this fucked game. She's wanted you forever. You're using her and you're putting me in the position of hurting her. And that's not fair to either of us. You've made your choices, Atlas. I won't be part of her pain, not like this." She took a deep, steadying breath before turning back to me. The anger lining her features was softer now, shaping into a sharp sadness—her lips turned down, her shoulders slumped. The sight of her like that—knowing I caused it— made me want to throw up. "Maybe it was for the best. I don't— I don't think I want that—whatever was developing between us —with you anymore, I don't think I'm capable of it. I'm your friend, Atlas." She took a deep breath, schooled her features back into that new, impenetrable mask she'd constructed. "And we can repair our friendship. I understand that you did what you did because you felt that you needed to. We'll figure the rest of our shit out later, the most important thing right now is that we get you out of here."

I opened my mouth to protest, but the look she shot me cut the words off before they had sound. It took every ounce of control I had not to reach for her, not to pull her to my chest and whisper against her hair until the frown lines between her brows softened. My body trembled with restraint as her words washed over me.

"Here?" I asked, suddenly remembering that we were in my childhood bedroom. Why were we here? How did we get here? "Where am I? What happened?"

Her expression softened into pity and she took a step forward, her arm raising and dropping at her side, like she was going to reach for me again but changed her mind. "Atlas—"

The walls of my room clouded over with black shadows, blurring the edges of my vision. My bed disappeared into the strange darkness—a darkness so deep and terrifying that it made the blackest of nights seem gray in comparison.

"Atlas?" her eyes, coated with worry, shot to mine. "Atlas what's happening? Something's wrong. This isn't me—this isn't succubus power. What—what is this?"

The shadows took my desk, my chair—and I knew with an unexplainable certainty that the objects it consumed weren't just covered in shade, they were gone.

"I—" I shook my head, trying to remember, to understand, like the answer was on the tip of my tongue, but I had no control over the muscle. "I don't know."

And then the darkness came for Max, her eyes widening as it separated us, her mouth opening into a scream, her lips shaping my name, but the shadows swallowed the sound. Long strands of her hair rose, blowing forward, her arms and legs floating in front of her as she was pulled away from me—down a deep, impenetrable black hole.

I reached for her, my own yell ringing through my ears, but my fingers grasped only at air.

Then, finally, the darkness took me too, and all I could do was linger in it, unable to move, unable even to breathe. My limbs no longer belonged to me, like they weren't even there.

I had no body. I was nothing.

I was empty.

I was alone.

"Atlas. Atlas, wake up."

I blinked several times, the edges of my vision blurry, too bright. "Max?"

My voice was hoarse, my throat aching and raw. Had I been screaming? Why was I screaming?

"Atlas, I'm going to get you out of here. Now. Let's go." She reached for my hand, clasping it in her own.

She felt colder than usual, but I clung to her like I was suffocating and she was the promise of fresh air.

Her eyes, usually warm and filled with shifting shades of brown and black, were black as night, pupils blown wide. They lifted in the corners as she smiled down on me.

Lifting my aching muscles up, I wrapped my arms around her. "You're safe. You're alive. You got away."

I repeated the words several times, like my own personal mantra.

The memories of that day flashed through my mind at lightning speed—Cyrus diving in front of Max, that scream of pain when she realized he was gone, her flashing away with his body, my father throwing me in a cell.

I pulled back from her, assessing our surroundings. The familiar cold walls of the cell boxed us in, the torturously bright light shining heavy on us.

I wore nothing but a stretchy pair of scrub bottoms, my body covered with unhealed gashes.

She ran gentle fingers over the long cut on my chest.

I shivered under her attention. Slowly, I lifted a hand to her cheek, my stomach fluttering when she leaned into the touch. My thumb traced the fullness of her bottom lip, breath lodging in my chest as her mouth parted.

"Atlas, I'm here to save you," she whispered, the whisper of her breath feathering against my skin. "I can teleport us out of here. I can bring you back to our team."

"Our team?" I whispered, my voice sounding more child-like than I'd heard it in a long time. How long had I been stuck in the labs? Hours? Years? "They're okay?"

Her lips curved into a soft grin. "Yes. They're all okay. Let me bring you to them. Come with me."

I nodded, unable to speak lest I break the spell she had over me. My arms tightened around her, bringing her into my chest. I pressed my face into her neck, inhaling deeply.

There was something off about her scent—or else whatever The Guild had been funneling into my system had my senses spiraling.

Still, I held her to me, feeling her heart beat against my skin.

"I'm ready," I whispered into her hair, barely able to contain the excitement clawing at my insides. Home. I was going home.

She stiffened in my arms, her skin suddenly freezing as she pulled away. Her dark eyes widened, the black bleeding into the whites of her eyes, swirling and spreading until it reached the skin, outlining the veins in her face in black. The lines spread, connecting and branching like roots, puckering the skin along her neck, her arms, slipping beneath the black cotton of her shirt.

"Max?" I ran my hands over her, as if my touch alone could erase whatever disease was spreading through her body. "Is this normal? Is this your power?"

She shook her head, chest heaving with panicked breaths as her fingers dug into my forearms, drawing blood. "Atlas, this is you. You did this."

"Me?" I took a step back, released my grip on her, and carved a crater of distance between us. "No—I," I turned, searching the room for something to help her, anything. "I didn't mean to."

"Why? Why would you do this to me? What did I do to deserve this?" Her neck bent back at an unnatural angle, her mouth opening wide as she screamed—the sound slicing through my gut with the force of a machete.

Black, curling smoke emerged from her mouth, her eyes, her nose. The veins of black ruptured through her skin until the light, golden-brown hue was painted wet and black.

"Max, no." I closed the distance between us, catching her as she collapsed, her eyes nothing but empty pits. "No, I didn't do this, didn't mean—" my voice cracked as tears blurred my vision, "I didn't mean to."

She was shaking in my arms.

No, I was the one shaking. Sobs racked my body as I held her, her breaths coming out in strangled, uneven coughs.

Until she stilled completely, her body nothing but a broken shell.

"My fault." I held her to me as I rocked, my head buried in her hair, searching for the last lingering vestiges of her scent. "My fault."

∼

THE SUN WAS bright as it bathed down on my bare skin. Max's dark hair fanned out along my pillow and over my arm. She curled into my chest, but I could tell from her breathing that she wasn't sleeping.

"You're awake, finally." I could hear the grin in her voice, even though I couldn't see her face. "I've been up for hours."

I pulled her tighter to me, basking in the feel of waking up next to her. My hands bunched around one of my black t-shirts, and I could feel her swimming in the material. I traced her side, her hip, my fingers feathering mid-thigh, where the coverage of the shirt ended.

Slowly, I lifted the shirt up, grinning at the way her body

responded to me, how even the smallest touch made her squirm with heated anticipation. I sucked in a sharp breath when my hand drew further up her thigh. She wasn't wearing underwear.

My dick throbbed, hard and ready against her hip.

A small giggle pierced the quiet. She enjoyed having this effect on me.

I'd spent so much time fighting it, fighting her. Why? When I could have had this all along?

I looked around the room, clocking my stash of weapons on the wall, the rest of our clothes strewn carelessly on the floor—not a detail out of place in the cabin. My chest tightened at the feel of being back here—the feel of being home. "When did we get here?"

"After I rescued you, of course." She turned, so that I was spooning her, my raging boner only raging harder against her ass.

Rescued me? From what?

"What happened?" My memory was foggy, and the feel of her ass against my dick wasn't much incentive to focus.

"Everything's fine now, we're all okay. It's all over."

"Over?"

She wound her hand together with mine, pulling my arm tighter around her for a squeeze. "We should get up, find the others for breakfast." She pressed a soft kiss to my fingers. "I promise we can come back up for round two after."

I let out a groan. "Why delay happiness?"

I wanted round two right now. I must've blacked out hard on something because I didn't even remember round one.

She laughed again, the sound breathy and soft, and a flutter set off in my chest at the pure joy of it. "We have a lifetime of happiness ahead, don't get greedy, Atlas Andrews. I promised I'd make pancakes for everyone this morning."

A lifetime—with this woman? How the fuck did I get so lucky? What the hell had I done to deserve her?

I had no idea, but I was ready to do whatever it took to earn it every morning that I woke.

With a grunt she heaved herself up and climbed off my bed, her hair tousled with sleep and round one.

My dick throbbed at the sight of her smooth, bare legs—at the way she looked at me with that fuck-me grin while wearing my shirt—my scent. "I'm going to need a second."

My eyes dropped to my lap and heat flashed in her eyes.

Her eyes.

There was something different about them.

I reached for her. "Hang on, come here."

She pulled away and moved to the door. "Come on, no one will think twice about some morning wood, Atlas. I'm hungry."

It took every ounce of control I had not to pull her onto my lap and make *her* think twice about it. But right now, with that coy look on her face, I couldn't deny her a thing.

Throwing on a shirt, I followed her to the door, down the hall, down the stairs, her hand eclipsed by mine.

She stopped short when the living room came into sight, then dropped to her knees with a scream that tore me in half.

"What—" I bent to pick her up and stopped when I saw what the cause of her distress was. "No."

I took the last remaining stairs in one jump, putting myself between her and the scene.

Declan was draped over the chair, a red line drawn down her neck, her hair bathed and matted in a pool of red. Eli was on the ground below her.

Or rather, his head was on the ground—completely detached from wherever his body was—his eyes wide and cloudy as they stared at me.

"No," I repeated, my heart racing in its cage as I tried to understand.

Max's sobs echoed behind me, the agony in her cry enough to raise the hair on my arms.

"Don't look." I said, my voice strange and unfamiliar. I repeated the words over and over, like I was trying to convince myself to do the same.

How did this happen? How did we not hear this? I took a few steps closer and then tripped.

My hand landed in a puddle of fresh blood, splashing my arm and face in red.

A strangled sob bubbled up when I saw what had been in my way.

Wade.

As dead as the others.

I cradled him in my arms, rocking back and forth. "How. How did this happen?"

"How? You know how, Atlas. Stop lying to yourself, stop lying to all of us." Max's hand was on my shoulder now. I hadn't heard her leave the stairs. "You didn't save them. You did this, Atlas. You weren't enough. You were never enough."

Her words cut through me like a hot blade.

I looked up at her dark black eyes and a fresh wave of panic scoured me as I noticed the red line drawn fresh across her neck. Skin that was smooth and prickling with heat and promise five minutes ago was now washed in red.

Her knees buckled, landing softly with a thud next to me. For a brief moment, her black eyes found mine, the sorrow and disappointment in their depths almost tangible, before the light behind them dimmed and her body landed on top of Wade's legs.

"No. No, this can't." I shook my head. "You can't be—" salty liquid lined my mouth. My vision blurred as my hands found her face, her lips, desperately searching for a pulse, for a sign that she was still in there, that this was just some terrible, sadistic joke.

But her skin was cold, like she'd been dead for hours.

My lungs pulled in nothing but the scent of death and decay.

I dug my face into my knees and rocked back and forth, trying desperately to either erase the scene in front of me or else join them in death.

My fault.
I did this.

12

WADE

"I still think you should have let me eat one of them. Such a waste."

It was the third time Darius had made this argument. After he secured what Ro and I had assumed was an abandoned vehicle, we'd driven a few towns over, just to be safe. Once there, we grabbed some clothes for the group, more groceries, and a couple of phones we could use without being tracked by anyone associated with The Guild.

But in that very town, I saw a familiar Guild face patrolling the area. He was with another man I didn't recognize, but they both carried themselves with the rigid posture of a protector hunting.

While it was possible they were hunting demons, something told me the odds were just as high that they were looking for Max.

"If either of them was attacked, it would flag this area," I ground out, clutching the wheel of the minivan as the trees zipped past us. We were taking it back to where we found it, twenty minutes outside of the cabin, once the obnoxious fanghole let slip that it was not so much abandoned as borrowed without permission from an old man who'd run into the local diner.

Honestly, it was half my fault. The car had fucking keys in the ignition. I should've put two and two together. My head was just all over the place. I needed to focus.

"I know, I know, we need to stay under the radar. You're in charge, incubus." He met my glare and winked—an infuriating hobby he'd picked up since the other night with Max. Like he just wanted to remind me that I'd not only been okay with him biting her, but that I'd been turned on by it. It took everything I had not to react, not to give him the pleasure of getting under my skin. "Bet they would've tasted rancid anyway. I've got better options for blood."

"Shut up," I muttered, pulling the car into the very spot it had been stolen from. Hopefully the guy hadn't noticed and was still chomping away on dinner. Last thing we needed was for the townspeople to take notice. Discretion was paramount right now. I was already antsy as it was, just knowing that there were Guild spies nearby.

"Do you two ever stop bickering?" A shadow of amusement crossed Rowan's face as he snuck out of the car and made his way towards the path we'd taken into town, muttering to himself as we followed, "I'm never getting roped into errands with you two again. Like a fucking mind-numbing married couple. No idea how Max puts up with you all. That's her real super power, if we're being honest."

"Well now he's just being mean," Darius whispered as he passed me, "no way in hell I'm the same level of mind-numbing as the twat-waffle incubus."

Twat-waffle? Where the fuck did this vamp come from?

His arms were straddled with about a dozen multi-colored bags (he'd insisted on buying reusable canvas bags, because "what's the point in saving the world if climate change kills us all anyway") until he looked more clothing rack than bloodsucking demon.

I rolled my eyes and followed them, once I was certain no one was paying us any notice. Miraculously, he hadn't drawn any attention in the twenty-foot trek to the woods.

We'd barely gotten two minutes into the bushy path when Darius stopped cold, the bags sliding off his arms, one at a time.

So fucking dramatic.

"What—" I swallowed the sentence when a dark red line seeped through the white shirt he'd borrowed from Rowan, carving a vicious slash down his back.

"What the fuck?" I closed the distance to him.

"What are you jackasses doing no—" Rowan's voice evaporated when he turned back towards us, his face growing grayish white. "What happened? Is it Max? Did you feel something?"

Was that possible through mate bonds? It'd been so long since true bonds were forged that we knew next to nothing about them. Still, I didn't blame Ro's mind for sliding instantly to her—Max attracted danger like a feather duster.

"Did you snag yourself on something?" I asked, desperately clinging to hope that the cut was Darius-caused and not some bigger problem.

"No. Not me. Fucking Eli. Always getting attacked. The kid's a goddamn liability. If I'd have known this would—" Darus's eyes widened. "Shit. Max."

Fuck.

Fuck. Fuck. Fuck.

Could we not catch one goddamn break?

Without another word, Ro took off towards home, surprisingly speedy and agile as he carved a path through terrain he was clearly familiar with.

Still, he wasn't as fast as we were, and when I stopped to check in, he shook his head and shoved his hands forward, brows bent with frustration as if he could push me along by sheer mental force. "Don't be ridiculous, go—I'll catch up."

So we did. We ran through the woods, trying like hell to remember the specific trails we took, the precise location of the cabin. But more than memory, it was Max that pulled us in the right direction, almost like I could sense her. I assumed the vampire could as well, since he was two steps ahead of me and showed no sign of insecurity or questioning about his tracking skills.

We'd be there soon, it was one scratch. Maybe Eli'd gotten cut up during a sparring session, or fallen in the woods. Or, or, or.

The possibilities filtered through my head, though none of them calmed me. I knew in my gut that nasty gash down Darius's back was the mark of an enemy. I just wasn't sure how many or from which group—demons or The Guild?

The trees rushed past my vision until they all blended together, just a mess of twigs and brambles in the chill air.

We were only about a mile out from the cabin when Darius stumbled, the momentum of his speed sending him careening in a series of tumbles until he was all just bent limbs and curse words.

Normally, I'd have found it amusing, but instead, my stomach sank. Vampires didn't just casually trip. And if they did, they didn't stay down, clutching a leg bent at a peculiarly not-right angle.

"What—"

Darius shot me a dark look, face pinched in pain as he pulled himself up and put all of his weight on one leg. "Don't stop, go. Get to her. Now."

I swallowed once, automatically bristling at the demand in his voice. I pushed it away and ran, moving my legs as fast as I could towards the familiar clearing.

My lungs constricted, not because I was tired, but because

my body couldn't find a way to process the panic and adrenaline flooding it. Now was not the time for another goddamn panic attack.

Please be okay, please be fucking okay.

I couldn't lose them, couldn't lose her—couldn't take another fracture in our team. I wasn't sure I'd survive it. Wasn't sure any of us would.

I exhaled as the cabin finally came into view, the relief only momentary.

There was a girl standing between the trees, and a few bodies scattered on the ground. My throat constricted as I scanned them, trying to verify that none of ours were down there. Seamus and Declan were wrestling with a wolf, their movements labored but practiced as they fought with each other.

For a brief flash, it reminded me of our early days in the academy, training with Seamus during long afternoons as he honed our bodies into the weapons they were today. They fought together with the kind of grace and awareness of the other that only came with time and practice.

I reached them just as Dec delivered a final blow to the wolf, puncturing her blade through flesh until it sliced up, under the ribs and into the heart.

When the creature dropped to the ground, her emerald eyes met mine, her entire body heaving with each breath she took. Blood splattered her face, her clothes soaked with it—but she seemed okay.

I spun around, my chest constricted.

Where the hell was Max? Eli?

I studied the corpses on the ground again, but all I saw were three wolves. There was no way Seamus and Dec had taken them all out solo.

Seamus's face contorted in pain as he dropped to his knees, his body exhausted. He didn't look old, but by demon-fighting standards, he was. This was probably the most intense and demanding face-time he'd had against demons in years.

As one, we turned towards the girl, as if we'd all just remembered she was there.

I ran towards her, coiled and ready to attack, but the dead look in her gaze locked me in place before I reached her.

"That was disappointing." She took a deep breath, shaking her head on the exhale. "And now the girl is gone." There was no emotion in her words as she studied her fallen companions. Instead, she collapsed onto the ground, as if she'd been shot from behind, her empty eyes meeting mine, just as dead-looking as they were when she was alive.

A dark shadowy liquid-like substance emerged from her nostrils, mouth, and eyes, collecting into a cloud above her that dispersed into the woods from which she'd come.

"What, the actual fuck," Declan clutched her side as she bent down to Seamus, "was that?"

Slowly, I reached for the girl's body, nudging her arm over until she was on her back. There was no mistaking that the girl was dead, but I checked for a heartbeat anyway.

Unsurprisingly, there wasn't one.

"Where's Max?" I spun back to Declan, studying her to make sure that she really was okay. She was coated in blood, yes, but it was too hard to tell how much of it was hers and how much of it belonged to the wolves. She was standing though; she couldn't have lost too much.

Repeating that over and over helped quell some of the panic clutching my limbs. If she was okay, Max and Eli were surely—

"Gone." Declan choked out another labored breath as she stared at a patch of grass, the blades wet from melted snow and fresh gore. "Teleported, I think. Took Eli and a vamp with her."

"Guess that means that she has her powers back then, at least?" I tried to shove the pulse of worry piercing through me.

If Max had her powers back, that meant that she could easily take on a single vamp, especially if she had Eli's help.

I took a deep, steadying breath, searching within for that ever-present pull I felt towards her, it strummed through me, a comforting pulse. But where it had pulled me to the cabin before, reaching and centering, I couldn't identify a starting point to access her now.

"Can you—" I swallowed, trying to ignore the feeling in my gut that knew the answer before I even voiced the question. "Can you feel her?"

Declan's brows furrowed. "What do you mean?"

"With the bond, I can usually sense her almost—can't you?"

She looked momentarily stunned by the question. "Yeah, yeah I can, usually. Though I've spent so damn long pretending it wasn't there instead of making use of it. It usually takes me a minute to feel it—I have to concentrate pretty hard." She sank into herself for a moment, her face blank. But then, her lips turned into a frown, skin blanching noticeably, even under the grime covering it. "I know she's alive. I can feel it somehow, though I can't quite explain how I know that," when her eyes met mine, I nodded. "But it feels like she's everywhere and nowhere all at once, if that makes sense?"

I swallowed back the bile rising up my throat. It was the same strangeness that I felt. When I tried to follow her before, to tug on the bond that I'd used when she'd teleported with Cy, it was so much easier. Now, it stuck, like a hose that had been kinked. "What the fuck do you think that means?"

"Hell."

Darius limped into sight, his jaw clenched tight as he studied the scene before him. His leg appeared to be healing quickly at least, and no new cuts had shown up—hopefully that meant no further harm had come to Eli.

"Hell?" Seamus's voice came out lodged somewhere between a croak and a whisper.

I'd nearly forgotten he was here.

While Declan was a little winded from the battle, Seamus looked downright drained. His chest was pumping in heavy, uneven gasps, and he leaned against a sturdy tree trunk, legs splayed in front of him, like holding even a seated position on his own was too much.

Darius swore. He picked up a large tree branch in his path and threw it with so much strength that it carved a chunk out of the tree that it hit. "It'll be the oath. He pulled her to him. Said this was going to happen next time he needed to see her. Just wasn't expecting it at the worst fucking time possible. Shouldn't be so damn surprised that it was though. Knowing our luck."

"He can't just do that without warning," Declan crossed her arms in front of her, posture rigid. "How the hell are we supposed to get to her?"

"He's Lucifer, he can pretty much do whatever the fuck he wants," Darius snapped. His eyes narrowed with rage, and I felt Declan's breath hitch. Sometimes it was surprisingly easy to forget that, until a few weeks ago, the fanghole had been one of our biggest enemies. Moments like this, when the strange teasing demeanor evaporated and the darkness floated to the surface, it was impossible to miss. "As for the second point? No idea. I suspect we'll have to wait."

"You can't seriously expect us to just—" she waved her hand in front of her, "wait here and do nothing."

"I didn't say do nothing. Happy to take suggestions, princess, if you have any bright ideas." His posture was rigid as he glared at her.

Dec's hands fisted at her sides and I could tell she was doing everything in her power not to bite back with venom. The two generally had a surprisingly good rapport, but right now the tension was dancing perilously close to a fuse.

We were all pissed off and, worse than anger, fucking terrified. Without Max here as the peacemaker, that left us all wobbling dangerously on a tightrope.

"Can't we just go back to Seattle—to your brother—and find her?" I asked. The thought of returning to hell, to Lucifer after just gaining my freedom made my stomach hollow out with dread. I'd do it though, without a second thought, for Max.

Darius arched his brow. "It's no easy thing jumping in and out of hell, incubus. Especially now, with the barrier as jacked as it is. Chances are high that, by the time we locate her, she'll be on her way back to us—like last time. The time imbalance between realms isn't predictable. Or that we'll make things worse for her by showing up. We knew this would be coming, it's just a shock because we thought we'd have more time, more preparation." Not that we could ever really be prepared for Max to just zip out of our grasp without a word. He waved his hand lazily towards the carnage at his feet. "It just feels more sudden because, for some reason, we weren't expecting things to get even worse than they already were—which, really, is just naivety on our part, what with the impending apocalypse and what not."

"But—didn't it take like a month last time?" Dec's shoulders dropped, as she added, "in the human realm side of things, I mean? Last time she—we—left?"

"Yes. A month." Ro's voice cut through the field like a blade as he surveyed us. "She's gone again, isn't she?"

He didn't look overly winded from his run, but there was a dejectedness about him that was hard to look at.

Dec opened her mouth to say something, but no sound came out for a few seconds, until she landed on a simple "yes."

"Lucifer. Hell." Seamus's eyes cut to Declan and then me, like he was waiting for one of us to announce he was on a hidden camera show.

I caught Dec's eye, both of us trying to silently weigh how much to tell him without checking in with the others. But they weren't here. And he was. He'd left everything behind to help us—and I knew that Max trusted him.

Dec nodded, reaching the same conclusion.

"Max told you that Lucifer is her father," I said, trying to figure out the best way to condense this shitshow so that it wouldn't overwhelm him, "well, she made a blood oath with him and broke it—"

"Broke it my ass," Darius muttered, but I didn't fight him on it. We all knew that the terms of the deal were jacked since the only reason she'd broken the deal in the first place was because of the time issues between realms. Nothing she could control. But Lucifer didn't give a shit about technicalities, not if he could abuse the power of manipulating the system for his own benefit.

"And now, because the oath was broken, he owns her will more or less," Dec scrunched up her nose, "I think. I don't really understand the terms or how it works, but basically, he told us he'd be able to bring her to him as a result of it."

"And Eli?" Seamus's eyes squeezed together as he pressed a hand into his side. The dude needed rest and medical attention ASAP. Protectors were stronger than humans and could heal pretty quickly, but Seamus was getting on in age and he'd taken on far more here than most protectors would survive even in their prime.

"He was touching her when she was pulled, so he'll be there with her." Declan bent down next to Seamus, her hands light and careful as she checked his wounds. I wondered if she felt the same tingle of jealousy that I did. Visiting hell was never high on my to-do list, but part of me hoped that when Max was inevitably pulled back to Lucifer, I'd be there with her. She nodded her head to Darius, a small grin tugging at her lips. "And see the fanghole? He's standing and doing okay. Alive. That means Eli is too."

"Yup," Darius stretched his arms above his head, his joints

cracking, "I'm basically an Eli-specific health monitor. So long as I'm standing and breathing, he is too."

Seamus's face crumpled in confusion at that, his skin slick with sweat as he tried to follow the conversation.

"What should we do in the meantime, just wait here?" I asked. We were already lost with how to go about rescuing Atlas. Now, with Eli and Max gone for who knew how long, our lack of direction became even more directionless.

I felt the mood drop around us all, if that was even possible. None of us liked the idea of waiting days here—potentially weeks—without Max.

"We work on getting Atlas out and on finding the shadow magic stores she mentioned."

It was Ro who answered, his voice calm and filled with more fight than I'd heard in it since he'd arrived here. His light eyes were haunted and hollow. Max had changed massively since coming to The Guild. I'd never really thought to consider how Ro had been handling all of it. He was harder than he was when he arrived, the puppy-like excitement cannibalized by something more lethal, more nihilistic. I couldn't blame him, but part of me wished the early excitement they'd shown up with could be preserved, bottled—that our world could have been as bright and adventurous as they'd arrived hoping it would be.

Well, the adventurous part had proven true anyway.

"Shadow store?" Seamus's eyes were still closed, each word looking like it pained him to shape.

Fuck.

We'd been so focused on getting Atlas out, that we hadn't spent much time talking about the shadow magic Max had found during the bonding ceremony. How had we not thought of asking Seamus about it before? He was high up in The Guild. Not right now, obviously, but generally speaking.

"The bond ceremonies," I closed the distance between us,

my body buzzing with the first prickling of hope I'd felt in days. "Max said they mix protector blood with a blade, a blade laced with shadow magic. Do you know where it's kept? How we can get to it?"

Maybe we could get to it before Max even got back—handle that one thing at least, without putting her in more danger.

Seamus's breathing grew more ragged, his pulse fluttering erratically against my palm as I held his arm.

The hand that had been clutching his side dropped to the ground as his head lolled to the side.

Fingers shaking, I shoved his shirt up.

Blood. So much fucking blood. And this close, I could tell that unlike with Dec, most of it was his.

"Hang on, wait—" Dec moved closer, shoving my hands out of the way, "fuck."

"Is that—"

Darius stood behind us, though I hadn't heard him move. "Werewolf bite. Nasty one from the looks of it."

Of-fucking-course it was.

13

MAX

All that I felt was pain—sharp and all-consuming, like it radiated from my pores. The sensation of drowning—sinking like an anchor into a deep, dark pool of water, as my lungs burned with fire. I lay suspended, clawing through the waves with a feverish desperation, never getting anywhere, until a soft light finally emerged.

I sat up, my breaths labored and heavy as sweat trickled into my eyes, the sting of the salt nothing compared to the way the rest of my body ached.

The room was dark, cold. My fingers dug into the rough stone ground for purchase, finding none. There was a blanket draped lazily over my legs. The fabric was impossibly soft, but I shoved it off of me—the weight of it was enough to make every inch of my skin scream, like I was being pricked by thousands of needles at once.

Where was I?

Where was Eli?

I craned my neck around, taking in the dark surroundings. I wasn't in one of Lucifer's cells, but I also wasn't in one of the more comfortable rooms I knew lined the labyrinth of his castle.

The space was large, open—but empty.

I was alone with nothing but the blanket and a statue in the corner of the room.

No, not a statue. A dark figure seated, unmoving.

"Lucifer?"

He leaned forward, forearms perched on his thighs as he studied me. There was no malice in his obsidian eyes, there was no emotion at all. It was equal parts infuriating and frustrating, never being able to read the man.

"Good, you're awake." His voice pierced the silence and the hairs at the back of my neck crawled to attention as he walked towards me, looking every bit the lethal predator that I knew him to be.

I refused to be his prey.

My stomach ached from where he'd sliced into me, but when I lifted my shirt to see the damage, there was only the soft puckering of a scar—the wound nearly healed over. "You stabbed me."

"It was necessary." There was no apology in his tone, his voice as impossible to decipher as his face.

"You fucking stabbed me." I heard the panic in my voice, echoing in the room. I crawled away from him as he prowled towards me, scanning the room for a door.

There, in the corner.

Behind Lucifer.

I didn't stand a chance.

"It was necessary," he repeated. He cocked his head to the side, eyes narrowed in focus as he studied me. I felt like an ant under the blaring sun, and he was the curious child holding a magnifying glass, watching in amusement as smoke curled from my body.

"Necessary? I thought you needed me? I could have died!"

Actually, why didn't I die? His blade was no ordinary weapon. The first time I saw it in use, it had nearly ripped Wade's life away.

"Yes," he crouched down, his fingers pressing lightly to my chin as he turned my head a few inches in each direction, the gentleness of the gesture so at odds with how he'd gutted me like a pig for slaughter. "You could have."

I ripped my face from his, my jaw tight as I met his eyes. "Why?"

He asked me to find The Guild's shadow store? I did.

He asked me to come when he called? I did.

Sure, I couldn't exactly control it, but I'd met his demand for a blood oath with little resistance.

I'd done everything he'd asked of me.

Not to mention that I was his daughter, for fuck's sake.

"If you died, you'd have been no use to me anyway."

"How can you be so callous?" My voice wavered, with anger more than sadness or fear. It disgusted me that I'd come from this man—that his blood flowed through my veins. I'd never been so acutely aware of the fact that being a father extended far beyond blood. Cyrus nurtured what this man in front of me sought only to destroy.

"Some things are worse than death." The sentence was little more than a whisper, so low that I wasn't even sure he'd meant for me to hear it. He gripped my face between his hands, firmer this time, as his eyes met mine.

A burning pierced through my skull and my vision swam. My body screamed with a vicious heat, the pressure building so strong that I was certain the hellfire had not only returned, but turned against me—punishing and brutal. Every muscle in my body locked into place and I was certain they'd all snap as one from the impossible tension. It made the general achiness I'd woken up to look like child's play in comparison—nothing more than a scraped knee from falling on the pavement. A loud, ringing scream echoed around us—all I could see was the heavy darkness behind my lids.

This—this was pure, unadulterated agony.

As quickly as the pain started, it abated, the shadow of it still ringing in my bones.

Lucifer dropped his hands roughly, like he was the one who'd been burned.

My chest lifted and fell in heavy, ragged pants as I turned to him, my jaw locked in a clench, my fingers buried into fists so tight I was sure I'd drawn my own blood.

A flicker of something flared in his eyes, there and gone so fast I was half-certain it was my mind playing games on me.

My body thrummed with an ache that went down to my marrow—but in that ache, I felt the stilted hum of something else, something familiar but dormant, thudding to life.

His nostrils flared, the lines of his face tense and sharp. He nodded once. "Again."

I started to ask what he meant, my chest heavy with fear, but before the muscles in my face could form a word, the blue haze of his blade sparked between us—before burying into my chest.

The pain lancing through me now made whatever I'd felt before seem frivolous. This was a pain that sizzled inside every atom of my body, attacking me from all angles at once.

A pain that had me begging for death—until I blissfully passed out from it.

When I woke again, my body so soaked with sweat that I felt like I was swimming in a pool of my own liquids, Lucifer was huddled over me.

The careful, polished facade from before was still radiating in his rigid posture, but there was a wildness in his eyes I hadn't seen before, his usually perfectly-styled hair tousled like he'd been gripping his fingers into it.

This time, he didn't wait for me to speak, didn't bother to

say anything at all as his hands roughly gripped my face, piercing into my head as he'd done before.

It hurt, I didn't doubt that. But my body had become so used to the pain, had almost begun to recognize it as a companion more than a threat.

"Again."

The blade didn't surprise me this time, the blue glow allowing room for one small hiccup of resistance, of fear from me, before it found its home again.

This pattern repeated for so long that I stopped counting, stopped protesting.

Eventually, it became like a meditation, my body growing simultaneously weaker and stronger with each foray into the darkness. The limbs attached to me felt no more mine than the ground that they borrowed for rest.

When I came to—who knows how long I'd been under, or how many times I'd been shoved into the murkines, I'd long lost track—Lucifer was sitting next to me, his arms dangling lazily on his bent knees.

The strange otherworldlyness of him hadn't left, the power he exuded as present as I imagined it always was, but there was a weariness about him. His black shirt was rolled to his elbows, his hair a mess, his skin clammy with sweat. Dark eyes met mine and there was no shield, no distant judgment or cold appraisal.

He looked like a man, one who'd been through the same heavy battle as me—weathered and shaped into something new.

I felt a strange kinship with him, an appreciation that I wasn't alone in the agony, even if he was the cause.

He took a heavy, labored breath, a strand of wet hair falling into his eyes as they dropped to the ground. "I've done all I can do." His mouth narrowed into a thin line, dipping slightly in the corners. He looked... sad. "Your powers are yours to shape and form. They crave connection. It is the only way to strengthen them—to bring them to where they were and then, hopefully, to go beyond that. It's the only chance you have. I've done all that I can do."

Slowly, painfully, he stood, his chest staggering in uneven breaths. Strange, to be aware of Lucifer's breathing. I'd long thought of him as being more like a god than a man—untouchable, impervious to pain or harm. This—this was a different version, a different shape of him than I'd encountered before.

Without another word, he left through the door, opening it wide enough for a large, furry animal to slip in through the crack.

A wet tongue pressed to my cheek, warmth spreading through my body as the creature curled around me, soft fur soothing a chill I hadn't noticed until it subsided.

"Ralph?" I pressed my head against his chest, fingers curled into the thick fur surrounding me.

A pressure in my chest released, comfort unfurling down to my toes.

With the first vestiges of peace clouding out the pain, I did all that there was left for me to do—drift into a deep, deep sleep.

∼

WHEN I FINALLY CAME TO, my body felt stronger, and I felt more *me* than I'd felt in a long time. I fucking hated Lucifer for what he'd put me through, and I'd have to process the trauma of it all eventually. But that need for revenge and healing was overshadowed by a ravenous hunger that I couldn't seem to satiate no matter how hard I tried.

Eli studied me, lips curved into a small grin as I shoved another piece of venison into my mouth.

"What?" I asked around a mouthful, no doubt looking as unattractive as I felt.

Eli's leg and the injuries he'd sustained during the battle had been healed up during the nightmare Lucifer had put me through.

"Nothing." The grin turned into a full-on Eli smirk, one that made the whisperings of a flutter stir in my belly. "I know you love your food, but this is next level, even for you. I think this is the fourth meal you've had since you woke up—two hours ago."

A shadow crossed his face, the teasing glint in his eyes eclipsed by concern.

I didn't want to talk about what I'd been through—and Eli hadn't pressed me on it.

That didn't change the fact that he was worried though. I felt his eyes on me whenever I wasn't looking at him, his focus carving a spark against each bit of skin it landed on. My awareness of him was stronger than usual, more insistent even than my desire for food.

I swallowed another too-big bite of meat, sitting up straight so that I could have a polite conversation and stop gnawing on everything in sight like a caveman. "What do we do now?"

Lucifer hadn't made an appearance since abandoning our little torture session, and while Ralph had kept me company for meals one and two, he left sometime during meal number three—no doubt to find Sam or his blue-eyed hellhound buddy.

"Sam said you'd need a day to recuperate, to heal your mind and body and some other yoga-sounding shit. He said after you eat a bit, to spar with me for an hour or two." He snorted, "apparently I'm so weak, he's not concerned about *me* pushing you too far. And then tomorrow, you're to check in with Lucifer, report any new information you've uncovered. He said he'd be around in the afternoon to continue the training regimen you developed with him last time you were here."

Sourness twisted in my gut at the thought of seeing Lucifer tomorrow. The man had put me through hell—something I probably shouldn't have been surprised about considering we were very literally in hell and he was also, you know, Lucifer.

That didn't mean I was excited for a reunion quite so soon.

I shoved my plate away, my appetite for it suddenly wavering a bit. Sam had been working with me on my training last time I was here, but his focus had been on strengthening my powers. Not on sparring.

"Sam's going to be really disappointed when he realizes that our training session is going to dry up as soon as it starts."

Eli took a deep breath, not meeting my eyes.

"What?"

His gaze cut to me briefly. "Have you tried to access your powers since waking up?" Leaning forward, he grabbed my hand, the feel of his thumb stroking my skin enough to send a shot of desire to the base of my belly. I pulled my hand away, shocked by the blast and his eyes widened with a brief flash of hurt before his usual mask cannibalized it. "After what Lucifer—" he cleared his throat, "after what you went through, I mean? Did he fix your powers? Find them or release them again or whatever?"

My face relaxed in surprise and I sat back, lifting my hands in front of me, considering. Had he fixed them? I closed my eyes, searching inside of myself for that familiar flicker of heat, of tingling energy.

A wave of nausea overtook my focus, my temples prickling with sweat as memories of that darkness came back, that pain.

I pushed it to the side, storing it in that box of shit to deal with later, the one overflowing now in the back of mind.

"Max!" I felt Eli lean closer, his voice filled with a tentative excitement. "Max, look."

The first thing I saw when I opened my eyes was how startlingly beautiful Eli was when he smiled. It was rare, these moments. He was always so aware of being observed, every expression a carefully-crafted shield. It wasn't that he didn't ever smile—his face was almost always twisted into one of those roguish, sardonic smirks I didn't think existed outside of romance novels. But he used that flirtation to hide from the world, to keep himself at a distance from everyone. Moments like this one were rare. His brown eyes, shot through with flecks of amber, shone with adoration as they met mine.

Something in that look made me feel not just desired, but like I was something precious—like I was someone worth fighting alongside of.

Like I was someone worth fighting for.

I wanted to trace the line of the smile, the way it traveled all the way up to his eyes, to memorize this rare glimpse of the real him before it disappeared. But when I moved my hand to do just that, I jumped back in my seat, startled.

Because the second thing I saw was that my fingers were on fire, the tips glimmering with the familiar, comforting heat.

"Oh my god," I whispered, my voice cracking with excitement. "My powers—they're back. Eli, this is amazing."

I reached deep inside, tried fanning the flames, building them up. They flickered and flared briefly, but then extinguished. It would take time to get them back to what they were before, but it was a start.

If I could access my strength again, it meant that we were finally, finally one step closer to saving Atlas.

"*You're* amazing," he whispered, his eyes narrowing softly as he studied me.

His hand feathered along my cheek, cradling it softly—touching just barely. I bit my bottom lip as lust coiled down my spine, stirring between my legs. His eyes latched onto my mouth, darting between it and my eyes, a silent question in the air between us.

My focus drifted to the last time we'd been together, how I'd broken down into a puddle after—to my realization after being with Wade and Darius, to that dream with Atlas.

Slowly, he moved to close the distance between us.

"Oh my god." I stood up abruptly. Atlas. How the fuck had I forgotten that dream?

"I'm sorry," Eli said, the words tumbling out in a rush as he watched me pace. "I didn't mean to push you."

I waved my hand at him. "It's not you, Eli. It's Atlas!"

Something unreadable flashed in his eye—hurt, jealousy maybe? "You're thinking about Atlas right now?"

"No, it's not like that—I just remembered a dream. That I had a dream while," I ran a hand over my stomach, "you know, Lucifer was torturing me and stuff." He flinched at the mention of torture, his jaw clenching with a rage both of us knew he could do nothing about. Lucifer could pretty much do whatever he wanted—neither of us was powerful enough to stop him. "I think he helped me to finally dream walk again."

"Oh." Eli sat up straighter, the corner of his mouth pinched as he considered. "You reached Atlas? Is he alive?" He shook his head, grunting. "I mean, obviously he's alive if you were able to reach him—" his eyes met mine, round and filled with excitement, with hope, "but is he okay?"

My stomach dipped at the realization that I had to crush that hope, or at least soften it—why did it seem like we never got to hold onto it for very long anymore? "I don't know. He seemed disoriented; something was very clearly up. They must be injecting him with all kinds of things." I closed my eyes, tried to focus on those final moments with him. Sometimes these dreams were vivid and clear, but other times they started to slip away the moment I woke up. This dream belonged to the latter category, probably because I wasn't at full strength. And, I was dealing with the whole mind-obliterating torture thing. "Something—something pushed me out. Something much, much stronger than me. It felt—"

Fear tangled into my thoughts and I felt my heartbeat quicken the closer I reached for it.

"Max?" Eli stood in front of me now his hands pulling mine from where they gripped my head, erasing the pressure with his soft touch. "What was it?"

"Fear," I whispered, my hands clinging to his as I stared up at him. "Absolute terror."

His thumb stroked my cheek and I realized, belatedly, that he was wiping away a tear. "You're okay. You're safe."

I shook my head, holding his hands to my face like he was my lifeline. "Atlas isn't."

I didn't have the confidence to voice it out loud, but I was pretty certain that the creature who pushed me from the dream-walk was a drude. Darius mentioned that they were nightmare demons, that they fed on a person's worst fears, using other people's weaknesses as a way to grow stronger.

But how would a drude have access to him?

Unless The Guild had managed to capture one at the ambush?

The thought that protectors, people who grew up with Atlas—hell, his own father—could use a demon to torture him, or other prisoners, made bile rise in my throat.

I'd met so many wonderful people—Seamus, Greta, Izzy—in my brief time at The Guild, sometimes it was difficult to parse that with the reality of the institution. Was The Guild truly so wildly and completely corrupt?

Surely Tarren would do something to help his son?

The Guild was so hellbent on extolling the evils of demons; surely, they wouldn't stoop to using those very *evil* powers to harm others?

I knew in my gut that it was wishful thinking—there were no bounds to the kinds of evil that shaped this world.

The division now was clear to me.

Evil was a term reserved only for those who used their power to oppress those without it, for those motivated by greed and a desire to keep those they deemed lesser down, for those who harmed for no other motivation than to gain more power, for those who profited from others' misery with a greedy eagerness.

Whether vampire or protector, that was the new code I would live by. I'd no longer think twice about cutting down those who betrayed it.

We couldn't help Atlas from here. As terrifying and frustrating as it was, I knew that the best chance Atlas had would come from me regaining control over my power—both so that I could reach him in sleep and so that I could teleport to him the second I was able.

14

MAX

"You're distracted." Eli swept my feet, catching me by the arms before I landed on my ass. "You're never this easy to take down."

My skin tingled under his touch, his hands lingering just a moment longer than necessary as he stood next to me, both of us breathing staggered breaths that had nothing to do with the fight.

I had no idea what was wrong with me, but I couldn't stop thinking about kissing him, about touching him—about pressing him up against the stone wall and climbing him like a tree.

"There's a lot to be distracted by." My voice was hoarse and breathier than I'd intended. "We are in hell."

When I'd woken with a ravenous hunger, I'd assumed that food would satisfy the craving. It was growing more and more clear, however, that I was starving for something more than nourishment.

My tongue wet my bottom lip, my body leaning slightly into him—not enough to be intentional or even visible to an outside observer, but enough to prove that the magnetism between us was growing impatient, demanding even.

The way his eyes heated when they dipped to my mouth told me that he was just as starving as I was.

At first, I thought it was just my succubus flaring to life after being suppressed and locked away again—hungry with want and eager to strengthen me the only way that particular power could.

But we'd come across two other people, when we'd snuck down to the kitchens for more food, both absurdly stunning in that way demons always were—and I didn't feel this needy draw to either of them.

It was just Eli.

His fingers traced down my bare arms where he held me, the simple friction enough to pull a small breathy moan from my lips.

I took a step back, breaking the spell he had on me.

He cocked his head to the side, brow bent in question. "Why do you keep doing that?"

"Doing what?" I took another step back.

He took one forward. "Pushing me away."

"I don't know what you mean?" One more step back in this dance.

A dark grin twisted his lips. I couldn't tear my eyes away from them. "I think you do know what I mean, Max."

I bit my bottom lip as my back hit the wall, the cool stone a welcome contrast to the heat blazing through me. Only now there was nowhere else for me to go, to escape him.

But he didn't pursue me further, his body still and coiled as he studied me with a ravenous hunger all but pulsing around him.

"Eli, we've been over this. We're fr—"

The smile evaporated from his face as he leaned into me, his forearms flattening against the wall on either side of my head as his eyes met mine—sharp and unflinching. "I dare you to say it, Max—dare you to tell me that we're just friends." I opened my mouth to do just that, my breath catching in my throat before he added, "but only if you actually mean it."

My heartbeat hammered like a wild animal against my chest, the thudding so erratic that I was certain it echoed around the room—it was echoing like a drumline in my ears at the very least.

Eli and I had been dancing around—and bouldering through—our attraction since the very first moment we met.

He'd been the first boy I'd given myself over to completely, but he'd also been the first to betray me, to crack my heart in half and stomp on the pieces.

I was over that pain; we'd worked through it and I'd forgiven him. And it had done nothing to abate the attraction I felt towards him, no matter how many times I told myself otherwise. The way my body lit at a single touch from him was undeniable, unavoidable, no matter how hard I tried to ignore it. To resist it.

The muscles in his jaw pulsed as he waited for my response, his eyes hard and probing as they bore into mine, the challenge in them clear and uncompromising.

"I want to mean it, Eli." I dropped my gaze to his chest.

"Why?" The word wasn't sharp or cruel, but the quiet demand in the question forced my eyes back to his. He wouldn't let me out of this conversation so easily.

Frustration flared in my belly at the double standard. "It's what you do, isn't it? It's what you all do—you push people away, don't let them get close, keep your distance—protect yourselves." A humorless laugh fell from my lips, settling in the tension between us. "And the thing is, it used to frustrate the hell out of me."

"And now?" His expression was unreadable, that impenetrable mask of his meeting and challenging my own, much more nascent one.

I straightened up, pulling an inch away from the wall, reclaiming my space even as it brought me closer to him. "Now, I see it for what it was—a valuable model. I understand now. This life we lead, the world we live in?" I closed my eyes for a moment, drew in a breath, desperately trying to shove my desire down where I couldn't reach for the temptation it taunted me with. "Letting people in, being consumed by someone in that way—it only opens us up to pain. And as much as I hate him for it, Lucifer was right. There's no room or time for grief in our lives right now. I can't put myself in a position of getting hurt like that because—" I wet my lips, meeting his eyes again, needing to make him see, to make him remember the lesson he'd already learned and mastered over and over again. "If I let myself get closer to you—to the others—if I fully give myself over to the bonds slowly threading between us—and then I lose one of you?" My chest felt heavy just at the thought. I was already too invested, already needed them all too much. "I don't know if I could survive that kind of loss. At first, I thought I could do what you do—" my focus fixated on his jaw, the way the lines grew sharper with every word I said, "just fuck, enjoy myself. But—" I forced my gaze away, back on his eyes, "I'm not built for that. I care too much about you to shield myself from falling deeper, from—" I shrugged, not entirely sure where that sentence ended.

The words dried up between us, the silence thick as Eli watched me.

After what felt like an impossibly long moment, he pulled his body back, no longer caging me in, but somehow, the new distance made me feel no less constrained, no less consumed by him. He took up the whole room; every breath I took was infused with the warm scent of him. No matter how badly I wanted to, I couldn't shake the feel of him, couldn't drag my eyes from every twitch of his muscles, every move he made drawing me in—like a moth to a flame, the consequences just as dire.

"You're so much stronger than us, Max." His fingers pressed against the bottom of my chin until my eyes met his, the tumultuous battle of emotions in their depths impossible for me to parse, but so mesmerizing I couldn't pull away if I tried. "All this time that you've been learning this lesson from us—one taught from an impossibly outdated book, a lesson only designed to ultimately fail you—we've been learning a much more valuable one from you."

He swallowed, and I greedily tracked the way his throat moved. "I can't speak for the others, but I can undeniably speak for myself. And it's taken me far too long to understand that shielding myself from caring isn't protecting me—it's suspending me in a never-ending agony, it's creating a life that isn't even worth living. But you—" His hands cupped my cheeks, his nose little more than an inch from my own as he ducked down to me. "You have shattered—completely obliterated—any shield that I've tried to erect. At first, I resisted the hell out of it, resisted you for as long as I could. Convinced myself that I could just fuck you and get it—get *you*—out of my system. Because you fucking terrify me—the way you made me feel fucking terrifies me. But you've also made me braver—the way you throw yourself into the things—the people—you care about. The way you give yourself completely to what you believe in. You're so fucking brave, Max. So much braver than all of us combined. And it would be nothing short of a goddamn tragedy if you lost that, if the thing you took away from losing Cyrus was that you should live your life like I've tried to do."

I blinked, losing the outline of Eli, my vision nothing but a watercolor of his features.

"And the ridiculous thing is," I heard the start of a gentle smile in his voice. His thumbs swept carefully across my cheeks, wiping away the tears raining down them. "Pushing people away? It doesn't even work. Because no matter how hard I tried to, it was impossible for me to fight. I am completely and undeniably in love with you, Max Bentley."

A sob clutched at my chest, but he swallowed it, his lips pressing softly against mine.

"You have the power to rip my heart out of my chest, to hurt me, to leave me. But I'm giving you that power anyway—gladly." His lips pressed to my jaw, the pressure so gentle it made my breath stutter. "Be brave with me, Max."

My heart caught in my throat and I couldn't manage a single word. Instead, I nodded once—it was enough.

Eli's lips caught mine in a searing kiss, his hands cupping my cheeks like he was afraid I'd still pull away.

I wouldn't. Not anymore. He was right. We were all likely to die—probably soon; I was done kidding myself. I wouldn't deny myself the chance to be with him all the ways that I wanted to. Physically, emotionally—real intimacy.

His tongue slipped into my mouth, tangling with my own. A deep, guttural groan reverberated in his chest as I met the depth of his kiss lick for lick.

My back was pressed against the wall, and this time I had no desire to resist the cage of Eli's arms around me.

He lifted me, my legs wrapping around his waist. I ground myself against him, desperate for the delectable friction, desperate for more of him.

His dick was hard and solid against me, and I could feel myself already soaking through my leggings.

Jesus fucking christ, I wanted every inch of this man.

His lips moved to my jaw, biting my earlobe on the way down my throat, each nip soothed with the wetness of his tongue. "God you taste good," he whispered, the words pebbling my skin and shooting a shot of blazing desire to my core.

Heat, so much heat I felt like I was going to combust if I didn't have him.

"More." It was half word, half moan, as I climbed down him. "I need more, Eli."

I peeled his shirt off, his body tanned and glistening with the sweat from our workshop—every muscle of his lean chest and abs outlined to perfection like he was carved from stone.

My fingers ran over his pecks, and I followed the path with my tongue, nipping playfully at his nipple. His breathing was ragged—hungry, and I could feel my succubus powers flare to the surface.

Every touch of his skin, every time I caressed him, I could feel his desire pulse through me as if it was mine. It was intoxicating, addicting.

With hurried hands, I unbuckled his belt, eager for what I really wanted, as he peeled my shirt off, my bra—fisting my boobs with a delicious roughness.

He reached for me, but I dropped to my knees in front of him, watching his face contort with pleasure as I fisted his dick, circling my thumb around the ridge of the tip. The sight of him like that—raw, uninhibited—filled me with power and made my mouth water.

Hungry and finally—finally—getting what I was really craving, I took him in my mouth. His groan flowed through me, down to my toes.

More, I wanted to be filled entirely with him. Relaxing my throat like Darius taught me, I drew him all the way in, my eyes watering at the size of him, need pooling between my legs.

"Fuck, Max," he groaned, his fingers curled roughly in my hair, thrusting until pain and pleasure tangled together. "Jesus, just the sight of you down there is enough to make me blow my load. I don't want to come yet—not until I'm inside of you and not until I taste you."

The heat in his words sent a mirrored heat raging in my belly as he knelt to the ground, taking my mouth with his. His kiss was demanding, a clash of tongues and teeth until I was dizzy with him. It was a dark contrast with the gentle way he leaned me back until my shoulder blades kissed the cold floor.

It should have been uncomfortable on the hard floor, the sharpness of the chill—but it just added another jolt of sensation down my spine. Everything felt good when my succubus powers were at the surface—even the things that normally wouldn't.

With a devilish gleam in his eyes, he moved down to my jaw, my neck, nipping playfully until he reached my left nipple. He bit down, harder this time, drawing a moan from my lips before he cooled the sting with his tongue, just as his hand slid past the waist of my leggings.

Needing no roadmap, his fingers pinched my clit and I saw stars.

"So fucking wet for me, aren't you, beautiful?" His voice was ragged, the look in his eyes filled equally with power and reverence. I was beyond the capacity for words as his fingers worked over me, the slick, slippery sounds echoing around us. With a wicked grin, he peeled my leggings off and stared at me, as I lay writhing and needy without his hands on me.

"Please, Eli," I panted, my body on the edge just from him watching me.

He blew a cool breath of air against my clit that had my back arching as if he'd fucked me.

Slowly—with agonizing precision—his tongue circled the skin around my clit, avoiding the sensitive bud, as he delved in, lapping me up like a man dying of thirst. Tasting me as he'd wanted.

My hips rolled forward, desperate for more. But he pulled

back from me, his trademark smirk plastered on his face as he peered up at me.

Could a person die from being this close to the edge and not being allowed to fall over it?

Because fuck it, it looked like Eli was determined to leave me tap dancing on that cliff.

Another cold breath to my clit. "Tell me you want me, Max." Another one. "Tell me that you want to come into my mouth until I suck you dry." His eyes narrowed on me, watching me squirm and rock with need, pleased with the effect his teasing was having on me. He sucked my clit, finally, his mouth pulling back almost as quickly as it touched me. "Your body wants me." He slid his fingers against me, the sound of my wetness obscene, "I want to hear it from you though."

"Fuck, I want you." My words were jilted, needy, breathy pants.

"And?" he asked, drawing the question out as he dipped his face towards me, inhaling deeply. Heat flared in his eyes and I knew he was getting as impatient with the game as I was.

"And I want to soak in your mouth until you're drowning in me."

His breath stuttered, eyes widening with surprise at my words. "Fuck you're perfect."

With no more fanfare, he took me into his mouth, his tongue stroking me as the flames inside of me built. I felt every lap of his tongue as if he was touching every inch of me at once.

'Oh my god," I whimpered, "yes, more."

Slicked with desire, his thumb circled the entrance of me before going further south.

I groaned, loud and desperate as two fingers slid into my vagina and one into my ass.

"That's it," he praised as I cried out at the fullness of him, "that's my girl—every hole is mine. Every part of you, mine."

The next swipe of his tongue was my undoing. Liquid

poured from me and Eli drank it up like a man dying of thirst, his moans almost as satiated and greedy as mine.

He took his time, not climbing back up me until he was well and truly finished.

As his dick slid against me, I clawed him to me, pushing him to the side until I was on top.

I slid myself against his dick, drenching him in me, my vision spinning with an all-consuming need for him.

His hands closed around my hips, rocking me harder against him. "That's it, beautiful. Ride me."

I didn't need to be told twice, I pulled him to my entrance, impaling myself on him in one slick motion, my hand pressed to his chest for purchase as I rode him with fast, hard thrusts.

"Fuck." His muscles contracted and tensed against my hand and I could feel him thickening inside of me.

It was my turn to see how long I could draw out his need before he exploded in me.

With a grin, I slowed my movements, lifted myself with my legs so that I was only riding the tip of him.

His head tilted back, a strangled chuckle pulling from deep in his chest. "Touche. God, you're per—" the words cut off into a groan as I squeezed myself around the tip of his dick and held there. Then, so slowly I thought I would burst with impatience at my own game, I slid all the way down his shaft.

Pure adoration and wonder radiated from his eyes as I started to ride him again, pulling him up to me in a seated position, so that we were skin-to-skin in as many places as possible.

I panted into his mouth, our lips grazing in feathered touches as I rocked. "Eli?" My voice was little more than a whisper as I felt myself climbing and stalling at the tipping point.

"Hmm?" he groaned, every muscle tensed as he tried to hold himself back for me.

"I love you too."

As if a flip had been switched, he took control of the pace, pushing me into an orgasm so intense my vision started to blacken. He swallowed my scream with his mouth, shooting into me with a groan of his own.

Waves of pleasure rolled through us, keeping us connected as he twitched inside me, his arms wrapped tight around my back, plastering me to him.

Something tightened in my chest, shifting and reshaping.

Heat flared against my skin, light flickering around us, basking us in warmth.

"Max, look," he whispered, voice strained and filled with awe.

It took everything to pull my eyes from him, but when I did, I saw that we were circled by a tall, thick ring of hellfire. It flickered and flared in time with my breath.

My powers were back.

With a vengeance.

15

WADE

Seamus was looking... bad. It had been two days since the bite and he still wasn't showing any signs of improvement. If anything, he seemed to be getting worse by the minute. Not a single lucid word had left his mouth since he passed out—just strange, incomprehensible mumblings and the occasional mention of Eli's name.

"We can't just leave him like this," Declan was pacing up and down the living room. This was the third time in as many hours she'd made this statement. "He needs medical attention. Proper medical attention, or else Eli and Max are going to come back to another fucking grave."

My stomach tightened at the thought of it. Seamus had always been more of a father to me than my own. While his arrival here was surprising, I couldn't deny the slight sense of ease I'd felt at knowing he was here with us, that he had our backs. It made things feel a little more possible, like we had an adult to turn to and tell us everything would be alright. It was childish, maybe, but it was true.

Werewolf bites were survivable for protectors. In fact, most bites caused little issue, healing with the help of the medical staff—vampire bites were the particularly iffy issue. And a small number of bites resulted in the protector turning into a werewolf like Atlas and Sarah, though I was starting to suspect those numbers were a lot higher than we'd been led to believe.

But Seamus was older than most protectors who found themselves up against a werewolf, and the bite location was deep into his abdomen.

So, not good.

It was sadistically ironic that Eli was the one who wasn't here. He was the best at field medicine.

Dec and I did our best with bandaging Seamus up, but we didn't have the supplies we needed, or a way to get them. A human hospital didn't have the things we needed, and while Cy had kept the cabin filled with protector first-aid basics, he wasn't equipped with the most up-to-date protocols for werewolf bites. Probably because the expectation of encountering one way out here was low as fuck.

"We can't just go barging into The Guild with him like this. That would be a sentence worse than death." I was reminding her as much as myself. For an hour, I'd been battling with just saying fuck it and taking him anyway. If he was going to die regardless, he'd stand a better chance there. And maybe his position, his tenure there would help?

I shoved the thought away—Tarren and the council weren't known for forgiveness or consideration. There was no nuance with Guild politics.

"Maybe we can find a way to get in touch with Arnell, we have phones now." Ro was sitting on the couch, passively watching Dec's errant pacing. Every few minutes, I'd catch him cutting his eyes to the door, like he was waiting for Max to show up at any moment.

Honestly, we all were. I felt her absence acutely. I wasn't sure how my brother and Eli had survived the wait for her return last time while maintaining their sanity. Two days and I was already willing to say fuck it, introduce myself to Darius's brother, dip into hell, and find her myself.

I'd tried finding her in my sleep, but either she was on a different sleep schedule than I was or I wasn't able to reach her through the realms without her having access to her succubus powers.

"That's not a bad idea." Declan paused, brows raised in question as her eyes met mine. "Maybe we can get them to smuggle us some supplies?"

Ro tensed, and I had a feeling he was second-guessing his suggestion. I knew from Max that he and Arnell had something going on, and I didn't blame him for worrying about putting him in more danger than he already was.

"Tell me again, about the mist." Darius burst into the door, ignoring the fact that we were in the middle of a conversation.

"There was a girl, when I showed up, after Dec and Seamus took out the last wolf, she collapsed to the ground and started leaking shadows." I ran through the list monotonously. He'd asked me dozens of times since it had happened, it wasn't like I had any new information.

"There's something off about her body." Darius leaned against the door frame, his expression hard and focused. "She smelled dead when I got here."

Dec scoffed. "That's because she was."

"I mean very dead."

"Can you be very dead? Isn't there just dead and not?" I asked.

He shook his head, frustration clouding his expression. "I mean dead for a while. Like more than recently dead."

"So, you think she was, what, a zombie?" Ro asked. "Are there zombies in hell? Is that a thing?"

Darius shook his head, then ran a hand through his hair, scattering dirt particles all over the white-blond strands. "The wolves smelled off too. Might be part of the reason Seamus isn't healing. Maybe there was something different about them."

They hadn't seemed different at first glance, but the world had been turned upside down so many times that encountering unusual wolves—or even a new species—wouldn't be the most surprising thing to happen this week.

I narrowed my eyes, studying the blackened ridges of his nails. "Did you dig them up?"

"To sniff them?" Ro's nose curled in disgust.

We buried the wolves a mile or two out after getting Seamus settled in the house. Darius hadn't mentioned them smelling off then.

He shrugged. "Something about the girl was rubbing me the wrong way, I needed to be sure. Hard to say if it's just the decomposition process or not—I don't exactly make it a habit to go sniffing carcasses days after killing them—but there's something off about the wolves. I can't place it."

"Great, just our luck that Seamus would get munched on by a fucking zombie wolf." I almost wanted to laugh at the absurdity of our rotten luck.

Darius narrowed his eyes, considering. "No, not like they've been dead for long, not off in the way the girl was off. Just off. Something familiar, but not. I can't explain it."

Dec opened the door to Cy's room, where we were keeping Seamus now, peeked in for a second, then closed it again. She'd been checking up on him incessantly, hoping for any sign of improvement. "No changes. Any ideas on the girl?"

Darius was quiet, lost in his thoughts for a moment, until I was convinced he wasn't even going to respond at all. "Not an idea, but the description of the shadow cloud sounds similar to a Drude. Legend says that they can travel in shadow form."

"So is it one of those then?" I asked, weirdly hopeful. One new creature we could handle. Maybe. But if a dozen were coming out of the woodwork, we'd be screwed. Even more screwed than we were. It was hard to create a playbook for the impending war when the players kept changing.

He shook his head, picking up on the pacing Dec had finally abandoned. "Not exactly, but maybe of the same kind of magic." He paused for a moment, one arm propping the other so that his chin rested in one hand. "When I was young, I heard tales from elders about shades."

"Shades?" Dec dropped onto the worn couch next to Ro, the bags under her eyes heavy and dark. She pulled a knitted blanket around her and breathed in deep, her shoulders relaxing a bit.

The house smelled like Max. I wasn't sure whether that made her absence better or worse—we could feel her all around us. It seemed unforgivably cruel that we didn't have her here—wrong to be living in her space without her in it too.

"Kind of like human legends of skin-walkers. I don't know much about them, they were always assumed to be a legend—stories told to terrify children, not that we needed much help being terrified in hell. They reanimate the dead, though only for a short time. The more powerful the body, the longer they can use it." He took a deep breath, a dark look crossing his expression. "I don't like this. First druden in the realm, now this."

"What does it mean?" Ro absentmindedly shoved his fingers through the woven holes of a stray corner of the blanket.

"It means that more than just the hell realm as I knew it has been disturbed."

Seamus moaned in pain, puncturing the tension in the room and reshaping it into a different kind of fear.

Darius nodded to the room. "He's not going to make it like that much longer. I give him three or four days—" Seamus coughed from the other room, the rattle in his chest audible even a room away, "maybe less."

I knew he was right, could feel it in my gut that Seamus wasn't long for this world if we didn't help him.

"Maybe Greta?" Ro shrugged. Greta was one of the nurses in The Guild. "Max seems to trust her, and she always knew that Max was something... more, didn't she? But she never told anyone. Helped her visit Ralph too, when he was down in the labs."

"That's the girl who gave Max the card key into the cells, right? Max mentioned her once or twice." Darius's features softened a bit.

Greta was one of the oldest working members of The Guild —hearing her referred to as a girl made my lips twitch into a small smile.

"Still no idea how to reach her—it's not like we have her number on speed dial." Dec leaned back into the couch, her body molding to it like clay. "And we can't exactly call The Guild and ask them to put her through either. It would put her at risk too."

Something jostled in my memory, capturing my breath in my lungs.

"Wade? You good?" Ro asked. The poor kid was so rattled and hypervigilant, that he noticed every small change in our demeanors, like he was constantly waiting for one of us to announce that our connection to Max was flaring, a clear compass to where she was.

Number.

In all of the chaos, I'd completely forgotten.

I ran to the coat rack and dug through my pockets until my fingers brushed along the edge of a scrap piece of paper. "Dani."

Dec shoved the blanket off of her lap and stood, eyes narrowing. "What about Dani?"

"When I made the first run for food, I ran into Dani—"

"And you're just saying something now?"

I shrugged, not wanting to get into the panic attack thing. Dec had enough to worry about. "Things have been a little chaotic, it honestly completely slipped my mind."

"What did she want? Did she follow you—say anything about Max?" Ro asked.

"She said she wasn't with The Guild, not really. That she knew some people who might be able to help us if we ran into trouble." I nodded to Darius. "Even said the fanghole could come if we trusted him. And she didn't seem concerned that I was clearly not just a protector, or that Atlas was a wolf."

Dec narrowed her eyes. "She's never mentioned anything like this to me before."

I shrugged. I wasn't as close with Dani as Dec was, but she'd always been the lone wolf sort. It didn't surprise me that she'd keep something likely to get her locked in a cell close to the chest. "Maybe she wasn't sure you'd be amenable. We spent most of our time being the lapdogs of the field division. It's only recently that—" I shrugged, "well, you know, things changed. We see the world differently now. Maybe she couldn't trust us until she was absolutely certain we wouldn't betray her."

She sank back down into the couch, nodding, her eyes focused on the floor. "Yeah. Good point."

Rowan squeezed Dec's shoulder before turning to me. There was a tenderness there that made my skin itch.

Sometimes it felt like I'd spent so much time locked alone that I didn't know how to be with my friends in the way that I used to. Like the shape I used to fill was just an ill-fitting costume now.

I licked my lips and offered the only words of comfort I could find. "It's possible she—or whoever that number leads to—will have access to medical care. Maybe they can help Seamus."

"You can't seriously be suggesting that we leave this place?" Darius's face was unreadable, his posture still and straight in a way only a vampire could pull off. "What if Max comes back and we're all gone?"

Another low, agonized moan sounded from the other room.

My fingers dug into my palms. Short of harming my team, I'd do just about anything to help Seamus. I didn't want to lay his ashes outside with his brother. Not if there was even a shadow of a possibility we could help him. "We can leave a note—and the number. When she gets back, we can meet up with her."

Darius turned to the door, ran a hand through his hair, considering. Every muscle in his body seemed coiled with indecision. "I don't like it. We're better off cutting our losses with him."

I took a deep breath and counted down from five.

Attacking him right now would not be good.

For us or for Eli.

"Plus there's a solid possibility that shade—or whatever the hell it was—will come back here. It knows where we are. We're basically sitting ducks if we just stay here," Declan said.

Darius was still as he considered her. "That doesn't mean that our only two options are stay here or call this Dani girl. We can find another place to wait for Max, to plan our next move."

"If we're just moving to another location, that doesn't help Seamus." I took another deep breath, trying to calm the anger flaring in my gut.

"Like I said," he shot me a dark look, "cut our losses."

Why the fuck was he being so cagey about this? Did he truly just not give a fuck about anyone other than Max?

I took a deep breath, but there was no expelling this flare of rage.

I lunged for him, shoving him against the wall, my forearm pressed into his throat as I reached for a blade. "You selfish fucking fuck."

I felt Declan's fingers at my arm, trying to peel me away, but I was stronger than she was. "Wade."

The fanghole cocked a brow, a malicious grin spreading on his face. "Suffocation won't kill me, incubus. This is just foreplay."

"Enough." The single word cut through the tension. "I say we call." Rowan's stare was hard and determined as it met mine. "Max would want us to do whatever we could to help him. We can't just sit here and let him die if there's a possibility of saving him. Max and Eli shouldn't come home to another pile of ashes to spread."

I felt the fight leave Darius's body at Rowan's words. I released him from my grip and took a few steps back, feeling the same effect on my own.

Rowan handed me a phone. "Call."

∼

Rowan's forehead pressed against the frosted glass of the window as he watched the trees zip by at lightning speed. "How far from town did she say it was?"

"About a thirty-minute drive," Dec said from the back.

Dani's directions were pretty vague and we'd only spoken for a few minutes. She didn't give us much information about where we were going or why. Just an address, a brief description of the place, and told us to ask for someone named Charlie when we arrived—that she'd let them know we were coming, whoever "them" was.

She called it The Lodge—a name as nondescript as her information. And when I pressed for more, she simply told me to trust her, that they were taking in protectors and demons alike who needed a place to stay safe. To come together.

We debated for an hour about whether that was enough to

go on, but when Dani texted that they had one or two medics stationed there, any arguing came to a halt.

It was entirely possible we were heading into enemy territory—that we'd be put on the defensive as soon as we got there, but we'd take the risk. Seamus didn't have another option.

My fingers curled tight around the steering wheel, the leather groaning its discomfort.

We'd been driving for hours, but had barely spoken.

Rowan left Max the address, hidden in a hollowed-out book he said she'd definitely check when she returned. I didn't press him on it—he knew her habits and the protocols they'd developed with Cy better than I did.

And on the off chance that the place was ransacked by more demons, we didn't want them tracking us down to this... Lodge place—so we couldn't exactly leave a note explaining everything in case they found it.

Seamus whimpered from the backseat and my focus cut to the rearview to check on him. He was sitting behind Ro, his clammy skin pressed to the window as Declan put her fingers against his neck, checking his pulse.

Her worried eyes met mine and my lips flattened into a line.

Thirty minutes. We'd get him there soon. They'd help him. They had to help him.

My gaze cut to Darius. He'd been surprisingly quiet during the trip. I'd half expected him to be like an obnoxious child on a road trip, but he sat behind me, eyes on the window, unblinking. There was a blankness in his expression, like he was there, but not, at the same time. The only sign of his early anger was in the stiff lines of his shoulders, the tight line of his mouth.

A siren blared behind us and, as one, we all straightened—Dec and Darius meeting my eyes from the back, and Ro shifting to stare at me.

This time, we were driving a very definitely stolen car.

While not ideal, it was necessary—no rental place would

give us a loaner without ID, and we couldn't risk making the trek on foot with Seamus as bad as he was.

Darius stole one for us and promised that, once we got Seamus safe, he'd deposit it somewhere an hour or two away and call in a tip.

Not a perfect solution, but it would theoretically wind up with the owner being reunited eventually.

It was a sporty, expensive car—a choice the fanghole justified by explaining that only a douche would purchase it in the first place, so they deserved to be robbed. But it was also a tight fit with five full-grown adults, and we wouldn't be able to explain away Seamus's condition if we were pulled over.

"Pull to the side," Ro said, jaw tight. "It's not like we can start a car chase with the cops. The whole point is to keep attention away from us."

I took a deep breath, considering, then pulled to the side.

No one breathed as the car pulled closer, then passed us.

As one, we exhaled. The car continued down the road, went through a red light a few hundred feet ahead, and then turned off the siren.

Declan shook her head. "All of that just to avoid sitting at a red light. Fucking asshole."

Ro snorted—the noise caught between relief and laughter.

Declan chuckled, the sound high and soft and light.

I couldn't help but join in.

The car felt lighter.

Except for Seamus, who was still unconscious.

And Darius. He'd just gone back to staring out the window, lost in thought, either oblivious to our moment of reprieve, or indifferent to it.

"What's with you?"

He met my eyes in the rearview, but whatever emotion was swirling in there was unreadable to me. "I don't know what you mean, incubus."

His voice was drawn, bored even, but I didn't miss the slight hint of warning there.

Declan's eyes cut to him, her brows bent in focus before she met my gaze in the mirror, confusion clear as day on her face.

She shifted to the vampire, nudging him with her shoulder, though they were already so crammed back there it hardly mattered. "Darius, if this place turns into a trap, we'll leave. Immediately. You have my word. But we have to try for Seamus. And I really don't think Dani will intentionally lead us towards danger. She caught us running that day at the ambush—with you. And she let us go."

Darius let out a nondescript grunt, not saying another word or even bothering to look my way once during the rest of the trip.

When we pulled up to "The Lodge" it looked more like an amusement park for relaxation. Dozens of small cabins lined the property, cratered in a small mountain valley.

Luckily there wasn't too much snowfall, but we'd still had to put some snow chains on to make it all the way up here. I sent a silent thank you up to whatever frat bro Darius had stolen the car from for having the foresight to keep them in the trunk.

"Where do we go?" Declan craned her neck between the two front seats, her eyes wide at the picturesque scene in front of us.

It looked like the kind of small town you'd see in one of those Hallmark movies—the tiny cabins warm and inviting and decorated with lights.

Snow coated the ground in giant fluffy mounds, smoke curling from chimneys.

I nodded my head. "I'm guessing the larger building over there."

I parked the car in a small lot, our temporary wonder evaporating as we maneuvered Seamus out of his seat.

His typically warm skin looked pale and ashy, caked under

layers of sweat. The bite on his side hadn't stopped bleeding, the bandages already seeped through with blood from the trip.

Carefully, I cradled him, one arm under his knees, one his head, as we walked towards what I assumed was the primary residence.

Ro and Dec's footsteps crunched softly in the snow along mine as we moved, all of us aware of the small trail of blood dripping along our path. No matter how many times we tried to close the wound, or at least put pressure to stem the flow, it wouldn't heal.

When I turned back, I realized that Darius wasn't following us. He stood by the car, his eyes scanning the cabins like he was looking for something—or someone.

"Let's go," Dec called, her words forming into clouds from the chill in the air.

For a moment, I thought he was going to get in the car and leave us here.

He stared at Dec, considering for a long moment, his jaw clenched so tightly I could see the tension from twenty feet away.

Slowly, as if every muscle in his body was resisting him, he walked towards us.

By the time he caught up, I was already knocking on the door, shifting Seamus's weight awkwardly as we stood back.

A girl with long red curls opened it, the heat and light from the cabin washing over me. A wave of smells hit me like a truck —warm spices, roasted meat, a subtle hint of clove.

"Can I help you?" Her smile was kind but hesitant.

My stomach growled audibly. How long had it been since we'd all had a proper meal? One cooked over a stove, not just from a box.

Her already wide eyes widened further as she took in Seamus. "Oh my god, is he okay?"

I shook my head. I wasn't sure who this girl was, if everyone here knew about the supernatural world, or if there were humans here too. "He needs medical attention. Dani said to ask for Charlie—she called ahead to warn that we were coming."

The woman stood taller, her almost child-like face flattening out into something more serious. "Yes, of course. Hang on."

She disappeared from the doorway and closed it. I took a few steps back, both to adjust Seamus and to get a better look at the place. I heard voices in the distance, but no one was within sight.

When the door opened again, a much less friendly-looking face greeted us. Dark hair, dark eyes, the build of a protector who'd spent a lifetime training.

For a moment, I thought I was staring at a ghost.

Dec stiffened next to me and I knew she was seeing the same thing I was.

Bishop Slate. Atlas's cousin, on his mother's side.

We'd been told he died on a mission.

Years ago.

"You." The single word was little more than a growl, more feral animal than human. His brows furrowed into an angry line and he sprang into action.

I turned, shielding Seamus with my body, but he wasn't coming after us.

In little more than a blink of an eye, he had Darius shoved against the wall of the cabin, the wood straining from pressure, the gleam of a dagger pressed to his heart.

Darius's lips twisted into a wild, terrifying grin—his eyes narrowed and taunting. "Good to see you too, Bishop."

16

MAX

"It's beautiful."

The River Styx had almost instantly become my favorite place in hell. A weird statement to make perhaps—hell was no amusement park or vacation site, but it was true. The dark shimmery water was still and serene, shifting in a rainbow of colors like an oil slick. I wanted to run my fingers through it.

Instead, I buried my hand into Ralph's luscious fur, grinning as he leaned into the pressure. It was good to have him near again. While I didn't want him anywhere close to the chaos going on in the human realm, I'd missed him. He was a part of me, and I didn't feel entirely complete without him around.

"It is." Lucifer's voice was filled with a quiet reverence as he stared at the infinite expanse of water. "Most dangerous things are."

I turned to face him, but found that I had moved several steps forward, my body unconsciously drawn toward the body of water. Ralph stood, closing the distance between us instantly, his wet nose bumping against my hand for more pets. I obliged.

The Guild acted like hellhounds were some of the most terrifying creatures around. But Ralph was sweetness embodied. Could he decapitate a demon in two seconds flat? Yes. But he was also a very good boy.

"Dangerous?"

Lucifer nodded, the longing still visible in the way he studied the water. "I would not touch it, if you hope to continue living. There is only one person who can guarantee your survival against the water's power—and he abandoned his post many years ago, whether by choice or not is unclear."

Something flickered in the dark depths of his eyes, a sadness maybe, or perhaps something darker—a regret?

"Someone you cared for?"

His lips pressed into a thin line, the momentary glimpse into feeling gone. "There is no one alive I care for. But yes, locating Azrael or his power source would be of great use to me. As with your birth, his disappearance has created many shifts in this world."

It was a surprisingly informative answer. Rarely did Lucifer offer more than a simple one-word grunt—and when he did, it was only if doing so resulted in a significantly longer chastisement of my many shortcomings.

"Azrael?" I'd heard that name before, in some lore or show, but it wasn't the one I was expecting. "Like the angel of death? I thought that Charon was the one who ferries souls across the river?"

"I've told you before—the mythologies you know are fractured versions of the truth." His words rang with a frustration and finality that I didn't feel like picking at right now. I had to choose my battles with him.

"Where do you think he disappeared to?"

"If I knew, it wouldn't be a disappearance, would it? Azrael and his river are of no concern to you right now. Just know that the magic in those waters is stagnant, but volatile. As drawn as you may find yourself to it, do not allow yourself to be overcome by your impulses—especially in this case. The amount of shadow magic in those depths would consume you on impact."

I wanted to press, ask more of Azrael, of the river, but I knew Lucifer well enough now to understand that this was his way of ending the conversation politely. Instead, I studied the shoreline, marveling at how still the current was—almost like the river was holding its breath, waiting for its master to return to release it. My gaze latched onto a lone figure, dressed in black, standing so close to the shoreline that a single misstep would find him toeing it.

Squinting, the lines of the figure grew clearer. "Is that Sam? What's he doing so close?"

Lucifer's jaw clenched, his exhale loud as he nodded. "He's as drawn to the river as you, though for different reasons."

I waited, silently praying that Lucifer would continue if I just bit my tongue.

When his eyes darted to mine, a knowing look in their depths, he continued. "His home is on the other side. He has not been able to access it since Azrael's departure."

Ralph let out an uncharacteristic whine, his tail wagging like he wanted to go to Sam. Their relationship was a peculiar one. And as much as Sam frustrated me, I'd be forever grateful that he'd not only sent Ralph to me, but taken care of him too in my absence.

I mean if Ralph liked him, he couldn't be as horrible as he seemed, right?

"Can't he just, you know," I made a popping noise with my mouth, my fingers digging behind Ralph's ear until he started thumping his back leg like a cartoon dog, "teleport to the other side?"

Lucifer's face lit up briefly with the vestiges of what looked almost like amusement, his eyes darting between me and Ralph, but when I blinked, it was back to the typical, impenetrable mask. "He cannot. The Styx is made up of a very powerful, very volatile form of shadow magic. Our magic is useless against it. The only way through is across. And the only way across is with Azrael—or his power source and someone strong enough to wield it. The dead have not fared well in his absence. I suspect there will be a reckoning for that soon. Our world does not do well without balance, and Azrael has always been the primary conductor of the scale between death and life. I do not know what the reapers have been doing in his absence, how they've been faring. If at all."

"Reapers?"

Lucifer's silence was answer enough—I wasn't going to get more on them or Azrael. He was already bored with that topic.

I tried another angle. "So that's why Sam stays here with you?" When Lucifer shot me a questioning look, I shrugged. "What? It's obvious you two don't exactly get along—or even like each other. But he has nowhere else to go. Also explains his general nihilism." I turned back to Sam, the wistfulness in the way he studied the Styx, the longing in his posture taking on a new form with this information. "It's kind of heartbreaking when you think about it. You've probably become the closest thing to a friend he has here."

Lucifer as your only friend? Fucking bleak.

"Samael's place here is a complicated one. One we have no time or need to discuss at the moment. You have far more pressing things to be concerned with and my time is limited with you." He studied me, his gaze sharpening as he scanned me, assessing. "I can sense that your powers have returned. That's good." Yeah, because he fucking tortured me until they reignited. Sanctimonious fuck. The small upturn of his lips—invisible almost—told me he knew where my thoughts had traveled. "Now tell me, what have you discovered in your time away?"

"I found the source of shadow magic you mentioned." I

tried to temper my excitement at the surprise widening his eyes—it was rare to catch Lucifer off guard, to impress him—but I could feel the smug grin pulling across my face anyway. "At least I'm pretty sure that I did, anyway. The Guild has a large stone, it looks like a much bigger version of your blade, and it sits in a pool of shadow magic. They've been using it to forge bonds between protectors. But it was how you said it would be—I felt an unmistakable pull to it. Power practically pulsed from it, intoxicating and impossible to ignore."

His eyes narrowed as he studied me. "How large was this stone?"

"I don't know—about," I estimated with my hands, feeling a bit ridiculous under his scrutiny, "this big?"

Something darkened in his expression, his jaw so tight he'd crack a tooth if he was human. "So my suspicions were warranted. They do have the Abraxas." He shook his head, eyes blazing as he stared at the river. I got the feeling Lucifer was very rarely off from his calculations—but it was clear in this case, he wanted to be. "And to use it for something so contrived. I wonder, then, when they stopped using stolen blades to manufacture their false bonds?"

The question clearly wasn't presented for me to answer, so I asked my own. "Abraxas?"

"Nevermind that, do you know where the stone is now?"

I shook my head, my chest tightening at the memory of the bonding ceremony. Something told me that if it was important enough to flare Lucifer's ire at just the mention of it, it wasn't something the council kept stored in an easy-to-access basement, carting out only when bonding new matches.

Not that I knew where the bonding ceremony had taken place anyway—I'd teleported in and out of it, drawn only by my connection to Atlas.

"Not an ideal answer." He sighed, his eyes landing on mine as he nodded once. "But that's a start. You've done well." I started to smile at the compliment before he added, "better than I expected you to, anyway."

I didn't bother stifling my eye roll. That was the closest thing to approval I'd likely ever get from Lucifer—which was maybe a good thing. I still wasn't sure what his intentions were, where I fit in this strange world-saving plan of his.

After what he'd put me through—what he'd put my team through—I didn't trust him for shit. For now, I wanted nothing more than to walk the tightrope with balance and focus—then when the time came, I'd decide on which side to fall.

But information was key, and I couldn't make moves until I had it.

"What will you do with it once you have it?"

He stiffened, his eyes darting from mine as the lines of his face sharpened. "Keep the hell realm from imploding and destroying all the beings here—and, most likely, all the beings in your realm as well. The details of which don't concern you yet."

"Lofty goals." I narrowed my eyes, focusing on him. There was something he wasn't telling me, I was certain of that much. It was rare for something to unsettle Lucifer, but I could tell that the true answer to my question—the one he wasn't yet trusting me with—did just that. "So what do I do now?"

He snorted, the sound strange coming from someone like him. "Other than finding it again, you mean?" His dark brow arched as he considered me, weighing how much to give, how much to let me in. I seemed to pass his assessment, somewhat at least, because he actually kept going. "We require three things to stabilize the shadow magic containing this world: the Abraxas, the nexus, and you. Right now, we have none of these."

I waved my hand awkwardly, from head to waist, stepping around Ralph in case the bulk of the hellhound was covering too much of me from sight. "Pretty sure I'm right here."

With a small yip that would have been better suited coming from a pomeranian than a giant hellhound, Ralph closed the distance between us again, leaning against me with so much of his weight that I stumbled slightly, wrapping my arms around his neck to keep from falling on my ass.

Lucifer glanced down at me, and I shrank at the clear judgment lining his face. The results of his assessment were clearly less ideal this time—whatever he was searching for was decidedly lacking. "Until you are at your full strength, you stand no chance of being of any use to me. In fact," he shook his head, shoulders tensing, "you're more of a liability than useful at the moment. The odds of you landing in enemy hands are significantly higher than you achieving your potential. Sometimes I think the wiser, kinder thing would be to keep you locked here."

I clenched my jaw, waiting for him to finish his thought, knowing full well that if the devil himself wanted to keep me a prisoner in hell, there was very little that I could do to resist.

"But," he said, drawing out the word as he nodded towards Sam's retreating figure, "he's convinced that your power will only strengthen as your bonds do. And unfortunately, there's very little that I can do to assist with that."

"Bonds? Like with my team, you mean?"

He nodded. "Life bonds have been absent for many years. But the mere fact that your friends were able to access you here, that they could pull through the barriers erected around this place and come into my domain uninvited—it is clear that they are returning. At least where you're concerned anyway. While you're here, we can train you—teach you to control the power you don't fully understand. But that power will only strengthen as your lifeforce is bolstered by theirs. It is the way."

"That's why you haven't killed them? Why you saved Wade near Headquarters that night?"

"I owed Serae and Wade's mother a favor." Serae was

Wade's aunt—a succubus that had been helping him, and later me, to control and use our powers. "It just so happened to be doubly beneficial for me in that I was able to use him to bring you to me."

"You'll let me return soon then?" I kept the hope from my voice as much as possible. Now that my powers were returning, I desperately wanted to return to the cabin. The sooner I did, the sooner I could rescue Atlas from the hell The Guild and that drude thing were putting him through.

"Soon, yes. Tomorrow in fact." His lips flattened into a thin line. "Though I'll expect progress from your end soon. We are running out of time and, like I said, we have none of the three things required to complete the ritual. You must train, every single day—not just sparring but your powers as well."

"Yeah, yeah, it's like a muscle," I said, echoing something he or Sam had mentioned before.

He flared his nostrils, looking down at me. "Yes well, mock all you want, but right now you're no better than a baby deer, all gangly limbs and little control. Prey. We need you to become a lion."

Tall order. I knew we were dealing with some serious shit, but a part of me enjoyed poking Lucifer, finding the cracks in his rigid demeanor. It was, perhaps, one of my deadliest coping mechanisms to date.

I pressed my face against Ralph, drawing from his strength, his comfort, to quell the anxiety clogging my airway. It was a lot—knowing that the literal fate of the world rested on my shoulders. According to Lucifer anyway. Part of me hoped he really was lying about everything, that his plan was truly nefarious—so that failing to live up to his expectations would actually benefit the world, not condemn it.

But hope was not the same as reality, and I could sense the world shifting, the realm collapsing, the stability and balance wavering. I knew that even if he wasn't telling the whole truth, he wasn't completely lying about what was happening either. It was hard to deny the truth when I was met with it at every turn.

"It's an honor, you know?" He cocked his head to the side, studying Ralph. "How that hound is with you. A mark of pure trust—something not often found in this place. The hellhounds here rarely let anyone but Sam within arm's reach of them. And they aren't even like this with him." His lip curled as Ralph nudged me with his head, preening at the compliment. "Then again, perhaps this one is defective."

Ralph growled, head bent forward as he turned towards Lucifer.

Would Ralph attack Lucifer? Probably not. But I didn't want to wait around to see if it was a possibility. Something told me that Lucifer's patience with the hound only extended so far.

"And the nexus?" I asked quickly, drawing his attention back to me and away from the staring contest with Ralph. "It's the third thing you mentioned."

"It is."

"Well—" I bit back a retort at Lucifer's deliberate resistance to offering anything that wasn't explicitly asked. It was one of his most infuriating qualities. Of which there were a fucking lot. "What is it?"

"The origin."

"Of what?" My jaw locked into place as I tried to melt the frustration simmering in my bones.

He was silent for a long time—so long that I actually started turning back towards the castle, tugging gently on Ralph to follow me.

If good old Lucy wasn't going to answer, there was no use wasting time out here when I could be training. I had to meet Sam soon for our session anyway.

"Of the realms," he whispered, stopping me in my tracks. I got the feeling he was trying to keep me around for a little while longer, though I had no idea why. Maybe even the devil grew lonely in this realm. "I believe it will be where the original ritual took place, during the creation of this realm. That kind of power leaves an indelible imprint. It is a power that will need to be channeled again—once more."

I turned around slowly, like any sudden movements would remind him of his general need to be cryptic and unhelpful.

"Believe?"

He shrugged. "That kind of power—where and how it settles, what it's connected or chained to—is unpredictable. I don't know that I would necessarily call this kind of magic sentient, but it has a way of staying hidden, revealing itself only when—and to whom—it sees fit."

Great. More unpredictability and half-answers.

"I'll need to find that too, won't I?"

His dark eyes found mine as he nodded. "I thought I would be able to handle that part. But with things as unstable as they are, I have a feeling I won't be able to leave this realm again until the ritual is completed. I'm now beginning to question whether the brief glimpses of your realm that I've allowed myself in the past year have caused things to," he gestured absently, "shift with more haste than they otherwise might have. It was reckless of me—I should've assumed that would happen." He shook his head, a shadow hollowing out his expression. "Even I make the occasional mistake out of eagerness, out of yearning. I've been searching for another way for me to leave this plane again, but I'm now quite certain that there isn't one."

I narrowed my eyes, trying to parse the flicker of something in his as they stared into me. Lucifer had a way of making it feel like he could not only peel back each layer of my thoughts until they were bare to him, but also rearrange and control them if he so desired. It clearly wasn't a skill that I'd inherited.

His secrecy made sense now. Perhaps his position was more vulnerable than I'd realized. He was always traveling, always on some secret mission. Was this why? Because he was stuck here, imprisoned again just when he thought he'd been granted his freedom out?

This was, perhaps, the first weakness of his I'd identified. The kind of information that could become a powerful tool down the line.

"Why?" I asked, greedy for more.

But his face relaxed into its typical mask, and I knew I'd get nothing more from him right now.

It was okay. For once, I felt like I'd emerged from a conversation with him the victor. Not only did I learn about his limitations, but I knew the exact things he was after—my power, the abraxas, the nexus.

And so long as he wanted me at my most powerful, I also knew he wouldn't harm my friends.

Not when they were so instrumental in obtaining that goal.

My power, the abraxas, the nexus.

I repeated the three things in my mind over and over again, until they were stuck there on an infinite loop.

∼

Fire flared along my skin, climbing the flesh of my fingers until it kissed its way along my forearms.

"Good. That's better. You're getting your control back." Sam prowled around me, his striking blue eyes tracking every flicker of flame, every muscle I flexed with a heady focus. "Again."

I sucked in a deep breath, fighting my urge to resist the request. It had been over an hour of this—me calling my fire, faster and easier each time. Then he'd have me throw it, get it to emerge around me, without touching me. Sweat caked my forehead, but I nodded, pulling and quenching the flames and then flickering them to life again.

When I thought I'd collapse from the effort, he handed me

a small cup of water, expression stern as he studied me. "Five minutes to break and then we work on teleporting."

My stomach sank at the thought, knowing that using that power took far more from me than summoning hellfire. And while I'd tried on my own a few times since feeling the renewed strength pulse through my veins, I hadn't been able to so much as move my body an inch.

Atlas.

Teleporting was the key to getting him back to us.

"No break," I said, panting as I finished the water. "I can start now."

"Very well." He leaned against the wall, the flicker of hellfire in the sconce above him licking strange colors of light against his face. There was a darkness there, in the depths of his eyes. And though Sam was often more teasing than Lucifer, I reminded myself that I'd do well not to assume that meant that he carried less power. That he was less dangerous. Something told me that the two men were evenly matched—otherwise, I had a feeling one of them would be dead by now. "When you're ready."

Twenty minutes of straining, and I'd managed nothing.

Ralph was growing restless as he watched me from the doorway, occasionally releasing small whimpers when I fell over or gripped the wall for strength. I felt his head nuzzle under my arm, providing a solid foundation to lean on after a particularly painful attempt.

"I'm okay." I scratched behind his ear, ignoring Sam's glower as he watched us. "Go back. I'll be fine."

Again. I'd try again and again until I was nothing but a husk. I wasn't leaving until I had at least some control of this power back.

My legs shook under my weight as I strained to reach for it, to visualize the sensation of my body dissolving and reforming into something new, to feel the air shift as I materialized in a new environment.

I fell on my ass, my chest heaving in deep breaths. "Fuck."

"Your frustration with yourself is making it worse." Sam's voice was void of emotion, but somehow that just made me angrier. It wasn't like I could turn off my own—like I could simply stop being frustrated just because he said so.

I used to be able to do this. And now, when someone I cared about depended on it, I couldn't. Frustration didn't even begin to cover the rage coursing through me right now.

"Go get the boy." At first, I thought Sam was speaking to me, but when I turned and saw Ralph heading to the door, turning back with one hesitant look in my direction, I realized he wasn't.

The boy?

"Why do you need Eli?" One hand digging into the wall nearest me for purchase, I drew myself back up to full height. I ignored the tremors pulsing through my body, the way nausea turned my stomach, and met his eyes with as much confidence and power as I could channel.

Sam and Lucifer hadn't been opposed to using my team against me in the past—harming them in order to motivate me.

As if reading my mind, Sam shook his head. "The last thing you need right now is more pressure. I'm hoping the boy will lend you strength. If—"

The soft echo of footsteps announced Eli's presence. The moment he saw me, his posture tensed, jaw muscles clenching as he threw a glare at Sam. Without a word he ran to me, his hands holding my face with a gentleness so at odds with the pure fury emanating from him now.

"What the fuck are you doing to her? She needs a break. You're going to kill her like this." Without moving away from me, he turned to Sam, teeth grinding as his heavy stare watched him.

"Neither of you give a fuck about her, do you? You just keep pushing, hoping she'll get strong enough to save your asses. You don't care that you're running her into an early grave in the process."

"She is plenty strong, she's just untrained." Sam arched one of his brows, amusement flashing briefly as he studied us. "It would take far more than this to kill her. And what she needs is to not be coddled. She is not fragile, weak—treating her as such is a disservice to the power flooding her veins. There are more dangerous things than a training session coming for her—the sooner she's equipped to handle them, the safer she'll be. Now," he narrowed his eyes and tilted his head forward, "why don't you make yourself useful and channel that rage you're flaring in my direction into something that can help her."

"I—" Eli opened his mouth, closed it, the lines of his face softening into confusion, and then, determination. "How?"

"Your bonds, as they are forged and strengthened, will ultimately allow you to transfer power—you will strengthen each other. It is one of the reasons they are so coveted, one of the reasons The Guild tries so hard to craft them in their own way." Sam turned to me. "Try again. Focus on your connection to him."

I pulled Eli's hands from my face and crossed to the other side of the room, not wanting to accidentally teleport half of him with me. I was still kind of murky on the dangers of teleporting and I'd seen enough sci-fi and fantasy movies to scare me into exercising care.

Closing my eyes, I searched within the compartments of my mind—I'd created so many different rooms in the past weeks, so many different boxes, that it was becoming cluttered and difficult to move through. But this time I didn't just hunt for my ability to shift through space—I hunted for Eli. It only took a few seconds for me to find the tether between us.

I usually saw it as a rope, my mind creating visualizations of a magic I didn't fully understand—manipulating it into something I could feel, reach for, use. This time, it wasn't just a rope—it was a thick, intricately-braided golden tether, flexible and strong. Impenetrable.

I reached for it, clasped my hands around the warm, soothing material, let it travel down to my toes, and then I gave it a tug.

"Okay," I said, feeling the smile in my voice—it was impossible to hide from the heady warmth now that I was holding onto it. Searching for Eli was like searching for the sun in the dead of winter—the light reflecting and refracting against the snow until it pulsed everywhere, the warmth fresh and intoxicating as it hit my cheeks. "I'm ready to try."

"Try?" Sam snorted. "You've done it."

I opened my eyes and found a familiar amber stare meeting mine—the flecks of gold shot throughout them not dissimilar from the shade of our bond in my visualization. "It worked?"

Eli's face split into a grin that made my knees wobble from more than exertion. "It worked."

"Again," Sam barked, still leaning casually against the wall—as if he was simply watching a boring chess match and not someone literally materializing through space.

I did it again. And again. And again.

I was exhausted and drained, but Sam was right. Having Eli with me helped, like there was a new store of energy that I could pull from.

Things were different between us now—stronger—and it felt like my power flared in his presence, like it wavered between us, not entirely his and not entirely mine.

Once I got the hang of it, once I became familiar with relying on our bond, I could even bring him with me when I teleported. It took considerable effort, but I could do it over short distances without dying from exhaustion.

Though when I tried to teleport with Sam, he didn't budge from the spot. Instead, I drained my strength as I pulled only myself to the other side of the room, my focus split on him and the distance between us.

It was a start.

And as much as I hated it, I knew Sam and Lucifer were right—it was a muscle. One I could grow strong through steady, consistent work. I just needed to nurture it.

Thanks to Cy and a lifetime of training, I was no stranger to this kind of work.

⁓

THAT NIGHT, curled into the warmth and safety of Eli's embrace, I reached for Atlas in my dreams. Dream-walking across realms was always more difficult, but I seemed generally able to do it when I focused on the energy bonding me to Six, to Darius.

This time, the moment I cracked into the seams of his dreamscape, I instantly felt the dark wrongness from before. I got little more than a glimpse—of Atlas curled in the fetal position, screaming as his fingers clutched at his head—before I was edged out, black curling smoke dissolving the image from my head.

I woke with a startle, my body coated in sweat, lungs gasping for breath as the sound of Atlas's anguish rang through my head.

Eli shifted next to me. "Max?" He sat up, hair tousled from sleep, and ran his arms frantically over me. "Are you okay? What happened?"

His hand reached for a blade under the pillow, but I grabbed his thigh, calming him, ignoring the flare of heat from his skin. "Atlas. It's Atlas."

Adrenaline eased into anxiety as his dark eyes darted between mine. "Is he okay?"

"No." I shook my head, my voice cracking. "No, he's not."

He wrapped his arms around me, hand cradling my face until I met his stare. "Max, you're doing everything you can. When we get back, we'll create a plan with the others, and we'll get him out. It's going to be okay."

Uncertainty echoed in his voice, like he was trying to convince himself as much as me.

"I—" I settled back down into my pillow, pulling him around me again. "I think I know someone who might be able to help?"

"Who?" His husky whisper caressed the shell of my ear, and I squeezed my thighs together.

Not now. My senses were heightened from letting the succubus flex inside me, but now was not the time to engage her other skills.

"Serae," I whispered, closing my eyes until the wave of lust dissolved into sleep.

The room was stunning, which shouldn't have surprised me. Serae was the type of person who dripped taste. She could probably make a paper bag look artistic and lush if she wanted to.

Dark velvet lined the modern furniture, one wall painted black and another pressed with an elaborate wallpaper that could have looked tacky under less a refined touch. Black and green plants carved paths down the shelves and bookshelves with their vines—pulsing with life as they wrapped around each other.

During my few sessions with her, we'd met in this room and I watched as she crafted it, using her power to mold the dreamscape as she desired.

"You're back." Her voice was a sultry whisper that trailed down my spine like a caress.

One second I was alone in the room, the next she was lounging on an elaborate chair, her full lips lifted in a small smile.

Today, she was dressed in a simple ivory silk slip that contrasted against her deep brown skin. Her dark hair was worn in long, intricate braids, pulled up in a tall bun.

Her skin seemed to glow with a vitality most people spent thousands trying to attain.

"I'm back." I smiled, taking her in, genuinely happy to see her after our time apart. Wade and I had trouble dream-walking to the hell realm when we weren't actually residing in it.

"That's good. Means you're still alive, still fighting. Don't lose that." She stood, crossed the room with a few graceful steps, and wrapped her hands around mine, pressing softly as her eyes narrowed with a playful mischievousness. "And my nephew? How is he?"

I studied her for a moment, considering, before she turned and dragged me over to sit on the burgundy couch.

With a soft, almost sad smile, she patted my knee. "What's troubling you? Is he alright?"

"He's," I searched for a word that would ring with truth, not wanting to deceive her, but not wanting to frighten her either. There was very little she could do for him from here. "Adjusting, I think. It's a lot, coming back into his whole world, feeling entirely divorced from it." It was a feeling I understood well. "I can tell he's still processing what Lucifer put him through." My teeth clenched at the thought of him locked in that cell for months on end. And for what? Just to draw me out and use him as a pawn? "That kind of trauma takes time to unpack."

"Mmm," she said, eyes narrowing as she nodded. "Yes, the boy has been through his fair share of changes recently. Time will heal. I hope."

"His father also learned the truth about him—or at least knows that he's not just a protector. He's always felt rejected by him, unwanted to some extent—in the shadow of his older brother. I think that being confronted with that rejection in such a tangible way, struck him with a precision, solidifying an insecurity that had never been truly confirmed before, if that makes sense?" Something about Serae's presence loosened my tongue, massaged my memory, allowing me to see my interactions and memories with Wade from an angle I hadn't noticed before, buried under my own shit. "And his brother, Atlas, was taken into Guild custody because he was protecting the rest of us." I took a deep breath, chest tightening at the memories of that day —it was as if I could see them play out before me again. "Wade holds a lot of guilt, a lot of anger." The words flowed from me as I told her things that I had only briefly allowed myself to consider. I'd been so involved in my own shit since Cy's death that I hadn't given Wade the consideration and time that I should have. I'd seen glimpses of course, here and there, echoes of the shadows clouding his mind, but he always tried so hard to mask his troubles, to protect us from them—to put me first. "I don't know how to help him, not when I can barely help myself."

Serae pushed a stray lock of my hair behind my ears, the sensation of her touch sending a relaxed tremor down my head. "You've all been through a lot, it is not expected that you will all come out of it as you were. Wade needs time to process, to heal. He's accepted his incubus nature, but that doesn't mean that he's found where he fits in the world he once inhabited. There has always been a darkness in him, one I think he assumed came from his demonic nature. I think he's probably only just realizing that it's a darkness harbored and nurtured by his father. That man," her eyes hardened as they met mine, "he represents everything wrong with The Guild—power hungry, selfish, rotten to the core."

"You knew Tarren?"

"Of him," she said, leaning back into the couch. She arched a thin, perfectly-shaped brow. "My sister spoke of him in a dream-walk with me once. He was beautiful, and she glowed under his attention, but she knew what he was."

"Why did she—" I shook my head, "sorry, that's not my place to ask, to judge."

"Why did she fuck him?" Serae didn't mince words. She grinned at the surprise on my face. "She gave her life to the cause. Lucifer needed a way into The Guild, needed to infiltrate, to get information—my sister carved a path. Once she set her eyes on someone, they didn't stand a chance. Tarren fell for her instantly." Serae shook her head, lost in a memory. "She was a hell of a woman. I think she probably fell for him a little bit too. Power attracts power." Her eyes darted to mine. "But a baby wasn't part of the plan."

"Tarren had no idea she was a succubus," I said, trying to remember what I knew of her, what I'd heard. "Thought she was a human."

A bright smile spread across her face, making her look even more stunning than she usually did. The joy spread across her skin, dancing as it laced her eyes. "Bet he hated how hard he fell. Would've loved to be there the moment he realized the truth—that she wielded more power than he ever would in her pinky finger." The joy melted into something softer, something sadder. "Anyway, I'm sorry that Wade was lost to me for so many years. We had no idea he was alive, that he existed. I only knew that she was gone."

"I'm sorry." I reached for her hand, squeezing it, finding my own grief echoed in hers when her eyes met mine.

She tilted her head, studying me as the wave of pain pulsed between us. Her free hand cupped my cheek as she nodded. "Yes, I believe that you are. Your pain won't always consume you, my girl. Neither will Wade's. You'll both find your way through it, to each other. Don't let yourselves pull back from the intimacy of it—there is great power in vulnerability, in trusting someone to share the burden you cannot carry alone.

Our kind, that kind of connection can infuse us with a beautiful power if we allow it to—if we don't let it destroy us. Now," she cleared her throat, and patted my thigh. "You did not come here to learn about our family or discuss my nephew. Why don't you practice here and now, unburden yourself with me. Ask what you came to ask?"

"How did you—" but the question evaporated with a look from Serae. It had long become clear that she could see and sense things that most could not. "Right. I was dream-walking to my other—" I dropped my eyes, guilt flaring through me, "I, um, Wade isn't the only one I'm bonded to."

Soft fingers lifted my chin until all I saw was the powerful confidence in her gaze. "Do not apologize for your connections. Humans have long expected a single relationship to do and accomplish everything they need, everything they crave. We know different. Connections, life bonds, like the ones you are forging—that is the most sacred power that we can tap. It demands trust, openness, an unflinching vulnerability most would run away from. Don't you."

I nodded, sat up straighter, tried to let her confidence, her wisdom, flow through my bones. "Right. Well, I was dream-walking to Atlas, Wade's brother. But there was this darkness manipulating the dreamscape, manipulating him. All that I felt was pain. It was so much stronger than me, and I could feel it draining him, draining me, even in the brief moments that I could push through to him before I was shoved out."

Serae's hands dropped to her lap, her jawline sharpening as she took in my words. It suddenly felt like the easy, languid peace of the dreamscape had been forfeited for a darkness, a creeping anxiety.

The careful warmth of the room seemed to darken, and I felt a chill raise the hairs on my arms.

Was that coming from her or was I just imagining it?

For a long time, Serae sat still, staring into the distance, frozen. Finally, she turned to me. "A nightmare." She shook her head, a sadness carving her features into a shape I hadn't seen before, but one no less beautiful than the other. "There is no defeating them, especially if it is not you it seeks. It's a battle between them. Nightmares are stronger than us. Creatures that feed on fear, that prey on a person's weaknesses—they will always win against our particular strengths. You will have a rough road ahead of you in saving him—I do not envy the many obstacles that litter your path. But the only thing you can do is get him away from the nightmare, remove its access to him. They require physical proximity to do their worst damage. And then hope that your connection will nurture his way back to you."

The silence stretched thick between us before she shot me a sympathetic look that made my stomach cramp with dread.

"Truthfully, girl, I have not encountered a true nightmare myself, but from what the stories say—you should prepare yourself for the possibility that death may be the kindest gift you can give him."

17

DARIUS

"How the hell do you know Bishop?" Wade asked. He was still holding Seamus, cradling him like a bride on her wedding day. If, you know, the bride also happened to be half dead on her wedding day.

I sighed, the deep breath plunging the tip of Bishop's blade into my skin.

Well, this was absolutely going to turn into the clusterfuck from hell I'd been afraid it would since the moment the incubus mentioned Dani's asinine plan.

Sure, let's go visit the small, secluded resort I terrorized years ago. The visit that eventually led to my being made into a lab rat, poked and prodded by The Guild's finest evil scientists. Because of fucking course.

I wasn't too worried about being the one who'd have to break the history down for everyone though, since it was taking all of my focus not to rip Bishop's blade from where it pressed threateningly against my sternum and bury it deep into his abdomen. Fucking prick. He clearly hadn't changed.

Let the record show that I was being the evolved, cordial

one in the scenario. Hadn't flashed fang, hadn't threatened decapitation. In fact, I was pretty sure I'd even said hello.

Protectors were fucking animals sometimes.

I would rise above this. One of the magazines Declan left me in the hotel had a whole article about affirmations, and mantras, and all that other new age shit that humans liked to pretend was actual magic. I couldn't blame them, living in a world of chaos and chance was a lot scarier than believing in something.

It was worth a shot. I had ten of them running on repeat in my head.

Affirmation 1: Don't kill Bishop...yet.

Affirmation 2: Actually, make that never. Max would probably be upset if I killed Bishop.

Affirmation 3: Do whatever you can to not upset Max.

Affirmation 4: There's a chance I'd have to kill more people here when they tried to avenge Bishop's death. Max hates it when people die.

Affirmation 5: Repeat Affirmation 3.

Affirmation 6: He was hardly a worthy adversary, killing him wouldn't be any fun.

Affirmation 7: His blood probably isn't even that good.

Affirmation 8: You're a strong, disturbingly good-looking vampire. You can do hard things—like not decapitate upon introduction.

Affirmation 9: If I killed Bishop now, then they probably wouldn't help us with Seamus, food, and places to sleep tonight—and it would be nice to have those things.

Affirmation 10: Oh, they've really built this place out since the last time I was here. Looks nice. I should get their contractor. Build Max something like this once the apocalypse settles down.

"Bishop?" Declan's face peered in the gap between mine

and the easy-to-anger protector-with-a-blade, scattering my mental flow. "How the hell are you alive? You, um, died," her eyes narrowed, surprise bleeding into focus, "like four—five years ago?"

"For fuck's sake, Bishop, let him go." A familiar woman charged at us, her thin fingers peeling the aggressive protector away from me. The man clearly hadn't changed in our years apart—all brawn, no brains, ready to jump into a battle he'd certainly lose. "I was afraid this was going to happen," she muttered to herself, "was warming up to explaining everything to him, but I wasn't expecting you for a few hours and things sort of got away from me. Been chaotic the past few months, as I'm sure you could imagine." Her dark eyes cut to me as she nodded, lips curling in a small, tentative smile. "Welcome back, D."

"Charlie." I grinned down at the pretty brunette. She was still as radiant as ever—light, golden-brown skin, a toned but curvy build, and dark eyes that saw and understood far more than she let on.

Those very eyes settled on mine, sparkling with a half-assed, teasing apology for her—judging by the surprisingly well-selected ring on her hand—rude husband. That look reminded me so much of Max that I wanted to hug her.

Gods, I hoped Max was okay.

"Explain." Declan had unconsciously positioned herself between me and Bishop, her eyes widening with the realization as she took a step to the side to give me some space. I ignored the bubbling warmth in my gut at the thought of her protecting me. "Please. What the fuck is going on? Bishop, how the hell are you alive? And where is Dani? Why did she tell everyone you were dead, when you are very clearly not? Why the fuck wouldn't she have given us a little heads up before we got here?"

"Before we get into all of this, can we maybe get a medic—

Dani mentioned you had one." Wade shrugged his shoulders, lifting Seamus into clear sight. "He doesn't have time for bickering, battles, or explanations."

Bickering, Battles, and Explanations—I'd read that book. Or at least the sparknotes version of it.

Bishop's shoulders dropped, the anger that crafted tense lines around his mouth loosening. "Is that Seamus?" With a quick glance between me and Charlie, he took a few steps towards the man, his fingers gentle, assessing, as he peeled back Seamus's fluttering eyelids. His jaw clenched as he studied him. "What the hell is wrong with him? Is he in—fuck was he bitten?"

"They're expecting him in the hospital wing." Charlie stared at Bishop, her voice brokering no argument. "Why don't you help—" she narrowed her eyes in question at Wade, before he gave her his name, "Wade—nice to meet you, I'm Charlie, Bishop's wife—get him to Greta and the others."

I smiled. Greta was here? Max would be pleased.

Bishop's jaw clenched as his eyes darted from me to the fiery woman next to me. "There's no fucking way I'm leaving you with—"

"There absolutely is a fucking way. Go." Charlie was several inches shorter than her husband, and significantly less muscular, but that didn't mean she didn't pack power into her presence. The harsh take-no-shit attitude dipped into a small, private look to Bishop. "I promise I'll be fine."

"If it helps," I added, ignoring the man's death glare, "I could've killed her years ago if I really wanted her dead. And —" I pointed to her with a flourish, "she's clearly alive and—" I winked at her, my grin growing at the growl that earned from Bishop, "flourishing."

"I'll go with you guys," Rowan said, gently nodding towards Wade and his heavy cargo.

Bishop nodded, and I sent a silent thank you to Max's

brother. Leaving Charlie with too many people he didn't know was only going to make the man act more like a neanderthal. He'd trust her survival better if it was just me.

"Explain." And Declan.

But everyone loved Declan.

"I've been here before." I shrugged, crossing my fingers in my pocket and hoping that she'd leave it at that.

The emerald fire in her eyes made it abundantly clear that hope would not become a reality.

"Dani told everyone that Bishop was dead many years ago," Charlie said, her voice calm and soothing as she studied me. "He wanted to leave The Guild, to stay here with me. And so they fabricated his death so that he could."

"Convenient," Declan said with a snort, but there was no malice in her eyes, just a little fraction of hurt. Grief was painful. And for whatever reason, she'd clearly experienced some with Bishop's fake death. "And Darius—how do you know him?"

"I attacked her, and then Dani captured me," I added helpfully, dodging Declan's elbow as it came bobbing at my stomach.

Charlie's hand swept to her neck, her fingers unconsciously tracing what was now a very small scar.

From me.

"Sorry about that," I said, surprising myself that I actually meant it. "You met me at a dark time in my life."

"Have you had a non-dark time in your life?" Declan asked.

"If you can believe it, I was even more fun back then," I shrugged, "if more murderous."

Charlie's eyes narrowed, again reminding me so much of Max that I half wondered if the resemblance was what had drawn me to this woman so many years ago. Sure, I tried to eat her, but even then, something about her fire had kept me from wanting to murder her. I'd had plans to turn her into a blood bag, sure, but a reusable one that I kept sparkly, clean, and happy. There was something very calming about her presence that drew me in. "You also saved me. So while, yes, you are an asshole for biting me, I've long forgiven you for it."

Ah right. Charlie had nearly died. I saved her—because, even then I had the rumblings of good-guy energy. But I'd forfeited my own freedom, letting Dani take me down in the process.

"And," she scrunched her nose, "I guess in a weird way, I wouldn't have my family if your trail of bodies hadn't brought Bishop here."

"You're welcome." I fingered the hole in my shirt that Bishop's blade had punctured. "But I do want to go on the record and say that I think you could do a lot better than him." I turned back to her, pleased with the reluctant amusement on her face. "Why did Dani send us here?" I studied the large, looming building before us. My memory wasn't perfect, especially because the last time I'd been here, I'd been letting the darkness more or less control me, but this building alone looked two or three times the size I'd remembered it. And there were dozens scattered throughout the clearing. "This place has changed a lot."

Charlie reached a hand out to Declan. "I'm Charlie by the way, Dani's told me a lot about you. She was really excited to report that you'd be joining us."

Declan considered the woman for a moment and then nodded, clasping Charlie's hand in hers.

"And as for why this place?" A soft smile lifted Charlie's lips as she opened the door for us and ushered us in. The restaurant I'd once met Charlie in was significantly larger than it had been last time—chairs, tables, booths scattered around a large room with a huge bar in the center. It still had the same homey warmth that it had back then, just with some major updates and extra space. "It's gotten a bit of an upgrade. The whole resort has, actually. We've added some extra buildings. Bishop and the others have been working tirelessly to make sure that we have enough space. And we've been keeping the books full—and removed most of our online presence—so that humans don't accidentally wander to our land anymore, hoping for a quiet vacation."

Curious stares met us from the scattered people working through their lunches. But when they saw Charlie's ease, the immediate tension seemed to release from them like dominoes.

"Enough space for what?" I asked, not bothering to hide my impressed perusal of the place. Bishop was a bit of a meathead, but the guy had done some really nice work with this place. Charlie deserved it. Even if I still didn't think that Bishop deserved her.

A fierceness flashed through her expression as she turned back to me, her mouth pressed into a grin that was as terrifying as it was pleased. "The Defiance."

"The what?" Declan sat on the stool Charlie pointed to, and I took the one next to her.

"Mer came up with the name." Charlie snorted. "Bit dramatic if you ask me, but she's used it enough that it's just sort of—" she tilted her head, nose scrunching, "stuck. Anyway, lunch service is ending, but I've got some leftover chicken pot-pie if that'll do for you both?" Without waiting for confirmation or further explanation, Charlie ducked to the back of the room, disappearing behind some saloon-style doors into what led to, I was sure, a much nicer kitchen area than the one I'd been in years ago.

"Well this is—" Declan shook her head as she took in the room. "Unexpected."

"You can say that again."

"Do you think we should stay?" she asked.

I held in my surprise that she seemed to be genuinely interested in my opinion on the matter and nodded. "There's always been something odd about this place. I found myself here years ago because I was drawn to it—even when it was considerably smaller and less populated. I'd like to find out why."

"Are you saying you liked this place before it was cool?" she chuckled, tapping her fingernails rhythmically against the counter. "Fucking hipster fanghole."

I bit back my smile

The same red-haired girl who'd initially welcomed us set two cups down on the bar counter—her lips split into a wide, pearly-white grin. "How about some water while you wait for food," she winked at me, "don't worry, Charlie's going to grab you a blood bag too."

Declan sipped the water around a bemused snort. "Thanks."

"Don't mention it," the girl said, her round, owl-like gaze locked on me with a familiarity I didn't reciprocate. "So, you're the infamous D, eh? I've heard a lot about you. Charlie says you're harmless." The girl's comically-bright eyes narrowed as she bent over the counter towards me, the threat clear as day. "But if you hurt her, or anyone else here again, I'll make sure it's the last thing you do. Got it?"

Declan choked on her water and turned to me. "How is it that you've pissed off every single person I've ever encountered from your past? Did you even try to be tolerable before Max?"

Before Max. I shivered at the memory. My entire world had reshaped and reformed around that girl. Fuck, I hoped she was alright.

I shook my head, trying to dispel the unwelcomed anxiety. I leaned in towards the girl, smiling as her arms tensed against the counter top. Had to give her credit though, she stood her ground—and knowing what I'd done to her friend, too.

"You're pretty brave for a human." A flash of pride gleamed in her eyes. "And don't worry. I didn't kill Charlie back then, and I won't now." People seem to be forgetting that I sacrificed my freedom to save her life. Would I do the same thing again if presented with the opportunity? Probably not. Then again, I wouldn't have met Max if The Guild hadn't played Evil Scientist on me. So yes, I would abso-fucking-lutely do it again. "Scouts honor. So long as no one hurts me or my friends, consider me no more threatening than a defanged vampire."

For a long moment, she studied me, turning my words over in those expressive eyes of hers before she nodded once and clapped her hands together like a judge pounding a gavel. "Excellent, I thought so—I had a feeling about you and Charlie was instantly onboard. Other than the first time she trusted you, her instincts are usually good. Welcome to the Defiance."

"People keep saying that," Declan grumbled, stealing my cup of water now that hers was drained, "and not explaining what it means."

"This lodge used to function partly as a resort, partly as an underground protector haunt. The latter I wasn't even aware of until a few years ago, despite the fact that I'd been running the restaurant for years." Charlie slid a piping-hot plate in front of Declan and the girl waited no less than two seconds before she started shoveling the warm food into her mouth. I didn't blame her, after the mediocre meals we'd made with canned food at Max's cabin, Charlie's cooking might as well have been the nectar of the gods. She slid her hand down her apron and looked up at me. "Don't worry, I didn't forget about you, D."

She tossed me a blood bag—the sort that hospitals used—and I plucked it easily from the air before it hit my chest.

Convenient.

Capri Sun, monster edition.

I stared at it, salivating, then looked around the room. The random spattering of people were watching us—attempting discretion by dropping their eyes whenever I turned to stare back, but I could feel their focus on the back of my head.

"Go ahead," Charlie said, tilting her head to watch me with

a coy, cat-like grin. "You're actually not the only vampire here, believe it not. No one will think twice about your dietary restrictions, so long as they're handled honestly and with consent. We all rotate with blood donations when we are able to." Her brows pinched together. "But if you go biting someone without their permission, that's a one-way ticket to getting kicked out of here, and probably with a blade through your heart if Bishop sees it happen."

Interesting.

"Hear that, Dec? Keep your teeth to yourself." I took a few long pulls of the thick liquid, thankful for the first taste of proper blood since drinking from Max a couple of days ago. This shit paled in comparison to her, but I had a feeling Max had long ruined all other meals for me. Still, this would do until she was back.

"You said this place used to be a resort." Declan had finally come up for air from her food, all but a few crumbs demolished. She was completely unfazed by the threats on my life. Suppose she was used to those by now, having given me many herself. She grinned as Charlie slid over a plate of fresh vegetables and fruits. Protectors always went googly-eyed at the sight of a balanced meal. Almost as insufferable about nutrition as gym bros. "What's the function of this place now?"

"Right," Charlie shook her head, "sorry, I'm kind of scattered at the moment. For the last few years, we've been taking in everyone. Mostly protectors, at first. But we've also got wolves, vampires—you name it. A lot of people choose to be anonymous about their backgrounds, when it's possible. Trust issues and what not. But we welcome anyone who doesn't feel welcome at The Guild, or who is trying to forge a different, unsanctioned path."

"You've probably noticed that things are getting extra wonky in the world," the redhead added with a conspiratorial wink. I'd almost forgotten she was there. "So now this place has become a community full of people wanting to help those who find themselves unrightfully under attack—a place for people to unite under a slightly less sanctimonious set of values."

"This is Mer, by the way," Charlie nodded in the direction of the eager woman. "She'll be helping you get settled into your rooms when you're done eating. We can give you a tour of the rest of the grounds once your friends can join us. Though I imagine they'll need food too, so I'll be sure to have some sent over to the medical ward." Her eyes met mine. "You'll find that a lot's changed since you last... visited us here."

A small, white furry thing hopped onto the counter, ramming its head into Charlie's hand. The creature's laser-like blue eyes landed on me, and I flew off the chair, landing unceremoniously on my ass.

Declan snorted, studying me from above with a smirk that made my cheeks flame. "A cat, Darius? Really?"

I stood up, dusting dirt and debris from my ass, and glared at the creature creeping towards me with interest. It let out a small meow and my lip curled in disgust.

Mer snickered. "You're not very brave for a vampire."

"To be clear, I'm not afraid of cats." I took a seat, tentatively, keeping one eye on the infernal beast as the three women shared teasing glances with each other. "I just don't like them. Feral, needy little things that clearly spend all their time plotting the demise of those around them. Like little demons in disturbingly furry packages."

When the cat inched towards me, clearly keen on ripping my throat out, I leaned back on the stool, nearly toppling it over again, while it swatted at the air where my chest had been.

Declan shook her head, a bemused expression stuck to her face with the permanence of a glue gun. "I've watched you literally disembowel people, and this is what has your heart racing like jackhammer? It's not even a cat. Barely a kitten—probably only a couple of months old."

"We have a family of strays that make their rounds through the grounds, so watch your back vamp," Mer said with a wink.

I cleared my throat, ignoring her, and focused my attention back on Charlie—keeping track of every move the beast made as it flounced between the girls. "And Seamus? What news do you have of him?"

That question ripped the amusement right off everyone's face. Good. Served them right.

Frown lines dimpled the corners of Charlie's mouth. "We'll do everything we can. Getting Greta here a few weeks ago was a big win—she's amazing. If he can be saved, she'll be the one to do it." She took a deep breath, her chest falling on a sigh. "But you know how these things can be. It's mostly a waiting game with wolf bites and we've been encountering a—"

"A what?" Dec prodded, leaning into the counter. Her brain was clearly going a mile a minute, devouring all this new information now that her ravenous hunger was sated. Protector mission mode, as Max called it.

"We're not sure if it's a new species of werewolf, or something injected in the venom that draws out the process, like a poison. But we've lost a couple to the bite in the last few months." Charlie squeezed Mer's shoulder softly and I wondered if they'd lost someone personally.

Why did I find myself caring if they had?

I cleared my throat, dropping my drained blood bag on top of Declan's empty dishes. "You said you had protectors here. All by way of The Guild? Or are they a different faction?"

Charlie cocked a brow, surprised by my question. "I won't reveal things about our guests without their permission. While we're all a lot more open about things than The Guild, we still honor the general need for secrecy and discretion. You'll have to talk to Bishop, to the rest of our community council before we tell you much more about what's going on here. As you know, information is a powerful weapon, so we have to be mindful about who we give the permission to wield it. Dani's already given us her vote of approval where you're all concerned, but we have to keep things honest and have a discussion with the rest first."

She leaned back against the shelves behind her, arms crossed over her chest. Now that I could get a good look at her, I noticed the dark circles under eyes, exhaustion drawing her expression down.

Made sense, she'd clearly not been idle in my time away.

The cat pounced onto the floor, disappearing behind the bar, and I held my breath until it made its way to the other end of the restaurant, finally putting a good thirty feet of distance between us.

"Your arrival was a bit more sudden than we expected, so we haven't all had a chance to speak about what your roles here will be—and with Seamus's condition, protocol got pushed to the backburner a bit," she added, nose scrunched in apology.

"I still don't understand why Dani didn't explain any of this to me before—on the phone, or in person." Declan straightened up on the stool, a trace of betrayal darkening her expression.

Unlike me, she wasn't used to being met with suspicion at every turn. Not from her friends.

I kicked my foot gently against hers, offering a soft smile when her eyes met mine.

"Knowing Dani?" Charlie and Mer shared a knowing smile, "probably didn't explain on the phone because she didn't want to give you the chance to overthink it. She's been going back and forth about finding a way to get you here specifically, Declan—but she knew that you don't lend out your trust to people easily." Charlie shrugged. "This place, with this many people from all over the world? What we're fighting for? It takes a leap of faith. She had to wait until she was certain you were ready to jump without looking back."

"Or without knowing what you were jumping into." The other woman, Mer, grinned a devilish, teasing smile. "Dani cares about you a lot—we just made her wait until she was certain you weren't a Guild lapdog anymore." She narrowed her eyes slightly, the warmth still radiating from them. "Dani also says you're very stubborn, so it was a matter of getting you to trust her enough to reach out once she gave you the option. But once she realized you were clearly already involved in your own covert, unsanctioned shit—" she raised her palms up when Dec stiffened next to me. "Don't worry, like Charlie said, we totally respect the need for discretion and privacy. We won't pry much, so long as we know you aren't aiming to harm innocent people."

"You seem human." I studied the girl, looking for any of the usual supernatural tells. It wasn't always obvious, but I typically had a decent gauge for this sort of thing, thanks to spending so much time with Marge back in the day. "How do you know so much about the supernatural world?"

"I'm dating an ex-Guild member, current werewolf." She shrugged. "And the people who live here—the ones around before this place became what it is now—they're my family. And now, so are some of the new people as well."

Declan cleared her throat, her eyes darting from me to the two women in front of us, discomfort and unease lining every tensed muscle in sight. "So we get Seamus help, then you have your community meeting about us, then what?"

Charlie cocked a brow, a shadow of a smile lifting the right side of her lips. "Then, like everyone else here, you'll earn your keep."

18

MAX

Eli finished his shower while I leaned against the large, oval window, staring at the calmness of the River Styx. I wondered now, if Lucifer gave us this room for the view, since he knew I was so drawn to the magic there.

Was it possible for him to be considerate, given the chance?

I honestly still wasn't sure. While he'd nearly killed me and my friends several times, he hadn't actually done the deed. And it was impossible to tell whether he would have intentionally succeeded. Plus, he was helping me get my powers back, no matter how questionable the process or how nefarious the reasons.

I wasn't shy or squeamish about crossing lines either. Since barging into The Guild with Ro and Cy, I'd taken more than my fair share of lives, done more than my fair share of highly questionable things. Some I regretted, deeply—others I didn't bat an eye at.

Maybe we all had a little darkness in us.

I'd just have to wait until Lucifer's shadier qualities revealed themselves in a clear light—then I'd know if they aligned with my values or not.

It was also possible that I was warming to him because this visit to hell was so much... softer?... than the others had been. Staying in the castle was a lot more pleasant when we weren't being holed up in the dungeon, starved, or repeatedly stabbed.

Granted, one of those things had happened on this visit, but I couldn't argue with the results.

The room Eli and I were in was large, the bed simple but incredibly comfortable. The decor was dark, ornate and had a grim sort of vibe to it, but I couldn't expect much else from hell. Or Lucifer.

Everything was cloaked in a blanket of darkness—but it was no less beautiful for that.

Even the daylight filtering into the room was cast in the gray, foggy haze that usually dissipated with dawn.

While the rest of hell didn't scream intricate opulence, Lucifer's small slice of it was like a gothic paradise.

"That shower was amazing. This place is kind of awesome when we aren't being tortured," Eli called from the bathroom, as if he was reading my mind. "Almost makes me question if hell really is the prison Lucifer claims it is. Why's he so eager to leave this place?"

"A gilded cage is still a cage, I suppose." I forced my gaze away from the mesmerizing aura shrouding the Styx

"Fair point. I suppose all my years in The Guild, hiding under lies and false histories could be considered the same." Eli emerged from the bathroom, one towel rustling through the wet waves of his hair, another perched precariously low on his hips. "I forgot to ask earlier. Did you reach the others?"

My eyes locked onto the small trail of dark hair that drew a perfect, delectable line from his sleek, defined abs, down to the equally glorious part of his body just barely covered by cloth. Heat blossomed in my cheeks and suddenly I wanted to throw away our plans to find Sam and start our trip home, for another romp in the bed. Our options in the cabin were significantly less roomy and private. Surely another hour here wouldn't kill anyone. "What?"

A cocky, knowing grin twisted his lips, the look so trademark Eli that it only made me want to jump him more. Jesus, this man knew what the fuck he was doing with that look of his, all feral hunger and heat. "After Serae." He closed the distance between us, until all I could focus on was the heady smell of the soap still clinging to his skin, and the water droplets drawing slow, curving paths down it. "Did you reach Wade or any of the others?"

His thumb traced my bottom lip, the feel of his skin against mine sending a bolt of need flooding between my legs. Without permission from me, my tongue peeked between my lips and lapped at the pad of his finger, the salty clean taste of his skin enough to pull a needy whimper from my mouth.

The cocky gleam in his eyes dissolved into a heat that matched mine. Slowly, he pressed his thumb further between my lips until it dipped in my mouth, my tongue and lips enveloping it eagerly.

"Fuck, I want you." He took a step closer to me.

A heavy scratching sound etched into the door from the hall, drawing my very reluctant attention.

With a ragged, deep breath, Eli took a few steps back from me, adjusting himself under the towel.

The distance made it slightly easier to swallow down my arousal.

Hadn't Eli asked me something? I blinked a few times, replaying the last few moments.

Wade, the others, my dream walk.

"No." I walked to the door and opened it, smiling at the sight of Ralph taking up the entire frame. If I had to be robbed of the possibility of fucking Eli, Ralph was pretty much the only uninvited guest who wouldn't earn my wrath from the disappointment. His tongue swept from my chin to my nose—and while I appreciated the affection, the drool I could do without. Wiping it off, I shook my head, chuckling at his eager hello. "After Atlas I was really drained, and then by the time I was finished visiting with Serae it was already morning. We'll see them in a few hours, hopefully."

The thought of seeing them all again reignited my excitement to get back. I knew they were alive, that they'd survived the ambush at the cabin. I'd know if they weren't—but I still needed to see it with my own eyes, to make sure they were okay.

It had been less than two days since we'd been torn away, but it felt like so much longer.

Ralph shuffled into the room, claiming Eli's free hand for some morning scratches.

A significantly larger shadow cannibalized me in the doorway, and I looked up into the bright, ethereal eyes of another familiar hellhound.

"You're back!" I wrapped my arms around the creature's neck, burrowing my face in the fluffy waves of its chest. While Ralph was still my favorite pup of all time, this hellhound had earned his own special place in my heart. He'd helped me out of a few tight spots in the past, and I had a feeling that he watched out for Ralph when I wasn't around. "I was afraid I wasn't going to get to see you before we had to leave."

"Max," Eli's face blanched as he reached for me, but he froze when the creature growled, the sound reverberating through my chest as I leaned against him. "Fuck. Be careful. Not all hellhounds are like yours. They're still extremely volatile and dangerous. There's a reason everyone who meets Ralph is terrified of him at first."

I peeled myself off the creature and with a narrowed glance and chuff in Eli's direction, he leapt onto the bed, making himself comfortable in the pile of blankets as Ralph settled into an awkwardly large ball at my feet.

"He won't hurt us," I considered the hound for a moment, holding his blue-eyed stare with my own, and shrugged. "I don't think he will anyway. He's had more than enough chances to swallow me whole in the past and hasn't. That's got to count for something, right?"

Eli grunted, tossing away his towel as he fished through the fresh clothes that had been left for us in the wardrobe. "Forgive me if that's not entirely comforting."

It took massive amounts of effort to pull my eyes away from Eli's dick and focus on the conversation. When I turned back to the blue-eyed hellhound instead, I could've sworn he was mocking me for the effort.

Could hellhounds mock? This one sure as hell could.

I narrowed my eyes at him and bent down to scratch Ralph's belly. It hurt every time I had to leave him behind, but I knew that with things as chaotic as they were, staying here with Sam and his friends was the best thing for him. Knowing Lucifer's fickle, impatient ways, I'd probably be ripped back into this corner of the universe in a few weeks anyway.

"Tell me again what we need for Lucifer's mysterious ritual?" Eli's words were muffled as he pulled on a shirt, covering the glorious spread of lean muscle on display.

I smothered my frown and ran through the list. "My power at full capacity, the abraxas stone—which we now know for sure the council has. It's just a matter of locating and stealing it. And then the nexus."

It was probably the third time I'd run through the items, but like me, I could tell that Eli held onto them like an anchor. After feeling directionless for so long, it felt like we were finally getting somewhere.

He nodded, then started to sit on the bed but changed direction with a startle when the hellhound shot him a daring look. Eli was right. While Ralph's friend might tolerate us, there was a predatory danger about him that Ralph never possessed around us. And while I was fairly certain that he wouldn't kill me, something in his energy made me less certain about Eli's chances.

Swallowing his pride and throwing furtive glances at the creature taking up most of the bed, Eli started collecting his blades and random articles of clothing from the room. "And he gave no hints about this nexus thing?"

"Not really, except that it's a place, not an object." But I shook my head, considering for a moment. "If he has any clue, he didn't share it with me. Just that it's the point where everything began."

Where would one decide to create a new realm? It all sounded so ominous and apocalyptic.

"You have your thinking face on." His mouth curled into a feral grin that I wanted to lick. "Care to share with the class?"

"It's a feeling more than anything." When he lifted his brows, signaling for me to continue, I exhaled my hesitance and did. "Well, it's just that we know that my—that Sayty's family was from the line that originally created hell. According to Cy anyway, and the stories she shared with him."

"You think they're still guarding it?"

"I don't know. There's got to be a way to trace back to them though, back to that moment and find out where they were. Her line was assumed dead, according to Guild archives—"

"Which we now know are not entirely accurate," Eli added, sliding his dagger into the holster at his waist. "They've rewritten history before."

"Right, and I mean," I shrugged, "I'm here. So we know the line didn't end. But Cy—" I swallowed back the wave of emotion, ignored the tightness in my chest, and tried to focus on the warmth radiating from Eli's eyes. "My last conversation with him, he mentioned that Sayty had a brother. A twin. Saif. He couldn't find him before—" I waved my hand awkwardly, "well before—you know. But maybe we could? And it's not impossible that he'd have information we could trace, a path to follow. Even just one breadcrumb could potentially lead us to another."

"Brilliant." Eli pressed a kiss to my forehead, and I could feel his smile lingering against my skin. Warmth tingled down my spine and I tried to ignore the flutter in my belly. Would it always be like this? This attraction between us? Now that we'd finally stopped trying to fight it, it was impossible to ignore. It was like Lucifer's stabby technique had done far more than reawaken my powers. The bonds that I'd starved for so long were flaring back with a vengeance that would obliterate us all. Thankfully, there were worse ways to die. "You're brilliant."

"It's nothing concrete." I didn't want us to get too excited. We were still a long way from what we needed. I leaned into his embrace, inhaling his scent—buried underneath the fragrant, fresh soap, I clung to the warm, familiar spices that were all Eli. "And even if we do find it—the nexus—I don't know that it's necessarily the ideal scenario. That we hand it over to Lucifer —that we're done—you know? I still think Lucifer is keeping something big from us, from me."

"Well, it's a start. And even if we don't give the information to Lucifer and Sam, knowledge is still power." He grunted, grabbing my hand on his way to the door. He paused, letting the hellhounds filter out first and lead the way. "Hopefully Saif keeps better company than your mom." He turned back to me, cheeks flushed. "Sorry, no offense to her of course. But I mean Lucifer and Samael? They're both a couple of raging dildos sometimes." The blue-eyed hound stopped short, causing Eli to stumble against the wall in his effort to avoid the collision. When the hound shot a sizzling glare behind him, I knew it was intentional. "Fuck. I swear this one hates me."

Lofty opinions of his master aside, I was honestly thankful for the hound's guidance. I still couldn't find my own way through this castle—there were so many winding hallways with towers and floors that were only accessible through a very specific path. It was a labyrinth built to make escape almost impossible.

"No offense taken, though I have no animosity towards dildos."

"Fair enough, raging dickholes then?" he asked, his brow arched playfully.

The hound growled, the sound echoing ominously as it reverberated around the hall.

"This oversized dog is going to tear me to shreds the first chance it gets," he muttered.

The hound added some extra pep in his step, clearly pleased with his attempts at terrorizing Eli.

"I still can't make my brain process the fact that she was actually, you know, *with* Lucifer." A jitter of disgust rattled through me. The devil might be pretty, but he was still the fucking devil. "And I think he legitimately cared for her too. As much as someone like him is capable of caring, anyway."

Eli furrowed his brows, bent in concentration for a few silent moments. "In a weird way, it kind of makes sense." He squeezed my hand as we found our way outside. "You're kind of the throw-caution-to-the-wind-and-run-full-force-into-danger type yourself, Max. It's not entirely far-reaching to imagine your mom doing the same, is it?"

"I prefer to think of myself more like the cautiously-walking-into-uncertainy-because-I-have-no-other-choice type, thank you very much."

"You freely spend your time with an absolutely ridiculous vampire, a feral werewolf, an incubus, and you act like your hellhound is nothing more than an overgrown golden retriever. I'm sure you look absolutely batshit to outside forces too."

Touché. When I narrowed my eyes at Eli, he wrapped a heavy arm around my shoulders and squeezed, his silent laughter rolling against me like satin.

There was a slight chill in the air as Ralph started circling around us at a fast gallop, his tongue lolling out of the side of his mouth.

"To be fair," Eli added, shaking his head, "it's hard to argue with the golden retriever thing sometimes."

I scanned the horizon, looking for Sam, but stiffened when a tall man I didn't know came into view. Ralph calmed his playing and resumed his place at my side, so that I was smashed between him and Eli.

The blue-eyed hound didn't seem concerned, and guided us towards the man.

Everything about the man screamed average—dark hair, dark eyes, dark clothes. There was a flatness about him though, like I'd pass right over him if he was in a crowd.

"Hi," I said, stretching the word out awkwardly as we came to a stop before him. His dark eyes landed on me, his focus heavy and almost familiar. "Do I know you?" When he didn't say anything, I did what I did best and just kept rambling. The guy wasn't giving off axe-murderer vibes, but he wasn't exactly a Care Bear either. "I'm—erm, Max, this is Eli. We were supposed to meet Sam here. Do you live at the castle?" Eli squeezed my shoulder, signaling me to shut up, his frame rigid against mine. "Right, I guess we'll just go back and wait for him."

"Why bother?" The man's voice was bored as his gaze lingered on the hellhound just a few feet from him. He was maybe the only person other than Sam and Lucifer who didn't seem startled by the creature. Instead, his thin mouth twisted into a lazy grin, before adding, "Sam's already here."

The blue-eyed hound growled, the sound low and deep.

"Um—" I scanned around us, trying to understand what the fuck he was talking about, but then the hellhound's bones started cracking. "Shit."

When I reached for him, to see if he was okay, Eli's arms wrapped around me and tugged me back.

Slowly, the hellhound shrunk, the black hair bleeding back to skin, its four legs shifting into two as it stood—until the only familiar feature left were the pair of otherworldly blue eyes boring straight into me.

"S-sam?" My mouth opened and closed like a fish searching for morsels of food as I stared at the—very naked—man in front of me and tried to completely rearrange everything I knew about him, the hellhound, and shifters all at once. "What the—how? I thought only werewolves?"

I was beyond full, coherent sentences.

Sam crossed his arms in front of his chest, not that it covered much up, jaw clenched tight as he turned to the stranger. "You should know better than to ruin my fun, Nash—I get so little of it, so it's precious when I do."

The man rolled his eyes. "I don't have time for this shit. I'm here as a favor to you and you're willfully wasting everyone's time."

"How?" I asked again, the word harsh and cracked as I mentally filtered through all of my interactions with the hellhound during my time in the castle.

Fuck. He'd heard us talking shit about him and Lucifer. Which meant he also knew that I didn't trust them.

Panic flooded my chest, making it difficult to breathe, until I remembered that I'd already told them both several times over that I didn't trust them.

Sam's brow arched as he watched my mental gymnastics, amusement twisting his lips into the shadow of a smile.

"Hang on—" Eli's brows lifted, a horrified realization sliding over his face. "You saw me naked." His lips flattened into a thin line, his normally playful eyes tight as they cut to Sam. "What the fuck you, dickhole? You can't just prance around as a hellhound without telling anyone—that's an invasion of privacy."

Sam glanced down at his very unclothed body, while I did

everything I could to keep from doing the same thing, to keep my focus north of the border. "Looks like we're even now though, doesn't it, you—" Sam grunted. "What did you call me? A raging dildo?"

I felt Eli tense against me, but grabbed his hand and squeezed. Now was not the time to attack Sam. In fact, never would be the time. Eli didn't stand much of a chance against an ancient in the first place. But Sam was, apparently, even more powerful than I originally thought.

Wait.

Did that mean?

My stomach dipped as my head whipped around to Ralph. "Is he—"

"No," Sam answered, before I could finish forming the question. "I'm the only one of my kind. The only one who can shift into a hellhound."

"Have you—" Eli stood taller, his grip tightening around my fingers. "Have you seen Max naked too? Because if she didn't know and you—"

"For fuck's sake," Sam ran a hand over his face looking suddenly as exhausted with Eli's presence as he had in hellhound form. "No. I don't make it a habit of seeing people in the nude. You just happened to whip it out before I even knew what was happening." A grin that danced between teasing and danger lifted the corners of his eyes. "Hell, it wasn't even a particularly impressive show. I hope for her sake, the girl's other prospects are little more—" he moved his palms apart, the distance growing, "well, more."

Eli didn't react, just chuckled at Sam's antics, any lingering anger gone at Sam's concession that he hadn't seen me.

We both knew that he was packing. And now, so did Sam.

"Can we get a move on, this reveal is all a bit," the stranger's jaw was tight as he studied us, not even bothering to hide his annoyance, "tedious."

Sam snorted. "You'd do well to remember that your invitation here is a conditional one as it stands, Nash."

"Nash?" I studied the man trying to remember where I'd heard that name. It took less than a second of sifting through my encounters to recall Darius's friend—er, sort of friend—who we'd spent an evening spying on. While there were some vague similarities between the vampire and the man before us, they were very clearly not the same person. "Is that a common name? I've met a Nash here before."

"You've met *him*," Sam said, cocking his head, a dark smirk shining in his eyes. "Nash often wears a glamour, especially when doing portal duty. Hard to be a guardian of the realm when everyone knows you—and what you look like. This adds a layer of protection." Sam's amusement only grew at the anger now radiating from Nash. "Once you know to look for it though, you'll be able to see through it easily. Kind of a useless parlor trick in that way, if you ask me."

"The entire point of a glamour," Nash said, words sharp and cutting, "is to keep it a secret."

Sam shrugged. "Serves you right for announcing my finale when I wasn't yet done with the game, old friend."

The word "friend" coming from Sam's lips didn't bring with it the warm tenderness the definition suggested. Whatever ease the two had with each other was nowhere close to a friendship.

As if the words themselves were magic, I watched the stranger closely, the unfamiliar features shifting and blending until I was staring at a very familiar face.

While he'd originally seemed average, the man now in front of me was anything but. His hair was a few shades darker than it had been, the lines of his face more defined and angular, and coiled, lean muscles were evident under his plain clothes. But it was his eyes that were particularly remarkable. They were a dark, cloudy gray that revealed a storm in their depths.

"It is you." I shook my head, the double reveal throwing my

entire concept of reality for a spin. "Hang on, did you portal us out last time too? Was that you, but with a glamour?"

The memory of that day was hazy, but I did recall a man there—one who'd been glaring flaming daggers at Darius. It fit.

Nash did nothing but tilt his head, a flicker of amusement in his expression, so brief I could've imagined it.

Our first introduction had been a short, tense one. And while the man clearly hated Darius, I hadn't exactly given him a reason to like me beyond that association.

Maybe he'd forgotten though? As a guardian, he was probably incredibly busy and dealing with loads of violent demons in hell. Odds were in my favor—ish.

"Please avoid elbowing me in the dick and holding a dagger to my neck this time, if you can, bloodbag." His expression didn't change, but that amusement I thought I'd imagined earlier, was flaring again in his eyes.

Well, he clearly did remember our encounter, so there went that possibility.

"Er," I cleared my throat, shrugging sheepishly. "Sorry about that. I've been under a lot of pressure lately. Sometimes it's easier to go with a more aggressive approach. When in hell and all of that."

Sam belted out a laugh, loud enough to startle me. I'd never heard such a genuine, unadulterated spark of emotion from him—and judging by the shocked expression on Nash's face, he hadn't either.

"Elbowed you," Sam bent down, hands clutching his knee —still naked as the day he was born, mind you, "in the dick." He turned to me, blue eyes shining with a warmth that pulled a reluctant smile from me. "I knew I liked you." The humor dried up into something softer. "You really do remind me of her sometimes."

I clenched my teeth, fighting back the surge of—sadness? pride?—that threatened to wash over me.

As if sensing the shift, Eli squeezed my shoulder and turned to Nash, eyebrow arched in challenge. "My money's on you likely earning the dick hit."

"Same," Sam echoed, the two of them sharing a glance, likely both shocked by agreeing on something.

"I'm glad to see that you're still alive, anyway," Nash's focus was on me, completely ignoring the others, "though disappointed that you're still keeping questionable company."

Without another word, he drew a blade and carved a thin line down his palm. Blood pooled in his hand and I watched, in awe, as he materialized a portal from it.

Where Claude and Darius seemed to require a consistent, stable portal—one that was currently functioning in Seattle—Nash seemed able to generate one anywhere. Like *he* was the portal, rather than the guardian of it.

I wasn't sure whether it had more to do with the instability of hell or that he was more powerful than the others, but I knew better than to ask. Sam had already revealed one of his secrets, I couldn't expect him to just hand the others over freely —not when the element of surprise could be the difference between life and death in hell.

"Alright then," I grabbed Eli's hand as we inched towards the portal. His grip was tight, and I knew he was already dreading the painful, debilitating tug between worlds. I turned to Sam and pointed with my free hand. "Don't think this whole hellhound-shifter discussion is over. After I've had time to process, you can bet your ass we'll be fully unpacking it next time I'm here."

His face split into a smile, blue eyes taunting and looking so much like the hellhound that it seemed absurdly obvious to me now that I knew the truth. "I'll be looking forward to it."

19

MAX

"Please," a dark, deep voice growled into the dark, "tell me how I knew it would be you?"

"Hi Claude," I mumbled, adjusting to the feel of having my feet back on the ground. The inbetween, usually a few moments of terrifying nothingness, had filled my ears with a soft humming song this time, like a woman far away calling to me. "Good to see you."

He shook his head, studying me. "Wish I could say the same."

I bit back a grin and the urge to tease him. Now was not the right time.

It was always a bit jarring to be faced with Darius's twin—as identical as they might be, the stark differences in how they carried themselves was impossible to not see.

Where Darius was always balancing between irreverent amusement and the darkness brought on by the tangled, warped shadow magic that corrupted him, Claude was polished, distant, a mask that only ever broadcast one emotion around me—annoyance.

Eli was crouched over, hands on his knees as he took deep gulps of fresh air.

We were in a large garden, but not one I'd seen before. Wherever we were, it was decidedly not in the janky back alley of Claude's Seattle bar.

"New portal spot?" I scanned the elaborate rose bushes lining the walkway down to a pond.

"Oh, I thought I felt something shift in the air," a quiet, ethereal voice murmured behind me. "I'm so glad you're still alive, Max Bentley."

Still?

I spun around, bemused, as I came face to face with Khali.

Dark, straight hair hung like a sheet down her back, framing a pale, thin face. She was dressed in a long, white nightgown, the lace and satin material speaking of a false fragility. I still had no idea what kind of supernatural creature Khali was, but she was one of the strongest I'd ever encountered.

Her magic had saved Eli from a certain death. The girl was anything but fragile.

"Hi Kh—" her name rolled into a grunt as she threw her arms around me, squeezing me in a surprisingly tight hug.

"Sorry." She pulled back, a pale flush coloring her cheeks as her dark eyes widened. "It's just so rare that I'm visited by a friend."

A soft smile tugged at my lips as I squeezed her hand. "Don't apologize, I'm glad to see you too."

"Khali," Claude stepped towards us, his annoyance with me bleeding into concern. His body strained with the invisible battle of trying to close the portal. "You shouldn't be out here. I haven't even closed this yet."

"I know, I can taste it in the air. I'm being reckless." She smiled a wicked grin and winked at me. "But with the world turning inside out, who could fault me a bit of recklessness?" At his groan of pain, her soft smile evaporated. "I really should be getting back." Her thin fingers squeezed mine, again the pressure stronger than I would've imagined her capable of. "I can sense you have to be hurrying on in your journey anyway, and I don't want to keep you. But if you're able, come see me soon. And it would be great if you could bring Darius too."

"Please don't," Claude muttered, wiping a fresh sheen of sweat from his brow. Like Eli, he was now bent at his knees, looking about two seconds away from vomiting everywhere.

Being a portal guardian seemed about as fun as going through Sam's training regimen.

I clenched my jaw at the thought of Sam.

My blue-eyed friendly hellhound, this entire. Fucking. Time.

"Goodbye, Max Bentley," Khali said, her voice like a chime on the wind.

And then, as quickly as she arrived, she left.

"I suppose I should be grateful to you," Claude said, a forlorn shake of his head.

"Why?" Eli made his way over to me, still looking a little pale, but mostly recovered.

Claude snorted. "I've gotten several months of peace from you and your trouble in my city." He frowned. "Not that dealing with fissures in the realm and an influx of hostile magic can be considered peace. Which, come to think of it, I'm sure I have you to thank for as well," he added, with a dark look down at me, "so maybe I'll just forgo my gratitude."

Several months?

The disintegration of the hell realm had led to some timing gaps in the past, but months?

Eli's eyes widened as they met mine, both of us ignoring whatever Claude was grumbling about.

Months. Were they still at the cabin?

Atlas.

Oh fuck. I clutched my side, squeezing my hip as I tried to get my breathing under control. Had he been under the spell of the nightmare, the drude, all of this time?

I leaned down, hands on my knees now, trying like hell not to vomit all over my shoes.

"It's okay, they're okay." Eli drew slow circles on my back, calming my panic even through the floods of his own.

"You okay?" When I looked up, Claude was hovering awkwardly by us, like he was stuck between wanting to help and wanting to get us as far away from his home as possible.

I nodded, catching my breath as I grabbed Eli's hand. "We need to go. Thank you for," I waved my hand in the general direction of where the portal had been, "you know, that."

"Wait, don't—" Claude took another step towards us, suspicion lining the curve of his brows, but I'd wrapped my arms around Eli and focused on getting us out of there before Claude found some reason to try and detain us. "Fuck."

Claude's clenched jaw was the last sight before the world bent out of focus and reshaped into an old ship yard.

"Where," Eli panted, nauseous and out of breath from teleporting so soon after portal jumping, "are we?" His eyes narrowed, taking in the shipping containers, the salty brine of the water a few feet away. "Did you bring us to where we were attacked by those vampires in Seattle?"

I shrugged, thankful for the soft glow of the moon to light our path. "I can't go very far with another person, and this was the closest place I could think of that wasn't super crowded in the city."

I wasn't wrong. The gravel-strewn alley was empty, the stones crunching and echoing as I took a look around, verifying that we were alone.

"So now we go to the cabin?" Eli ran a hand through his hair, muffling the waves up in a way that made him look like a model on a photo shoot. "I can steal a car."

With a deep, slow breath, I closed my eyes, reaching for the others. I couldn't tell if they were all together or not, but I knew, at the very least, that they were alive. I could feel the shadow of our bonds, growing stronger, more in focus, the harder I focused on finding them.

"I don't—" I shook my head, trying to hold onto the feeling. It was going to take practice to get a hold of this whole thing, but we didn't have the time for me to learn. "I'm not sure that they're at the cabin. I think it would be better if we just followed the," I felt my cheeks heat under his perusal, "you know, the bonds."

I felt Eli grinning at me before I even opened my eyes, like his warmth flared through me.

Fingers brushed softly against my cheek, his lips pressing with surprising gentleness against my lips. "Are you finally accepting the fact that we're all a bonded group then, Miss Bentley?"

There was a suggestiveness in the way he used my last name—since it was his too—that sent a pulse of heat through me.

When I opened my eyes, my lids heavy with desire, I stared into his, slipping into the amber pools. Words fell flat on my tongue, so I simply nodded, trying like hell not to give in to my libido here, in the middle of an industrial district in Seattle.

As if sensing my struggle, Eli grinned, pressing one more quick kiss to my lips before putting some much needed distance between our bodies. "Good. Then let's go find the others using your cool new spidey senses."

They weren't particularly close, so it took ten jumps before we landed somewhere in woods I didn't recognize.

"I think," I panted, strained from so many teleportations with Eli attached to me, "we're close."

He looked down at me, face tinged gray with nausea. "Thank the gods. Much more of this and I'm going to pass out."

I nodded, my own stomach feeling hollow and full at once. "Same."

"Does this ever get easier?" He bent down, tucking his head between his legs. "Because as much as I love being wrapped up in your arms, I almost prefer flying."

I bit back a grin as I joined him on the ground.

Eli hated flying.

Hunting demons? No problem. Riding along in a metal contraption in the sky? The guy acted like the world was ending.

It was oddly endearing.

"Feels like spring." His face peeked up as he took a deep breath. "I wonder how long we've been gone."

The thought sent a fresh ripple of nausea rolling through me. The others were probably freaking out with our absence, but more than that I was worried about Atlas. How long could he survive being tortured by his worst fears?

As soon as we found the others, I'd rest long enough to get back to full energy, but then I was going after him.

"How much further, do you think?"

I closed my eyes, sank into the feel of the others. I frowned, noticing a rift.

"What's wrong?" I felt Eli stiffen against me.

"I think they're separated. Close by but in different locations."

"Who's closer?"

I focused, trying to differentiate between the bonds. It was going to take practice, letting myself learn and lean into this. It was like all five of them had pathways in my mental labyrinth, some more vibrant than others. Atlas was the dimmest of all.

I couldn't be sure whether that was because he was bonded to Reza now, or because he was—

No—I refused to go there. I shook my head and stood up, lowering a hand to Eli.

"Wade and Darius. They're close, maybe only a few miles."

"Let's walk it then," Eli said, heaving himself up and twining his fingers through mine. "I don't think I can stomach another shift and it's probably best to tread carefully. They're definitely not at the cabin, and we have no fucking clue what we're walking into."

I nodded, quietly relieved that I could catch my breath for a few minutes. My powers were back, sure, but I'd never teleported so many times before, with this level of intention and precision. It was fucking exhausting, and my body ached the way it did after the world's longest day of sparring. If that day also occurred during a bad bout of the flu.

We walked in silence for about an hour, both of us tensing at any rustle of the leaves, hyper-alert.

After the first mile, I hardly even needed to focus on the bonds to guide me, it started to become second nature to just let myself move towards them—my body practically buzzing from the nearness after days apart.

Had it really been months for them?

Eli was right, the air did have a distinctly spring feel—and we'd left in winter.

His fingers tightened around my hand, stopping us as we came to a clearing. "What the hell?"

A little ways in the distance—a roof peeked into the skyline.

"You think they found a bigger cabin?" I asked. It made sense. If we'd been gone for months, I couldn't imagine them holed up in Cy's for that long.

"Maybe," he frowned.

Anxiety fluttered in my stomach, the fear I'd been trying to ignore since Claude's suddenly making itself known.

Months. We'd been gone literally for months. Who knew what the others had been through in our absence.

He took a deep breath, studying the unfamiliar trees

surrounding us. "At least this isn't Headquarters. So we know The Guild hasn't hunted them down."

It sounded like he was trying to convince himself of that as much as me.

"Dec isn't here though."

My chest tightened at the possibility she was alone. Maybe we should've gone after her first?

When I focused on her bond, I could feel it flaring, like she was getting closer, like she was making her way back here, almost? It was hard to parse, hard to follow the nuances of this strange connection.

"Stop." Eli's finger looped under my chin, lifting my focus back to him. "Don't spiral on me, Bentley. We'll get them, find out what the fuck this place is, and then," he shrugged, "then we'll go get her. It'll be—" a red laser landed between his eyes "okay."

I shoved him behind the nearest tree, grabbing my dagger as I crouched low. I felt him do the same, the moment he grasped what was going on.

When I looked up, I saw three people inching towards us, then when I spun back around, ten more.

"Fuck."

Too many for us to take on the traditional way.

I called the hellfire to my free hand as Eli and I moved away from the large tree trunk and pressed our backs together.

"Fire! They're going to attack, be careful," someone called from above, like they were hiding in a tree, scouting for an ambush.

Where the fuck were we and how the hell did Darius and Wade get here?

The muscles in Eli's back rippled against me. "Where are our friends?"

The people surrounding us closed ranks, but no one moved to attack.

"How did you find this place?" one of them asked, their voice gravelly and filled with warning.

Were they Guild? Demons? I couldn't be sure.

My fingers tightened around my dagger and I balanced my weight on the balls of my feet, preparing to lunge or parry at the slightest provocation.

A figure lunged forward, breaking through the circle of people in a flash of speed that made distinguishing features impossible.

They stopped in front of us, with their back to me.

What the fuck?

For a moment, I was stunned—no one shows their back to an enemy, especially not when they're armed with a blade and hellfire.

After a moment, I traced the familiar lines of their back, the unmistakable platinum hair.

"Darius?"

"They're with us, do not touch them." His words were barely more than a growl as he inched backwards until his back touched the tip of my blade.

I dropped it at my side.

He held his breath, like he was waiting for something, then someone must've gestured something, because his shoulders relaxed.

He spun around, eyes nailing me to the spot. I fell under the spell of that mesmerizing golden and black gaze, my heart thumping in its cage at the pure anger—hunger—that I found there.

"You're back." He wrapped me in his arms, burying his face into the crook of my neck and inhaling deep, slow breaths, as if searching for and savoring my scent. "Fucking finally. It's been nearly three months."

"Max?" A familiar voice yelled in the distance. "Is it really her? Are you really here?"

Another body crashed into us, tightening me into a sandwich of muscle and warmth that had me aching with need, despite all the people watching us.

"Wade?"

His answer was a kiss to my neck, his tongue against my skin like he needed to taste me.

"Gods you smell good," he groaned, his grip around me tightening and pulling a growl from Darius as he pulled me back into him too. "Don't ever do that to me again." He shook his head against my neck. "I know it wasn't your fault, but fucking hell, I don't think I can handle that again. Make him take us all next time. He can't just keep you like that."

"It's been like two days for us," Eli said, from somewhere near the man-muscle blanketed around me.

Slowly, and against the wishes of my needy pussy, I extricated myself from their arms, catching a good look at them. "You're both okay? You're not hurt?"

"We're okay." Wade's eyes locked onto mine, the nebulous haze of the incubus blurring darker blues and purples into his irises.

I scanned them both anyway, the tightness in my chest needing proof. They looked good.

Wade's hair was freshly buzzed, the stubble lining his jaw neatly trimmed.

Darius's hair was tousled in messy fuck-me waves, the skin along his arms silky and unblemished.

Neither of them looked starving or hurt. Of course, we'd guessed that Darius was fine by Eli's lack of dying, but I also wasn't sure how their blood tie worked across realms. Hell, they were so rare that we hardly knew how accurate they were when they were standing right next to each other.

"Dec?" I looked between them, then remembered that there were other bodies around us. "And where are we?"

"She's on a scouting trip," Darius said, his jaw tensed, eyes unblinking as he drank me in.

"And okay," Wade added. "Should be home tonight or tomorrow."

"And the 'where the fuck are we' part?" Eli echoed, darting curious glances to the people around us.

Wade turned to them, nodded to someone I couldn't see.

"Let's give them space," an unfamiliar voice called.

Rippled murmurs and the sound of feet walking through the brush signaled their departure—a departure very much blocked from my field of vision by Darius's solid chest.

He was running his fingers over my jaw, my neck, my arms, like he still wasn't convinced I was standing before him.

Wade's hands massaged into my back, kneading out an ache that I hadn't realized was there.

I leaned back into him, closed my eyes, moaning into the pressure. "That feels so fucking good."

When I opened them, Eli and Darius's eyes were locked feverishly on my mouth.

I felt Wade against my back, his dick thickening with every heavy, panting breath I took.

Their hunger raked against my skin as if it was my own, until it felt like it had been months since I'd seen them too. The heat of their focus pulled another involuntarily breathy groan from my lips.

As if that single sound sealed it, Darius pressed his mouth against mine, his tongue searching, demanding as it forced its way into my mouth. It was no gentle clash of teeth and tongue, but wild and probing and filled with the tingling pleasure of just a little bit of pain.

Wade's arms wrapped around me, one cupping my boob, the other dipping into my pants as he licked, kissed, nipped the tender flesh at the base of my throat.

Liquid pooled at the juncture of my legs and I gasped when Wade's finger slid against my clit.

Another set of hands—Eli's most likely—pulled my pants down, ripped off my shoes until I was bare from the waist down.

My body felt hot with fever—the need to have them all suddenly so strong I thought I might combust.

Wade paused his languid perusal of my neck and jaw long enough to pull at my shirt, but Darius simply ripped it down the middle, refusing to break our kiss long enough to pull it over my head.

I heard clothes drop to the forest floor as Darius lifted me, gripping my thigh so that my legs wrapped around him. He leaned me back against the tree, the rough bark scratching and aching with a pain that only heightened the heady sensation of his dick rubbing against me.

When I looked down, I saw that his dark pants were wet, coated with my need.

"Pants," I whispered, into his mouth, biting down on his bottom lip hard enough to break skin, "off."

He groaned into me, the taste of his blood washing against my tongue, delicious and metallic.

Slowly, gently, and so at odds with how he'd been kissing me, he shifted my weight and kept me against the tree while he dropped his pants.

His dick was hard and heavy against me as he slid against me, the sound of my slickness echoing obscenely in the woods around us.

My eyes latched onto Eli, and then Wade, both of their expressions heavy with need and the promise of satisfying it next. For now, they seemed just as excited to watch. Something about their eyes on me while Darius made me squirm made me throb with excitement.

Fuck yes.

I wanted this.

I needed this.

I was vaguely aware of the fact that neither of them had answered the 'where the fuck are we' question and that there quite possibly were still people scattered in the woods around us, our show on full display.

I just didn't fucking care.

Darius pushed into me, bringing my focus back to him, the wild gleam in his eyes shining with a daring glint as he slid home.

Yes, I was most definitely letting this happen. I should probably be ashamed by the fact that Wade and Eli were watching Darius fuck me, but something about the way their eyes tracked every lift of my chest, every shape my mouth made as I moaned through the pleasure only turned me on more.

It was like every flicker of desire they felt echoed in me until it was impossible to deny, cocooning us all in a shared, intoxicating lust.

"Harder," I whispered, my voice deep and cracked.

With a wicked grin, Darius obliged, pumping into me over and over again. "Does my girl want a little pain with her pleasure?"

I dug my nails down his back, drawing blood in answer.

He hissed.

Leaving one hand to help hold my weight, his other stroked up my chest with enough pressure to carve soft indentations into my skin. He slowed his thrusts, made me focus on the feeling of him teasing, kneading me. With a dark smirk, he pinched my nipple. The spark of pain shot through me and I clenched around him.

He grunted, trying to maintain his composure, his control, as his hand went higher, stopping as it reached the base of my neck.

I let out a needy whine, demanding something I didn't even know to ask for.

"That's it. Let's push you further." His fingers wrapped around me, a perfectly-fitted necklace. He thrusted forward, tightening his grip slightly with each pump.

My vision swam as I clung to him, the ecstasy of giving myself over to him, of basking in the feel of him inside of me, filled me with a renewed focus until it became overwhelming.

Liquid slid down my thighs, coating us both with every roll of my hips. The lack of control over my breath—something so essential and powerful—the surrender to him, elevated everything.

"That's it, little protector," he said, each word punctuated with a thrust, his hand on my hip firm so that he controlled the power of our cadence, "gods, you're fucking perfect. Look at me." I opened my eyes, finding his fixed on me, wild, powerful, and filled with reverence. "Come for me. I want to feel you clench around me, tighten around me like a warm little vise." He squeezed harder. "Three months without this perfect fucking pussy," He drove into me faster, as he added more pressure, blocking my breath, "let me feel you surrender to me the way I surrender to you every day. Every hour. Every goddamn breath I take."

I saw stars as I came, my moan fractured from his grip, but he released it until I was screaming my pleasure into the air between us.

He drove into me, faster, harder, and then followed me over, until we were both relying on the steadiness of the tree to keep our knees from buckling us to the ground.

Not for the first time, I sent a silent shout out to Greta for hooking me up with birth control months ago.

Slowly, I slid down, collapsing as Wade gripped my arms, keeping my knees from hitting the ground with too much force.

The feel of his skin, warm and soothing against mine made me feel drunk with a renewed desire.

I pressed my palms into the forest floor as he collapsed around me, hard and ready.

Without a word, he speared me on his dick, the movement easy and wet with my own desire and Darius's cum.

My sharp gasp of surprise melted into a needy moan.

"More. I need more." I leaned back as Wade fucked me.

Darius crouched down in front of me, a wicked, feral grin twisting his lips before they disappeared against me, his tongue and teeth scraping against my clit as Wade pounded into me from behind

Looking up I saw Eli a few feet away, naked and glorious, and fisting his dick.

"Mine," I growled.

He walked forward, and I took him deep in my mouth, the taste of his pre-cum salty on my tongue.

But still, I wanted more. I wanted them all inside of me, filling me to the brim.

As if reading my mind, they shifted, and I whimpered when Wade pulled out of me.

"I know baby, just wait a second."

He kneeled down on the ground, soundlessly communicating with the others until Eli sat down and reached for me.

I knelt over him and slid down until his dick found its home. For a few seconds I rode him, grinding, my desire building as his compounded it.

My succubus sensitivity flared to the surface, until every touch felt like a mini-orgasm, until every wave of lust that built in them echoed in me tenfold.

The lust made me dizzy, until I wanted nothing but to exist in this moment with them for eternity.

I felt Wade move in behind me, his legs over Eli's and on either side of me. His hands massaged down my back, sliding lower and lower until one of his fingers started circling around and lightly entering my ass—and then he stuck it all the way in.

Surprisingly, it sent a bolt of tightness to my lower belly as I clamped around Eli, my head dipping back against Wade's chest as he pinched my nipple.

When he pulled his finger out and gripped my hips, settling himself hard and thick against me, I tensed.

"Trust me," he whispered, the feather-light touch of his breath sending a rippling heat against my skin. "Lean back."

He was still soaked with me as he slid into my ass, both of them filling me up with a pressure that had me shaking. It hurt at first, but once he made it past the threshold, the pain morphed into an explosion of pleasure, like every nerve ending in my body was screaming in ecstasy.

"That's it," he said, his hands on my hips, guiding me to ride them both, slow at first, as Eli squeezed my thigh, his thumb rubbing delicious circles over my clit.

"Fuck," I closed my eyes, the sensation almost too much to process.

I felt someone grab my arm and then the heat of Darius's mouth as he nipped and licked his way to the inside of my elbow.

Eli took one of my nipples into his mouth, biting down just as Darius's teeth pierced my flesh, pulling deep, intoxicating gulps of my blood.

Eli stopped, his hand squeezing my thigh, like he was going to protest, but I felt Wade shake his head at my back, and he relaxed back into me, his dick throbbing inside of me.

It should have felt wrong, all of us together like this, but it didn't. I searched myself for shame, but came up with none, just the intense rightness of being surrounded by them.

A flash of possessiveness coursed through me, branding me with heat.

They were mine.

All of them were mine.

And I was theirs.

I understood that now, could hardly comprehend why it had taken me so long to acknowledge—to take what was mine all along.

Power surged between us, encircling us as we fully gave into the desire that had been a shroud around us for so long—complete, absolute surrender.

I rolled my hips again, building momentum and climbing to that cliff, as they joined me.

"Fuck," Wade hissed in my ear, "I'm so fucking close."

"Me too," Eli said, his teeth nipping at my neck, "Jesus Max, you tighten like that around me again and I'm going to blow."

I squeezed around them both, the sharp, tandem intake of their breath like a bolt down my spine. With a harmony of moans, the three of us came, both of them filling me to the brim as Darius took his own fill at my side.

We collapsed in a pile of sweat and limbs and warmth, the gray light of the early dawn welcoming us to a new day that felt like a new era.

20

MAX

After lingering for a few minutes in the joy of simply existing with each other after so much time apart, Wade carried me in his arms. Not because I was too weak to walk—if anything, I felt stronger than I ever had before, like their strength was amplifying my own—but because, like me, he craved the closeness of my skin against his.

I didn't take in the surroundings as we walked. Instead, I carved my finger along the smooth lines of his body, claiming and tracing his arm, his shoulder, his chest, grinning to myself as his flesh pebbled and shivered at my touch.

His soft brown skin glowed with an almost inhuman, ethereal light, basking in the power of intimacy he pulled from us all. The realization that he'd gone months without feeding the incubus in my absence sent a wave of guilt spearing through me.

If Lucifer managed to pull me away from him again, I'd need to make sure that Wade was the first one I dreamwalked to.

His brows bent into a scowl. "No frowning."

My thumb massaged the divot between his eyes as I grinned up at him. "Look who's talking. Where are we going?"

"Our cabin," Darius said.

The thought of Darius and Wade sharing a cabin together made me squirm with amusement. But hope was buried underneath that too. "And where are we exactly?" It was wild how easily the sexfest had completely pushed pragmatics out of my brain for an hour. "What is this place? Who were all those people back there?"

"This is The Lodge," Darius answered, his hair made golden by the sun as he came into view behind Wade's shoulder. "We found out about it from that purple-haired girl who works for The Guild—Dani. It's composed of a bunch of protectors—both ex-Guild and other lines—and supernatural creatures who either need protection or want to help protect. They're more or less stepping in to do the job that protectors have always said that they're going to do but don't actually follow through with. Kind of like a secret vigilante group that helps whoever needs helping—everyone is welcome here, so long as they aren't deliberately harming others."

It sounded strangely like the answer to my new moral guidelines, and I felt an odd rightness about this place shift into place.

Morality wasn't black and white, but that didn't mean there weren't still ways to help people. If anything, it made fighting for people more imperative than ever.

It's what had originally drawn me to The Guild in the first place—Ro and I had always dreamed about becoming protectors so that we could help people. Use our power and position to protect those who couldn't help themselves. It was one of the reasons the truth about The Guild, about the supernatural world, had been so disappointing.

Oh my god. My chest tightened, leaving no room for air. Ro.

"And my brother?" I spun around, as if he might suddenly

appear amongst the cabins and houses. Now that the lust haze was fading, panic started to flutter low in my belly. "He's here, too, right? And Seamus?"

I shoved at Wade's arm, silently asking to be put down, but he simply held on tighter, pulled me closer to him. "They're both okay." He pressed a kiss to the top of my head. "Ro is on the mission with Dec. Aside from his constant worrying about you, he's been really thriving here. And Seamus—" he shared a look with Darius at his side. It was so odd, seeing them not bickering, to think that they'd lived months alongside each other, working together—that they could communicate with a look, the same way the rest of Six had always been able to.

Darius shrugged. "No use hiding or sugar coating it, they're going to find out eventually." He turned an apologetic glance to Eli. Seamus is a wolf. He was bit during the attack at your house. It's the reason we couldn't stay and wait for you there. He was dying."

"What?" This time, I shoved harder at Wade's chest until I dislodged myself, landing with a soft thud on the pads of my feet. Darius was carrying my shoes and clothes, and I was swimming in his black t-shirt, the hem almost at my knees. My focus latched onto Eli, his face suddenly pale, lip curled in concern as he processed Darius's words. "But he's okay?"

"I need to see him," Eli said, voice raspy, "now."

Wade gripped Eli's shoulder, but his eyes didn't leave mine. "He's alive, he made it through the transition. He's just," he tilted his head, considering, "struggling a little bit. Tex is helping him with the transition."

"Why is he struggling? What's wrong?" My voice was higher than usual, and I took a breath, trying to calm down, to compose myself and my worry if only for Eli's sake. "And who is Tex? Do you trust them?"

Darius's lip curled, but Wade ignored him and nodded. "Yes, we trust the people here, for the most part—they haven't given us a reason not to yet, and they could've killed us dozens of times over if that's what they really wanted to do. They're also the only reason that Seamus isn't dead right now. Tex is a wolf. Another protector who's gone through the transition. There are quite a few here. Seamus's transition has just been extra intense because he's older and—"

"We think there might be a different line of werewolves," Darius added as he walked up to the last cabin in the long row we'd been weaving through. He unlocked the door and nodded inside. "Some of his symptoms have been strange and hard to predict. But he's one of the lucky ones. He's strong. Most protectors they've seen with this bite have died." He cleared his throat awkwardly and spread his arms. "Welcome home."

"A different line of werewolves?" I tried and failed to keep the panic from rising in my voice like bile.

Darius tossed his keys on a small table and kicked his shoes off, looking so strangely domestic in this space that it threw me off balance in contrast to the direness of the conversation. "It makes sense, with Druden and other creatures showing up. Why not add freaky shifters into the mix."

Eli ran a hand through his hair. "I need to see him. Now."

Wade clenched his jaw and nodded. "I can take you, but you should prepare yourself." He met Eli's eyes on an exhale. "He's lost a lot of his memories. Shifts in and out of it, but it's possible he won't recognize you, won't know who you are."

Nausea swept through me as I grabbed Eli's hand, squeezing it softly, trying to lend him my strength.

But he didn't need it. A shadow crept into his expression as he took in Wade's words.

"Okay," he said, pressing a soft kiss to my lips. "You stay here, I'll be back in a bit."

"I can go with you."

Wade shook his head. "No, they won't let you both in. I'm not even sure they'll give Eli the okay without the council's permission. And you need to clean up, rest a bit before you meet with Charlie. I'll take him. Darius just gets on everyone's nerves in that wing, so he should stay here with you."

The council? What the fuck was this place?

"For once, I'm grateful that people find me insufferable," Darius muttered, a small grin tugging at his lips.

"Soon." Wade kissed me, his tongue slipping into the seam of my mouth and tangling with mine briefly before he pulled away with a groan. "We'll be back soon."

They left and Darius grabbed my hand, tugging me through a small, minimally-decorated but cozy living room area, with stacks of novels piled on either side of the TV and to a back room.

"Kind of small and doesn't smell as good as your place, but it's clean and they're letting us stay together. There are five bedrooms, and we've been using four, but we'll figure out the logistics of sleeping arrangements later."

"This place kind of feels like The Guild. Middle of nowhere, cabins to house people." It wasn't as fancy as the cabin Six had, but similar all the same. "A mysterious council that makes the rules."

"I think they modeled it after that style. Convenient way to keep people close and protected. And, like I said, there are a lot of ex-Guild people here. And from what I can tell, their council is very deliberately created as a representation of all the people here—a true community council that disperses power, rather than revels in it. But yes," he turned back to me with a cocky grin, "the branding could do with some work."

There was an amusing bounce to his step as he walked me through each room, pointing to various things they'd obtained in my absence, rehashing arguments between Wade and Dec about chores, and reliving his video game victories over Ro. He seemed relaxed, almost excited by the idea of a home.

It made sense. He hadn't really had a home in years—a

place to settle into, people to trust. Warmth spread through me at the idea that Darius fit—not just with me, but that he'd been finding his way with the others in my absence too. And even through all of the chaos, all of the uncertainty, I couldn't keep the smile from my face.

He stopped when we got to the bathroom, popping the light on and pulling me inside. It was small, minimal, but clean—and large enough for us both to comfortably stand in.

"What are you—" My words muffled around his t-shirt as he lifted it off of me, tugging it gently before pulling off his clothes too.

The sight of him naked in front of me, his eyes hungry and focused on mine, sent a renewed surge of heat to my core. Fuck, this man was gorgeous.

The shit-eating smirk on his face told me he was fully aware of his effect on me.

"Shower," he said, turning to start the water, running his hand under the stream to check the temperature. "Figured you'd want one after your travels, but I'm not ready for you to be out of my sight yet."

With a soft grin, I let him tug me underneath the water with him, groaning as the water beat down against my skin, the beads carving transfixing paths down our skin. It was fucking amazing.

I pressed my lips to one drop as it traced the line between his pecs, licking it up. There was something so divine about the taste of the water mixed with him.

He spun me around, his dick hard and thick against my lower back. Like me, he was more than ready for another round, but he ignored it.

Instead, he pressed a feather-light kiss against my neck, licking the water droplets against my skin, before grabbing a bottle of shampoo, the steamy air filling with the scent of vanilla and almonds as he squeezed some into his hands.

He tilted my face back, dousing my hair in the steady stream, before he dug his fingers gently through the strands, lathering the soap and scrubbing my scalp.

It felt almost as good as sex, him washing away the dirt and grime. With a knowing grin, he pulled out a twig and my cheeks heated, recalling our carnal devouring of each other in the middle of the woods.

"I've missed you, little protector." His voice was quiet, vulnerable, as he rinsed my hair and massaged conditioner into the strands. He rubbed soap along my arms, my back, my ass. There wasn't a demand in the touch, no need for sex, even. It was an intimacy of care, so at odds with the roughness of how he'd taken me in the forest that it made my stomach flip and my heart thump at an uneven pace. "I think," he paused, clearing his throat, eyes meeting mine as he tilted my head back, searching. "No. There's no thinking about it. I know. I love you. I've loved you from the moment I saw you outside of my cell. You were like a light, waking me up from a long, impenetrable, nihilistic slumber. But even before that, before The Guild, I was lost."

His hands ran through my hair, rinsing the conditioner. "You found me. Helped me find myself again."

I turned around to face him properly, mesmerized by the softness in his gaze.

He cupped my cheeks, the vanilla mixing with the familiar scent of him as he studied me, the reverence in his gaze almost tangible. "You've given me something to believe in again, something to fight for, a reason to give a fuck about more than my own base needs and desires."

He kissed me, his tongue slow and searching—hot in its hesitance.

His thumb traced gentle circles along my arm, his lips dipping to my jaw, my clavicle, but then he pulled back, brows furrowed.

I leaned into him, needing more, frustrated by his pause—but I sobered up when I saw the question in his face as he rubbed my shoulder, over and over.

"What's wrong?"

He rinsed my arm, then pulled me from the shower, both of us dripping wet on the floor as he wiped condensation from the mirror.

At first, I didn't see anything. But when I looked closely, I noticed an almost invisible, shimmery design creeping up along my shoulder. It was almost like a vine that reached to my back shoulder blade, and traced down the curves of my side.

"What the hell?" I rubbed my hand furiously over my skin, but it didn't disappear.

Darius studied my reflection in the mirror, his fingers tracing lightly against my skin. "I think it's a bond mark. I—" his brows furrowed, "I've never seen one before."

"Oh." Something Serae mentioned before floated back to the surface. That incubi and succubi used to have shadow marks when they were bonded. They occasionally carved temporary runes into their skin to mimic some of the power and connection they afforded. "Why now? I've had—"

I cleared my throat, letting the sentence fill the room in my silence. That hadn't been my first time having sex with any of them.

Darius took a deep breath, his fingers unceasing in their perusal of the mark, my skin heating at his touch. "I can't be sure of the reason, but bonds have always been more than carnal pleasure. It's a decision, a commitment, an intimacy that both parties have to give themselves over to completely."

Be brave with me, Max.

Eli's words rang through my ears with a new clarity. Something big had shifted between us in that moment, something that carried over into how I saw the others too. I'd gone all in and so had they.

We'd surrendered to each other, completely.

It wasn't sex that strengthened the bonds, it was trust, the willingness to be vulnerable, even in the face of rejection and pain.

I tilted my head, studying Darius's reflection in the mirror now, instead of mine. Was that…?

Turning around I shifted his shoulder towards me, ran my thumb over the lines that were only a shade darker than skin. "I think you have one too."

Every muscle in his body tensed as his eyes met mine, wide and hesitant, like he was afraid to look for himself. But when he dipped his gaze down, the fear evaporated. A giant grin lifted his lips, his eyes gleaming with pride as he ran his hand along his chest and arm.

Something about the hope on his face made my chest ache.

Darius had always seemed so fractured, so lost.

The pure adoration as his gaze met mine made my vision blur with tears.

He pressed a kiss to my lips, his fingers trailing the mark along my ribs. "I told you that you were mine, little protector."

With careful hands, he lifted me against the counter, entering me in one swift thrust. Where our union an hour ago had been rough and demanding, this was gentle, cleansing—a testing union of more than just bodies.

I tilted my neck, suddenly desperate for his bite, and rolled my hips along him in slow, languid thrusts, every inch of his dick that sank into me sending sparks of pleasure down to my toes.

As his teeth pierced my skin, I whimpered, needy and drunk on him—unable to keep the ecstasy of his nearness locked down.

"I love you too, Darius," I whimpered against his chest, pressing my lips against the evidence of that love.

He froze against me, body tensing as he pulled his face back to meet mine, my blood staining his lips. I pressed mine to his anyways, needing his tongue tangled with mine.

"Mine," he whispered into my mouth, the word a promise, a prayer, as he thrust into me again. "Mine."

And then, we both shattered.

∼

"Not bad, right?" Darius sat down on a dock, leaning back on his palms as he stared at the expanse of water before him.

Not bad didn't even begin to cover it. This place was stunning.

The water was almost turquoise in color, reflecting both the sky and the evergreen trees surrounding it. The mountains in the distance added a mirrored reflection in the vast pool, like a painting.

This place was the sort of beautiful that was so stunning it didn't seem real. Even standing here, I was half convinced I'd stepped into a painting or a dream.

It was spring, but there was still a crispness in the air, and I knew that the water would be freezing. Still, I found myself wanting to jump in anyway, to swim through the water and comb the floor of its depths for a few minutes.

"I've never heard of this place," I said.

Darius shrugged. "I imagine that, for the last few years at least, that's by design. It's called Lake Cadaver Resort and Lodge. Carved out by a glacier centuries ago."

I scrunched my nose up and turned to him. "Lake Cadaver? What kind of name is that?"

His face brightened into a grin and I felt my insides going all twisty and gooey at the sight of it. "Legend says that the bottom of the lake is lined with the bodies and bones of an old serial killer's victims. Not exactly great for tourism though, so most people just call it the Lake at the Lodge."

I took a deep breath, letting the calm, cool air settle in my lungs. Lake Cadaver. I repressed a shiver. It was odd for a place so beautiful to be named for something so gruesome. I supposed, like with all things, there was always a balance between light and dark. "I like it here."

Darius's lips twitched into a sad smile as he watched me lean over the dock and comb my fingers through the easy waves colliding into the wood. "I thought you might. It's changed a lot since I was here last, but it still has the same lure that it had before."

"You've been here before?" I wasn't sure why that shocked me—of course Darius had a life before his captivity. I knew that there was a gap between when he left his brother and sister in Seattle and when he ended up in the labs, but the realization that we still knew so little about each other's histories caught me off guard.

My life had been so simple, so uneventful compared to them. Sure, the circumstances of my birth were unique, but most of my life was just a rinse and repeat of training and hanging out with Ro in the middle of the woods. Until recently, I'd lived my most extreme experiences vicariously through books.

"This is where I was captured." He nodded to the other side of the lake—it was large enough that I couldn't see where it ended from here, all of it surrounded by mountainous terrain and woods. "There's a ledge over there. Big scary battle," he waved his hands in the air, "It was all very exciting. Dani brought me in."

"Declan's Dani?" I squinted, trying to imagine the scene playing out on the tall cliffs still speckled white with the remnants of winter. "She's the reason you were captured?"

"I'm the reason I was captured," he said with a chuckle, "she was just in the right spot at the right time. I grew careless towards the end. I rarely stayed in the same place for very long, and I knew there were protectors hunting in this area, but something about this place—I just couldn't leave it. Not sure why."

I leaned back, my fingertips slipping through the wooden slats. A heavy peace, a yearning, had settled over me since the shower. The fantasy of settling down, somewhere like this place, building a routine, cocooned in the beauty of the woods—I could see how that would be difficult to abandon.

A life on the run, your life constantly in danger—it was a difficult way to live. Home was a powerful sensation, and one you couldn't help but chase when you didn't know where to find it.

"Thought you both would be out here." Wade walked down the dock, his footsteps echoing as a pair followed him.

The shorter of the two, a woman, was beautiful, but there was a severeness to her posture, to the dark depths of her eyes—a quiet strength, the kind that was earned. Still, a grin lifted her expression as her eyes met mine.

There was something about her that flattened out my typical instinct to withhold my trust until she earned it. I liked her immediately.

The man at her side was clearly her partner, the way his arm brushed along hers as they walked, the way his gaze softened only when he looked at her. His eyes were far less inviting than hers, but not cruel.

Something about him reminded me of the day I met the members of Six—of Atlas.

If Atlas's tendency to protect his circle by treating everyone outside of it as a threat had a look, this man wore it like a pair of comfortable jeans.

"This is Charlie and Bishop," Wade said as they reached me. "They more or less run this place."

Charlie scrunched her nose, extending a hand to me. "It's run by the community, we're just today's greeting party." She glanced down at me, a conspiratorial gleam in her dark eyes. "Honestly, I've been dying to meet you."

The man, Bishop, didn't seem up for the gesture. A muscle in his jaw pulsed as he glared down at Darius.

Darius, as always, seemed either unaware of the man's dislike or unbothered by it. Maybe even a little pleased by the effect he seemed to have on the man.

I stood, swallowing my smirk and shook her hand. "Thank you. For keeping my friends safe, for giving them a place to stay while Eli and I were—er, away."

I had no idea how much these people knew about us, about where we'd been.

Her smile brightened, making her look even more stunning, the sun casting her light golden-brown skin in an almost ethereal glow. "It's what we do here. Take in strays. We've heard a lot about you, Max Bentley. Your friends have been incredibly worried." She cut a teasing look to Darius and Wade. "Almost obnoxiously so. Kind of amusing to see the vampire so bent out of shape over someone, if I'm being honest. But now, it's good to have you here, safe and well."

"Are you a, um—" I cleared my throat, not certain how to ask the question at the tip of my tongue politely.

Her eyes narrowed, humor radiating from her. "A protector? No." She scrunched her nose again, considering. "Well, not really. I've lived my life assuming I was completely human, but I inherited the restaurant from an uncle who was a protector. I only learned about the supernatural world because of D."

Bishop bristled, which only made Darius grin one of those snarky grins of his.

Was he D?

He was still sitting on the dock, his legs dangling over the edge, He glanced up at me, looking sheepish. "I attacked her, Bishop saved her—let's not delve too intensely into the past."

He winked, conspiratorially. "Makes Bishop even crankier than his default, which is quite the accomplishment."

"Bishop is Atlas's cousin," Wade added. Explained the similarities. Though, beyond the dark hair and eyes, it was mostly the general grumpiness that hinted at their relation. Was grumpiness an inherited trait? I had no fucking clue. "He used to be on Dani's team. Faked his death years ago and everything. Has been hiding out here, creating the Defiance all this time."

Bishop grunted. "You keep using Mer's ridiculous branding, and she's going to start getting ideas that we're keeping it. That, or it's going to stick—and then we'll never be rid of it."

"I don't know." Darius's face stretched in thought. "I kind of like it. It's growing on me. Has some real aggressive agency to it."

Bishop shook his head. "See what I mean?"

"The Defiance? What exactly does that mean?" I asked, following Charlie as she started to walk back towards the clusters of buildings. The guys had started to clarify, but I still had so many questions—questions that got put on the back burner when my libido went into overdrive. "Is it like an army?"

Charlie shook her head, her hand slipping into Bishop's with the ease and familiarity of a couple who'd been doing it for years. "This place was abandoned for many years, but the property's always been monitored by my ancestors. When they opened up the resort years ago, it acted in part as a sanctuary for other protectors in their line," she tilted her head toward Bishop, "non-Guild protectors. Then, in recent years, my uncle used the place as a sort of safe haven for turned wolves and those on the run from The Guild. I lived here for years none the wiser about the supernatural world."

Non-Guild protectors.

Could that mean my mother's line? Was it possible she had been here? Had she lived or vacationed here before her mother brought her to The Guild?

The lingering potential of connection, of getting to know her better somehow, even through the ghosts of her past, made my chest ache with longing. I'd learned so much about where I came from, but all that did was open more paths of unknown history—paths with no clear direction to tread.

I ducked under a low-hanging branch as Charlie and Bishop walked us through the grounds. I hoped wherever we landed, there would be food. I was fucking famished. "How many people live here now?"

She shrugged, a trace of laughter in her voice. "I've stopped keeping track. Some people stay, some leave, and—" she paused for a beat, her shoulders tensed, "and some die. But we're preparing as many as we can."

"For what?"

Darius and Wade were uncharacteristically quiet on either side of me. I could tell that they respected Charlie. Bishop too, no matter what history there was between him and Darius.

"For whatever is coming. A war, most likely, though we don't yet have an army large enough to fight it." She stopped walking, turned around, and studied me for a long moment, her dark eyes peeling back layers, though I wasn't clear what she was hunting for in that gaze.

How much had Wade and the others told them? How much could we trust them with? How much were we keeping from each other?

She nodded once, satisfied with her search. "Look, I can't predict the future and I don't know what that something that's coming is, but the line of protectors who've kept this place as a sanctuary for years have lived by very few guiding principles." She counted each one with a finger. "To help people who need it, to keep the balance whenever possible, to interfere only when injustices demand it. And those are still our goals—will remain our goals—in broad strokes. But it's clear that something big is coming, something unprecedented. And it's coming for all of us. There are more demons, more humans being attacked, unpredictable surges of power. The world is changing at an unsustainable pace, and when humans finally learn the truth, we'll all be in danger. We're going to do whatever it takes to save and protect as many people as we can. Ideally, we can shape the new world to the principles The Guild should have abided by all along."

"There's more than one battle on the horizon." Bishop's voice was soft and low, but rang with a heavy clarity. "And the divisions fashioning them are complex and unpredictable. We're shaping an army, making sure that our people—demons, protectors, humans—have a place in the future, whatever that future might look like."

"While we don't know the details, Max, I don't want to lie to you. We did hear about what happened at Guild Headquarters." Charlie resumed her walking, leaving us no choice but to follow. "We know that you are more than you seem. That you and your team are likely at the center of this change, though they've been particularly tight-lipped about things when our council has broached the subject. We just haven't fully decided if you're a weapon to be fashioned for or against us. Until you give us a reason otherwise, we'll assume the former. We'll fight for you, alongside you. But make no mistake—if the latter becomes the case, we will take you all out. There's too much to protect here."

Wade squeezed my hand, calming the rush of panic flooding my body and preventing any kind of verbal response.

Because while I desperately wanted to claim that I was of course a tool for the greater good, I knew that deep down I had no idea what I was capable of.

No idea what would happen when Lucifer had his three requests, when the hell realm collapsed or reformed. Something told me that if any of his enemies—or even The Guild—got a hold of me, found a way to use my connection to the shadow magic against me, the world would be monumentally screwed.

No fucking pressure or anything.

And as kind as Charlie was, her threat was clear. I got the sense that she and the others here wouldn't hesitate with carrying it out if things came to that.

A gentle bristle of leaves preceded a soft thud.

And then a small, surprising scream released from Darius as he jumped two feet into the air.

"Infernal beast," he yelled, shoving a small white ball of cotton off his shoulder where it had landed.

Wade and Bishop both broke into deep, barking laughs, the tension dissolving like ice in a desert, while Charlie politely tried and failed to conceal her amusement.

"Max, meet Shadow." Wade pointed to the small kitten weaving between Darius's stiff legs. He looked like he'd stepped on a landmine, too terrified to so much as breathe for fear of setting it off. "She's kind of adopted Darius."

"More like adopted the practice of stalking and tormenting me. I swear to the gods that this isn't a normal cat. It's a demon in disguise."

Wade snorted. "So are we, jackass."

I bent down to pet the cat, pleased when it rubbed its face into my palm with a deep, vibrating purr.

"You're right, Darius," I picked her up, my heart melting as she burrowed into my chest. "She's absolutely vicious."

21

DECLAN

"Alright," Levi said, letting the wide-eyed teenager go back to his fathers, who were huddled together in the corner of the room looking scared but confused. "They won't remember anything. At least not anything to do with the portal."

I nodded, hardening myself against the pain I knew the family would be feeling in a few hours when they realized their daughter was gone and not coming back.

Levi was Eli's half-brother. The two hated each other—or at least Eli hated Levi, I wasn't exactly sure where Levi stood with their relationship. He was a pretty closed book on everything. And finding him amongst the smattering of familiar faces at The Lodge had been almost as big of a shock as finding Bishop alive and well.

Levi's place here made sense though. He'd always been such a nebulous figure, not entirely wrapped up in The Guild the way that the rest of us were, always operating on the outskirts.

More surprising still was the realization that Levi wasn't just a protector.

Of course, after three months, I still had no fucking clue what the hell he was. He clearly had no inclinations to share with the class. He'd given us zero information about who the fuck his father was.

Or what his father was, more like. He wasn't in the picture, but he'd clearly gifted his spawn with powers that reached beyond the protector spectrum.

The only confirmation I had that he was something a little *more* than I'd believed was his ability to blur the memories of humans, but his secrecy led me to question whether there was more he was hiding.

Still, I couldn't complain, as frustrating as he was. His ability made him a hell of an asset on these missions.

Vampires could lightly compel humans, so when they were being careful, humans rarely remembered those encounters. Sloppy vampire attacks were the reason for all the conspiracy message boards that humans liked to frequent in the dark hours of night, when the existence of monsters seemed all the more possible.

With werewolf attacks, intervention was rarely needed. Those humans almost never survived. And when they did, they often made sense of the encounters, revisioning the experience as if it were with an irregularly-sized wolf instead, or a bear.

Lust demons were far more rare and almost impossible for humans to detect, to trace back to the source. Humans just felt consumed with ecstasy, and then, slowly, they died.

But now that there were large-scale attacks constantly, and new kinds of demons emerging from the woodwork, it was becoming increasingly important to cover the supernatural community's tracks, for as long as we could.

It was a mission we would inevitably fail, and soon—but we were buying as much time as possible.

Our mission had been a quick one, but turned out more complicated than we'd expected. We thought the family had been attacked by a vampire—there were a few reports of blood-drained victims in the area and animal attacks. A lot of the demons newer to this realm were less interested in erasing their footprints—they didn't have lives here yet worth protecting.

But when we intercepted a more recent call reporting a girl disappearing, it seemed that a vampire hadn't attacked the family at all.

Instead, a portal had been ripped open, their eldest daughter pulled through to who knew where. It explained some of the heightened attacks in the area, but it was shocking all the same. By the time we'd arrived, the portal seemed to either have closed or moved somewhere else, unreachable.

When we walked in, the family had been staring at a spot in their backyard, the son holding his hand up and waving it through the air like he expected his fingers to catch onto something. He'd been the one who'd watched her fall through, who'd called the emergency line.

Convincing a human that they'd been attacked by a rabid wolf instead of a werewolf was a lot easier to do than explaining away their sister's disappearance into thin air before their very eyes.

"They can't stay here." I scanned the yard through their window, trying to notice a shimmer or suggestion of a seam. Was it really gone or was it just dormant for the time being? I considered tracking down Claude, but I knew he wouldn't be able to do much. Last we'd heard from him, the barriers between the realms had been wearing thin in places, tearing in unexpected locations that set the whole world off balance. "Portals are too unstable, we have no way of knowing if it will open up here again when we leave. Or if it's even really gone."

Levi cracked his neck as he tilted his head from side to side, looking as exhausted and drained as I felt. "We burn the place down." He shrugged, surveying the land, the huddled family.

"With any luck, they'll assume their daughter was lost to the fire and try to move on with their lives—somewhere else."

I took a step back, like he'd struck me. "You can't seriously be suggesting that we take everything from them now? They might never see their daughter again as it is. To take even more from them seems so—well, heartless."

"They won't see their daughter again, Declan. She's gone. The best we can hope for is that she met a quick, painless death the moment she stepped through. Humans aren't built to survive that kind of magic. Even supernatural creatures die from that kind of power, especially when it's an unprotected entry point like this one."

I knew he was right. We'd heard reports of demons appearing in random locations, torn apart from the shadow magic of unstable portals.

"I know it seems harsh." His lips flattened into a tight line. "But it's the cleanest option we have. They can't stay here. We don't want them coming back. They can go start a life somewhere else. It's hard, but they're lucky."

"How the fuck is any of this lucky?"

He shrugged, and I noticed that he seemed to be actively trying not to look back at the family, like their trauma and pain were contagious. Maybe he was right. "The portal could have taken them all. It didn't. They still have each other. That seems pretty lucky to me, all things considered."

I took a deep, heavy breath as I swallowed down the fight building in my throat. I knew he was right, pragmatically speaking. The world was practically imploding. It had literally torn open in their backyard. But that didn't make any of this easier, any less cruel. "How many more do you think there are?"

Unguarded portals? Human deaths? Families affected by the imbalances in our world? I wasn't sure what question I was even asking him.

"Honestly?" He shook his head. "I have no idea. More than we can assist with or even find, that much is certain."

I ground my molars together, searching for a problem I could actually solve—and I found myself looking everywhere in the small room but at the family in the corner.

"Any news from your mom?" I asked him, nodding to Ro and the others that it was time to go.

"Atlas?" He studied me for a moment, considering. "He's not doing well."

My teeth clenched and I nodded, knowing that I wasn't going to get much more out of him. Levi and Eli's mom was still at Headquarters, doing everything she could to slowly feed us information.

Guilt churned low in my belly, knowing that we'd eventually have to tell Eli that the half of his family he tried to pretend didn't exist was working closely with us...and that his father was a werewolf.

Still, even with that sorry state on the horizon, I'd give just about anything to have him and Max back.

Living without them, trying to create a semblance of a life at Lake Cadaver, with the Defiance, felt like I was leading a shadow life. Things just felt empty, wrong, without them with us.

I would take on just about anything the world had to throw at us, but I wanted my team at my side. They were what made this fight worth fighting.

"How bad?" Ro asked, as he joined us, the others keeping a little bit of a distance. They trusted us, but it was clear that we were still outsiders.

I couldn't even blame them. Joining the Defiance was a ballsy move, one that would be met with death if The Guild caught wind. They had no proof we wouldn't go running back to our families with a list of names and locations.

The corner of Levi's lips turned down.

I clenched my teeth. *Bad* bad then.

I gripped the hilt of my blade until my knuckles cracked from the pressure. "We need to get him out of there, take the labs down—do *something*. We can't just leave them down there."

Atlas. Sarah. Who knew who else was down there now with the council and Tarren on a massive power trip.

"Burn it all down is nice in theory." Levi shrugged, a cruel grin on his lips. "But in practicality, we don't have the capacity to take on the council. Not if our goal is survival."

Fuck survival, I wanted fucking justice.

"I get that Atlas is your friend," he continued, "but we can't sacrifice everything we've built for one person. When we have the numbers, the strength to take on The Guild, we will. But you have to remember that not everyone there is an enemy—and it's not going to be easy to parse those with us from those against us once The Guild's truths are revealed."

"Still not going to share what the long-term plans are?" I asked, grinding my teeth together to keep the anger from lining my voice. "I think we've proven you can trust us."

Ro set his hand on my shoulder and squeezed.

He wanted Arnell and the others extricated safely too—we all had people we loved in the clutches of a council that wasn't working for them.

"I don't know, Declan. Going to tell me where my brother is? Or the girl he follows around like a lost puppy? Or how she wields fire and teleports? Or how you came to learn what you have about Guild histories? Or where exactly you and your team fit in this chaotic mess of things? Or—"

"Okay, okay, we get it." Ro shot him a dark look. "We're all keeping secrets."

"Yes," Levi nodded, "and you and your group have been allotted more than your fair share. We've trusted you enough to let you in, to provide you shelter and a purpose for now, but if you want in deeper, that's on you to rectify."

Fucking asshole.

I understood his frustration, but I was so fucking sick of secrets.

But honestly, as annoying as Levi could be, it was a surprise that the Defiance told us as much as they had. And they'd saved Seamus, so we owed them. But why keep secrets at all? We already knew where they were, we knew—fuck.

I glanced at Levi. "Your memory trick. That work on protectors and demons too? Or just humans, like with vamps?"

His lips flattened into a thin line again, jaw muscle pumping as he said nothing.

That was why they'd extended as much rope as they had. Levi could distort any memories on the surface if he wanted, if we betrayed them. Or they'd just kill us, whichever was easier, cleaner.

A shiver shook me to my core at that kind of power. Our histories, our memories—that was what made us who we were.

The Guild had already proven what could happen when history was distorted by malevolent pens.

We just had to hope that Levi—and any others like him—was as moral as the Defiance led us to believe.

After committing arson and getting the family to a safer locale, our trip home was uneventful. I tried to sleep through it, my mind concocting dreams of Max that alternated between the horrifying and the salacious.

But as we pulled onto the long winding road that led to the entrance, my heart stopped.

A familiar *thrum* pulsed through me, one I always associated with her.

Wait.

Could she—

I gripped Ro's hand where it lay next to me on the seat,

focused on the feeling deep in my chest, an awareness growing, a familiar pull.

Ro turned to me, brows lifted in concern. "What's up, you okay? Bad dream?"

"I think," I squeezed his hand, my smile so big that my cheeks strained with the pressure. "I think they're back."

We hardly waited for the car to stop rolling as it turned up the drive, ignoring Levi's cursing as we bolted. I felt Ro at my back as l I followed the strange, surreal sense that brought us to the front door of our cabin.

With a deep breath, I turned the knob, hoping like hell I wasn't just imagining things.

"Hey, you're back." Eli's face lit up with a genuine, rare smile that instantly transformed him into a younger version of himself. He closed his arms around me, engulfing me in a hug so tight that it literally took my breath away.

I heard Ro calling for Max as he pushed in behind me, heard the collision of his hug when he found her, the heavy grunt as they both lost air from the squeeze.

"You're okay?" My question came out strangled from the pressure of Eli's hug, but I didn't care.

He was here, he was back, and in one piece it seemed.

His response was just a grunt, as he gave me one big squeeze and finally pulled back a bit so that I could see him properly. "I'm okay. You?"

I nodded, sniffled, and looked down, embarrassed by the glaze of happy tears that blurred my vision.

"Oh Dec, such a softy." I heard the grin in his voice as he ruffled the top of my head, mussing up my hair like I was a dog.

With a shove, he backed off.

And then I saw her.

Dark brown eyes met mine over Ro's shoulder. Her smile was bright and white and filled with so much radiance that my heart literally stuttered at the sight of it.

I knew it would be a few minutes before Ro let his sister go—and she held onto him with equal ferocity—so I contented myself in the meantime with simply laying eyes on her.

She was safe.

And even from here, I could tell that she looked happier than she had when she'd left. There was an ease in her smile that had been completely eclipsed by grief before. I wasn't sure how long the trip to hell was for her—judging by the pattern, probably far shorter than it was for us—but something about her energy felt renewed, more solid.

She pressed her lips to Ro's cheek, making a loud suction sound with her kiss that had him shirking away with a groan and wipe of his face. Seeing the sibling ease and bond between them tightened something in my chest.

Using the brief reprieve from his affection, she ran, closing the distance between us, and flew into my arms with the force of a tornado.

Before I could prepare myself for it, her lips were pressed into mine, her smile salty with tears that I didn't even realize I was shedding, as she squeezed me to her—like she'd missed me almost as much as I missed her.

My heart beat heavy and erratic in its cage as I clung to this girl, letting the familiar scent of her surround and envelop me. It wasn't even a scent I could name with any concrete clarity—she smelled like the sun, like a campfire, like an open field of flowers, like home.

"I missed you," she whispered against my mouth, her forehead pressed to mine as her fingers carved trails through my hair.

Every touch was electric, my entire body buzzing with the closeness of her.

It took me a second to realize that she was being openly affectionate with me—like in front of my team, not just in the stolen, secret moments that we'd only ever shared before. The kiss wasn't overtly sloppy or demanding, but the intimacy of it, of our friends witnessing it, made me dizzy with delight. I hadn't realized how much I craved it.

I knew she'd been with all of us, but never openly—never like this.

Something had changed while she was gone, something finally snapping into place, where it had been misaligned before. The resistance I was so used to between us, the constant tug between friendship and something more, finally seemed to have crossed the invisible finish line.

Hopefully for good.

∼

"A FUCKING HELLHOUND?" Wade mouthed soundlessly, indigo eyes wide with shock as he snorted. "This whole fucking time? What a dickhole."

Max and Eli shared a laughing glance as they recounted different parts of their—for them—brief adventure in hell, while we did the same, filling in the gaps that Darius and the others had left out when they'd initially arrived.

Dinner was filled with the best food I'd ever had. Not because it was particularly great, though Charlie's food was always fantastic, but because she was back, eating next to me, her arm grazing mine every now and then as we all filled each other in on the things we'd missed, like her body missed mine in the way mine missed hers.

Things weren't perfect—not safe or whole. There were moments throughout the meal when we all felt Atlas's absence acutely, a sharp stab through the chest when we paused in our mirth for a moment, glances meeting and darting away in a shared grief.

I needed to fill them in on what Levi said earlier, but I couldn't bring myself to do it yet. Didn't want to breach the easy humor of the evening—hearing about Sam's secret party trick, and Max's excitement about getting her powers back—with Levi and his mom.

It was so rare to see legitimate happiness on Eli's face, that I wasn't ready to watch it disappear behind the usual shadows that crept behind his eyes whenever he thought about his family. Not when he'd had less than a day to process what happened to Seamus.

Ro seemed to read my mind, offering brief overtures about our mission—recounting the ones that came before it—while I tucked in to my food, savoring the flavors and tastes in a way I hadn't been able to in months.

It was quite late for dinner, but Charlie's restaurant never seemed to be empty, and there were a few Defiance members I'd seen around the grounds a few tables away. So we kept our voices down when we needed to and avoided topics that we couldn't discuss with outside ears close by.

Every molecule in my being seemed acutely aware of Max, every sense heightened by her nearness.

I nearly choked on a bite of lamb when her hand crawled slowly up my thigh, under the table, her fingers dipping close enough to graze my clit through the fabric of my pants.

That simple touch sent a bolt of fire rippling through my spine, the sensation somehow heightened by the knowledge that it was a secret moment between the two of us—the message clear that even though we were all together, sharing in our nearness, she wanted me individually.

I hid the pulsing need behind a well-practiced mask, I met her eyes—the dark desire mirrored there enough to instantly melt it away.

I slid down in my chair, unconsciously sliding her hand towards me again, my body craving something I'd normally be too shy to acknowledge or ask for in public. But now, something about the taboo nature of it sent an erotic thrill through me.

Her knuckle ran along the seam of my pants, from my clit down to the wet heat already radiating from my core, a firm promise in the gesture that had me half ready to abandon this team dinner altogether.

As happy as I was to see Eli, I was burning to get Max alone—and I was afraid if I didn't soon, I was going to jump on top of her in front of everyone.

My head pounded with want, the pull I always felt to her loud and insistent, unwilling to be caged after so long apart.

I sipped my water, desperate to relieve the heat, when she stroked me again and I choked, sputtering the liquid back into my cup.

"You okay, Dec?" Eli cocked an eyebrow at me, and something about the teasing gleam in his eyes as they darted between me and Max had me half convinced he knew exactly where my head was.

I cleared my throat. "Fine. Wrong pipe."

Another stroke, this time her thumb circling my clit with a slow, languid stroke.

The corner of her mouth tilted into a knowing smirk as she took a bite of bread.

My pussy throbbed, like it was aching to close around her fingers, to rub against her thigh, skin to skin and delicious heat.

My thong was soaked, and I squirmed in the discomfort of it, in the aching need.

I pushed my chair closer to the table, sat up straighter, and tried listening again to the conversation. Ro and Darius were talking about... something. Though the way Darius flared his nose, his eyes latching onto Max with a want I felt in my bones, told me he was just as aware of the need building between us as Eli was.

Max didn't seem to care. Her hand dipped into the front of

my pants, her fingers slipping through my slickness with the practice of a master.

I bit down on my fork, spilling the piece of fried potato on the table before it could reach my mouth.

"Oh," Max said, arching her brow, "finders keepers."

Using the same fingers that had been stroking me two seconds ago, she picked up the bite of food and ate it, her tongue and lips sucking my juices off her fingers as her eyes met mine.

Wade groaned, the indigo in his eyes bleeding with the dark black of his pupils. Incubus. Of course he could feel the tension, he was fucking feeding off of it.

Thank the gods Ro still seemed oblivious to how bad I wanted to fucking maul his sister at least.

Slowly, I slid my hand over her thigh, pressing my palm to the mound of her, pleased to feel that she was as hot and needy as I was, that I wasn't the only one affected by the desire building between us.

She rolled her hips forward slightly, like she was trying and failing to prevent herself from grinding against me in the middle of the restaurant.

Max's breathing was fast and heavy, and I was hypnotized by the chaotic rise and fall of her chest. She was about as feral and ready to combust as I was—despite the teasing confidence of her fingers. We were both on the edge of losing control entirely.

After a tense pause in which my team all held their breath in a haze of lust, while Ro went on about Charlie's cooking, none the wiser, Max pushed back from the table.

"Er," she cleared her throat, her eyes darting around the table, unable to meet anyone else's, "I'm going to call it for the night. Very tired. Goodnight. See you in the morning."

Her words were stiff and robotic as she stood, her gaze

dropping to meet mine briefly, her pupils blown wide as the succubus energy engulfed me.

With a wave to Mer, who was sitting on the opposite side of the restaurant, she left.

For a moment, we were silent, while Ro stared after his sister looking slightly confused and concerned.

"If you're not going after her," Darius's eyes met mine as he took a long pull from the blood bag clutched in his hand, his fingers nearly puncturing it with the force of his grip, "then I will."

"Yup." I yawned, long and exaggerated as I shoved away from the table, cringing at the metallic groan of the legs on the floor. "Also tired. Long day. I'll help her back and get her settled in for the night."

I all but ran for the door, not giving anyone the opportunity to stop me, hearing only the collective exhale from the others and Wade's low, drawn out "fucking hell" as the door closed behind me.

It was late, so it was dark outside, no light except for the reflection of the moon on the lake and the sprinkling of lights from the various cabin windows.

I didn't see Max, but I took five steps before a hand wrapped around my mouth and pulled me to the back side of the building.

I started to scream and clenched my fists, ready to fight, instinct taking over, before I swallowed the noise as Max pressed her hips into me.

Her eyes were dark, hungry, and the moment she peeled her hand from my mouth, she replaced it with her own.

Our lips met in a clash, as she slid her knee between my thighs, twining our legs together.

Her tongue stroked the roof of my mouth, sending a bolt of raging need low in my belly. I groaned into her, grinding against her thigh as she did the same. Her hands wrapped through my hair, around the back of my neck, pulling me down, closer and harder against her.

"Fuck, I've missed you." The words were little more than a whimper turned into a moan when her hand slid down the front of my pants, soaking my lips with my desire as she spread me.

She ducked down to her knees, her eyes sparkling with mischief as she pulled my pants down to my feet. The cool air hit my soaking pussy like a fucking slap, my hips bucking forward at the urgency of my want.

Fuck. This was reckless. There were dozens of people on these grounds at any given moment—anyone could come out of their cabin for a nighttime stroll at any second and find us like this.

"Max!" I scanned the immediate vicinity, making sure no one was watching us. I could still hear scattered voices in the restaurant, but no one was in sight, and we were in shadow, burrowed between the restaurant and the forest. "Someone is going to see."

"Let them see." Her eyes met mine again, both begging and demanding. "I need to taste you. Now. I don't want to wait another second."

A needy, mewling sound reverberated in the back of my throat as her mouth closed around me, any pretense of calling this off made impossible now by the waves of pleasure swallowing me whole.

"Fuck, that feels good." My head fell to the back of the wall as she licked and sucked. When she shoved two fingers inside, petting along my G-spot, my knees went wobbly.

She pressed her forearm across my hips, stabilizing me against the wall with a surprising strength as she continued feasting like she hadn't eaten in weeks.

Her fingers pumped faster inside of me, her lips sucking on my clit with almost too much force.

My head went dizzy, my heartbeat erratic, as I squirmed, the sensation riding the edge of being almost painful with how good it felt. But her arm remained firm, keeping me there no matter how much I squirmed, her pace unrelenting and punishing until my orgasm ripped out of me. I shoved my fist into my mouth to swallow the scream tearing through my chest as Max kept going, her pace slowing as the sensitivity mounted, but building back up again into another wave.

My legs turned to jelly as my knees buckled, and I slid down the wall until my face was next to hers. She pressed her mouth to mine, as a strange, not-entirely unpleasant tingling sensation engulfed me, the world going topsy-turvy and then black.

I closed my eyes tight, growing dizzy from the surplus of sensations, but when I opened them again, we were standing in the cabin—in the room I'd been sleeping in.

So her powers really were back—and stronger, more controlled than they'd ever been.

Generally, teleporting made me nauseous and exhausted, but the lust shrouding us was so strong, so demanding, that any discomfort slipped nearly unnoticed.

I kicked off my shoes, letting my pants slip to the ground as I made quick work of Max's clothes.

"Fuck, you're beautiful." I shoved her gently back onto my bed, groaning at the smooth, warm skin, the hard peaks of her nipples, the way her hair waved and sprawled out over my pillow.

There was a new, dark iridescent mark carving around her arm, her side. "Is that a tattoo?"

I combed my memory of our last time together. I'd spent hours memorizing it, knew every inch and dip of her skin. This was new.

"You got inked in hell?"

She cleared her throat, a small, shy grin tugging at her lips. "It's a bond-mark."

I nodded, my stomach tightening at the word, like a need, an ache inside of me knew the gravity of it, the reverence—my brain just needed to catch up. Later.

I had questions, but now wasn't the time to ask them. Instead my eyes traced the complex lines and curves of the mark as I pulled my shirt and bra off, wanting as much of my skin against hers as possible.

After peeling her leggings and panties off, I found her hot and soaked, her pussy glistening with need. I crawled onto the bed, sliding my tongue over her, my own clit pulsing when she moaned, like her pleasure was my own. I kissed and nipped along her firm stomach, pressing my knee to her core as she thrust against me, soaking my leg with her desire.

When I took her nipple into my mouth, teasing the hard bud with my teeth, she arched off the bed, her breaths little more than gasps and desperate pants.

"Please, Declan," she whimpered, her voice cracked and raw as my fingers slid down her stomach, her thigh, teasing. "Gods I want you. I feel like I'm going to fucking combust."

This was what I wanted every day for the rest of my life—Max splayed out on my bed, hot and ready for me, shivering at my every touch, begging for my mercy.

I took her bottom lip between my teeth, my stomach tightening at the taste of her as she gasped, hips thrusting forward along my thigh.

She raked her nails down my back, pressing my hips down until I was pressed against her, my entire core throbbing at the friction.

My chest slid against hers as I rode her, my fingers slipping through her folds, thumb circling her clit, until she was a writhing mess beneath me.

"Yes," she moaned, head tilted back, so that my lips and

teeth could find the sensitive skin along her neck. "Yes, just like that. Oh my god," she tried riding my hand, but I wouldn't let her control the pace. This was my turn. I stopped moving my fingers inside of her, stopped grinding against her until my own pussy clenched in frustration at the halt.

A needy, cracked cry left her lips as her dark eyes met mine, flaring with heat and power.

I took that power and made it my own. Slowly, I slid down her, not breaking eye contact, as I lifted her thighs over my shoulders and blew air against her clit.

"Fuck, fuck, fuck," she whispered, fists clenching into my sheets as she tried to hold herself still under my teasing.

Holding this power over her was fucking divine. Everything about her was intoxicating.

When she stopped moving, I grinned, licking her, my mouth closing around her as I pumped two fingers in, then three. She tasted amazing—salty and hot and mine.

Her walls clamped around my fingers as the orgasm ripped through her, her body jerking with the force of it as I ate her out.

"Oh," she panted, chest heaving in ragged breaths, "my fucking," she pulled me up to her, taking my lips with hers as our bodies wound together, "gods."

Both of us were still slippery, unsated as our legs slid together, grinding on each other as we licked, teased, bit, and held each other.

Every inch of my skin was aware of her touch, a single finger on my back as erotic and enticing as the touch of her tight thigh against my core.

She dipped her hand between us and my entire body spasmed when she lightly pinched my clit.

We slid against each other—tangled limbs, sweat, desire, and heat. Our pace picked up as our eyes met, mouths open and gasping into each other as we drew closer to another release.

She pressed her forehead to me, panting and whimpering from the intensity.

"Your mine, Max Bentley," I whispered into the air between us.

She pulled back, meeting my eyes again, their depths dark and filled with power as she nodded. "Yours."

She kissed me as we both exploded, swallowing each other's screams of pleasure until I couldn't be sure where mine ended and hers began.

22

MAX

The room was dark, impossibly cold. I watched my breath form into small, transparent gray clouds in front of me.

Squinting, I saw a figure, huddled into a ball next to me. They were naked and trembling. And almost glowing—the only thing I could see, like they were the light source for this room. If this could be called a room. It felt more like a void.

I inched forward, hyper aware of how silent it was here, how alone we were in the darkness.

It was the heavy sort of darkness that I could feel all the way to my bones, like I could lose my grip on reality if I wasn't careful.

When I reached the ball of trembling limbs and lean muscle, it skittered away before unfolding with a long, anguished cry.

Dark eyes met mine, wide with fear and pain.

"Atlas?"

The sound of my voice made him flinch, his head twisting in each direction at awkward angles, as his breaths came in panicked, rapid gasps.

"No, no, no, no," he repeated over and over again, shifting away from me each time I got close.

"Atlas, talk to me, what's wrong? What's happening? Where are we?" This was no Guild lab room. This was a cold, dead abyss that made Lucifer's dungeon-dark cells feel like luxurious glamping getaways.

My fingers reached for him, seeking his warmth, but he leaned back and screamed, the sound deep and guttural, sounding more wild animal than man as he started to thrash and crawl further away from me.

Tears clouded my vision as I tried to process what I was seeing. I'd seen Atlas in bad shape. Watched as he fought for control against his wolf.

This was different.

He wasn't battling a part of himself here, he was swallowed whole by something malevolent. Something powerful.

His limbs were thinner than I'd ever seen them, his body covered in cuts and wounds that should've healed almost instantly on a werewolf.

I crouched down, a few feet away from him, suppressing the shiver down my spine, the strange wrongness of this place that had the hair at the back of my neck rising to attention.

We weren't alone here.

I couldn't see another presence, couldn't see beyond the few feet between us, but I could feel it, cloying and ominous.

"Atlas," I whispered, reaching forward but making sure that I didn't touch him. My touch seemed to cause him pain—a realization that sent a dagger spiking through my chest.

His body trembled, his hair covering his eyes in dark, greasy strands as he rocked back and forth.

"You aren't real," he whispered, the words masked through a sob, "you aren't real. Go away, go away, go away."

The words grew louder, more powerful, until the darkness

became so thick that I couldn't see through it—could no longer make out the frail shape of him.

I tried to inhale, but my breath got stuck, my throat and chest tight as I clawed at my neck, trying to breathe.

My head went dizzy as the seconds slipped into minutes, I reached forward, trying to find him, to find something, but eventually all I could do was claw at my throat as I curled into a fetal position, like I could open my airway if I just ripped my skin open wide enough.

Panic overwhelmed me as I tried to scream, but without air I was voiceless.

No, this was wrong.

This was a dream.

A dream.

A dream.

I had power here.

This realm belonged to me as much as it belonged to the druden.

I shook my head, pushing away the overwhelming fear that sizzled in my veins, my eyelids tight as I welcomed the darkness, reshaping it as my own.

I shot from the bed in a gasp, my lungs angry and demanding as I pulled in air.

"Max?" Declan rose next to me, her eyes searching for mine, her fear visible even in the darkness of the room.

But even the night felt bright after that place.

"What happened? Are you okay?" I felt her shift out of the sheets, heard her switch on the lamp, watched her scan the room for an enemy invisible to her.

I closed my eyes against the light, giving my body time to adjust to being back on this plane. Panic still clung to my ribs like rotten meat as I tried to pump air through my lungs, pinching my thigh to ground myself in the present.

"It was a dream," she said as she wrapped her hands around my arms, pulling my hands free from my face. "It wasn't real."

It was a dream, yes. But that didn't mean it wasn't real. Because it was. So real that it would be hours—maybe days—before I would be able to shake that cloying darkness.

Her hands cupped my cheeks and, slowly, I opened my eyes again, the outline of her perfect face blurred through the film of tears.

"You're okay, Max, it's okay." Her voice was gentle, reassuring. It called me back, grounded me better than I could do myself.

I nodded, several tears shaking free down my cheek from the movement. "I am," my voice cracked as I tried to hold back my emotion, "but Atlas isn't."

"What?" She froze, her fingers trailing gently down my neck. "What happened?"

Pain seared at her touch and I flinched.

I stood up, made my way to the small mirror on the wall and noticed deep, black gouges down my neck. I lifted my hands, my fingers aligning perfectly with the marks..

I did this. But these were not normal etchings. I should be healed, or healing by now.

"Max?" Concern boiled in her voice, the calm finally outweighed by fear. "What happened?"

"We need to get the others."

∾

THEY'D BEEN ARGUING for twenty minutes about the best way to handle the situation while I paced through the micro living room, the dream with Atlas on repeat in my mind. I could see it so clearly it was almost like I was watching an overlay of the encounter on top of the living room.

He'd seemed so small, so frail, a fragment of the hard, fearless leader I'd always seen him as.

Broken.

"I'm going to go get him." I stopped my pacing to find all of them staring at me, wide-eyed and clench-jawed.

"Absolutely not."

"Max, you just got back, don't be ridiculous."

"We have no idea what kind of dangers you'd encounter there."

Declan took a deep breath, shared a glance with Ro. "We don't know the details, but we know that things in the labs are bad. Very bad."

"What do you mean you know?" Eli narrowed his eyes and took a step closer to her.

Dec didn't meet his gaze, keeping her focus on the wall behind him as she straightened her back. "Evelyn has been trying to get access to the labs when she's able to without raising suspicion. She saw him—and it's bad."

"Evelyn." Eli's voice was hollow, dangerously low. "As in my mother, Evelyn."

Dec sniffed, nodding. "She and Levi work for the Defiance. They have for years. She's our highest-ranking contact still in The Guild at the moment. If there was a way for us to safely get Atlas out, she would have told us."

"Our." Eli's hands closed over the top of the entertainment center until the wood groaned from the pressure. "So you're one of them?"

"For fuck's sake," Wade stood up, "we don't have time to get into the politics of this shit. We trust Levi, Eli. I know that's hard for you to hear, but he's saved our necks more than once while you two were away. And Evelyn—" Wade's eyes softened as he stepped closer to Eli. "She's the reason Seamus is alive. She raided the medical ward at The Guild and got the stuff we needed in time to save his life. So yes, you have a complicated history with your family, I get that. I'm not exactly operating with the most tolerable bloodline myself. But this is bigger than that."

Eli's jaw locked, his eyes dark and filled with an emotion I couldn't parse, but he didn't argue.

"Chances we can get Charlie and the others to help with an extraction?" Ro asked. His hair was still mussed from sleep, his shirt tugged on inside out.

Wade shook his head, punched his fist into the couch before he started pacing, the steps stiff and erratic with barely-contained anger. "They're not going to risk taking on Headquarters and Guild Council until they're certain they have the numbers to win. They won't take that risk. There's too much to lose, they've built too much to chance failing now."

"Maybe if we—" Dec started, but I cut her off.

"It's me," I said. "It has to be me. I can get in and get out. As far as we know, I'm the only one who can."

Darius was peculiarly silent, leaning against the wall across the room, his eyes tracking me like a predator.

"We don't know that you can actually teleport to him." Ro ran a hand over his face, groaning in frustration. "They have so many wards down there, so many protections in place—more, now. And Tarren knows you can teleport. They'll be expecting you to do that."

Probably. But we didn't have any other options.

"We can all go." Eli's voice was even, his mask back in place. "We stand a better chance with all of us."

"I don't think I can carry you all," I said. What I didn't say was the larger truth—that having them all there would be a distraction, more for me to worry about. I stood a bigger chance of losing them all if we all went. I wouldn't save Atlas just to turn around and immediately lose any of the others.

I tilted my head from side to side, felt the strength from the bonds flexing inside of me. The space where I felt Atlas was withered, a hole that had my breath stuttering in my lungs. We were running out of time. How many months could a person stand against a nightmare and survive? I was panicking after just a few minutes.

"I'm stronger now. Stronger than I've ever been, maybe. I can do this." My voice was clear, unwavering. "You just have to trust me."

"Give us two days." Declan grabbed my shoulders, forcing my eyes back to that emerald gaze that had taken my breath away a few hours ago. "If we can't come up with a better plan by then, we'll all go to Headquarters. The old-fashioned way. He's survived for months down there—two days won't break him. We'll get him out." Her lips wavered slightly. "And Sarah."

My stomach sank. In all of my concern for Atlas, I'd nearly forgotten that Sarah was stuck in that hellhole too. Was she being tormented by the drude as well?

I clenched my teeth, dropped my gaze.

She narrowed her eyes, brows furrowed, a question taking shape on her tongue.

"I'll call a meeting with Bishop and the others in the morning." Ro sighed. "Let's try to get some sleep and we can talk about this again when the light is up."

A few minutes later, I curled into Declan's side, my legs entwined with hers. We didn't speak, and I just pressed my head to her chest, listening as the erratic pace of her heartbeat eventually slowed into sleep.

It took me half an hour to realize that I was afraid to close my eyes for intervals longer than ten seconds. I was afraid of falling asleep, falling back into that void of misery.

A void that Atlas had been alone in for months.

Bile rose up in my throat at the realization. I'd been letting myself sink into my team, feeling more alive than I had in a long time. While he'd been suffering.

Charlie, Bishop, the rest of the Defiance, or whatever they

called it—I was pretty sure that we could trust them. There was a rightness about this place, a grounding I felt here that I hadn't felt in a while. I wasn't sure if it was because the bonds with my team were strengthening, or something about them, this place.

But as much as I believed their hearts were in the right place, I knew with an even greater certainty that Atlas wasn't a priority to them in the way that he was to me.

They wouldn't be wrong to refuse going after him. There were so many people here that needed their protection, that relied on their anonymity and clandestine missions. For fuck's sake, I'd seen toddlers running about the camp grounds.

We couldn't ask them to sacrifice this small oasis they'd created. They'd proven that protectors and other demons could thrive in a community together, could care for one another and protect each other.

This was something I had to handle. I was sick and fucking tired of waiting—for Lucifer, for my powers, for answers.

It seemed so clear to me now. *This*—waiting—was our Achilles heel. We spent too much time planning for things to be perfect, going with the flow, waiting for things to align with an imaginary timeline and moral code—when things never once went how we'd planned them to go.

This was something I could do, I knew it. I felt it in my bones.

I was going to get Atlas out of that hellhole.

I was going to get him out tonight.

And the first step?

I needed to dream.

To make a long-overdue visit.

It was still dark when I woke up again, Declan's breathing still deep and even. Her face was just an inch or two from mine, her expression softer than I was used to seeing—peaceful.

I gave myself thirty seconds to memorize the lines of her face, the curve of her nose, the smooth skin along her neck. My hand reached forward, to touch the soft flesh there, fingers hovering just slightly above her, before I pulled them back.

Slowly, I peeled myself out of the bed, careful not to disturb the blankets or the mattress distribution too much. I quietly rifled through my bag until I found some fresh clothes and used the light glow of the moon to change into them.

My hands swept along my thighs out of habit, looking for the one thing I couldn't leave here without. My blade.

I vaguely remembered setting it on the table in the living room, while I'd been pacing like an animal in a cage, back and forth, listening to the others.

Fuck.

I set my hand on the door handle, took a deep, steadying breath, and turned it slowly. The wood groaned slightly as the door opened and I froze.

Dec shifted onto her back, her arm splayed above her head, but her eyes were still closed, her breathing still steady.

When I had an opening large enough for me to squeeze through, I did.

The room was dark, silent, but my eyes had adjusted enough to the night that I could see the general shape of furniture. I got to the small, weathered table and started to panic.

My blade wasn't on it.

I swept my hand along the rough grains, as if the blade had simply camouflaged itself, ran my fingers over the woven rug underneath, in case it fell.

Fuck, fuck, fuck.

Where the hell was it?

Had I left it somewhere else? Did one of the others grab it and put it away somewhere before we all split for bed?

I looked one more time, took a deep breath, and then stood back up. It wasn't ideal, but I'd go without it.

I was weapon enough.

"Looking for this, Little Protector?"

The words were softly spoken, barely even a whisper, but loud enough to send a bolt of panic tingling down my spine. My neck twisted, as I searched for the familiar voice.

Darius.

He was sitting in the corner of the room, buried in shadow, his eyes peeking out behind stray waves of hair, watching me like a predator—my blade clutched in his hand as he balanced the tip on his knee.

For a few breaths, we simply stared at each other, unblinking—the challenge in his eyes clear.

"What are you doing up?" I asked, my voice cracked and quiet.

He arched a brow, sighed, and stood up. His steps were like those of a lion as he closed the distance between us, his eyes never once leaving my face.

When he stopped, he was close enough for me to catch the minty scent of his toothpaste.

I craned my neck to meet his gaze, my heart beating like a jackhammer. Darius couldn't stop me from teleporting, of course, but I'd hoped to buy more time before the others caught on to what I was doing.

He sheathed the blade at my waist, his lip curling into a devilish grin that inspired both fear and excitement in equal parts. "I had a feeling you'd be going on a moonlit stroll tonight. Thought I'd join you."

"How?"

"I know vengeance when I see it, and you were too easy to appease tonight." He bent closer, until our lips were just a few inches apart. "You're stubborn. Far too stubborn to abandon your plans so quickly, without a fight. Not when you're confident that you're right."

I bit down on my lip, hoping like hell I'd at least convinced the others—enough to hold off their suspicions till dawn at least.

"You can't stop me."

His fingers grazed my cheek, the gentle touch lethal in its own way. "I know that. I'm going with you."

"No." The word came out louder than I'd intended, and I froze, listening for movement in the other rooms. I lowered back to a barely-audible whisper, "You can't."

"You don't have the strength to carry us all with you." He took a step closer, until his thigh brushed my hip, his hand resting on the small of my back. I got the feeling he was trying to touch as much of me as possible, in case I decided to try teleporting without him in the middle of his plea. "But you can carry one. So carry me. Let me help you bring back your wolf."

"It's not safe." I tried to move back again, but his grip tightened against me, unwilling to break contact.

I was right. He knew that so long as he was touching me when I teleported, he'd come along for the ride.

"I'm aware." He somehow pressed even closer against me, sending my stomach plummeting for a completely different reason. Threat and seduction were always so intertwined with Darius. "But I'm a vampire. Much harder to kill than the others." His eyes narrowed as he tilted my chin up to meet them. "And I'm more familiar with that cesspool they call a lab than you are. I can help you find him."

"You realize, right, that you're asking to break into what was once your prison? I helped you break out of there not once, but twice. And now you're asking to go back?"

"Not asking." A dark grin lifted his lips, spread to his eyes. "Begging."

I stared at him, considering his offer. My gut still told me to leave him here. To go this alone.

"This," his hand dropped to my shoulder where the bond mark was etched beneath my shirt, tracing the path of it along my arm and side. A shiver rippled through me at his touch. "Means that we're in this together from now on. You're strong, Max. I don't question that. But just this once, let me come with you—don't fight me." His fingers dug into my waist, sending a bolt of desire between my thighs. "Use me. On this mission, especially, let me be your weapon of vengeance. I've earned it."

I heard someone shuffling in one of the rooms. Whose, I wasn't sure.

There was no time to find out.

"Don't—" I bit my lip and shook my head once, "don't make me regret this."

I wrapped my arms around my vampire and pulled him through space with me, clinging to him as we dissolved and reformed alongside each other, my body alive with the closeness of him.

He was right. I was stronger with them around me.

It only took a few separate shifts before we landed outside of a familiar, dilapidated hovel.

My chest pinched at the memory of fixing this spot up for Ralph, at the realization that Ro had spent days here, alone, with nothing but his grief and the biting cold.

Darius twined his hand through mine as a long, shrill alarm rang around us.

It was the same one that sounded during the ambush a few months ago.

"What the hell?" Darius glanced around, searching for a threat. "Did we set off an alarm trigger somehow? What's happening?"

I took a deep steadying breath and grinned into the night. "Izzy."

23

DARIUS

Before I could form my question, she wrapped her arms around me and pulled me through space.

It was easier and less disorienting than it had been—and would continue to get easier as our bond strengthened. But that didn't mean I didn't still feel it.

I swallowed back the nausea, only for another wave of it to hit me hard in the stomach when I caught sight of our new surroundings.

"The labs." The word tasted like bile on my tongue as I came face-to-face with the walls that had drained my life away for four fucking years.

A hot, hollow rage simmered in my bones as I breathed in the familiar scent. Bleach, cleaning equipment, and various tinctures that only went so far in covering the blanket of blood, gore, and misery that truly built these halls.

Max squeezed my hand, her head tilting to the side in question.

I nodded. "I'm okay." And I was. Because while we were standing in the belly of the place that tortured me for years, it was also the place that brought me her. Still, it was surprisingly empty. Especially given all we knew about what had been going on down here lately. "Where is everyone?"

Max grinned, her eyes dark and wild as they found mine. "I dream-walked to Izzy. That's why I didn't leave immediately after everyone went to sleep."

Izzy. It took me a minute to place the familiar-sounding name in my memory.

Max's friend. The one who'd threatened to murder me.

"I like her," I said, a wistful smile tugging at my lips. She had Max's fire, her fearlessness.

Max pulled me further down the hall, towards the light emanating from the cells. "Told her to create a diversion and then evacuate as many people as she could, gave her directions to Charlie's place, just in case, and told her to bring only those she could trust." She smiled. "I imagine she has most of the teams scattered all over the place chasing invisible monsters."

Smart girl. I beamed with pride at her quick thinking. Perhaps this rescue mission wouldn't be as haphazard as I'd feared.

There was a plan, and one filled with all kinds of fuckery meant to mess with The Guild.

I liked it.

That smile melted off my face as Max abruptly stopped, her gasp of horror echoing around the sterile room.

The cells were crammed full of demons—both living, breathing demons, and the remnants of those that weren't. Whether they were killed by the so-called researchers here or from fighting each other, I wasn't sure.

It took a lot to turn my stomach—I literally survived on blood—but even *I* found this hard to look at.

There were piles of bodies in the rooms, discarded like expired meat. Pieces and fragments of body parts and organs I didn't want to examine too closely littered the ground and walls over every overcrowded room.

Several of the demons who were still alive looked practically catatonic, hooked up on IVs that drained them.

"What the hell? How is this even worse than last time I was down here—I didn't think it was possible." Max pressed her small hands to the window of one cell, where a girl no older than fifteen huddled in a small corner with one arm, the wound where her other had been festering and rotting as a feral wolf prowled around her.

They were pitting them against each other, trying to weed out the weak.

Why? This didn't make any sense. The stronger demons were the bigger threats to them.

A shiver rippled down my spine.

I never had a good feeling when I was down in the labs, but something had shifted here, revealed itself—become even more nefarious and twisted than I could have ever imagined.

The thought of Max getting stuck in one of these cages made my blood go cold.

"Let's go." I tugged her back against my chest, her solidness leaning into me enough to ground me, to remind me of my purpose. It was her. Her happiness, her survival. That was all I cared about. And both were compromised the longer we stayed down here. "We can't save them all. Where's our wolf?"

She shook her head, eyes wide and lips quivering as she tried to pull away from the sight in the cell. With a deep, steadying breath, she tugged us once more, until we dropped on the other side of a different cell.

We were in a hall I wasn't familiar with. The rooms here were less violent, the smell of blood and death better disguised.

Max turned, scanning the wall of windows. "They're draining their blood."

I narrowed my eyes, focusing on one man in front of me. He looked around my age, though I couldn't quite tell what kind of demon he was. His veins were black around the needle, the blood leaking into the bag tinted with something strange.

"It's not just their blood," I whispered, stepping closer to get a better look. There was a shimmer in the liquid, the shade of red darker than it should've been. Was that—

"Shadow magic," Max whispered, following the line of liquid with her eyes like she could feel it flowing through the tube. "They've found a way to isolate and pull it from the demons." Panic cannibalized her expression as her eyes started to flutter. "Atlas. We need to find him. Now."

Her hands shook as she moved from cell to cell, the quiet calm and confidence from before now abandoned. When she came upon the cell at the end, a soft "oh," escaped from her lips as she fell to her knees—hands pressed against the glass as she stifled a sob.

Pain pulsed through her, so strong and harrowing that I felt it mirrored in my body.

When the occupants of the cell came into sight, I understood why.

There were three people in there—Sarah, Atlas, and someone I didn't know.

None of them were touching, none of them even visibly moving.

Instead, they were each huddled in a corner of the small room, naked and trembling—Atlas and Sarah covered in a sheen of sweat, their veins a sickly grayish-black and visible through their skin.

The third figure looked much better off, his body half there, half billowing black shadows that crept towards the other two. His eyes were pure black, bent in concentration.

Every few seconds, his body would break down more, until he was dissolved almost entirely into black shadow. The waves of black rammed into the wall, like he was trying and failing to escape. There was a thick, dark band around his ankle—the lower half of that leg the only part of him that seemed unable to fully change into his shadow form. A dark bag attached to a needle in his foot filled with a steady drip. They were siphoning from him too.

Druden were incredibly strong, their power almost entirely stemming from shadow magic. He was likely their prized prisoner.

Max rammed her hands against the glass, her eyes wild and wide as she called to the wolf.

He either couldn't hear her or didn't have enough strength to respond, to react.

Her panicked expression turned towards me and I felt my chest crack in half at the sight of her. She felt others' pain so acutely. It was like watching her break over her father's body all over again.

Tears streamed freely down her cheeks as I bent down next to her to wipe them. I scanned the hall looking for a tool, for something to break down the wall, but I knew that it was futile. The Guild was run by assholes but, for the most part, they were competent assholes.

She closed her eyes tight, face scrunched in focus as her hands tightened into fists. "I can't—" a sob pulled through her chest, "I can't teleport inside."

I nodded, swallowing down the unexpected emotion rising in my throat. Witnessing her pain hurt me more than my own.

My teeth clashed together, jaw muscles twitching as I studied the drude. "They've found a way to block that kind of magic. The drude can't escape either. I don't think," I narrowed my eyes, noticing the bleak, empty expression on the demon's face, "I don't think he's pulling from them by choice. The Guild is siphoning his power, siphoning what he's pulling from them."

He was the siphon.

Was this how they'd learned how to isolate and draw out

shadow magic so easily? Wolves didn't have much, it wasn't the foundation of their magic, but he was using their power to amplify his own, converting it.

I ran a hand over my hair, feeling helpless as I tried to comfort her. Fuck, this was messed up. We'd come this far. We had to find a way to help them.

Hell, I didn't even particularly like the wolf, but I wouldn't wish the fate of these cells, of these fucking piranhas, on anyone.

Fire flared from Max's hands as she pressed them into the unbreakable glass, heating it to unspeakable temperatures.

Still, it did nothing.

"You can't go in there," a soft voice sounded behind me and I jumped—frustration and panic flooding my system at the surprise.

I should have heard her, should have been keeping watch, but I was distracted by Max's pain, by my helplessness. She deserved better than me falling apart because I couldn't control my own emotions.

We both craned our necks to see who'd intruded into the otherwise silent hall.

A tall, white woman with blond hair and biting blue eyes stood a few feet away from us. Her face was all sharp angles, her posture rigid as her stare locked onto Max.

Max stiffened. "Reza?"

The girl arched a perfectly-plucked brow and crossed her arms over her chest. "Figured it was you—that Izzy and the others were acting on your orders. Always ready and willing to follow your lead."

Her voice was arch, and I kept my focus between her and Max, trying to decipher if this was a girl I was allowed to eat and kill.

She nodded to the window, eyes darkening when they

landed on the three miserable figures in there. "You can't go in there."

"Reza, please," Max stood, so I did too, trying to edge myself between them in case the girl was more dangerous than she looked. I knew better than to underestimate The Guild. Never again. "We need to get him out, he's going to die."

The girl studied Max for a long moment, then nodded, her body relaxing slightly. "I know. I've been waiting for you, expected that you'd come for him a hell of a lot sooner than you did." Her lips curled in disgust. "*You* can't get in there. But *I* can."

Max took a step back, surprise etched in plain lettering across her face. She tilted her head to the side, eyes narrowed as she watched the girl. "You're—you're going to help me?"

The girl, Reza apparently, clenched her jaw, her nostrils flaring slightly as she scanned the empty hall. When she turned back to face us, she'd deflated slightly, her harsh edges and attitude softening into disappointment, into fear.

"I didn't know." Her voice cracked, but she shook her head slightly and took a deep breath. "What they're doing down here—it's not right. I'll help you get to him if you promise you can get him out of here, away from them."

The two women stared each other down, an understanding passing between them.

I wasn't sure what their history was, but I could tell in the lines of tension in Max's body that it was a complicated one. Fraught, even.

Max straightened her posture, turned to me briefly with a nod, then met Reza's eyes again. "Deal."

"Follow me." Reza led us through a maze of halls and rooms that I'd never been in before. She had a keycard with a photo of a woman who looked a lot like her, but wasn't. She was older, more severe looking in the image, with cropped hair and a sharp jaw.

Some doors required her to prick her thumb on a blade she kept on her thigh.

I nodded, impressed that she didn't seem to grimace or fawn away from the pain.

"Once I heard the commotion, I checked on the cameras to verify that you were down here, then I did what I could to clear the way," she said, brows arched, clearly pleased with herself. "It won't buy you much time, but hopefully enough." She turned back to Max, a flash of panic halting her step. "You can still do that teleporting thing right? This whole plan is hitched on the premise that you can—that you can take him with you. Quickly, before they throw him back in his cell. Whatever Izzy's done to sound the alarms, it won't clear these halls for long."

Max nodded.

The girl's shoulders sagged with relief. "Good. Okay. Then let's do this."

"And you?" Max asked, as we ran after her. "Your mother—the others—they're going to know that you helped us."

There wasn't accusation in her voice, only curiosity.

Reza's jaw clenched tightly, her hands balled into fists at her sides. "I don't care what they find out. As long as you get him out of here. They're going to kill him." She shook her head. "It won't be the end of the world for me. They'll punish me. Badly, probably. But they won't kill me. And my mother will do what she can to soften whatever blow the council gives." Then, with a note of bitterness, she added, "she won't let her precious legacy disappear or be tarnished if she can help it."

With a final shove of a heavy, solid metal door, she led us into a room, stopping short. A short, stocky man that I was all too familiar with stood in the center of it.

"Good, you're still here." Reza pushed further into the room.

Max stiffened, fingers flexing on the handle of her blade when she saw the man. "Sal?"

I clenched my jaw at the sight of the man—he'd been the primary instrument of my torture during my time here.

"You." His lips curled in disgust, a flash of recognition in his eyes when they landed on me. His finger hovered over a button, beady eyes darting for a weapon or alarm to sound, no doubt.

Max spun on Reza, hand lighting with hellfire. "You set us up?"

Reza rolled her eyes and pulled out her dagger. "We need his blood and mine," she shrugged, "well my mother's line anyway," to open his cell. Precautions have tightened since you've proven particularly adept at breaking people out of this place."

"Reza!" Sal's face drained of what little color it had, spittle flying from his lips as his eyes darted between us. "You can't betray your kind." His lips curled as he shook his head at her. "Your mother will be disgusted that you've let them in here." He took two wide steps, his arm lifting towards a lever that I was all too familiar with. He was going to sound an alarm—alert the others that we were here. "You—"

In a flash, I closed the distance between us and snapped his neck, the loud crack echoing in the control room. They'd given this place quite a few upgrades since my stay.

Reza's eyes widened, her face contorting in rage. "What the fuck have you done? I didn't bring you here to fucking kill him."

"This man is—" I paused, shifting his body more comfortably in my arms, "*was* a fucking monster. A sadist—and the nonconsensual kind, to be clear. I'm all for those who rock that lifestyle with permission." I blinked, refocusing at the flash of confusion on the girl's face. "He lived his entire adult life torturing people for pleasure down here. He won't be missed."

When my gaze met Max's, she simply nodded, any look of disappointment I'd expected to see reflected in her eyes replaced by an unfazed acceptance.

"He's right." She turned to Reza. "And we don't have time

for this. Anyone who gets in our way will meet the same fate. Open Atlas's cage. Now."

Reza took a deep breath and, for a long moment, I thought she might abandon us here. Instead, she shook her head and rushed over to a complicated panel, filled with small reservoirs and buttons—each one labeled with a number.

"He's in cell 47. Only five people have access cards to get this room. So from here, the protocol is a little more lax. Sal and I have to drop our blood in the coordinating reservoir at the same time, then push the button. It needs to be fresh from the vein." She turned to me, judgment and disgust practically licking against my skin. "So we'll need to be quick and hope that the fact that he's dead won't matter. Then, the cell will open for exactly thirty seconds. If you don't get him out before then, it will close and we won't be able to open it again for two hours without a council member present to override it. When it opens," her eyes cut to Max's, "everyone with clearance will be alerted that there's a breach. You'll need to leave immediately. Take him, go, and never come back."

Is that what she considered fucking lax? Gods, protectors were fucking paranoid.

Then again, I supposed we'd given them plenty of reason to prove that paranoia valid. We were, in fact, breaking in—and out.

Max considered her for a long moment. "Why are you doing this? You won't see him again. And you love him."

Her jaw locked in response as she glanced from Sal's corpse, back to Max. "That's *why* I'm doing this." Her expression hardened, posture straightening as she unsheathed her blade. "And before you say it, yes I know that he doesn't love me—I know that it's always going to be you. But I deserve to be more than someone's second choice." She reopened the cut on her thumb and walked over to me. "I don't want him to die, and I don't want to be forever tied to someone who spends every ounce of his energy wanting someone else." She cut Max with a dark look. "For months, the only word he's spoken is your name."

She sliced Sal's wrist with less care than her own, then held her finger and his arm above the spot with a number 47 etched into it.

Max watched the blood pool in the small divot, a flash of indecision on her face before her focus cut to me. Her eyes were wild with more emotion than I could decipher in the flash of time I saw them.

She took a slow, steady breath, arriving at some decision I couldn't follow.

She closed the distance between her and Reza with more speed than a protector could muster.

Then with a muttered, "Sorry, Reza," she split the girl's wrist with her blade and squeezed her arm, pulling and dragging her so that the entire board was washed in her blood.

"What the fuck are you doing?" Reza's eyes widened with surprise, then darkened with anger as Max shoved her away and repeated the process with Sal's body.

"No one deserves to die here, rotting away like this." With a wild, dangerous grin she turned back to her. "All of their power stolen?" She shook her head. "I'm letting them out. All of them."

"W-what?" Blood drained from the girls' face, until her skin was almost translucent with panic. "Bentley, you can't. That's not why I brought you here. Atlas. You're supposed to just take Atlas. I get that it's bad down here, but that doesn't mean you have the right t-to—Max, this will destroy everything."

Max shrugged, fire burning behind her eyes as she spared the girl little more than a second glance.

She was fucking magnificent. If it weren't for the potential threat on our lives at the moment, I'd bend over that panel and fuck her senseless.

"Thank you for your help, Reza." She nodded once in the

girl's direction, but continued her work. "I won't forget it. But I'm not leaving with the labs still standing and stocked full like this. If you don't want to join us for this part, then I suggest you get out. Now." She craned her neck to face the girl. "While you still can."

Reza grunted in disbelief, but as she watched the unilateral focus and power pulse from Max—so strong my own veins were practically marinating in it—she stumbled, took a few last lingering glances at us both. When her gaze landed on Sal's limp carcass, her breath hitched. And then, without another argument, she bolted, her sneakers squeaking on the floor down the hall as she turned the corner.

Max turned to me, unconcerned with the hasty departure or the threat of cavalry that would likely be ushering through those halls any moment, and took a deep breath. "No going back now. Ready?"

Fuck yes.

I dropped the sorry sack of a flesh suit at my feet and joined her in hitting all of the buttons. Warning alarms cut through my eardrums as the place lit up with red, flashing lights.

I had absolutely no idea if this was going to work, but it was worth a shot.

"Get them out," she said, hands lighting with fire again. She dug her fingers into the panels, let the flames spread—the electrical equipment sizzling as it fried. "All of them."

She was locking the mechanisms in place, giving us more time to get them out. Genius. Her powers wouldn't work against the material they used to contain the demons, but they never considered that a demon might have access to their tech.

"Meet me at the front of the labs." She turned to me, skin glowing by the light of the fire.

Gods, she was radiant.

A fucking goddess.

And she was mine.

"Fucking now, Darius. Go."

My cock strained against the zipper of my pants as I grabbed her face in my hands and stole a quick, hard kiss.

"Burn it all down to the fucking ground, little protector," I whispered the words against her lips, my heart—and dick—throbbing with pride. "I'll bathe in the ashes with you."

I felt her smile against my mouth.

"Now," I pulled away, reluctantly dragging my eyes from the fire blazing in hers. I ran to the doorway but turned back long enough for a quick wink before disappearing through it. "I'll get the others. You go get our surly wolf. We have a war to start."

24

MAX

The metallic, briny smell of the blood and gore still lingered beneath the bleach that they'd used in an attempt to cover it. Even the smoky fumes from my fire frying the control panel couldn't erase the scent of death that caked this place. It lingered, like a fresh lining in my nose.

My body shook with rage from what The Guild was doing here, but my hands were still as I washed their sins away. My fire flared over the room, disintegrating all the *work* they'd done, the control they held.

With a final sweep of my surroundings, I teleported to Atlas, trusting Darius to get as many of the prisoners to their safety as he could, before I took this place down.

Because my disgust made one thing clear—it was going down. I'd burn it until it was nothing more than ash.

I realized, with a breathtaking clarity, that my life had been a series of things happening to me—of me passively reacting and responding. No more. I wasn't taking shit on the cheek anymore.

I was taking control of my life.

I was going to do what should've been done the first day I found Ralph and Darius down in these fucking cells.

I had all of this power—it was time I used it for something I believed in.

The door to Atlas's cell was open now, the others around him already empty—their occupants no doubt seizing their chance at freedom the moment it was in sight.

The drude that was locked in their cell was gone, no sign of him left.

Even with the bind on his legs, feeding off the other two had probably supplied him with enough energy and strength to quickly disperse when the opportunity struck.

Sarah and Atlas were still huddled in their corners, oblivious to the shift in the air, to the fire and chaos that was screaming through the halls.

I ran to him, my heart cracking in half at the way his body trembled.

His hands gripped his dark, sweat-soaked hair, several inches longer than it had been the last time I'd seen him. His eyes were pinched tight, cheeks hollow and dusted with an uneven, scraggly beard.

The room smelled stale, even though the people who worked down here had been doing their best to hide the horror of their work.

"Atlas." I set my hand on his shoulder, tentative, his skin cold and clammy to the touch.

He flinched, pinched his eyes tighter, gripped his hair with renewed strength that had several strands ripping at the root. He rocked his body forward and back, his head slamming into the wall behind him each time.

"Atlas," I whispered again, pulling my hand back as tears clouded my vision. "It's me. It's Max."

A tremor rolled through his body at my name, but he pushed himself further into the corner, head shaking.

"No, no, no," he repeated, his voice little more than a whimper. "My fault. My fault."

I swallowed down the emotion, dug deep down to find the strength that he needed. Carefully, I cupped his face in mine, pressed my forehead to his, and closed my eyes. "It's me, Atlas, I'm here. I came to get you out of here. The others, your brother—we're all safe. *You* saved us." Tears rolled down my cheeks as I searched within me for that damaged cord that tied us together. "Please. Please let me save you now."

I knew that the hellfire wouldn't harm me. Knew from experience that it probably wouldn't hurt Atlas either. But Sarah was here too and we needed to go before there was structural damage. Fires did more than simply burn, and I had no desire to be buried under the rubble of this glorified cemetery.

"Please," I whispered, pressing my lips softly to his. I hadn't even meant to do it really, it was like there was a strong magnet pulling between us, resistance futile.

When I opened my eyes, he was peering back at me, pupils blown wide until all I saw was black, no sign of the wolf at all.

The only emotion in his eyes was fear, strong and solid as he shook his head.

"Max?" He pulled back from me, head crashing hard against the wall. "You can't be here. You can't. You—" His eyes darted around the room frantically, searching. "You have to go. Before you die. You always die."

When I made no move to leave him, he shoved me—a gentle pressure. A sob ripped through him. "Go. Please. No time. GET OUT."

His voice reverberated around us, loud and filled with an agony that tore through my ribs as if it were my own.

I shook my head, stifling my own sob. "I'm not leaving without you, Atlas."

"It's not real." His voice was hollow as he snorted. He shook his head again, rubbed his eyes into the palms of his hands. "Not real. You're not real."

A loud, metallic clang echoed around us. I had no idea how much damage my flames had done, how quickly the fire was spreading.

We didn't have time.

In retrospect, I probably should have waited to commit arson until after we were out and safe, but something had come over me after seeing what they'd done here—my patience wrung out like a rag.

I had no idea how much time Izzy and Reza's diversions would buy us, but I had a feeling it was running out.

I couldn't heal the invisible wounds in his mind, but I could do my best with the physical ailments.

If he didn't have his own power, I'd give him some of mine.

With a deep breath, I closed my eyes and pressed my lips to his again. I clung to the tether between us, pushed as much of my power into it as I could, felt my heart flutter in my chest as it gave to him.

And gave and gave.

My hands gripped his chest, the side of his head, as I focused on funneling my strength into him, on healing as much of him as I could. The magic didn't have specific injuries to latch onto, but I focused on sensing his life force and pushing as much of mine into him as I could.

I gave until I reached that tipping point, the one I'd slowly learned would leave me comatose for days if I crossed it. We didn't have the luxury of me giving more than I could, not right now.

He inhaled sharply against me, his mouth cracking open into a loud, deep scream against my lips.

But still, I felt it working, fixing and strengthening what it could, leaving the rest for later.

When we were safer.

When he could unpack whatever trauma the nightmares had unlocked and rained down upon him.

Months. Fucking months. My breath floundered in my chest at the thought of him endlessly confronting his deepest fears. I'd shared two brief dreams with him and still felt the terrifying ache they'd left in my spine, the scars invisible but there all the same.

His breathing was ragged, his chest lifting and falling in an unnatural cadence as he fought me, as he fought to decipher reality from the dream world he'd been locked in.

"Atlas," I whispered, falling back on my butt to give him a few inches of space. "This is real. Me and You. I'm here. This isn't a dream. This isn't a nightmare." I picked up his hand, pressed it against my chest, let him feel the heavy pounding of my heartbeat. "Focus on my pulse. Focus on me. Breathe."

I took a deep, slow breath, and watched him mimic the pace.

After a few long minutes that seemed to stretch into eternity, his head lifted slightly, eyes finding mine. There was so much pain, so much turmoil and distrust in their depths—but there was a brief flicker of hope too.

"Max?" His voice cracked on my name. "It's really you?"

I exhaled in relief, a fresh wave of tears blurring him from my sight. I nodded rapidly as they fell down my cheeks, squeezed his hand against my chest. "Yes, Atlas. It's really me."

The air grew thicker with smoke as the fire made its way closer to us.

We were almost there. Almost.

He considered me, neither of us breathing as he brought a hand to my cheek, then pulled away to stare at the liquid glistening on his fingers. He pressed those fingers to his mouth, tongue peeking out to taste my tears—like he couldn't manage to trust any one of his senses on its own.

"Atlas," I wiped my eyes, and turned to Sarah. She was just

as lost inside of herself as he had been. I'd need his help getting her out of here. Sharing my strength with him had cost me some of my own. "Atlas, we have to go. Can you stand? Can you walk?"

I hoped like hell that my healing had helped some of his atrophied muscles—had given him enough strength for this journey.

His jaw clenched as his gaze met mine again, wild and angry. He nodded.

"Good." I stood up, pulled him with me, and stepped out into the hall. I grabbed a stack of hospital gowns and handed him one before I bent down next to Sarah, tugging one over her.

Unlike Atlas, she didn't seem to respond to my touch at all. Her head rolled back, her body doll-like as I quickly dressed her and pulled her into my arms.

Atlas was at my side in an instant and grabbed her from me, cradling her against his chest.

Another loud crash sounded, startling us both. I'd never successfully transported with more than one person before, but if we did it in short spurts, I hoped it wouldn't be too draining.

I wrapped my arms around them both and pulled us to the entrance of the labs.

A wave of nausea from the jolt of carrying two people washed over me, but I swallowed it back as the world reformed and settled around us.

Where the hall had been eerily quiet and empty twenty minutes ago, it was now filled with chaos.

People ran—in human form and wolf—as they sought safety, breaking their chains and ripping out IV bags, blood and magic splattering the floors and walls, as they clashed into each other. They weren't fighting, weren't using the freedom to continue the brawls that had been forced on them in their individual cells.

They just wanted out.

I left Atlas with Sarah briefly, needing to make sure that all of the cells were open. They were. There didn't seem to be a living soul in sight. Just the broken and abandoned bodies, discarded empty shells of the demons they once were. I clenched my jaw and felt the pain of their loss flare deep and heavy in my chest.

We'd done what we could. It wasn't enough to erase the pain of this place, but it was a start.

When I returned to them, my blood went cold for a new reason.

"Atlas?" The familiar voice echoed down the corridor, sharp and threatening. Familiar blue eyes cut into me with a vicious glare. "You. Of course, it's fucking you."

Tarren.

My teeth squeaked with the force of my grind as I clenched my jaw.

I walked, unblinking, until I stood next to Atlas. The last time I'd come face-to-face with his father, he'd taken mine from me.

My fingers itched to grab the blade at my thigh, to carve out his heart with a ferocity that would make even Darius flinch from the violence of it.

Atlas's warmth, his pain washed over me, freezing me in place.

No. I couldn't do that. Couldn't bring the same hurt I'd felt onto him or Wade.

The muscles in Atlas's jaw worked as he turned to me, depositing Sarah in my arms.

My knees buckled under her weight.

Where was Darius? Panic whipped through my body as I craned back to the fire, hoping like hell he was out of here already, that he was somewhere safe.

Without another word, Atlas walked towards his father, his steps sure and steady.

I shifted Sarah's weight slightly. "Atlas?"

"What are you doing? What have you done, son?" Tarren's words were biting, but I could see flashes of sadness in his eyes as he surveyed him. "Atlas, I—"

Before he could finish the sentence, Atlas wrapped one arm around Tarren's shoulder, like he was going in for a hug.

But then he plunged the other straight into his chest.

I stopped breathing—couldn't even blink through the shock.

"You hurt her." Atlas pulled his hand back, fingers wet and red, holding the warm, deceptively large heart of his father.

Tarren's body buckled at the knees and crashed to the ground. His eyes opened wide with surprise, but were otherwise empty.

Dead.

He was unquestionably dead.

Without another thought for the man, Atlas turned back to me and dropped the heart at my feet. "Let's go home, Max."

Darius turned the corner, his eyes, sparking with adrenaline, cut from Tarren, to Atlas, to me. He nodded once, a dark grin twisting his lips. "Well done, wolf. Though I'm sorry I didn't get to take him out myself. Would've enjoyed torturing him for a few days." Then, he turned to me, assessing me from head to foot, nodding again when he was satisfied that I was unharmed. "Izzy and the others are outside. It's a little," he narrowed his eyes, "intense."

Fuck.

Izzy. I'd nearly forgotten.

Atlas grabbed Sarah from me, either oblivious or unconcerned with the dark blood he smeared all over her in the process, and we followed Darius.

It was quick work moving through the once-beloved building. I caught a brief glance of the cafeteria as the front door came into sight. Longing gripped at my chest, remembering my first time walking into that room. With Ro. With Cy. It was the first time I'd laid eyes on Eli, on Atlas. It was hardly even a year ago, yet it felt like I'd lived ten lives in that time.

A man stood in the hall, a few feet from the door outside. He was tall and thick, dressed in a heavy black robe that contrasted deeply with the pale white skin of his hands. The wristbands and center clasp were adorned with The Guild crest, but he was unfamiliar to me.

The brief glimpse of his forearms revealed black veins that bulged beneath his skin like poison, not unlike what I'd noticed in the demons locked downstairs.

He pulled back the large hood, revealing a bald head and entirely unmemorable face—nose and eyes small, features flat. It was difficult to pin down an age—he could just as easily be seventy as thirty. There was something about his eyes, dark and swirling, that felt wrong. Dangerous. It wasn't the intensity I'd grown accustomed to in other demons. It was something else entirely.

There were no eyebrows visible on his face, but if he'd had any, his expression gave the impression that he'd be arching them. His lips were pressed flat, but I had a feeling that he was laughing at us.

My mouth dried up at the sight of him, and I could feel Darius's curiosity, confusion, and anger radiating from him in equal parts as we all came to a standstill, unsure who—or what—we were dealing with here.

"So, you're the girl." The man, who I figured must belong to the council, turned his head, studying me—whatever he found in his assessment clearly lacking. "Consider your declaration of war heard—loud and clear. I can't speak for the others, but I know I, personally, will enjoy watching your defeat."

I stood taller, suppressed the wave of repulsion ripping

through me at the metallic wrongness of his voice. My fingers itched for my blade, before I remembered I was a far more powerful weapon than any metal could be.

Fire flared to life through my fingers and I drew a line of it between us, a shield of sorts to keep the others safe.

I felt Darius coil, ready to spring at my side, reading his moves and patterns with the ease with which I knew my own.

"We'll meet again soon, girl," he said, not taking his eyes off the blazing barrier in front of him.

He didn't seem afraid of the fire—if anything, he seemed almost envious of it.

My flames cut towards the man, hot and angry and mobilized by the rage I'd been fostering for years. But the councilman seemed unconcerned, only met my eyes briefly and then disappeared from sight.

"Did he just—" Dairus's eyes narrowed as he studied the spot that had held a man only one second ago.

"Teleport," I finished for him. "I didn't think protectors could do that."

Other than me—but I was more than just a protector.

Darius, frowning, reached for my hand as the flames died from my fingers. "They can't."

When we made it to the door, crisp fresh air beat against my skin. I invited it into my lungs, stunned by the sight before us.

Dozens—probably hundreds of people stood outside. Some of them wore familiar faces—Izzy and Arnell at the front—others carried themselves with the wear and tear of life within the labs.

"Max!" Izzy was eyeing a particularly frail girl who was leaning against a large tree when she caught sight of me.

Her body crashed into mine with a momentum that had me falling into Darius at my back.

"Thank the gods you're fucking okay." Her words were mumbled against my ear as she squeezed the life force out of me. "I was about two days away from hunting you down myself."

"Good to see you too, Iz," I pulled back and studied my best friend closely.

The bags under her eyes were fuller, darker than I'd ever seen them, but the flare of focus in her gray eyes was more vibrant than ever. Through the exhaustion, she'd come alive—found a focus, a sense of purpose that molded and shaped her into something even stronger than she was before. Which was saying something because she'd been a fucking force since the very moment I'd met her.

We had a lot of catching up to do, but it would have to wait.

"Did you get everyone out?" I asked.

I knew, at the very least, that the council had moved the younger students, the ones not yet assigned teams, to a secret location a few states away, in an attempt to keep them safe after the ambush—so no one unable to protect themselves would be harmed tonight.

"Of course I did." She arched a cocky brow, then scrunched her nose in confession. "Well, Arnell did most of it. He hacked into their tech with the ease of a warm knife slicing through butter. Main building is clear. Pulled the teams a few miles away like we'd planned and then I made sure that everyone who's with us stayed behind. Called in every favor I had, and it took some serious work but," she shrugged, scanning the collection of protectors who were eyeing the freshly freed demons with more than a little trepidation and fear. A few seemed to have a vampire pinned who was snapping his mouth with a ferocity that spoke of a dangerous hunger. "I think we mostly pulled it off. Of course, we've lost our layer of anonymity and secrecy in the process. We won't be of any more help to you here—we've played all of our cards."

I squeezed her hand and walked into the strange crowd. Good.

I knew from the moment I stepped foot into our dreamscape that Izzy, Sharla, Arnell, and whoever else was with us, wouldn't be spending another night at Headquarters. There was no going back from this. And after tonight, I'd make sure that there was no Headquarters to return to.

While many of the lab's former occupants were scattered around the grounds, I had no doubt that several had made haste with their unexpected freedom and dispersed. We just had to hope that they wouldn't go on an attacking spree.

It was a problem for another day.

Most of them, however, seemed too weak to get very far. All of the demons remaining looked far weaker than Darius and Ralph had after their horrendous stay in the labs, so I knew that Tarren and the council had amped up their tactics. Massively.

The Guild was a rabid animal that had been backed into a corner—lashing out with a surge of strength.

Even though everyone looked more or less human at the moment, it was easy to tell Izzy's collected protectors from the demons in the labs. The latter were predominantly either naked or dressed in hospital gowns that had seen better days. They were also almost all trembling with fear and the remnants of whatever drugs had been pumped into them to suppress or drain their power.

A few demons were coiled a few feet away, ready to attack—either each other or the protectors surrounding them—but the confusion and chaos had thankfully kept too many skirmishes from breaking out.

My fire flared to life, carving a tall hedge of flames between them, stopping three demons mid step.

The intensity of the hellfire pulled everyone's attention to me.

"Listen," I cleared my throat, not entirely sure how to rally a large group of people who'd spent a lifetime learning to hunt each other. "Er, right."

My eyes met Darius's and he nodded, his hand finding mine in a show of solidarity.

"The Guild has lied to everyone." I projected my voice as loud as I could into the silent, wide-eyed crowd. This message, I directed at the protectors, some looking confused, others mobilized by the events of the evening. "Fabricated a history of our world, of the hell realm. They've been stealing magic from the demons they keep in the labs—not to protect humanity or their supposed values—but to take the only thing they've ever cared about. Power." I shook my head, trying to gauge how much I should reveal, how much I should tell them. But I'd had enough of lying, enough of half-truths. "No more. Because, honestly, The Guild is the least of our concerns. The sudden presence of the council, the urgency and shift in Guild tactics, the magical surges, the hell-realm breaches. These things are indicators of a larger problem. An existential one. The realms are dissolving, the magic crafting them is warping in unpredictable, uncontrollable ways. If we truly want to save humans, our loved ones, each other—we have to work together."

My voice broke into the wind, and I paused, searching for what else to say. So many scared, angry, hesitant faces met mine.

But then my focus cut to Arnell, his dark eyes glistening in the soft light. He clenched his jaw tight, his lips twitching in an almost imperceptible smile, urging me to continue.

"There is a place not far from here. A place where protectors, other demons, and humans live and fight for a better world together—a place of community, of accountability. I'm extending an invitation to every one of you here, to join the community that we have become a part of—and if they won't have us all, then to create something new with us instead—" I honestly had no idea if Charlie and Bishop could house this many people, but we'd jump that hurdle when we met it, "to fight to protect each other as we take on whatever this new, strange world will throw at us." I paused for a moment, took a deep breath, "It has always been so, but we declare it together now—from this night forward—The Guild and their council are an enemy to us all."

A few of the demons from the labs bristled, glancing at each other with skepticism etched into every line of their bodies. It was to them that I directed this next part.

"You don't need to fight with us, of course. We won't force anyone to join us. You're free to leave this night, to forge your own path, if that's what you prefer. I wouldn't blame you if you found trusting a stranger difficult, especially after what The Guild has put you through." I took a deep breath and straightened my spine, the hundreds of eyes pinned to me like tingling sparks along my skin. "You're free to leave this place, so long as you do so peacefully. But make no mistake, if you attack or harm anyone who hasn't directly harmed or threatened you, we will hold you accountable. You don't have to join us, but if you go against us, the peace between us ends."

"So you're really just going to let us go?" a thin man with matted red hair asked. His arms were crossed, muscles tense with distrust.

I took a deep breath, cut my eyes from Izzy, to Darius and Atlas, then back to the redhead. I nodded. "Yes. We all deserve the chance to choose where our allegiances lie." I cocked a brow and took a step closer to him, pulling my fire back so that it left nothing but a line of scorched grass in its wake. "This is yours."

A short white woman with kohl eyes glared at me. "What reason do we have to trust you?"

Izzy snorted. "Um, did you miss the part where she just burned down the lab and made sure you weren't in it when she did? I'd say that's a pretty damn good first impression."

I rested my hand on her shoulder, pulling her back before Izzy-best-friend-mode activated fully.

"Just so we could become soldiers in this supposed war we're expected to buy without question?" The redhead shook his head. "Kind of seems like moving from one prison to another."

I didn't blame him for his distrust. It was warranted—I honestly had know idea what the fuck I was doing.

Hell, I'd only just met Charlie and the rest of the Defiance and I *still* had no idea whether Lucifer was leaning more towards good or evil. He seemed to fluctuate in my estimate as frequently as the sun rose.

But I was convinced, indisputably now, that if good and evil did exist, The Guild was the latter. It was the one thing driving my moral compass now. And the only thing I could do was just go with it. "Like I said, you're free to go. And I don't really have any answers or guarantees if you choose to join us. We're sort of figuring things out as we go. The apocalypse, unfortunately, did not come with a thorough instruction manual. I'm simply extending the offer to join us, if you want it. If you need a place to go or a purpose to filter your anger and strength through. Otherwise, so long as we don't get wind of you attacking innocents, you won't hear from me again."

The man's posture remained tense, but he didn't push any further.

"We're taking down The Guild—the council that runs them—whether you're at our side or not." Darius's voice was strong and deep as it projected over the group. His eyes were wild with light.

The hazy glow of dawn softened what had seemed like dozens of glowering faces, revealing the fear and anxiety that coated us all.

While some of the demons and protectors had split off from the group during my bumbling speech, winding their way through the woods, bent on their own paths forward, others eyed me—each other—with curiosity. Some, even with hope.

I wondered how many people in the labs were former members of The Guild. I was certain Atlas and Sarah weren't the only ones.

We needed to get a move on. I heard rustlings in the distance, shouts, and knew that the team members Izzy and Arnell had sent out would be back soon—and filled with a rage I didn't want to face just yet.

Even if it was only Atlas, Sarah, Izzy, Arnell, and Darius coming back to The Lodge with me, I couldn't teleport us there. I was drained from lending so much strength to Atlas.

And judging by the numbers Izzy had gathered, there would be far more people joining our trek back than just the six of us.

Hope bloomed sweet in my chest, curling through my limbs like a cool breeze.

This—whatever this was, exactly—wasn't nothing.

I had no idea what this revolution would look like tomorrow, but the promise of it sparked a new clarity in my bones.

We had each other, and that was a hell of a lot to fight for, to hold onto.

"We need to go," Arnell said, nodding to the group of people gathered behind him.

I turned around, studied the large, castle-like building that stood tall and ominous behind me. "You're certain everyone is out?"

Izzy nodded.

Sirens roared their fury into the early morning air, the fire alarms screamed their agony around us, preemptively receiving the message I was going to send loud and clear.

My last conversation with Cy reverberated in my mind, louder and with a new sharpness.

Cy originally left The Guild because he no longer believed it served the greater good.

Seamus stayed because he wanted to fix things from within, to mend the broken system, rather than destroy it and start anew.

I hadn't been sure where I stood—had been straddling the line between both approaches.

Until now.

I was done working with a system that did nothing but try to break us—a system built and designed for us to fail.

I'd seen first-hand what The Guild stood for—how they lied to, tortured, and used so many of us. No more.

Cy was right, and I'd honor his death by leaning into that truth.

It was time to break this fucking system and act. To live by a code that we all believed in, one grounded in truth.

With a deep breath, I pulled the spiraling heat deep into my center, stoking and nurturing the flames until I felt like I would combust.

And then on an exhale, I let the heat flare out of me, as hot and angry as anything hell could conjure—the perfect mirror and extension of my rage.

Flames licked up the walls of the beautiful building I'd entered only months ago, naive with wide-eyed excitement. I threw my arms out to the side, watching as my fire scorched the grounds that I'd spent so many mornings running through with Ro.

Smoke billowed from the training center where I'd met Izzy, trained with Six, been forced to fight to the death against Darius.

I left only the cabins, the small spaces of home that the teams created together—a small token, an offering. Let them gather their things, their communities, and decide for themselves where their loyalties would lie from this moment forward.

If The Guild wanted to destroy us—wanted to mobilize against us—fine.

Let them do what I did and rise from the ashes.

We'd see if they had the same strength.

My muscles relaxed at the sight of my flames—vibrant shades of orange and blue and purple. As beautiful as they were deadly.

We stood there, together—Darius brushing up against me on one side and Atlas on the other—watching with awe, with pride, as the very power The Guild feared swallowed it whole.

25

ELI

"Wake the fuck up." I shoved Wade again as I tried to swallow the panic threatening to clog my throat.

"Whmm," he mumbled, bleary eyes barely opening at first, but when he caught sight of my expression, they rounded wide with concern. He sprang up, expression thunderous as he rummaged around through his things on the floor, no doubt searching for his blade.

"She left. Declan and Ro are in the living room." I threw a hoodie that was laying casually over his lamp at him. "Get dressed. We need help."

"And the vamp?" Wade's voice was muffled as he pulled on the sweatshirt and followed me to the cramped living space.

Ro was pacing feverishly, his hair sticking out at every direction, whether from sleep or from taking out his frustration, I wasn't sure.

Declan's eyes were fire, her voice cracked with gravel. "We're assuming he went with her. That they went to get Atlas." She rubbed the tension in her forehead, eyes pinched tight. "I should've fucking heard her leave. I can't believe I slept through that."

"Do we have any idea when she left?" Ro asked.

I'd been pretty restless in the night, woke up once to take a leak, but hadn't heard anything.

Declan sighed and shook her head. "Could've been hours ago." She bunched the bottom of her t-shirt tight into her fist. "Fuck."

"Every fucking time she leaves with that fanghole, it's bad news." My jaw hurt from grinding my teeth together so hard.

The last time she'd ditched us with him, she wound up locked in Lucifer's dungeons. Who knew what the fuck would happen to her now.

Declan considered me for a moment. "She's stronger now. Maybe—"

Hope clenched at my chest too. If Max could pull off her asinine rescue mission, it was possible we'd start the morning with Atlas and Sarah back where they belonged—with us.

But The Guild was an entity, and as powerful as she was, she was still just *one* girl.

And a deeply unpredictable vampire.

Tarren was also a formidable opponent in his own right, especially if the force of the entire council was stacked behind him.

Everyone was hunting for her. The moment she stepped foot on campus and was spotted, she'd be on a nonstop mission to get him and get out as quickly as possible.

I tugged my boots on with more force than was necessary. "If she'd just fucking waited until morning, we could have helped, could've gotten them out of there together."

Generally, I both loved and hated how impulsive Max was, how much she threw herself into the things that she believed in. Right now, I only hated it.

Declan snorted, her brow arched. "It's entirely possible we would have held her back though." Her anxious hands ran through her long hair, snagging on tangles as she absentmindedly combed through it. "Fuck, I hate feeling useless."

I froze. That was it, wasn't it? If any of us had any chance of getting Atlas out, it was Max. And Darius was the strongest after her.

Wade too, though his powers were better suited to things other than a rescue mission.

We were the fucking B-team, and we'd been benched.

"It was too easy—when we discussed this earlier." Ro stopped his pacing long enough to rest his forehead against the wall, eyes pinched tight together, the shadow of defeat dipping the rigid lines of his shoulders a few inches from where they'd been. "We should've known she'd do this. *I* should've known. If she really thought Atas was that close to death, there was no chance she'd wait until we could assemble a cavalry to get him."

I nodded, my stomach aching. "Especially if she thought we might stop her."

Declan sighed. "Or hold her back."

Ro stiffened, lifted himself back in his—as Max liked to call it—mission-mode posture. "We need to reach out to Bishop and," his eyes cut to mine briefly with apology, "and Levi. They might be able to help us get a team together. Headquarters is only a couple of hours away from here."

"And we can make some of that time up since it's the middle of the night," Wade added, the dazed expression he'd worn when I'd woken him up abandoned at the threshold of his room. "Less cars on the road. Declan has a lead foot."

"Be ready to leave in sixty seconds," I called over my shoulder, as I went back to my room to hunt down every weapon I had to my name.

◡

I KNEW that I was going to have to suck down my pride and talk to Levi. What I hadn't prepared for, was that he, along with Charlie, Bishop, and a few of the others I hadn't yet met, would already be up and gathered together in the main building—huddled over the bar of the restaurant.

Their serious, hushed voices dropped as one when they saw us standing in the doorway.

"What happened?" I generally wasn't great at reading the room, but even I could tell that the number one thing fueling the atmosphere, before we'd even arrived, was tension. The kind so thick you could taste it in the air.

Charlie glanced from Bishop to the others, all of them locked in a silent conversation that loudly reestablished what we were to them—outsiders.

Just when I expected her to shut us out completely, to send us back to our cabin with a stubborn chastisement, she let out a heavy breath instead and turned to me.

"Something big is happening. At Guild Headquarters—but we're getting conflicting information. Evelyn sent word that there was a greenlight for an all-team, top priority mission in Seattle a little over an hour ago." My stomach turned at my mother's name, but I didn't interrupt her—because Max was at Headquarters. My stomach sank. "Several of them realized pretty early that there was a security breach and were heading back to check on things. We're not really sure what's going on, but we've never seen a Guild pattern like this—this many teams, a series of ambush descriptions in Seattle that aren't mapping onto our own surveillance. And Evelyn, she's usually got pretty high clearance for this stuff but—" Charlie shook her head, "she has no idea what's going on. She—and most of the others—are locked out of the system. The alert has never been raised this high—a full evacuation—not even after the ambush on Guild grounds a few months ago."

"Max," I said, not bothering to hide the small smile tugging at my lips.

Levi, who I'd been doing a really great job of ignoring up until this moment, furrowed his brows and took a few steps towards me. "What about her?" His gaze cut over all of us crowded in the doorway. "Where is the little firecracker, anyway? Haven't gotten to say hi yet."

My hands balled into fists at the weird endearment, and then clenched even tighter when I caught the knowing smile in his eyes. Dick.

"She took off with Darius." Declan stepped around me and walked further into the room, which was probably for the best since I was notoriously not great at keeping my cool around my family. Especially not when I felt like the one being deliberately kept in the dark. "We think she's most likely going to break Atlas out."

"Well," Levi snorted. I couldn't tell whether he seemed impressed or annoyed. "I'd call her and tell her to turn around, because shit is clearly going down there right now."

"She uh," Ro cleared his throat, "didn't exactly drive. She most likely teleported."

Bishop's eyes narrowed on him. "How long ago?"

"I'm guessing around the time you got word that shit hit the fan so to speak," I said.

Levi's lips quirked into a grin. "You think she's the one responsible for this?" He scratched his jaw, holding my eyes as his grin dipped into a frown. "Hm. Impressive."

"We need a team, if you can spare one." Ro directed his ask directly to Bishop, and I got the feeling that the two of them had developed a good working rapport in the months I'd been gone.

Bonus for us, because that heightened our chances that Bishop would say yes to him.

He crossed his arms. "No."

Charlie set a hand softly on his bicep. "Bishop—"

He shook his head. "We're not risking anyone for an impulsive girl we barely know—not when shit is," his dark eyes cut to me, "as you say, hitting the fan. We have no idea what we'd be sending our people into, and we're not risking any of them until we have more information and more time to assess. Not an option."

"But we don't have time to assess," I said, my words clipped as I tried to reign in my anger, "she's in trouble *now*."

Every second was precious—there wasn't a chance we were going to just sit here and wait for them to have a meeting and talk in circles about the best options. Max could be fucked this very second.

The thought nearly sent me to my knees.

Levi's stare was leveled at me, had been since the moment I walked in. He shrugged. "I'll go."

Ro nodded his thanks when I was stunned silent. "We'll need a vehicle. Can you spare us a car or two? We don't need anything else from you—we just need to get to her. Now."

"I'll go too." Charlie was rummaging behind the bar counter, her head only emerging above it when she had two sets of keys dangling from her fingers.

Bishop snorted.

When he realized that she wasn't kidding, his expression darkened. "Absolutely not."

Charlie shot a dark glare at him, the two locked in some silent battle of wills until she arched one of her brows in challenge.

Even through my frustration, I could admire her tenacity. She reminded me a lot of Max, in so many ways.

"I mean this with all of the admiration for you in the world, but you're basically human. You're not nearly strong—or trained—enough to take on a single protector," Bishop said, his words soft, tender almost. "The entire Guild? We have no idea what you'd be marching into." He shook his head, every muscle in his body lined with tension. "I'm not losing you."

"Bishop," she rested a hand on his cheek and he pressed into it, "this is what the Defiance is here for—" he grunted at her use of the name, which only made her smile, "to help people when they need it. Right now? Max needs it."

He wrapped his hand around hers, squeezing it against him, his eyes boring into hers.

I cleared my throat and averted my eyes. It felt like I was trespassing on their intimacy.

With a deep breath, Bishop grabbed the keys from his wife and turned around to face us once more, the stiffness in his expression paved into resignation. "I'm going. Charlie will stay here and run point on communication." He tossed Levi one of the sets of keys, then nodded to the door. "Let's go."

For a moment, Charlie looked ready to argue, but when Bishop's eyes cut to her stomach, she swallowed whatever resistance she'd been ready to spew and nodded.

Before they reached the door, Levi stopped, brows furrowed as he pulled a vibrating phone from his pocket. "Hang on."

"Can't you take the call on the road?" I muttered, running my hand through my hair as I glanced at the others. "Literally every second counts here."

But he ignored me, walking away—further into the bar and farther away from the cars—the phone pressed to his ear.

I bounced on my feet, the adrenaline coursing through my body with nowhere to go, unable to hear anything but the occasional grunts and contextless one-word responses that Levi spit into the phone.

Levi froze, pressed a finger into the ear that didn't have a phone against it.

Something was wrong. Was he talking to mo—Evelyn? Did something else happen?

Fuck, Max needed to be okay. I needed her here. Now.

Jesus fucking christ, I wanted to be on that road yesterday.

Panic gripped me in its vise, my breaths little more than uneven, broken gasps at air. My body started to shake as I tried to focus, tried not to kill my fucking half-brother for taking goddamn forever to finish his phone call.

But I couldn't stop trembling. What if it was about her? What if she was hurt? What if she was dea—

I felt like I was ready to combust, like if I didn't see Max in two seconds, I was going to burn the fucking world down.

Heat flared through me.

"Eli," Declan's voice was sharp as her hand wrapped around my forearm. "What the fuck?"

"I'm just antsy," I muttered, pulling my arm from her. "I'll be fine in a second."

"No dude," Wade pointed at my waist, "look."

An unbidden, irrational fear that he was pointing at my dick—that it was like, I don't know, missing or something—clogged my throat with another wave of panic.

I patted at it with my free hand, the one Declan wasn't holding hostage at my side, just as my eyes dipped down. Relief poured through me at the familiar—ahem, large—bulge in my black pants.

It was fine. The dick was there.

But a bright light blinked into focus in the side of my vision, and I jumped—a sharp scream pulling from my throat without my permission.

My left hand, hanging a few short inches from my dick, was on fire.

I ripped my arm from Declan and started shaking my wrist, like the flicker of fire was water and could disperse with a little effort.

Did not work. For the record, fire was not water.

Bishop came up behind me and shoved me outside as the flames crawled hungrier and higher up my hand, my wrist, my forearm.

"Eli," Declan followed us, and ran in front of me, her eyes latching to mine. "Breathe. Calm down. This is—" she shook her head, face reflecting the same shock that I was no doubt feeling underneath the pulsing panic that tended to take over when you were, you know—on fucking fire. "I think you're conjuring hellfire. Like Max's hellfire. You just have to control it. Breathe. Calm down. Focus."

"Calm down?" My voice was higher than I recognized it ever being. "Hellfire?"

The flames flared, burning into the ground with a sizzle and the smell of char.

Fuck I hoped that was just grass and not, like, my skin or something.

Bishop swore and sent Wade and Ro in for a fire extinguisher. I held my arm as far from my body as I could, blinking as sweat dripped into my eyes.

She nodded, eyes cooling, expression flattening into the typical strong, Declan stability we always needed to set shit straight. "Breathe with me, okay? In and out. Do what Max does—visualize it pulling back inside of you, the more you try to dispel it, to push it out, the more it will spread."

"Gotta say," I stammered, voice still high and unfamiliar, "pulling fire into me, not exactly aligned with a single instinct that I have right now."

She bit back a small grin and nodded. "Understood. Do it anyway. Just remember, Max's fire has never hurt you. Think of it as an extension of her. It's just Max. Not fire."

Just Max, not fire.

I closed my eyes, pinching them tight enough to dispel the glow of the flames from my sight.

The soft pressure of a fire extinguisher sounded around us, and I was vaguely aware of Bishop yelling something.

Heat trailed along my arms, and I knew the fire was growing, spreading.

I did my best to ignore their panicking.

Max, not fire.

I inhaled, counting to five, then exhaled, slow and deep.

Max, not fire.

Her smile flashed through my mind, the quiet strength she seemed to wield even when she wasn't trying; I remembered the awe I felt, every time I saw her produce hellfire, the ease with which it seemed to move with her, a part of her—an extra limb.

I imagined her face, her body—watched as she relaxed, and pulled the fire back into her, the flames rescinding into her skin and dispersing through her like vapor.

Max, not fire.

"Eli—Eli, open your eyes," Declan whispered in the air between us. "You did it."

Not entirely believing her, I opened one, flexing my once-flaming hand in front of it. It was just a hand. Wiggling my fingers, I opened my other eye, then looked at Dec—both of us smiling.

"I'm not on fire." I chuckled, never so happy to see skin on my hand in my life.

"Yeah," Wade said, "we can see that." His brows furrowed as he stared at my hands. "But how were you ever on fire at all?"

Right. That was a good question. If I hadn't been so focused on the whole self-combustion thing, I would've probably had the wherewithal to ask it myself.

"You were clearly channeling Max." Declan shrugged. "I just have no idea how you were able to do it. Or why now."

Wade took a step closer and shoved my t-shirt sleeve up,

revealing the barely-visible design winding around my arm. "Guessing it has something to do with this."

Bond marks.

I jerked him off me and shoved my shirt sleeve back down.

Bishop's eyes cut between us, question and confusion clear as day.

Get in line, my guy—this was new to me too.

"Well," Levi walked over, tucking his phone back into his pocket. His gaze cut from me to the crisped ground at my feet. "Looks like you and your girlfriend have a lot in common. Apparently, she burnt shit down tonight too."

"The labs?" I asked, scuffing my feet over the ruined ash, like swishing the char around might make it disappear.

Levi grunted. "Headquarters."

"Yeah, but which part?" Wade asked.

"All of it."

∽

ALL THERE WAS for us to do was wait at this point. According to Levi-via-Evelyn, Max was nowhere to be found when Guild teams finally showed up to the campus.

And apparently Max wasn't the only one missing from the scene. Every demon kept in the labs, and dozens of team members were unaccounted for. In the wind so to speak.

All that she'd left in her wake were piles of ash and debris.

"At least she can control her power." Levi stared down at the visible reminder of my little pyro mishap. "Mom said she kept the fire contained well enough to prevent what would certainly have been a widespread wildfire."

My focus caught on a single tree that had burned down during my panic.

I, clearly, did not.

Thank the gods that one was isolated from the rest of the forest.

"If she has that kind of control, she definitely meant to burn down The Guild then," Bishop said, his expression blank.

Declan snorted. "Well, yeah. Do you blame her?"

He shrugged. He'd been incredibly silent since Levi's revelation, lost in the mind-trap of his thoughts clearly going a mile a minute, though he shared none of them with us.

Levi scratched the back of his head, an unreadable expression on his face. "It will certainly escalate things now."

"Do you think they'll retaliate?" Charlie asked. Her lips had been pressed into a tight, worried line for nearly an hour now—anxiety clear as day, though she did her best to try and hide it.

"For destroying their largest foothold in the States?" Levi shot her a look that screamed *Are you fucking serious?* even if he didn't put words to the sentiment.

Charlie rolled her eyes and let out a breath that was half grunt, half sigh.

Bishop massaged his temples. "We don't have the numbers—the power—to fight them if they do."

Declan ran her fingers over the patch of ground that used to be grass and was now ash, clearly still fucking confounded by what I'd done. Get in line. I kept staring at my hands every two seconds, just to make sure I hadn't turned into a raging matchstick again.

She looked up at me. "Where do you think she is now?"

Ro, who'd been particularly silent since Levi's call, smiled. He nodded down the path. "Here."

Just on the horizon, I could just make out a blob—and when I squinted, that blob dissected into multiple figures, all of them making their way up the winding hill that would bring them through the main entrance, straight to us.

As one, we took off, sprinting to meet them.

My heart full on stopped in my chest when I saw her face, clear and bright, like I was a fucking lovesick teenager.

Probably because I was.

I crashed into her, grabbing her into a hug so tight that it would probably do damage to a human, and breathed in the familiar scent of her hair. It was buried under a healthy layer of smoke.

"Atlas." Wade pulled his brother to him in an awkward side hug, crushing Sarah between them. "You're okay."

Judging from the dark haze in his eyes, the way his mouth didn't even lift into a grin at seeing us, I'd say he was probably anything but okay.

A long way from it.

But he was alive. And he was here.

Darius found Charlie and Bishop, ignoring Dec's attempts to berate him for leaving without us.

"There are more of us," he said, "about two miles down the road. We didn't want to bring them to your living room, so to speak, without the okay from you first."

Bishop narrowed his eyes. "So you brought them to our doorstep instead?"

Max, pulling away from Dec's grasp, smiled sheepishly. But the half-apology was at odds with the shining strength in her eyes—the clear confidence that she was right. "You said you needed an army, right? That you couldn't take on The Guild or whatever darkness is coming without one?"

He nodded, jaw clenched like a vise as he studied her, a fuse of barely-contained tension sparking in his dark glare.

"Well," she shrugged, "I've brought you one."

"From what I understand," Charlie grinned, "seems you've already single-handedly taken on The Guild yourself."

"I had help—a lot of it. And The Guild is more than a single location." A shadow crossed her features, and I found myself fighting the desire to pull her into a hug and lock her in our cabin for the next two years so that no danger could touch her again. "I've simply declared war."

"So," Levi looked at her like she was the most amusing toy he had in his toy box, "exactly how big is this army you've brought?"

Max grinned, her eyes wild with challenge. "Big."

26

MAX

I'd slept for at least twenty hours after our arrival, the adrenaline of the showdown at Headquarters long since leaked from my body. It left only a heavy lethargy.

The fire itself hadn't used too much of my energy, but the strength that I'd lent to Atlas had drained my stores more than I'd realized at the time.

Wade left a note by my bedside, filling me in on what had happened while I dozed.

Charlie and Bishop were meeting with their council, creating a plan to handle the sheer number of people we'd bought back with us—from vetting them, to caring for them, to finding them shelter.

We had a lot of work to do, but I knew that Charlie would persuade them to take on the task.

I saw the decision in her hard stare, before she'd even uttered a word.

The multitude of their army had grown, more than doubled. But they'd welcome them all.

It was what they did here. It was why they existed in the first place, why Dani had guided us here.

And I would do everything that I could to help them adjust —from building new living facilities, to training, to organizing missions.

Whatever she and the rest of the council determined necessary, my labor would go to them.

But first, before I could get started on any of that, I had to speak to him.

The others had left me to help them hours ago, after a long, unnecessary attempt at arguing over my protection detail. Their bickering woke me up long enough to remind them that I'd more than proven I didn't need protecting. Not here.

Atlas was the only one who'd stayed behind.

My chest squeezed at the memory of him reuniting with the rest of his team.

After the shock of our arrival wore off, the excitement of seeing him again pulsed through them all.

Only that joy hadn't quite extended to him.

He hadn't said a word since we made it back to the cabin. Hadn't spoken to any of them.

Hadn't even smiled when his brother pulled him in for a hug.

There was a darkness, a heaviness that seemed to cloak him now.

It made the surly, often-angry Atlas of before seem downright jovial.

I pressed my hand to the door, took a deep breath in as I prepared myself to push it open.

He hadn't come out of Wade's room once. Not for food, not for anything.

I knew that my power had healed most of his physical injuries, but I had no idea how to go about healing his mind, his heart.

The door creaked on its hinges as I pushed it open, the

room basked in darkness, despite the fact that it was early morning.

It took me a moment to find him, but he was pressed into the far corner of the bed, seated, his back pressed as far back into the wall as it would go, his head leaning down as his wavy hair curtained around his face.

A shiver ran down my spine at the sight of him there, like that. It was the same exact position I'd found him in at the labs, like his body had committed the posture to muscle memory. Like it was the only way he knew how to exist anymore.

I could tell from the cadence of his breathing that he wasn't sleeping, though he made no acknowledgement that I was in the room.

"Atlas?" I whispered into the darkness, almost afraid to disturb him.

His body tensed at the sound of my voice, but he made no other indication that he'd heard me.

The plates of food the others had left him sat untouched on the bedside table.

He'd showered and changed into a fresh pair of his brother's sweats, but I had the sense that he hadn't otherwise moved an inch since we got here.

The mattress groaned as I crawled onto it, careful not to touch or startle him as I made my way towards him. I leaned back into where the bed met the wall, a few inches away from where he sat.

His hands rested on his lap, his fingers clenched in uncomfortable looking angles, like they'd been stuck there for hours.

Slowly, I set my hands on his. When he made no attempt to resist me, I turned slightly until I faced him, and pulled them gently into my lap.

My fingers dug and massaged into his hands, slowly loosening the stiff muscles there until his hands resembled hands again, and not the lobster claw-like formations they'd forced themselves into.

"Atlas?"

His chest lifted and decompressed quickly, like he was repressing a sob—the sound made louder by the absolute silence of the cabin.

He didn't respond, but he didn't pull away from my touch either, so I rubbed his wrists next, then his forearms.

Every muscle I touched was coiled tight, his body locked inside of a trauma response.

Tears blurred my vision, but I didn't let any fall as I moved up his arms inch by inch, forcibly relaxing the tension that had built up.

When I reached his shoulders, I touched his chin, tilting it slightly until I could see his face.

His dark eyes were glazed with liquid as they found mine, tear tracks silently carving down his cheeks.

"Oh, Atlas," I pulled him to me in a hug, relaxing slightly as his arms wrapped eventually around me.

He held me tight against him, tighter than I'd ever been held, as his body wracked with sobs.

My own chest ached, my throat tight with emotion as I held him to me with equal force. I pressed my nose into his neck, letting the familiar scent of him wash over me.

"It's okay," I said, my voice thick, "you're safe. You're back. You're home."

I repeated the words over and over, until it sounded almost like a soundtrack, convincing myself of the very things I was trying to convince him of.

He was here.

We'd rescued him.

He was home.

He would be okay.

But deep down, I had no idea if it was true. Serae's warning had been ringing through my mind nonstop since I'd spoken to her.

His body trembled against mine as he buried his face into my hair. He pulled me to him until I crawled into his lap, allowing our bodies to stitch together until he was touching as much of me as he possibly could.

I had the feeling we both needed this, the touch. To feel each other, to understand that this was real, he was okay. We were together.

His grip on reality was tenuous, his mind constantly tug-of-warring him back to that place. I wasn't sure how I knew it so certainly, but I knew it all the same, with a truth that settled deep in my bones and cracked me in half—until his pain was my pain.

I could feel it threatening to swallow me whole, dragging us both into the darkness until we sank like anchors, rotting hand in hand, bones locked together for the rest of time.

We held each other as the minutes bled together—until I felt real enough to him that he could begin to distinguish his nightmare landscapes from reality.

My fingers carved paths through his hair, tracing his scalp, the lines of his back, his arms, as I muttered soothing things to him.

After what could have been ten minutes or two hours, he loosened his grip on me, pulling back until his eyes could latch onto mine.

Fire sparked through my veins as we studied each other. It was an intimacy, a closeness we'd never allowed each other before.

There was so much emotion brimming in his black eyes that so often swirled with yellow—anger, shame, but most of all, fear.

I hadn't seen a sign of his wolf since finding him in the labs, and I found my chest aching for that part of him too. How far buried would that part of him be? Did The Guild have the tools to steal it away entirely?

Atlas's fingers trailed along my neck, my cheek, gently touching every inch of me that he could reach as he fought to ground himself here, with me.

This was real. I was real.

I willed the words into being between us, hoped that he could feel them if he wouldn't hear them.

When his thumb swept over my bottom lip, heat flared low in my belly, and I begged my body to ignore it, to push it away.

Now wasn't the time for lust.

And I wasn't sure that there would ever come a time for that with Atlas.

Not after everything.

But something inside of him sparked at whatever expression slipped past my wall, and he swept his finger over my lip again. His eyes traced the path that his thumb carved, down my jaw, along my neck, the visible shiver of goosebumps no doubt signaling the effect he had on me—no matter how loudly I pressed my body, my heart, to forget it.

His pointer finger traced my collar bone, dipping along my chest, before he came back to my bottom lip again.

I shivered despite myself, my heart suddenly drumming a furious rhythm against my chest, like it was trying as desperately to reach him as I was. "Atlas."

His eyes locked on to my lips, as his thumb stroked delicious tingles down that path again "I watched you die." His voice was little more than a croak, like his throat was relearning how to work, the words flat and grating in the silence of the room. "Hundreds, maybe thousands of times."

I couldn't speak, could barely breathe, every molecule of my body alert with the deep sadness etched into every line of his face.

His eyes darted briefly to mine, before finding my lips

again, like they held all the answers he sought. "I watched your lungs stop breathing until you choked on air that wouldn't come. I watched you die hundreds of different deaths, each more gruesome and painful than the last. And every single time, it was my fault. No matter what I did, I couldn't protect you. Any of you." His voice was gravelly and cracked, like he was trying to hold back another wave of emotion. "Until I was just alone. Always alone."

I didn't have that kind of restraint. My vision swam.

Atlas wore guilt like most men wore clothing.

From the moment I'd met him, even through his piercing distrust of me, I understood that everything he did, every thought he had, was structured around protecting the people he felt responsible for.

It made perfect sense then, that his nightmare of nightmares involved watching the people he cared about slip through his fingers over and over again.

And for months on end?

Until reality and the nightmare blurred into one?

I had no idea what that kind of trauma would do to a person.

His fingers trembled against my cheeks as he traced my tears.

I pressed his palm to me, held it there before he could pull away again, before he could withdraw back into the shell he'd hardened to protect himself.

"Atlas," I held his cheek in my hand, forcing him to meet my eyes. "You can't be responsible for us all. You can't carry our lives on your shoulders. You'll buckle from the weight."

"I can't lose you again, Max." His voice caught on my name, the sound of his pain like a dagger to my chest. Dark eyes bored into mine, a flicker of fight so deep in their depths that I had no idea how to claw it to the surface. "I won't survive it."

My chest tightened at the familiarity of his pain.

I saw the mirror of my own fears reflected back at me.

Atlas pushed everyone away because the thought of losing the people he cared about shredded him.

The easiest solution was to simply stop caring. Until he couldn't.

And then the drude made him confront that pain, that fear on an infinite loop.

We stared at each other, our faces mere inches apart, every breath syncing us closer and further.

His lips brushed up against mine, the touch so light it could almost be an accident.

My body came alive at the contact, need slicing down my spine, deep in my belly.

His expression shifted, his eyes growing hungry with something I didn't recognize, but my body seemed to respond to.

I tensed, started to pull away. "Atlas, we shouldn't. We can't. Not now."

He held me to him, his dark eyes meeting mine now, unflinching. His fingers cradled my neck, my cheek, the back of my head, until all that I saw, all that I felt, was him.

His lips ghosted over mine again, and I felt the echo of my shiver reverberate through his chest.

"Atlas." I pressed my hands into his chest, pushed against his grip. "I can't keep doing this. This push and pull." Tears rippled down my cheeks, but his hands collected every single one as he held me there. "It hurts too much. *You chose* her. We talked about this."

It was the one discussion we'd had during the only dream walk I was able to actually reach him in. Before the drude kicked me out.

He flinched, like I'd slapped him, but he still held me there. His forehead dipped to mine, and I could feel his jaw muscles clenching as he fought his own hurt.

"From the first moment I saw you, I was terrified of you,

Max. And I haven't stopped being terrified a single moment since." His voice was little more than a whisper, so fragile and soft that the slightest breath could shatter it. "Of losing you. I didn't want to let myself care about you, didn't know how to open myself up to the pain that comes with it. I saw it as a weakness. One that I didn't want. I didn't want you."

Pain lanced through my chest, angry and hot.

"I didn't know how to protect you from me. I didn't *want* to want you. Told myself over and over again that it was just the wolf, not me, that kept tracking your every move—that sought you out in every room, that craved even a single glance from you, that lit on fire whenever you touched me." He paused for a moment, rolled his forehead against mine. "But you became the only thing I wanted. And it had nothing to do with the wolf at all. I was fucking kidding myself—I was done for from the first moment that I laid eyes on you. So then I decided to settle on protecting you. On doing what I could to keep you safe." A dark, humorless chuckle pulsed from his lips. "But I failed at that over and over and over again."

He pulled away, until he met my gaze. "I lived your death a thousand times. And even after experiencing that pain, I still wanted you. Even when I thought I'd lost you forever, I still didn't regret wanting you. I only regretted not letting myself have you while I had the chance." He shook his head, jaw muscles working to fight back the emotion in his eyes. "I will always want you, Max. I thought I could protect you from that, from me. But I'm a selfish fucking prick. I don't think I'm even capable of not loving you for your own good. I don't think I ever will be. Because in all of that darkness, in every nightmare, you —the light that you carry, the one that emanates out of you like a fucking beacon—it's the only thing that kept me floating."

It was maybe the most I'd ever heard him say at once before —every word rushed out in a single breath, tumbling in the air between us.

My eyes streamed, and Atlas, clutching my face between his hands, pressed gentle kisses along my cheeks as he cried too.

"You're here. You're real." He whispered the sentences over and over again, like he was willing himself to believe them. "Not a dream. Please don't leave me again. Please, please find a way to forgive me. I'm sorry. I'm so fucking sorry, Max."

His lips found mine, salty with my tears and his, and suddenly all of the hurt and anger I felt melted, not gone entirely, but flatter, transformed—the logical voice that had been warning me against letting him in again, silenced by the rabid pounding of my heart.

We'd both resisted this for so long, found ways to justify and explain away our attraction, the depth of our need—it was like a dam was collapsing, the wood splintered and fraught from restraint.

Until it burst.

I deepened the kiss, groaning as my tongue clashed with his, as the taste of him filled me. Heat pooled deep in my belly, and I felt the responding growl vibrate in his chest.

He came alive with need, the shell he'd been just minutes ago breaking in half and releasing a hunger that rivaled my own.

I rolled my hips against him, a shot of pleasure shooting through me at the feel of him hard and ready beneath me.

His fingers dug into my hips, forcefully moving me against him—harder, faster.

I bit his lip, scratched my hands down his back, nearly ready to come simply from riding him, fully clothed.

He ripped my shirt from my back, tearing it with the force of his urgency. Then, pulling my sports bra down he licked and kissed down the column of my neck until he pulled a hard peak into his mouth.

My head fell back in ecstasy as he sucked and bit, the mix of pain and pleasure rolling through me in equal measure.

But I needed more.

With a growl he shoved my pants down, dipped his fingers between my legs until they were soaked in my desire.

Apparently, he needed more too.

With trembling fingers, I shoved his sweatpants down, my mouth watering at the sight of his cock—hard, demanding, and already pulsing with a bead of pre-cum.

We made quick work of the rest of our clothes, a mess of limbs and hurried grunts, until he slid over me, pressing my head back against the pillow, and into me.

I moaned in pleasure as his lips met mine, his tongue tangling with mine at the pace of each thrust.

At first, the movements were hurried and urgent—the kind of explosion that only came from months of repression, like if we didn't take each other now, we never would. It was the same hurried thrusts as the first and only other time we'd fucked.

But I felt the shift as he slowed down, as he pressed his forehead against mine, his hand cupping my face as he rolled his hips against mine.

His other hand massaged and teased my nipple, going lower and lower with delicious restraint, until he circled my clit.

His tongue followed the path, down my neck, my chest, my belly.

I grunted in frustration, wanting his dick back inside of me, but he kept going, nipped playfully at my hip bone, until he found my clit with his tongue—turning my protests into pleas for more.

He swept his tongue inside of me, his scraggly beard doing delicious things against the sensitive flesh there. He held me still, kept me from full-on humping his face with a lean forearm pressed across my stomach.

The resistance, the denial of movement, only amplified

every sensation, made me crave every touch, every breath that he bestowed.

His groan vibrated against me as he ate me out like a starving man.

"This," he rasped, dark eyes darting to the abandoned plates of food on his bedside table, "is the only meal I've been hungry for." He swirled his tongue over my clit, eyes watching my every reaction with a ravenous hunger that bordered on wonder—on obsession. "The only taste I've wanted on my tongue for months." Teeth scraped against me, until I squealed and squirmed against him, on the edge of ecstasy, my lungs offering me nothing but breathy, needy pants. "The only sounds I've wanted to hear." Two fingers slipped inside of me, the sound loud and slick as he worked me. "Let me feast on you, Max, let me taste my own surrender on your lips."

His lips closed over me again and sucked until I couldn't find the edge any more—there was only falling.

My vision blurred from the force of my orgasm, every inch of my flesh his as I turned to jelly.

But he wasn't done.

He worked me, reading the waves of pleasure that pulsed through me, until the first orgasm rolled into a second, even more powerful one.

"Fuck," he whispered, licking up every ounce of liquid I gave him, "I could come just from watching you."

The walls of my pussy throbbed, begging for more.

A feral need took over.

Like hell was he coming anywhere but inside of me.

Clawing at his shoulders, I pulled him up, shoving his shoulders down and rolling until he lay where my head had rested only a moment before.

I speared myself on him, my body craving the fill of him as my fingers dug into his chest.

His breathing picked up, eyes filled with rapture as he watched me ride him.

"How do you usually like it?" I asked, every inch of me flaring to life with the energy of his lust. I wanted him to feel as high on this moment as I felt.

His hand gripped my thigh, kneading into it with a punishing force as he sat up, lips hot against my neck. "Anything I've ever liked pales in comparison to this." His fingers dug into me, as he pulled me as far down onto him as I could go, like even that wasn't enough. "Pales in comparison to you." He rolled me back for a moment, only to pull me back down with more force. My fingers dug into his shoulder blades, carved trenches down his back. "There is only you, Max. That's the only thing I want. Whenever, however you'll have me."

I clenched around him, the openness in his face, the honesty in his eyes almost as hot as the feeling of his dick hard and demanding inside of me. "I'm yours, Atlas. I've always been yours."

Something shifted in him at my words. And for all of the initial softness, Atlas was no gentle lover—the feral edges of his nature seeped into our union like vines. The dark black of his eyes cut through with a thin streak of gold, and my breath stilted with happiness.

They'd taken a lot from him, but they hadn't managed to take the wolf, his inner fight, after all.

We clung to each other with a wild desperation as we fucked, our bodies slick with heat and sweat and need that controlled us both—one we'd fought for months. No more. When we kissed, I tasted blood, our mouths a battle of tongue and teeth as we pushed each other to the edge, both vying for ownership of the other— for submission.

There was a loud crack, then a crash, then we rolled from the now lopsided mattress—the bed frame broken and forgotten.

That was fine; the floor, messy and sturdy, was more suited to our war than any bed could be.

I bit down on his shoulder as my orgasm tore through me, my pussy spasming around him, still vying for control, for his surrender. And she received it. With a roar, he followed me over, his teeth buried into me as we pulsed together.

We lay like that, framed in a haze of our lust, no sound but our uneven breaths, as we clung to one another.

I felt fuller than I had, maybe ever.

More right.

Complete.

27

MAX

It was dark, the air filled with the briny freshness of the sea. Soft waves trickled to the shore, breaking at my feet before the sea pulled them back, out of reach.

I bent down, my hand hovering a few inches above the water.

"I wouldn't." The voice was cold, dark. Familiar.

Craning my neck around, I got a look at him. Tall, ominous as always, dark eyes glittering in the night, like they owned it. "Lucifer? Where are we? Did you pull me back here already?"

His dark brow arched as he studied me. "Interesting. You have enough power to pull me into a dreamscape—something that no demon has had the strength to do in decades, mind you—yet you're weak enough not to recognize that you're doing it. You're a girl full of contradictions, aren't you?"

I fell back on my ass, rested my forearms on my knees as I studied the lake in front of us. It reminded me of the Styx, but the waves were a crystal blue-green—the vibrant color somehow visible even in the dark.

"How could I pull you to a dreamscape? I thought that was supposed to be almost impossible across the realms." I'd only been able to manifest dreams with Wade because of our connection.

For a long moment, he said nothing, just stared out across the sea, no land on the horizon in sight.

A soft wind blew through his dark hair, disrupting the usually rigid style he wore. The dark cloak was wrapped around him.

"I'm not entirely sure." His eyes narrowed, frustration evident in their depths. Lucifer didn't like being in the dark on anything. "You must be near a portal, some kind of magical juncture. That, or your power has grown immensely since we last met." He shrugged, studying me. "Perhaps both."

I closed my eyes, focused on the power coursing through me. "I feel more powerful. More alive than I have in a long time."

My skin tingled, power and connection flowing through every vein, every bone.

He studied the ground for a moment, considering, then sat down on the rocky shoreline next to me. "Your bonds have strengthened. Considerably, if I had to guess. Seems you and your team have finally found a way past the childish will-they-won't-they you've been exhausting me with since the moment I met you." A small almost-grin tugged at the corner of his lips. "Unfortunately, that means Samael won our bet."

I physically had to restrain my eyes from rolling. "Yes, well, not all of us are as freely giving of our love as you are, unfortunately."

He snorted, the sound startling a small jump from me. It was so human-sounding that, for a moment, his hard edges softened into something else, a ghost of who he used to be, maybe.

There was an ease about him in this dream realm, the hard, intimidating mask he so often wore abandoned in sleep. Or perhaps with a realm between us, he didn't see the need to wear it.

Did we all do this? Hide ourselves from each other? Erect walls to protect us from pain, from love?

"Touché." He picked up a pile of small, uneven rocks, studying them with interest as the sandy stones tumbled from one hand to the other. "I'd almost forgotten how real these dreams could feel, how intricate."

I didn't say anything, just watched the usually hard lines of his back relax a fraction.

"You remind me of her," he whispered, eyes still focused on the gravel in his hands, "a lot. She," he cleared his throat, straightened his spine again, "she would be proud of you, I think. I'm sorry that you never got to know her."

A wave of emotion got stuck in my throat. I sniffed, stared out at the water until my vision cleared.

I didn't know how to have this kind of conversation with him. There were moments when I could forget entirely that he was my father, that I had this whole family history that didn't involve Cy or Ro.

Remembering felt almost like a betrayal to the home I loved.

"You're different here," was all I managed to shape into words.

He sniffed, nodding. "The magic of this realm, the power you wield, makes it difficult to keep guards up. It's one of the greatest strengths dream demons possess. Some think it's about lust, sex. But there is real power in rendering your enemies vulnerable in this way."

I studied him. "Is that what you are? My enemy?"

A shadow fell over his expression, a flash of something that looked almost like pain. "I am not your friend."

A strange knowing churned deep in my gut, a suspicion I'd been wrestling with for months hardening into a truth.

"The ritual," I started, clearing my throat, "the nexus, the abraxas stone, my power. Once we have your three things, what will happen?"

His jawline sharpened, his eyes not meeting mine as he dropped the gravel back to the ground and wiped his hands along his pants, dispelling the finer remnants. "You will act as a catalyst, a filter for the barrier to sift through. The final anchor."

His eyes darted to mine briefly, then cut back to the water. It was long enough for me to see the sharp sting of regret in their depths.

"I won't survive it, will I?" My voice was hollow, but somehow, even though I was certain that I knew the answer to my question, I didn't fear it.

"I've tried. I've been looking for a way, another solution—" he took a slow, deep breath, then shook his head. "No, I don't think that you will."

My throat tightened as I nodded.

Was this what he'd been doing?

All those times he'd left on some mysterious mission?

Trying to find a way, a magical deus ex machina that would allow me to survive this war I'd been thrust into the middle of?

Strangely, my chest squeezed at the sentiment.

His distance made so much more sense now. Why allow yourself to get close to a daughter, to become invested in her life, if you knew that she was destined to die?

"The blood oath," I said, with a small chuckle, knowing with a vicious certainty that this was the real reason he wanted control over my will. It wasn't to bring me to hell for training at his every whim. It was to ensure that when it came time to sacrifice myself, I wouldn't back down.

I'd broken the oath, I'd have no choice when it came time for the ritual. No way to refuse, even if I wanted to. He ultimately controlled my actions, until he relinquished that power.

I wouldn't though—I couldn't. Not if my survival would mean everyone else's demise. It was a failsafe he didn't need.

Both of us sat there in silence as the heaviness of the moment fell over us. His hand wrapped around mine, surprisingly soft—gentle, even.

But he wouldn't look at me, wouldn't meet my eyes.

Instead, we just lingered in the loud silence, the waves a soft, mournful battle cry.

I felt dizzy, armed with this knowledge, but also oddly calm.

If the alternative was the realms collapsing into each other, everyone in hell and everyone in the human realm dying? Well, my death seemed like a bargain.

My toes slipped into the water, an arctic chill slicing through me.

I heard Lucifer's voice, but couldn't make out the words. Instead, the water engulfed me, pulled me under.

My lungs fought for air as the cold numbed my limbs. I searched for light, for a way to the surface, my mind wrestling with the possibility of simply sinking to the bottom, letting myself drift like an anchor to the hidden depths below.

Something sharp tugged at my chest, a sudden urge to fight ringing strong through every bone in my body. I clawed my way to the surface, my vision blacking at the edges as I fought to stay conscious.

But it was too far, too hard.

A hand closed around me, then another, tugging me forward.

I gasped with my whole body as my face broke the surface.

Darius dragged me to the beach, where the others were swimming to meet us—all of them soaked, eyes wide with panic.

The dreamscape was gone, replaced by the crystal calm of the lake, of the forest surrounding it—beautiful.

"What the hell happened?" Wade asked, as Darius, dripping wet, picked me up and cradled me in his arms, tugging me against his chest.

He was trembling, but not from the chill, his eyes wild with fear as they scanned every inch of me.

The full moon beat down on them all like a spotlight—Declan, Atlas, Wade, Eli, and Darius.

All of them strong, all of them mesmerizing.

Something must have called to them, pulled them to me.

I felt their panic, felt their fear radiate through me, clawing and demanding.

"It was a dream," I said, my voice wobbly as my body fought for the oxygen it had been denied. "Just a dream. I must've sleep-walked out here by accident." I met each of their eyes, willing them to believe it, to feel it. "I'm okay."

And for now, surrounded by them all, I was.

Even if I knew now that it couldn't last.

THE WORLD UNDONE

Don't miss out on the final installment of Max and her team's epic story!!

The world as we know it is quickly unraveling, and it's up to Max, Team Six, and the Defiance to stop The Guild Council before it's too late.

Be prepared for action, adventure, banter, and spice.

ACKNOWLEDGMENTS

This book wouldn't be possible without the support of my family and friends. You know who you are, and I couldn't be luckier to have you in my life. Thanks for always encouraging and pushing me to chase after my writing worlds.

Special thank you to my editor, Kath, and my cover designer, Michelle. This book is so much better because you've all contributed a piece to it. Thank you.

And to my very own 'Ralph,' thanks for keeping me company while I wrote this series for hours and months and years on end.

Printed in Great Britain
by Amazon